GAME CHANGER

Game Changer

KAYLEE LOSEY

Smitten Publishing

For all of us who like our book boyfriends a little damaged
and aren't afraid of a little red flag or two...
this one's for you.

Chapter 1

Gabriella Cabrera-Perez had been wide awake since quarter to the butt-crack of dawn. It was her first day at a new job. New job, new state, new beginnings. She had moved all the way from Maryland to take this position as a finance lawyer at Warren & Blakely, a major law firm that offered a variety of specialties and law services. It was true that many of the larger firms in Maryland often bred lawyers into six-figure politicians, but there were several factors that drew her attention to the small town of Traverse City, Michigan, instead.

For starters, she hated politicians. She had no desire to become one or be near them. Every firm she had worked for since she was a pre-law student at Yale seemed to be grooming her for an outstanding career in politics.

No thanks.

Along with the surprising perks of getting away from people who, in Gabriella's mind at least, were nothing more than career criminals, there was another incentive pulling her toward the small lakeside town. The alpha and omega, the core value and supreme ruler of all decisions, the one factor that would always and forever trump all other factors- Family.

Yeah, family was a big deal in the Cabrera-Perez household.

Gabriella's family was here, therefore she would be here, too.

"Gabby! Are you done in there yet?" Lola, her sixteen-year-old sister, called from the other side of the bathroom door.

"Lola! *Un minuto, por favor!*" Gabby snapped back. Why she had come to her parents' house before her first day of work was a mystery.

She supposed there was something about big moments needing to be shared with *la familia* that had been ingrained in her brain since her first big moment- her birth.

Gabby looked in the mirror and smoothed down her nearly-black hair in its new edgy bob. She couldn't remember the last time she'd had short hair. Her hair was thick and caught somewhere between straight and wavy- the perfect salt water, beachy look. But now it fell just below her jawline and she was annoyingly self-conscious about it, constantly tucking it behind her ear, smoothing it down, or touseling it.

When she'd made the decision to chop it, she was going for professional. All business. Boss lady vibes. Something that said "Yeah, I'm a woman in a male-dominated field. I've got phenomenal breasts and a fine ass, but none of that will stop me from kicking yours!"

Let it not be forgotten that she was also young in a field in which people prided themselves on being seniors, and she was Cuban-American where most of her colleagues were white. Most of them were also privileged enough to come from exceptionally wealthy homes. Not that there was anything wrong with being old, white, or wealthy, but...she stuck out. A lot.

She exhaled. "Don't think about that now, Gabby. You got the job. You're a total boss bitch, and anyone- man or woman- would be a damn idiot to mess with you."

Finally she pulled the door open to find her young sister leaning against the wall in her pajamas, scrolling through her phone.

"How do I look?" Gabby stood with one hand on her hip, looking eagerly at Lola.

"Damn, sis! Look at you!" Lola exclaimed as she looked up from her phone screen, "H.B.I.C. in the house! Seriously, Gabs, you're throwing out *major* boss lady vibes."

Gabby grinned widely. Right, this is why she stopped at her parents' house before work.

"That blazer- that skirt! *Your eyebrows!*" Lola continued, "It's official. I want to be you when I grow up."

"Thanks, girl, I really needed that," Gabby said, squeezing Lola into a hug.

"Not so tight- I gotta pee!" Lola squealed. Gabby let go and watched as her sister leapt into the bathroom behind her and closed the door.

In the kitchen, her dad was already filling his Thermos with coffee and grabbing his lunch box off the counter, ready for work.

Gabby's parents, Carlos and Evelyn, had emigrated from Cuba to Florida when they were kids- teenagers, actually. They were eighteen, had just married, and were looking for a new life. A new place to start a family. Shortly after arriving and settling in Miami, they established jobs and wasted no time before procreating. Her dad was an agricultural worker for several years before switching to construction, and her mom worked at a tailor shop before deciding to start her own business as a seamstress and work from home so she could take care of her kids.

Isabel was the oldest, followed by Gabriella and Marco, who were twins. The three of them were born and raised in Miami, and once Gabby and her brother were out of high school and onto college, her dad had taken a better job in Michigan. At Walker & Sons he moved up the ladder from construction worker to foreman, and was now supervisor at the very same company.

Oh, and once they'd gotten established in Michigan, they started procreating. Again.

Lola was the first Michigan-born baby, then Roberto, more commonly known as Robby, and then Elisa.

Gabby prayed her parents didn't move again because she had no idea what she would do with another three siblings.

Family and hard work. That's what mattered. Gabby and her siblings had been told over and over throughout their childhood that as long as they worked hard and knew they were putting in their best, they would have a life to be proud of. It was something that stuck with her to this day.

"What's the project today, Dad?" Gabby asked, pouring herself a cup of coffee and being sure to pour it away from her silky white blouse and over the sink.

"Another house over on South Cherry," he replied. "There have been a lot over that way lately. Renovations, demolitions and rebuilds."

"Sounds like you're staying busy then," Gabby said, taking a small sip of coffee. Pure, untouched black coffee. There really was nothing like it in the morning.

"Every year the town seems to get more and more young people, so I don't think I'll be out a job anytime soon," Carlos smiled and gave Gabby a quick peck on the cheek before meeting his wife at the door to do the same. He turned and faced Gabby again and his smile seemed wider. "I'm glad you were able to find a job so close. It's going to be good having you around again. Oh, and good luck today, hija. Show 'em who's boss." He winked, and then headed out the door.

Gabby's mom shuffled back into the kitchen, still in her slippers. "Have you gotten used to the city yet? Do you know where everything is?"

She had only been in Michigan for a little over a week, and was still getting used to things. Finding out where all the good food places were, the bars, the nightlife, the lake. She couldn't believe the number of wineries and breweries the place had, and couldn't wait for her brother to take her on a tour of them all. Maybe not *all* of them in one day, but if she was going to live in the wine capital of Michigan, she was going to check them all off her list eventually.

"Not yet, but I was hoping Marco might get a chance to show me around. We need to catch up anyway. I saw there were a bunch of ways to do wine tours, and I've always wanted to do one," Gabby said as she sat down next to her mother.

Marco was and always had been a social butterfly. He knew everyone's drama, the ins and outs of every town, every community, every relationship. He was a walking gossip encyclopedia and Gabby could never quite figure out how he did it. Like her, Marco was still very career-focused and had worked hard to get into Princeton to study architecture. He now worked for a commercial building company designing shopping malls, restaurants, office buildings, and hotels. Out of all the Cabrera siblings, Gabby did well, but Marco made the big bucks.

"He stays busy," her mom sighed, holding her coffee mug with two hands. "But he still makes time to stop in from time to time."

"Mom!" Robby bursted into the kitchen like a tornado, "Who's picking me up from practice? It goes until 5:30, and I'm always starving afterward." He flung open the fridge to find his lunch neatly packed for him and yanked it out, letting the refrigerator door slam shut behind him. Gabby was certain she heard something fall off its shelf, or at least fall over. "Oh, hey Gabs!"

"Good morning, Robby."

"But anyway," he quickly flicked his attention back to their mother, "some of us were thinking about maybe going out to eat together right after practice. A team bonding sort of thing. I guess Kolbe said his mom was going to take a few of us out to eat. If that's okay with you. But I'll need some cash?"

"Aren't you old enough to get a job yet?" Evelyn teased. She stood up and grabbed her purse off the counter. "Here's a twenty. Don't use it on junk please, and if there's anything left over either use it to tip the server, or put it in the savings in your room."

"Thanks, mom." Robby snatched the crisp twenty-dollar bill from her hands and stuffed it in the front pocket of his backpack.

"I can't believe he's starting high school next year," Gabby said, shaking her head slowly as she watched her youngest brother slip back down the hall. "Not even next year. In like, four months! The school year is almost over."

"It'll be good to have you here for it," said Evelyn, "He'll be so excited for you to go to his games."

"Marco says he's quite the ball player. Really lives up to the *Cabrera* name."

Evelyn smiled, "He uses that a lot, too. Robby and Miggy, like it's some sign from the universe that he's going to be the next big one."

"Maybe he will." Gabby looked at the clock on the microwave and sat up. Looking down into her half-empty mug she felt the coffee turning acidic in her stomach. She still had plenty of time to get to her new building, but wanted to make a good impression and get there early.

"I should probably get going. I don't know what morning traffic is like, and my new building is right in the middle of downtown. Parking could be disastrous."

"Good luck, *hija*. Not that you need it. We know you'll be amazing. They'll be completely in awe of you by the end of the day," Evelyn said sincerely. She stood to give Gabby a hug and a quick kiss on the cheek. "Will we see you tonight?"

Gabby nodded, "Yeah, of course. I'll stop by for dinner."

The traffic wasn't nearly as bad as what she was used to, and finding a parking spot was a piece of cake. The town had seemed so busy over the past week and half, but she supposed the wineries, breweries, and the lake must just bring in a lot of tourists who weren't active this early on a Monday morning.

She sat in her car and waited for a few minutes. Showing up to work at a law firm thirty minutes early wasn't unheard of by any means. Hell, she'd been known to go in an hour or two early in Maryland. But she didn't have a case. There was nothing to work on, and the only people inside would be far too busy to show her around or give her any sort of welcome. When it was about fifteen minutes to eight she hopped out of her car and made her way up to the tall building.

A man with sandy blonde hair, a neatly trimmed beard, and a wide, muscular frame was just ahead of her. When he reached for the door handle and pulled it open, he stopped slightly, turning to give her a thorough look over, and she took the time to do the same. He filled out his expensive suit, which was probably Armani or Versace, with powerful shoulders, a broad chest, and a tapered waist. The guy definitely worked out, and she found her gaze lingering just a little too long over his deliciously sculpted shape, wondering if it really was as impressive as she was imagining beneath the suit.

Oh, crap. Dios mio, why am I imagining what this man looks like without clothes on?

Her eyes snapped up to his face when she realized she was starting to stare. He had deep, ocean blue eyes, his eyebrows were a few shades darker than his hair, and he radiated masculine power.

For a fraction of a second, she noticed he was sliding his own gaze down her body as he held the door open for her, over her form-fitted blazer and white blouse tucked into a sleek pencil skirt, down to her black T-strap pumps. His eyes turned stormy when they met hers and she could've sworn they blazed with flecks of orange and gold before he smiled at her.

It wasn't a friendly, welcoming smile. No, it most certainly was not.

It was a smirk. A devilish one, at that. There was heat, temptation, and challenge. All rolled into that one little twitch of his lips.

She felt a sudden wave roll through her, like a heavy wind taking her breath away and leaving her hollow. Then she regained her composure and stared back into the storm behind his eyes. Whatever was brewing behind those mischievous eyes of his, she could weather it. She arched one perfect eyebrow and did a quick sweep, head to toe and back, of his body before looking away as though bored, and breezing past him and into the building.

Chapter 2

Emerson Yates sat at his desk in his office, tapping a pen to his chin as he stared off into space. He wasn't completely zoning out, he was just thinking about that hot chick he'd held the door open for only minutes earlier. He'd watched as she walked past him and that back view was equally as enticing as the front.

Gorgeous, big brown eyes surrounded by thick lashes.

The fullest lips he'd ever seen- and they were bare. He was used to women using glosses and lip-plump serums, but hers were all natural. He wanted to fucking taste them. Suck them between his teeth and feel her moan course through him.

The buttons on her blouse were stretching just the slightest bit, straining against the size of her breasts. Only the top two buttons were undone, and her top was conservative, but it didn't hide the fact she was sporting a pair of tits that would be a generous handful- even for him.

Her curves in that skirt made his mouth water, and her ass was just asking to be grabbed onto. Squeezed. *Goddamn,* he'd love to hang onto it while he-

"Emerson," Tyler Watson's voice snapped clean through his dirty fantasy. "We've got a meeting in the conference room downstairs. Fifteen minutes."

"Kay," he replied flatly, still at least trying to hold onto where his brain had been taking that day dream.

"You good, man? You look like...I don't know, like you're still half asleep or something."

Emerson forced himself to blink and then looked over at Tyler who was still holding onto the door knob. Clearly he'd only intended to pop in and give the announcement. "Oh, yeah, I'm good. Just, uh, hey, do you know anything about a new associate? There was this chick I saw downstairs in the lobby. I hadn't seen her here before, but she looked like she worked here."

"There have been a few new hires," Tyler said, "I don't know their names though. Why? Did she look familiar?"

He shook his head, "No, not at all."

"Probably not our area then. Maybe Brody will know."

Tyler was currently a legal intern, and had been since December. He was a good kid, a fucking brilliant one, with a good head on his shoulders. He wanted to be one of those lawyers who actually did something good, made a difference in someone's life who had simply been dealt a bad hand. Tyler always talked about kids who were part of the generational cycle of poverty, drug use, and incarceration. It's all they grow up knowing, so of course they end up following in their parents' footsteps.

Of course, he was in the wrong fucking place for that kind of rewarding work. He knew Tyler had only taken the internship because it was paid- law school isn't cheap- but the kid was *good*. He knew his numbers, he was meticulous when it came to legal documents, and he had yet to bring anyone the wrong files or the wrong coffee. It was the little stuff that mattered sometimes, and Emerson was contemplating forgoing his rule about never begging. He just might beg the kid to stay on full time when his internship was finished.

Warren & Blakely was vicious, highly competitive corporate law. The offices on the floor where Emerson and Tyler now worked handled finances, bank loans and delinquencies, bankruptcy, and collections. It was boring as shit sometimes with the amount of paperwork and legal documents to read through, but it paid well, and every now and then there was a high-stakes case that had added bonuses.

Other floors in the building handled things like wills and estate law, contract drafting, employment law, taxes, and antitrust law. Asleep yet?

Yeah, most of the time it was pretty boring, but there was a major case coming Emerson's way and he was more than ready for the challenge. There had been a class action lawsuit filed against Alpha National Bank for seventy-five million dollars, and Alpha was hiring Warren & Blakely to take care of business.

Normally high dollar cases like that were given to partners or seniors rather than associates, but Emerson's boss had personally told him that he'd be right for that case. It would be long and grueling, and it may take months or even a year to settle, but it would be worth it. Winning a case like that would not only give him his choice of law firms anywhere in the country, but he'd be able to set his salary and still have firms begging him to join them.

Oh, and there was quite the bonus for winning a case like that. This Alpha case would more than double his salary if he won. Which he would. Because he was the best guy for the job.

"Are you going to the meeting?" Emerson asked before Tyler could slip back out of the office.

"Interns don't usually go to those things. Plus, Tanner put a stack of documents on my desk the size of Mount Everest, so…"

"You should come anyway. See how those things go. You've got two weeks left of your internship before you graduate and leave me," he said, giving his best pout. "Unless…"

"I'm not staying here, man. It's great that you can help banks get more money than they deserve from people who are already struggling and not feel a damn thing about it," Tyler said, "but I swear every time I open another lawsuit, another bankruptcy, and think about who's really suffering on the other end and how we're not helping *them*…my soul is crushed just a little bit more."

Emerson let out a heavy sigh as he stood up. "Five months. Five months here and I've taught you nothing. Their problems are their problems. You have bills to pay, student loans to pay back, you need to worry about *you*. It's not your job to save the world. It's not your job to make sure the Mom-and-Pop shop on the corner is making enough money to get by- they should. That's their job."

"Spoken like the son of a real *family values* politician," Tyler remarked.

"Whoa! Was that sass? Were you giving me shit just now?" Emerson clapped a hand on Tyler's back as they headed out the door together. "Damn, Ty, I didn't know you had it in you."

Emerson's father, Johnathan Yates, was a sitting United States senator. He was also an asshole. Quite possibly the worst person he had ever met, to be perfectly honest. As if the complete absence from his childhood weren't enough- with the exception of photo shoots to make their fucked up family look like a vintage Americana wet dream- the times Johnathan had been around made Emerson yearn for the neglect.

There was no warmth, no affection, no approval from Johnathan Yates. He was cold, career-driven, and a professional fucking liar. He would stand on a podium and preach about family values- how every family needed a mother and father present, how children were gifts that should be cherished, how family was a divine privilege that no one should take advantage of.

L-O-L.

But the people ate it up. Though maybe that shouldn't be as surprising as Emerson always thought it was. His dad was a good looking guy. That thick, sandy blonde hair, a solid bone structure, and the impressive height ran in the family. And don't forget the charm. That twist of his lips that turned up into the perfect smirk, the casual raise of an eyebrow, the intense gaze that seemed to make women's panties drop instantly. Yeah, Emerson had definitely inherited that, too.

He had his mom's eyes though. Dark blue and piercing. His dad had blue eyes, too, but they were a cold like ice and never turned quite the stormy gray-blue that his mom's did when she was upset.

And she was upset a lot. That's what happens when your husband cheats time and time again, becoming less careful, less worried about who in the home is going to walk in on him and mistress number twenty-two, twenty-three, twenty...whatever.

The Yates family was too focused on keeping up appearances to ever actually do anything about all the affairs. His mom, Corrine, was a trophy wife, and she knew that to be the deal. She was pretty, blonde, and from a respectable family, which basically checked all the "wifey material" boxes for his dad.

Even though Corrine had been a stay-at-home mom, she'd rarely spent time with her only son. She busied herself with charity events and dinners, making appearances at benefits to make her husband look good. Emerson was tempted to feel bad for his mom at times but couldn't help the gnawing recognition that she had chosen that life. She never left her husband after everything he'd put her through, and that was her choice.

Emerson cleared his throat and cleared his head of those thoughts as he walked into the conference room, taking a seat near the head chair and gesturing to the one next to him for Tyler. Yeah, he'd successfully coerced the intern into joining the meeting.

He took out a folder with a legal pad and pen, ready to take notes on upcoming cases, but when he looked up he froze.

There she was. Those sexy lips that woke up some of his most sinful day dreams, thick black eyelashes surrounding maple brown eyes. Her posture, her expression, everything about this woman was tailor-made to shove a man to his knees and state that *she* was the head bitch in charge.

A scene played through his mind where he was literally on his knees in front of her and she was in that tight little skirt, one stiletto-encased foot on his shoulder, digging in as he got ready to fucking worship her.

Well, fuck. That was new.

Her gaze dragged over him for a quick beat and they locked eyes for a millisecond before she looked away again with that same look of disinterest she'd given him earlier.

Huh. Also new.

It irked him, to say the least, that she seemed so indifferent. Bored. Not interested. But hey, he was nothing if not determined. Headstrong and stubbornly persistent. And women were his forté. He could smooth-talk and persuade anyone to do just about anything, but women? Women were his sweet spot.

She sat down in the chair across from Tyler's and the steady flow of various men and women in suits and ties, skirts or pantsuits, filed in and filled out the long conference table.

Emerson nudged Tyler's elbow and made a subtle gesture toward the woman sitting across from them. He raised his eyebrow in a question- *You recognize her?* And Tyler's usual poker face faltered. His eyebrows shot up and he mouthed *"damn"* under his breath.

Yeah, well *damn* was an understatement, but he took the reaction to mean no, Tyler hadn't seen her before either.

One of the senior partners stood in front of the long table and began the meeting. Emerson did his best to take notes and pay attention, but was getting increasingly annoyed with himself and his wandering eyes that seemed to have some sort of magnetic pull toward the mystery woman across the table. He made mental notes about her with each in-voluntary glance her way. Her nails were manicured, painted in a subtle peachy-nude color that was professional and in no way ostentatious. Her lips, he confirmed again, were bare. No gloss, no lipstick, no stain. And *fuck* did they look juicy. He'd never focused so much on a woman's lips in his life.

Her skin was flawless caramel and cream, and her hair looked black until the sun caught it just right and he realized it was a deep, coffee brown. Normally he liked long hair on women. Something about it was fun and flirty, easy to grab onto when he was hitting it from behind. But hers fell below her jaw, not quite long enough to rest on her shoulders, and when she tousled it to one side before shaking it out, the motion went straight to his cock.

Not the time, bro. Not the time.

"And we have finally reached a decision on the highly anticipated Alpha National case," the droning voice of senior partner, Tom Bow-man caught Emerson's attention. He dragged his gaze from the woman's perfect throat- he'd been imagining licking it, sucking on it, watching it curve back as she pressed her head into his pillow- to the much less appealing short, balding, bespectacled man who had the floor.

"This was a tough call, and I know it's completely unorthodox, but we don't think we could put this case in better hands," Tom said. "We've watched this associate's work from a distance and seen nothing but results. Everyone, we are proud to be handing the case over to-"

Emerson smoothed a hand over his tie but refrained from getting ready to stand up already, wanting to at least pretend he was shocked and humbled by their decision.

"-our newest associate, Miss Gabriella Cabrera."

Emerson stopped short, hand on the arm of his chair, glancing around the room for some sort of explanation. Tom had specifically told him a week ago that he was the best guy at Warren & Blakely for a job of this magnitude. What the fuck? Who the fuck was-

And then she stood up. The woman he'd been eyeing, studying like a goddamn psychopath for the last half hour.

He felt his gaze turn steeley as he watched her make her way to the front of the room and shake Tom's hand. She smiled, beaming, and even her smile was fucking perfect, but he couldn't appreciate it. Not now. His jaw clenched and he hesitated to let his breath out all the way.

Was this some sort of sick joke? He couldn't trust a goddamn thing right now. He wasn't even sure his chair wasn't on some sort of trap door, waiting to be opened so the floor could swallow him whole.

He felt Tyler shift uncomfortably in his seat next to him. Of course Emerson had told Tyler he had this case in the bag. They'd spent hours at his brother's bar downtown coming up with what kinds of shit he'd spend the extra money on once he'd won the case. Tyler had far more reasonable and responsible ways to invest the extra cash, but all Emerson wanted was a timeshare in Hawaii. He'd visit a few times a year and bang local twenty-somethings in their hula skirts.

The hollow applause died down before Emerson even realized his colleagues were clapping for her. He might've been the only one who didn't, but who fucking cared? That was his case. She'd worked here for an hour and a half and was already taking his caseload.

"Hi everyone, I'm Gabriella Cabrera-Perez," she announced through her plastered-on smile, "I knew about this case when I was hired, but had no idea until about an hour ago that I was up to take the lead on it and I am honored. I'm thrilled to have such a strong start here at Warren & Blakely, and I am going to make you all proud. And lots of money."

Tom chuckled heartily at the last comment and gave her one last pervy handshake before she went back to her seat.

Emerson didn't realize he was watching her again, like a hawk- or a serial killer in the shadows- until her eyes flicked up to his. She didn't look away this time. He knew how he was glaring, he could practically feel the room grow darker as his eyes swirled stormy blue. Gabriella met his stare, then raised one perfectly waxed eyebrow in challenge. She knew that case was supposed to be his. She knew she'd snuck it right out from under him.

Like he said, Warren & Blakely was viciously competitive. Kill or be killed. Slay or be slain. He'd give her this round, but she was about to find out exactly what happened when someone tried to beat him at his own game. She may not know it yet, but this was fucking war.

Gabby was back in her office, already buried in legal documents, learning every piece of information she could possibly absorb about this case. The research was the boring part, but it was necessary. She'd developed a fool-proof plan for organizing and was meticulous about her routine when it came to approaching cases like these.

She was grateful, however, for the number of assistants Warren & Blakely had to offer. Around noon, a tall, young intern with a friendly smile, short black hair, and warm chestnut skin popped into her office. He'd introduced himself as Tyler Watson and said that he was an intern, or the "office bitch", on the sixth floor, and let her know that if she needed any files read and summarized, copies made, or a Starbucks run, he was her guy. He also welcomed her to the building and congratulated her on the case. She couldn't help wondering what the hell a nice kid like that was doing in a cut-throat corporate law firm, but reminded herself that he was an intern. A little seasoning, and he'd toughen up a bit.

Just before six o'clock, she still felt like she'd barely made a dent in all the case information. She knew she could stay as late as she needed, but her stomach was growling. She'd only brought a small southwest salad for lunch, and although she could easily have something delivered, she knew her mom was cooking.

In the week or so that she'd been back, Gabby had eaten more home-cooked meals than in the past decade combined. She was used to take-out and food-prepped meals, but after being reunited with her mom's homemade cooking, she didn't know how she could possibly go back to microwaved enchiladas, chopped salads, and chicken and rice for dinner every night.

Blowing out a breath after the next growl rumbled through her stomach, she accepted defeat for the night, and decided to start cleaning up. She wasn't even at her desk anymore. She was organizing files by category and the only place that had room for all those stacks was the floor. So here she was, sitting with her legs out, ankles crossed, and pumps kicked off, surrounded by legal documents on the floor.

There was a knock on the other side of her office door, and she stood abruptly, holding three different stacks of files in her hands. Hastily toeing her way back into her heels, she called out, "It's open!"

The door creaked open slowly and standing in the doorway was that man from earlier. Well, from earlier in the meeting, and even earlier than that at the front door this morning. His tie was loosened and he leaned casually against the door frame.

"You're still here," he remarked. And *oh...God...*that voice? He's got to be kidding with that voice, right? It was deep and rich, low and gravelly, naturally husky like its sole purpose was seducing women or reading romance audiobooks at the very least. "Long first day, huh?"

He looked down at the floor where several more piles of documents were neatly stacked, then back up to her. Then she remembered that look he'd given her in the meeting that morning. After Tom had announced their intention to give her the case. He'd been pissed, but otherwise composed. The way he'd stared her down, she was surprised he hadn't leapt across the conference table and attacked her.

"I suppose," Gabby replied, nonchalant. She dropped the files in her arms onto her desk and stepped toward him, taking control of the situation. It was her office, and she'd be damned if she'd let this guy intimidate her in her own office. "We haven't been properly introduced. I'm Gabriella Cabrera-Perez." She extended her hand politely.

His eyebrow ticked up and stayed there.

Are eyebrows supposed to be sexy?

"That's quite the mouthful. Got any nicknames?"

"No," she stated, piercing him with a look she hoped he felt in his bones. No way in hell was she about to tell this guy he could call her Gabby or Gabs or any of the names her family or anyone close to her used out of endearment.

He hummed. "Well, I'm just going to call you Gabe, because that's easier for me."

"Gabe?" she repeated flatly. "That's a boy's name."

"It's 2021, how do you know? You can't just slap genders on shit these days."

Gabby rolled her eyes. "You can call me Gabriella."

"Sure thing, Gabe," he said with a wink. She narrowed her eyes, annoyed. Finally he took her hand in his and shook it. "Emerson William Yates, since you want to be so formal."

"That's quite the mouthful," she said, throwing his own line right back at him.

A slow, devilish grin dragged across his lips and his blue eyes sparkled like sapphires. "So I've been told."

Gabby scoffed and pulled her hand out of his grip as he chuckled quietly to himself at his own pervy joke. Now she really wanted to smack that cocky, sexy, playboy grin right off his face.

"They must've made you think you'd be getting the Alpha case. I wonder what made them change their minds."

His features immediately darkened and she grinned, triumphant.

Emerson recovered quickly, looking indifferent as he said, "Eh, more free time, I guess. I won't be the one sitting on the floor buried in legal documents until nine o'clock at night."

"Oh, I'm sure. More free time to enjoy those private rooms at the local strip club or roofie a college girl's drink at the bar," she said coolly.

He laughed, and that damn smirk still wouldn't wipe off his obnoxiously handsome face. "That's an astounding assessment you've made of me."

"Yeah, well, I'm a lawyer. I read people."

"Mhmm…" Emerson eyed her for another moment and she kept her poker face, her indifferent, resting bitch face. "Well, I'll leave you to it. I'd hate for you to get behind on your first day."

"How thoughtful of you."

"If you're here too late and find yourself getting lonely, feel free to send me a message." She was sure he deliberately let his eyes linger over her chest before sliding his gaze back up to her face, that stupid, cocky, playboy grin back in place.

Instead of feeling absolutely disgusted like she knew she should have, her heart fluttered and her vaginal walls clenched. *Ugh!* What the hell kind of reaction was that? Her lady bits were betraying her brain, and that was *never* a good sign. Luckily she made sure her face didn't show it. Instead, she curled her lip and scoffed derisively.

"Don't count on it," she replied, her response clipped and definitive. Of course her attitude didn't faze him one bit. If possible, his grin grew more wicked and those damn blue eyes twinkled mischievously.

This guy…Emerson Yates…he was dangerous. Not in a serial killer, serial rapist kind of way- she didn't actually think he would roofie college girls' drinks. But he was dangerous in the way that made her brain and her body disconnect. The way that made her silently wonder what types of things he could do with her body, how those strong hands and that taut, muscled skin would feel against hers. All while simultaneously sending off alarm bells. The guy was a walking red flag, and she needed to stay the hell away.

Emerson backed away, pulling the door shut as he called out, "Have a good night, Gabe!"

The door closed before she could call out a retort. *Dammit.*

One day in and she'd already made an enemy.

Chapter 3

Emerson threw back his second shot of Jameson and slammed the glass back down on the bar. "This is fucking bullshit!"

"Did you talk to Tom?" Tyler asked, wincing harshly at his first shot.

They were sitting up at the bar at Trojan Horse, the downtown sports bar that was owned by Tyler's older brother, Chris Watson the third, and his best friend, Jett Miller. Emerson had intercepted Tyler on his way to his car and made him walk down the short block and a half to his new favorite place to drink, bitch about work, and pick up women. Occasionally. He didn't really need to pick new women up- he had a veritable smorgasbord of willing sexual partners that were just a text message away- but he was always willing to add more names to the list.

"That jackass," Emerson snapped. "I tried, but he fucking dodged me. He knew I was pissed and turned into a little bitch. Slipped out early while I was on my way to his office. He was all fucking shifty-eyed, looking over his shoulder. He knew. He fucking knew I wasn't going to take it laying down."

He grabbed another shot glass and tossed back the amber liquid. Upon arrival, he'd taken a seat on a bar stool and ordered six shots of Jameson- three for him, three for Tyler- but he had a feeling he'd be consuming most of them at this rate.

"Rough day at work?" Tall, dark, and handsome Chris Watson had pushed his way out of the kitchen and now stood on the other side of the bar. "Xander said you came in here on a mission." Chris surveyed the four empty shot glasses in front of them next to the two full ones that remained. "Was that mission to get hammered and make an ass out of yourself? Because if so, you can take your shit somewhere else. I don't need that drama. My bar doesn't need that drama. We get enough publicity."

Emerson's eyes slid involuntarily to the white and blue number twelve baseball jersey behind the bar and scowled.

Ugh... Quinn Casey and his shrine. That fucking dick.

Okay, it really wasn't personal. The few times Emerson had been in the baseball All-Star's company, he actually didn't mind the guy. He was all right. His annoyance, his dislike, his...contempt for the guy was purely based on principle. Quinn Casey was engaged to Raelyn DeRose. Emerson used to be engaged to Raelyn DeRose. It's primal biology- you can't like a guy who has fucked or is fucking a girl you're with or were once with. A girl you once thought of as *yours.*

Sure, the reason Raelyn was no longer his was entirely his own fault, but...that was beside the point.

Chris, Jett, and Tyler had grown up with Quinn, and the locals knew he frequented the bar in his off season or during his and Raelyn's visits to see their families. Since the previous summer anyway, the bar's business had skyrocketed because of the cocky son-of-a-bitch. While Emerson was glad the bar was thriving and his friends' business was doing well, he didn't appreciate the giant shining spotlight on their friend; he had to force himself to look away from it every time he sat at the bar. The constant reminder of what was quite possibly the biggest fuck-up of his life and the consequences of that fuck-up.

But the past was in the past. And right now he had another unbearably sexy woman to be pissed off about.

"I'm not going to make an ass of myself," Emerson said flatly before taking his fourth shot. He shoved the last one at Tyler. "Just got fucking played at work and I'm pissed off. I need to blow off some steam." His eyes caught sight of a particularly curvy redhead wearing black leggings, and a silky green top that showed enough cleavage to leave little to the imagination. "Or maybe I just need to fuck away some of this frustration."

The redhead turned and caught his gaze and he winked. She blushed in response, biting her lip to conceal that girlish giggle she didn't want to come out.

The image of a sassy brunette with flawless skin and full lips flooded the forefront of his brain long enough for him to remember the exact color of her eyes. He blinked.

What the fuck was that about?

He turned back to the guys at the bar and reached for another shot glass, but Tyler had apparently given into peer pressure and taken the final shot, so he ordered a Heineken.

"She's cute," Tyler said, after a glance in the redhead's direction. "Not as cute as *Gabriella Cabrera-Perez* though." He wiggled his eyebrows obnoxiously at Emerson.

"She is *not* cute."

"You're right, she's not," Tyler agreed. "She's fucking gorgeous."

"No...she's not."

Okay, yes, she was. But he couldn't let that distract him. They were at war.

"Who's Gabriella...whatever-whatever?" Chris asked curiously, placing two bottles of Heineken on the bar.

Emerson grinned inwardly at the darker-complected mini-me he'd created over the past six months. Tyler was a fantastic student. He wore impeccable suits, was always neatly groomed- he'd even started growing a beard a few months ago and always kept it perfectly trimmed. They went to the bar together after work, drank Jameson and Heineken, and Tyler was an excellent wingman. He rarely took girls home himself, even when Emerson offered his own wingman skills. That might be the only thing he hadn't managed to do- Tyler wasn't a ladies' man. It wasn't his fault or anything. The kid was smooth, and could lay down a good line just as well as any bachelor on the prowl. He just didn't seem interested.

Oh, right, and the whole *good-guy lawyer* thing. But he still had a little over a week with Tyler. He was determined and almost always got what he wanted. He wasn't giving up yet.

"She's the reason we're here," said Tyler. He looked meaningfully at Emerson as though asking if he would like to take it from there. When Emerson grunted, Tyler continued, "Tom, one of the senior partners, told Emerson he'd be 'the best guy' for this new case- a major case with a *huge* payday if he won- and this morning, they announced they were giving it to Gabriella. A completely new associate at the firm. It was her first day and she got this case everyone's been anticipating for weeks."

"No shit?" Chris raised an eyebrow at Emerson, "So, what, are you pissed that you lost to a girl?"

Emerson glared, "Girl? She's not a *girl*, she's a fucking She-Devil."

Tyler and Chris both laughed.

"All day, man. I had to listen to this all day," Tyler said to his brother. "I went into her office to talk to her...introduce myself. She seemed nice enough."

"Nice?" Emerson narrowed his eyes. "*Nice?* You think the fucking bride of Satan seemed *nice?*" He shook his head. "No no no, Ty. She's a lawyer. A corporate, relentless, cut-throat she-demon. She's like a praying mantis. Luring you in with her enticing, delicious-looking lady bits. She'll treat you to a good time and then- Bam! Rip your goddamn head off before you even finish coming."

While Tyler and Chris, clearly not appreciating the gravity of the situation, burst into laughter again, two more familiar faces joined them at the bar.

"What the fuck did I just walk in on?" Jett Miller pulled a bar stool out for his girlfriend, Zoey Nunez, before taking his own seat next to Emerson.

"Emerson has a new arch-enemy," Tyler explained. He told Jett and Zoey the same thing he'd told Chris and, if possible, Emerson seethed even more.

"Wow, so you're saying that someone promised you something and then went behind your back and...betrayed you?" Jett summed up. "Huh, how'd that feel?"

Emerson let a heavy, hot breath out through his nose. He didn't miss the connection his friend was trying to make, but chose to ignore it. Or just be an ass about it. "It felt like I should've fucking expected it."

Jett rolled his eyes and ordered himself a Labatt Blue, and "the new usual" for his girlfriend.

"No more gin and tonic?" Emerson asked, glancing down the bar at Zoey. She and Jett had started dating back in late November and had already bought a house and moved in together almost three months ago.

It was fucking nuts, in Emerson's opinion, but he couldn't deny they made sense together. Even if Zoey was a ten, and Jett was a curly-haired dork with no game. Jett was a good looking dude, but how he'd managed to land someone so hot- not to mention six years younger than him- was a mystery. The guy was painfully awkward in front of attractive women. He used goofy accents and was always cracking corny jokes. But apparently that worked for her. And if he was being honest, he was happy for them.

Chris placed a rocks glass in front of Zoey. It looked like her usual gin and tonic with a lime on the side.

"Different gin," Zoey shrugged simply.

Quickly getting back to the issue at hand, Emerson hummed. "I have to make her quit."

"What?" Tyler asked.

"I have to make her life at the firm so fucking awful that she quits. Can't stand it. She cracks. And then the case- and the six figure pay day- is mine."

"That's insane. What are you going to do? Put fake spiders in her desk? Booby-trap her office so a bucket of water falls on her head when she walks in?" Jett asked.

"I like where your head is at with this talk of boobies, but no. I wouldn't do anything so juvenile."

Chris chuckled. "'I'm too mature for that' says the guy who still laughs when someone says 'booby-trap'."

"I was thinking bigger. We need to dig into her history, see if we can find any dirt on her. Where is she from? Where did she work before? Did she have any unprofessional relationships there? Did she give Tom a blowie on her first day and that's why he gave her this case instead of me?"

"When you say 'we', I really hope you don't intend on involving me in that," Tyler said.

"Of course you're involved. You're on my side, aren't you? You're my legal assistant. You'll do the work I fucking give you." Emerson was zoned in on his target now, his mind swirling with ideas, different ways to break his new nemesis.

"Technically I'm the whole floor's assistant. Which also means I'm Gabriella's assistant, too."

Emerson sat up straighter and the corners of his mouth curled up devilishly.

"Oh god, I think that's the face the Grinch made when he decided to steal Christmas," said Jett.

"Tyler, Tyler…" Emerson sighed, putting a hand on Tyler's shoulder, "You're probably the smartest person I know- besides me, of course. I think you know exactly what I need from you."

"Oh boy…" The intern looked to be holding his breath.

"You've already established a relationship with her, right? A friendly rapport, if you will."

"I literally stopped in her office once today to introduce myself. She didn't ask me for anything else all day," he argued.

Emerson ignored him. "You, my friend, are going to go behind enemy lines. You're going to collect intel and report back. Tell me her daily routine, where she eats, what she eats, how she takes her coffee. You're going to find out *everything* you can. What she likes, her weaknesses, find out about her relationships, her family- no detail is too small."

"Emerson, bud, I think you're losing it," Tyler said, with a furrowed, concerned look on his face.

"This is fucking war, Ty," Emerson replied, pounding his beer bottle on the bar top. "I'm getting my case back. And I'm going to make her leave. For good."

"Or," Zoey's feminine voice cut through Emerson's wicked thoughts suddenly. "What if you just look at the silver lining? It's sort of extreme, don't you think? The things you're talking about? Couldn't you get in trouble? What if you end up losing your job?"

"I'm touched you're concerned, sweet cheeks, but that's not going to happen," he said confidently. The use of a pet name was clearly unappreciated as Jett responded with an intense glare.

"Okay, but maybe it would be best to just embrace it. Life is full of surprises, right? So, you didn't get this case and you thought you would. That's okay," Zoey shrugged. God, she was so cute and naive. "This anger you're feeling is probably completely normal. Maybe you feel like you failed, but remember, with all failure comes growth. As long as you can accept it, you can grow from it."

Emerson stared down the bar, past Jett who had put his hand on top of Zoey's. Her eyes were pretty hazel globes of optimism. He set his gaze in a steely glare. "Wow, Zo. That might possibly be the dumbest fucking advice I have ever heard. Congratulations."

Jett punched Emerson's arm. "Don't talk to my girlfriend like that! She's just trying to be helpful, and you didn't even do anything to deserve it. Jesus, listen to you, talking about having an arch-nemesis like you're actually in one of your damn superhero movies. I think she's right- you need to accept it and move on."

Emerson rolled his eyes before he looked back at Zoey. His brow furrowed. She looked...upset. Like she was pouting or...

"Are you crying?"

"No," Zoey squeaked.

But her lip was quivering, her eyes were glossy with tears, and her breathing was heavy but controlled, as though trying not to let out a sob.

"You made her cry, you asshole! Apologize to my girlfriend right now!"

"Shit, I'm sorry!" Emerson exclaimed, putting his hands up defensively. "Fuck, I had no idea she was so sensitive." This earned him another punch in the arm and he winced, rubbing his bicep.

He took another look at Zoey, taking in her full appearance this time. It was early spring, and in Michigan, Mother Nature was a bipolar bitch, going from sunny to snowy one day to the next. Today was a sunny, seventy degree day, and Zoey was wearing a light yellow cotton sundress with short sleeves and a scoop neckline. Of course this neckline drew Emerson's attention directly to her chest. Her tits looked amazing as usual. This was something he noticed frequently, but even he wasn't dumb enough to voice this out loud in front of Jett. His eyes lingered at her phenomenal cleavage, noticing the swells of her breasts looking more rounded and pronounced. Trailing down, he stopped where the cotton was clinging over her lower abdomen.

Zoey was petite and tiny, but there was the smallest protrusion that hadn't been there before. Was it odd that Emerson paid this close attention to a girl he wasn't with and absolutely had no chance to be with? Perhaps. But what could he say? He had a true appreciation for the female form.

"What's the new gin, Zo?" He asked slowly, eyeing the clear, bubbly glass in front of her. He hadn't even realized it was her second one. She never drank that quickly.

"Hm?" Zoey's eyes went wide, then darted from her drink, back to him, then to Jett.

"The new gin. You used to drink Hendrick's- occasionally Bombay. What did you switch to?" He paused and watched her freeze, mouth partially open. "You're drinking Sprite, aren't you?"

"Um…" She hesitated before caving, "Okay, yes, it's just Sprite!"

"You're pregnant?!" Emerson shouted.

"Yeah," Zoey smiled brightly through the few tears that remained. She wrapped a hand around Jett's arm who smiled with her. "Yeah, we're having a baby. We're due in November."

Emerson shot a look across the bar at Chris. "You knew about this?"

Chris nodded. "Well, yeah. For about a month now, actually. Victoria and I told them our news…"

"You and Victoria are having another one?"

"We are. In September," Chris smiled proudly.

"Congrats, man! Sophia will be a great big sister," Emerson replied. Then he turned his attention back to Jett and Zoey. "What the fuck, you guys? What the hell is wrong with you?"

"He gets a congratulations, but we don't?" Jett asked.

"No! No, you don't get my congratulations! *They* did it right! What are you thinking? You're not even married! You're not engaged! You guys have been together for like…five fucking minutes! You couldn't keep it wrapped?" Emerson was suddenly furious. He'd finally gotten Jett into his social circle, worn him down as a friend, and now he was going off and having a baby. "You practically live here, Jett. You can't bring babies into bars. Where the fuck are we going to hang out? What about video game night? What about me? We're friends now. When am I going to see you?"

"Seriously?" Jett raised an incredulous eyebrow. "What about *you?* That's why you can't be happy for us?"

"So, are you just going to take her down to the courthouse? Have you bought a ring yet? Do I get to be the best man?" Emerson's questions flew out of his mouth with barely a breath between words.

Jett looked to be suppressing a laugh. "Um…I had no idea you were so traditional. No, we're not going to the courthouse. No, I don't have a ring yet- we just bought a house, which is pretty damn well suited for a family. I think that's what matters more."

"And that would be a *hell* no on the best man front," Chris chimed in.

"This is just great. Just. Fucking. Great." Emerson sighed heavily again and took a long pull from his beer. "This might be the worst fucking day of my life."

"You just made my pregnant girlfriend cry, so I'm having a hard time feeling bad for you right now," Jett said. He wrapped his arm around Zoey's shoulders and kissed the side of her head.

"I said I was sorry," Emerson grumbled. "And I am, Zoey. I'm sorry for making you cry and I'm sorry your selfish boyfriend couldn't be bothered to use a rubber. I should've known, though. Your tits are bigger. They look fantastic."

Jett looked like he wanted to throttle him for a second before Zoey smiled genuinely. "Thank you, Emerson, that means a lot."

"Any time," he said with a wink. He was beginning to think his night was going to have a turn-around; normally if he gave Zoey any kind of compliment about her appearance she would scoff or roll her eyes, and Jett would glare or punch him- usually in the arm or shoulder, but he hadn't pissed him off enough for a face or gut punch. Yet.

Remembering the flirty redhead from earlier he turned in his bar stool to look around for where she'd gone off to. It wouldn't take long to get her to come home with him. A new face, a new body to explore, a new pussy to get lost in. Yeah, that would clear his head and help him focus, and he needed to be on his A-game tomorrow at work.

"Better move fast," Tyler said, nodding toward the front door of the bar. "She's on her way out with her friends."

God dammit. Sure, he'd like the distraction, but no way was he chasing a girl down when she was only three feet from the door. That was a good way to look desperate. Or like a creep.

He let out a frustrated groan and slouched into the back of the bar stool. Tonight was really, *really* not his night.

Chapter 4

"You would absolutely not believe this guy, Marco." Gabby sat back in her lounge chair on the patio and tipped back her full glass of Chardonnay. "It was like talking to the Devil himself. Underneath all that charm and those eyes- Marco, his *eyes!* I hate him. I hate how much I'm attracted to him, and the fact that he's attractive makes me hate him even more."

"Sounds like you guys would have amazing hate sex," Marco grinned over his far more modest pour of wine.

"Hate sex?" Gabby curled her lip. "Marco, that's not a thing. And if it is, it shouldn't be."

"It's absolutely a thing," her twin insisted. "It's for those instances, such as this one, where you find yourself physically attracted to someone who is in all other ways completely repulsive. Like this Emerson fellow."

Gabby rolled her eyes and took another deep swill from her wine glass. "I don't really know him, to be perfectly honest. He held the door open for me this morning at least, but the way he glared at me after Mr. Bowman announced I had the case...you should've seen it. He was practically burning Superman eye-laser beams into my skin."

After Emerson had left her office that evening, she had taken her time picking up her office, not wanting to run into him in the parking lot since he seemed to think she needed to stay longer- not that it mattered what he thought, but...just as a precaution, anyway- and then headed straight to her mom and dad's for dinner. Marco and his husband, Max, had been there and could immediately tell that something was bothering her. They'd been gracious enough to wait until the rest of the family had cleared from the table before peppering her with all their questions.

When her mom had asked her how her first day at the new job went, she'd focused on the positives: She'd gotten a huge case that everyone at her office was talking about and they'd made the announcement first thing that morning. She couldn't go into too much detail about the case, but she did mention that it came with a substantial bonus if she won.

As soon as Marco had discovered the reason she seemed off was because of a man, he'd insisted on heading back to her place with her for some good old fashioned wine-and-gossip time. So, here they sat on the balcony of her condo, sipping Chardonnay and gossipping like aged southern belles on a porch swing.

Max slid the glass door behind him as he came back outside with the remaining bottle of wine and a chiller to set it in. Bless his heart.

"It sounds like this guy has never been told no before," Max suggested, taking a seat in the patio chair next to Marco. "He probably just assumed he'd get the case and is pissed that he lost to a woman."

"I wouldn't be surprised. He looked so perfectly put together. Like he'd never done a single piece of manual labor in his life. Like he's always had people to do that stuff for him. Like maybe he'd look down on someone who comes from a background like mine," Gabby said.

"People probably say that about me, too," said Max. He had a point. Max was also tall, with perfectly quaffed blonde hair, hazel-green eyes, and a stunning bone structure. A great, square jawline, a straight nose, and a permanent tan. He had a sort of pretty-boy look that was just a touch more masculine than her brother's. Max was like one of those guys who could pass for a construction worker model in a *Playgirl* magazine. He had enough masculinity and muscle to make a girl swoon, but that didn't change the fact that he waxed his chest.

"It's different, I think. Emerson..." Gabby shook her head as she tried to put it into words, "he's just got this arrogance about him. It's like a cloud surrounding him and it infiltrates the room as soon as he steps in. I mean, he told me to send him a message if I got lonely. Who the hell does that? And he stared at my breasts for a solid five seconds as he said it."

"Gross," Max scrunched up his nose.

"You know what makes it even worse?" Gabby continued, "I bet that works for him. I bet he gives these forward advances on women all the time and he just has them eating out of the palm of his hand."

"Well, maybe those women will, but not you," Marco said definitively. "You, my dear sister, are better than that. You have class and self respect, and you would never fall for some bullshit lines and a pretty face."

Gabby blew out a long breath. "I just wish I could do my job without being surrounded by all these trust fund assholes trying to mansplain everything and thinking they're better than me."

She stared out over the glass railing to the view of the lake. There was absolutely nothing shameful about where she'd come from and how she'd gotten where she was. She'd earned it all herself. She couldn't have done it without the support of her family and all their hard work, of course. Her parents had risked everything, left the only life they'd ever known, and worked their asses off to give them a good life. Without them and their guidance, she didn't know where she would be.

Some people, however, particularly in her field of work, were raised to believe that people like her were below them. That they were born superior, as if it were a divine right that had been granted to them at birth.

"That's fine," Marco said with a shrug. "Let him believe he's better, and then show him how wrong he is."

"Exactly." Max nodded. "You're where you are because you worked hard to get there. You were your high school valedictorian because you worked for it. You earned your SAT scores and every other outstanding achievement that made Yale- an *ivy league school*- pay for you to go there. That means something. You're a badass, girl. Fucking show him."

Marco sat up and held out his wine glass, his brown eyes bearing into her identical ones. "To giving him hell!" Max raised his glass and Gabby smiled, feeling a little proud and a lot badass.

"To giving him hell," she said coolly, joining her own drink into the circle and clinking glasses.

Gabby got to Warren & Blakely a solid twenty minutes early Tuesday morning to get a head start on the day and all of her paperwork. She needed copies made so that she could have backups, and she had about ten thousand more pages of legal briefs to examine. She thought of that intern who had offered to read and summarize documents for her and silently hoped he'd stop by again.

In previous jobs, she'd rarely made use of interns and assistants because she wanted things done a certain way and she didn't want stupid mistakes that could have easily been avoided if she'd just done the work herself. With a case this big, however, she figured she just might have to suck it up and accept some assistance.

Stepping off the elevator onto the fourth floor, she had to squeeze by two men in blue maintenance uniforms moving a large desk down the hall. She smiled politely and let them get by her before making her way to her new office. Turning the key in the lock, she pushed her door open and froze.

Her office was significantly more bare than the previous day.

Her desk was gone.

Gabby looked around curiously, wondering if there was a note or a memo that she'd missed about being moved to a different office, but saw nothing. Quickly, she slipped back down the hall and managed to catch the two maintenance men as they were halfway into the elevator.

"Excuse me, did you take that desk out of room 408?" She pointed to the desk and gestured down the hall toward her office.

"Yes, ma'am. We got the work order first thing this morning from a Mister..." the scruffy, bearded man looked to be thinking, "Gates? Something like that. It was in the email."

"Yates," the other provided.

Of course.

"Well, that wasn't necessary. I hate to ask you this, but is there any way you can take it back? That was in my office and I didn't authorize the removal of it."

The two men looked uncomfortably at one another and hesitated. "I'm sorry, ma'am. We got the work order, so you'll have to take that up with our supervisor or the...Mr. Yates, was it? The guy who initiated the order."

Gabby let out a frustrated sigh. "Great...okay, well I'll be in touch with your supervisor then. Thank you, guys."

"Sure thing."

"Sorry about that, ma'am."

Gabby waved them off before heading back down the hall. "Not your fault."

Unbelievable. Fucking unbelievable.

She slammed her office door behind her and sighed, looking at the empty space in front of her. Part of her wanted to storm down the hall to Emerson's office and ask him what the hell he was thinking, but she didn't want to give him the satisfaction of knowing he'd pissed her off. So instead, she pulled her laptop out of her bag, set it on the wide window ledge and pulled up Wayfair, in hopes of finding a new office desk by the end of the day.

By 10 a.m., she was back on the floor, sitting in the same organized mess as the previous evening. At least seven different stacks of documents were in front of her in an arc, and her laptop was now at her side. She had kicked off her heels and shed her blazer, and was reading the same line for the ninth time when there was a soft knock on her door.

"It's open." She didn't bother getting up off the floor or trying to make herself look more presentable. Her coffee had worn off and all she cared about was getting through this next stack of documents.

The legal intern from the previous day popped his head in, then after a curious glance at the sight before him, he slowly stepped into the room and shut the door behind him. "Um...Miss Cabrera? You don't have a desk..."

"Yeah, I'm redecorating," she said, her eyes flashing up to him and back to her work.

"O...kay?" He looked around again awkwardly. "Emerson mentioned that you looked like you had a lot of work to do, and I thought I'd stop in and see if I could help you at all. It's sort of the biggest case in the office right now and I don't mind reading some of the boring stuff and going over it with you. I've been told I pay pretty spectacular attention to detail."

Gabby let her gaze travel back up to him, eyeing him critically, "Emerson sent you?"

"No, I wouldn't say he sent me. Just that he mentioned in passing that you had a lot more work going on than anyone else in the office right now and if I was going to offer up my stellar office bitch skills, why not help the attorney with the biggest caseload?"

"Office bitch skills?" Gabby repeated, nearly laughing. "His words or yours?"

"Originally his, but I've accepted my role. No use candy-coating it."

Gabby considered for a moment before resigning. "Sure, yeah, I could use some help. I usually try to do everything myself, but I'll be here until tomorrow morning if I want to get through all of this today."

She gestured to an empty spot on the floor in front of her. "Tyler, right?" He nodded, sitting on the floor and stretching his long legs out in front of him. She thought he looked like he was trying not to laugh. "What? I know it's not exactly practical..."

"Or comfortable," he said with a grin. "Maybe if you got some of those pillow things the Japanese sit on when they have meals."

"Maybe that's my plan, and the pillows just haven't come in yet."

Tyler raised an eyebrow and smirked. "He had your desk taken out, didn't he?"

Gabby opened her mouth and Tyler began to laugh. "Is he always that terrible? Or is this like a newby hazing sort of thing?"

"He does enjoy hazing the interns, but you're not an intern. This is just..." Tyler shrugged. "Emerson doesn't get told no a whole lot. And he's really used to getting things his way."

"I suspected that."

Tyler laughed again. "You know, I'd love to be able to tell you he's just one of those guys who's not so bad once you get to know him, but...he honestly is sort of an asshole. You just kind of...get used to it."

Gabby made a face. "Get used to it? Why hasn't anyone ever tried putting him in his place? Knocking that ego down a few pegs?"

"I think his ego is like that monster in *Hercules*. You can try chopping its head off, but it'll just grow three more."

She was quiet for a moment, remembering that confident air he had about him, almost visible like a cloud that followed him around and kept away anything that would tell him he was less than amazing at everything. Maybe it was less like a cloud and more like a forcefield. Super powers to come with that Superhero bod- of course his name would be Ego Man, and he'd fight crime with untouchable confidence, unwavering arrogance, and a piercing sapphire gaze that made lady parts want to melt and say to hell with feminism.

"Well, maybe the massive ego-dragon just hasn't met its Hercules yet."

But he was about to.

Emerson peered out his office window at the darkening sky, overcast with storm clouds. Of course he was beaming from the inside out after his move this morning. He felt pretty satisfied that he was sending Gabriella the message that he was the boss around here and he could remove her just as easily as he could remove her furniture from her room. Or at least, that's what he was hoping.

His office door pushed open and he turned to see Tyler closing the door behind him. He found himself somewhat disappointed that it wasn't the She-Devil coming to yell at him about the desk.

"Where the hell have you been?" Emerson snapped.

"Working," Tyler replied. He dropped a thick file folder on his desk and scowled. "You took her desk out of her office?"

Emerson grinned smugly as he leaned back in his chair. "I didn't move anything. I put in a work order. That desk was ugly as fuck and way too big. The other day when I stopped in, all her shit was on the floor, so I thought I'd free up some work space for her."

"Oh, so it was an act of kindness?" Tyler replied skeptically. Of course he knew better.

Emerson shrugged, "I'm a thoughtful guy, what can I say?"

"You're an ass."

He could only laugh to himself. "So...did you figure anything out? Gather some intel?"

Rolling his eyes, Tyler reluctantly sat in the chair across from him and began listing things off. "She is from a big family- five siblings, one of which is a twin-"

"She has a twin?" Emerson sat up, grinning mischievously as new dirty thoughts swirled around his head. "That could be interesting. Maybe I could fuck her twin."

"That *would* be interesting, especially considering it's a twin brother."

"Dammit," he sighed. "Okay, what else?"

Tyler continued, "She likes her coffee black, hates jelly-filled donuts, but loves the long custard-filled ones-"

Emerson chuckled, "I've got a long custard-filled one she can have."

Tyler glanced up, clearly exasperated, "How old are you?"

"Keep going."

"Her favorite food is surprisingly a bacon cheeseburger- she doesn't look like she eats a lot of those. She reads romance novels, loves spending time in Barnes & Noble, and going to the beach. She loves baseball and her favorite team is the Miami Marlins, closely followed by the Tigers."

Emerson stared at Tyler incredulously. The guy had clearly missed the whole point. "What the fuck, Ty? I'm trying to destroy her, not date her!"

"You asked for information."

"All you did was bring me her fucking dating profile! I expected more from you."

Tyler rolled his eyes. "Well, don't you think it would've been weird if I'd asked her what her deepest secrets are or what she's afraid of most while we were just sitting there trying to work?"

"Not any weirder than whatever the fuck kind of conversation you clearly did have," Emerson retorted. "Are you taking her out for a nice seafood dinner later? Maybe share a strawberry milkshake with two straws while you gaze into her eyes?"

"I'm not trying to date her either. We were just sitting there and...I don't know, talking between reading."

"Aw, that's sweet. You gonna ask her to go steady and wear your varsity jacket?" Emerson teased. He wasn't sure why the idea of Tyler and Gabriella sitting across from each other at dinner or sharing a nice conversation over glasses of wine was making his muscles feel hot and tense, but he wasn't about to let it show, so he shoved it down.

Tyler glared and moved on. "She's got a shitload to do with that case. Honestly, you might've dodged a bullet with that one."

"You don't think I could handle it?" Emerson challenged, suddenly feeling competitive. "*I* could handle it, Ty. *I* should be on that case."

"I never said you couldn't handle it," said Tyler, putting his hands up defensively. "I just know you and how much you like to fuck around. You wouldn't be able to do that with a huge caseload like hers."

"I don't fuck around when it comes to my job. Other things, sure, but not my job. I'm the fucking best lawyer at this firm."

"Says the guy who had time to put in a work order to remove his new 'arch-enemy's' desk," Tyler replied, arching one eyebrow.

"That's different. I'm letting her know what's up. Showing her this is *my* territory and she has no fucking business on my case."

Emerson didn't like the way Tyler was looking at him, as though he'd lost it.

"Did you pee all over her office, too?" Tyler teased. "I hear that's a good way to mark your territory."

"I thought about it." He hadn't. That would be gross, but he felt the need to show Tyler he would do absolutely anything to prove his point.

To prove that he could get her to leave *and* take her job. To prove that they didn't need her here because he was plenty good for the job.

"Is that all you got for me?" Emerson asked, "That she likes long walks on the beach and Sylvia Day?"

Tyler looked confused. "Sylvia Day?"

"A romance author. Erotic romance, actually," he explained. "You should look into some of those books, Ty. All these women write their fantasies out, right where a man can look at them, but we walk right by them all the time. Why do you think women always say yes to another night with me? Because I know what they fucking want."

"Interesting...I had no idea you took your hook-ups so seriously," Tyler said, looking rather surprised and impressed.

"Hook-ups?" He was offended. "I give those women a goddamn romantic fantasy experience, Ty. If there were a theme park based on romance novels, it would be my bedroom, and I would be the main fucking attraction. I would be the ride. *All* of the rides."

"Well, excuse me, Romance King."

"In the bedroom I prefer Master or Daddy, but I suppose King will suffice."

"Gross. I'm not calling you either of those things. Ever," said Tyler. "I just meant that I didn't realize you did your research. I'm impressed. I sort of...I don't know, I guess I assumed you were one of those guys who just makes it all about himself."

Emerson gasped. "Tyler! I'm offended! No- what's worse than offended? Appalled! I'm appalled that you would think so little of me."

"Sorry."

Emerson folded his arms over his chest. "I don't think you mean that."

Tyler rolled his eyes, "Okay, well I didn't mean to insult you. I'm sure you truly are the romance grand master of your bedroom."

Unable to stop the crooked grin that pulled up the corner of his lips, Emerson shrugged as if it were nothing. "I really am."

Tyler pushed himself out of the chair and stood. "Well, I am going to go get some more work done. Do you need any copies? Anything read? Summarized? Analyzed?"

"Are you going back to *her* office?" Emerson pictured the two of them sitting on the floor, talking and getting to know each other, enjoying each other's company amid boring legal documents. He didn't like it. But why?

Because she was his enemy, and Tyler was his friend, obviously. He just didn't want Tyler getting too close and spilling his plan. That was it.

"Probably. I'll try to dig up more dirt for you, though I don't know what good it'll do. She seems like she can hold her own. I don't think she will scare easily."

Thunder rumbled outside and Emerson turned to see that it had started to rain at some point during their conversation.

He agreed with Tyler that Gabriella didn't seem like she would scare very easily. He remembered her presence as she'd walked into the conference room the previous morning. The way she carried herself, equally strong and graceful. Her curves were feminine and enticing, and they made his mouth water, but he knew better than to try his usual moves on her. She radiated empowerment and her gorgeous brown-eyed gaze demanded respect. A real-life Wonder Woman.

No, she wouldn't be easy to scare off. But when had he ever backed down from a challenge?

The rest of the workday went on with relatively little to report. Emerson was surprised to find himself increasingly annoyed every time someone entered his office who wasn't Gabriella. They crossed paths only once in the hallway, and she had barely even looked at him. It was as though she couldn't see him at all. His smug grin went completely unnoticed and instead he only felt more aggravated.

Unable to focus much after that, he decided to cut out earlier than usual. The rain was a full-on downpour when he got down to the lobby, but he was pleased to see Gabriella ahead of him, opening an umbrella beneath the overhang outside. He quickened his pace until he got to the first inside door, not wanting to miss her, then pushed the outer door open slowly.

"Hey there, Gabe," he said with what he knew to be a very charming grin.

She glanced over her shoulder at him, then narrowed her eyes in concentration. "Oh hi...Emmett, right?"

Emerson stopped short. His charm faltered for only a fraction of a second, but it was long enough for her to register it. *God Dammit.* She gave him a sly grin, and that wicked sexy look went straight to his dick.

He cleared his throat and composed himself again. "Emerson, actually."

"Oh, that's right. I've met so many people today." She waved a hand dismissively, trying to appear innocent, but he knew she was full of shit.

"Ty said you were working on the floor again," Emerson said. "You know, you might as well get rid of that monstrous desk. You'd have a lot more workspace."

Now it was her turn for her expression to falter and he grinned.

She shrugged. "Actually, it was sort of a monstrosity. I think I need something prettier, you know? Not so...brobdingnagian."

His eyebrows shot up. "I'm sorry? Is that English?"

"It is. It means unusually and unnecessarily gigantic."

He chuckled immaturely to himself. "Ah, yes. I've got something like that. No one's ever complained about it though."

Gabriella scowled. "Has anyone ever told you you're exhausting?"

He grinned again. "I've been told I know how to wear a woman out."

This time she shook her head and rolled her eyes, then started off toward the parking lot. Frustrated with himself that he hadn't checked the forecast and didn't have an umbrella with him, he hesitated before following her into the rain.

He jogged the few paces it took to catch up with her, then snatched her umbrella out of her hand. "Allow me." He ducked under it while shielding both of them from the rain and gave her a wink.

She gaped at him but had to quicken her pace to keep up with his longer strides. She was wearing those sexy heels again.

"You're unbelievable!" Gabriella huffed.

"Because I'm so good looking? Yeah, I get that a lot, too."

Her sigh mixed with a groan, and he couldn't help imagining hearing that sound in a different context. The crotch of his pants was starting to feel tight.

"Which one is your car? I'll walk you to it," he offered when they entered the parking lot together.

He was looking out into the sea of black, white, and silver cars, most of them Audis, Beamers, and Lexuses. When she didn't respond, he looked down to see that she was looking up at him as though he'd sprouted a second head. "What?"

She blinked and looked away. "Nothing. And it's fine, mine is just that Lincoln over there." She pointed to a newer model Lincoln in deep red that was only a few cars away. "Where's yours?"

Emerson looked around for his all black Lexus RC. He always parked in the same spot near the front sidewalk, but that space was empty.

Gabriella slid the umbrella from his hands as he stared on in confusion. "Oh, that's right! Yours was that Lexus with the battery that died! What a bummer. I just hate having my car towed."

She backed away toward her Lincoln and he swore he could see her devil horns poking out through that dark hair of hers. Her grin was wide and triumphant and just plain evil.

That. Bitch.

"Have fun walking home, Edmund!" She winked and was laughing as she slipped into her car and shut the door.

He could see her laughing still when she pulled out of the parking lot, leaving him standing alone in the rain with nothing but himself and the realization that he had severely underestimated his opponent.

Chapter 5

When Gabby got to work on Wednesday, she practically held her breath as she opened the door to her office. After her amazing car-towing prank, she knew Emerson was likely to hit back hard. Would he go *Home Alone* and set up a torturous maze of broken glass, hot door knobs, and swinging beams from the ceiling? Would he go high school senior-prank style and release livestock in her office? Her eyes went wide and her breath caught at the next terrifying thought- bugs. *What if he put bugs in my office?*

That was ridiculous. He couldn't possibly know that she was terrified of bugs. Literally all of them. Butterflies were okay to look at...from a distance. But she really was not a fan of any sort of creepy-crawly critters.

She exhaled and pushed her office door open. Nothing had changed. Her desk was still gone, though two chairs still remained, and the filing cabinets on the wall adjacent to the window were still in place.

Stepping into the room, she knew she should have felt at ease, but the fact that there was nothing glaringly obvious wrong with the space put her on edge. She felt like she should be waiting for the boogeyman to jump out of her closet.

Gabby shook those thoughts out of her head and told herself to stop being paranoid. She pulled her laptop out of her bag, took a large gulp of coffee from her tumbler and took a seat in her desk chair. According to a notification she'd received that morning, her new desk would arrive that afternoon. She'd paid extra to have it shipped in one day so that she could stop feeling so ridiculous about working on the floor.

She had just gotten all of her files organized in an arc in front of her when there was a light knock on the door. "It's open," she called out, not bothering to take her eyes off the file she was currently reading.

"Hi, Miss Cabrera?" An older woman with dark brown hair and stylish thick-rimmed glasses poked her head into the office. "My name is Alice Goldman, I'm one of the paralegals on this floor. I just wanted to come in and offer my congratulations!"

Gabby's eyebrows pulled together in confusion as she looked up at the woman again. "Congratulations?" She must have been talking about the case. Or the new job.

"Yes!" Alice beamed. She clasped her hands beneath her chin and looked like an over-excited school girl watching her crush walk by in the hallway. "On the baby!"

"*Baby?*" Gabby repeated, eyebrows shooting upward into her hairline.

"Yes, I heard that you're pregnant, and I'm just so excited for you!" Alice said, still smiling brightly. "Babies are just the best, aren't they? Now, I know you're doing the single mom thing, and that's totally your choice, but I think you owe it to yourself- and that baby- to at least figure out who the father is so you can let him know. I know we *independent* women think it's easier to just do everything on our own, but maybe the man will step up, right?"

Gabby stared in awe as she let all this new information reach her ears. Unable to come up with a proper response she simply nodded at Alice and thanked her for her advice. Once Alice was out of the room it finally registered what had happened.

A rumor? Really? How juvenile. She fumed silently, but pushed through and forced herself to concentrate on her work. Easier said than done. By noon, she had received at least a dozen visitors stopping by to offer their congratulations. Worse was when Tom stopped in and asked sincerely if she thought she would be able to work on such a big case while pregnant. He wanted to know if the pregnancy hormones would get in the way of her ability to think and reason critically as was required.

Of course, she knew she wasn't pregnant, but that question had pissed her off regardless. What was it about a woman's ability to reproduce that made men feel they were less competent and less capable of doing their jobs just as well? What had all these men learned about *female hormones* that led them to believe women turned into blubbering, inconsolable nit-wits? Seriously, sexual education in this country was a joke.

"Tom," Gabby said firmly, "I'm not pregnant. And even if I were, I assure you there is nothing that would stop me from being able to do this job."

Tom gaped at her through his wiry spectacles. "You're...*not* pregnant?"

"No. I'm not sure where the rumor got started, but I can assure you with one-hundred percent certainty that I am not with child." She stared him down for a few silent moments. He looked confused before nodding and backing toward the door.

"Well, good. I was concerned I might have to add another associate to the case. Mr. Yates, perhaps-"

"Definitely not," Gabby said, definitively. "I am fully capable of doing this on my own. Baby or no baby."

"But...there is no baby?"

"Correct," she nodded.

"Well, okay then. Good," Tom inclined his head briefly. "Carry on."

Gabby rolled her eyes when the door shut and sunk back into her chair.

Around two o'clock, her new desk arrived and she showed the movers where to place it. It was a white L-shaped desk with a built-in filing system, and plenty of storage space, without being bulky like the one that had come with her office. She was finishing up her organizational system when there were two short knocks on her door. The door swung open slowly before she had a chance to respond or answer it.

"Congrats, Gabe!" Emerson's low drawl made her stomach clench with annoyance as she looked up at him. "A new job *and* a baby. Wow, you modern women sure know how to have it all."

Gabby narrowed her eyes at him. He was looking far more smug and pleased with himself than when she'd last seen him getting drenched in the rain. The memory brought a smile to her face.

"What the hell is your problem?" she asked. "Are you in high school? Telling people I'm pregnant *and* I don't know who the father is?"

"Brilliant, right?" he replied, his blue eyes glittering like sapphires. "It's an oldie, but a goodie. I can't believe you're not even going to try figuring out who the father is. Think of your baby, Gabe. Doesn't it deserve to grow up with two parents?"

She rolled her eyes and sunk into her chair behind her desk. "You know, I really like you more when you're speechless in the rain." Her eyes met his for a moment and she grinned. "Did you enjoy your walk home?"

Emerson frowned as he took the seat across from her. "I wouldn't expect a She-Devil like yourself to understand, but I caught a ride with a *friend.* But thank you for asking."

"A *She-Devil?*" Gabby repeated, amused. "Wow, that's a new one. And I can honestly say I'm surprised to hear you have friends. Congrats."

"I wouldn't be opposed to taking you to meet some of these friends," he said, scratching his perfectly trimmed, close-cropped beard. "I understand we'd have to go at night, of course. When the sun is down so you don't melt or whatever."

"That's so sweet of you," Gabby laughed, "but I think I'm going to be a little busy tracking down all my potential baby-daddies. There are just so many of them."

Emerson chuckled and his smile actually struck her as genuinely handsome and pleasant. Obviously he was a good looking guy and he knew it- anyone with eyes would know it- but he had an easy smile that made his features look relaxed. When he smiled that way, he seemed far more real and approachable. It made her smile with him.

A brief silence settled over them and she couldn't help looking at him. He was annoyingly handsome, as always, and wearing a deep blue suit. The shirt he wore was white with a light blue check pattern, and with the combination of his tie, the whole effect truly brought out his sapphire eyes. His sandy blonde hair was thick, a little longer on top, and short on the sides. And of course the short, closely cropped, meticulously groomed beard that he must trim every morning. It was always the same length, and she wondered if he was baby-faced underneath, or if he'd still look like the epitome of masculine perfection. He emitted power, strength, and smooth, sexy confidence.

In her careful observation of the gorgeous specimen across from her, she noticed his glittering sapphire eyes had gone stormy, and realized his gaze was fixed on her mouth. She ticked up an eyebrow curiously before deciding he was definitely staring, so she licked her lips slowly. Bit her bottom lip. His Adam's apple bobbed and he licked his own lips. She wasn't sure why she felt so satisfied with herself that he was attracted to her. Maybe because he was so obviously attractive himself, and it had been a while since she'd really felt like she'd caught a man's attention?

A slow grin crossed her lips as she continued to watch him shamelessly watch her.

Something between a grunt and sigh escaped him and he muttered, "God*damn* those lips look fuckable."

"Excuse me?" Gabby snapped.

Emerson blinked and his eyes met hers, looking alarmed. Clearly he had *not* meant to say that out loud. "What?"

"What did you just say?" Gabby eyed him critically.

"Nothing." He smoothed down his tie and cleared his throat before standing up. Color crept into his face and he grinned. "It's a compliment, really."

"Oh, is it?" she asked, glaring at him as he backed toward the door.

"Of course," he said with a shrug. He bumped into his chair as he took a step back, paused, and righted it before carefully stepping around it and toward the door.

"Get out of my office, Edward." Gabby folded her arms over her chest and stared him down.

In an attempt to divert her attention from his obvious blunder, he opened the door and called over his shoulder, "Congrats again on the baby, Gabe!"

Once she was alone in her office again, she let out a heavy exhale and shook her head. Just when she'd thought he was almost bearable, he'd gone and said *that*.

But she couldn't help smiling. Discovering his attraction to her felt a lot like being handed brand new ammunition.

It was Friday, and Emerson was pleased to see that Gabriella was still having people stop by and offer their congratulations on her pregnancy. No matter how many times she shut it down and insisted there was no pregnancy, he was there to assure everyone that she was just embarrassed that she didn't know who the father was.

Another consequence of his brilliant rumor was that he discovered she was single. She never tried insisting that she would definitely know who the father was because she had a boyfriend, and something told him that she wasn't the type to do much sleeping around, either. Why this new information eased his mind, he wasn't sure. She was obviously attractive. Fucking gorgeous. He wouldn't be surprised if she caused accidents when she walked down the street, running errands on her lunch breaks. That was probably all it was. He was physically attracted to her and didn't like the thought of some other schmuck not fully appreciating her lips or those curves, or those big brown eyes and thick black lashes.

Fuck.

He adjusted himself in his dress pants. He didn't want to be attracted to her, but there was no denying it. Sneaky little siren that she was. She'd been intruding on his thoughts since Monday and he hadn't been able to push her out of his mind. Even last night when Taylor had shown up for their usual Thursday night fuck-fest, he hadn't been able to get Gabriella out of his mind. It was fucked up.

There he was, in his bed, with a perfectly hot, perfectly eager, willing, naked woman. And yet...when he'd turned her around and sent both of them toppling over the edge of ecstacy, Gabriella's face was the one he'd imagined. When he'd wrapped his hands in Taylor's caramel-brown hair, he'd wished it was a much darker shade of brown clenched in his fist. Her sexy little mouth, licking and biting that bottom lip as she sat across from him. Her feminine sigh and the graceful slope of her neck.

God dammit. Get it together!

That didn't mean anything. It especially didn't mean he had *feelings* about her. All it meant was that she was hot and he wanted to see her submit to him. That was it. It was perfectly normal to want to see her arching her back as he pounded into her from behind. It was normal that he'd imagined Gabriella's plump lips wrapped around his cock instead when Taylor had gone down on him the previous night. The woman was trying to emasculate him. Show him that she could do his job better. Of course he'd been imagining her like that.

Emerson didn't do feelings. They never worked out for him. They never lasted. He'd get bored and move on eventually. He'd been that way ever since junior high when his first girlfriend, Miranda, had invited him over to her house to "watch a movie". They'd fooled around a little, but when he'd taken a quick bathroom break, he'd been intercepted on his way back to her bedroom by Miranda's older sister, Natalie, who was a sophomore. A sophomore with a lot more experience. Natalie had pulled him into her bedroom and shown him the light- and that sex was fucking awesome. Even when Miranda came looking for him and found the two of them hastily pulling their clothes back on, he really struggled with feeling bad about it. Come on, he was fourteen and just had sex. How could anyone expect him to feel bad?

That basically set the tone for his dating career. He tried to stay out of relationships, because they always ended the same. Every now and then someone would keep his attention for a little longer than usual, but in the end there was always someone new. Someone more exciting. Someone different.

That's why for the past several months, he'd crafted a careful system- a rotation- of women he slept with on a regular basis. It was a schedule that ran like a well-oiled machine. Taylor was part of that rotation. She came over on Tuesdays and Thursdays at 8 o'clock when she didn't have to work late at the bar on Union street. Then there was Haylie. She came over on Monday nights and usually slept over so she could leave directly from his place to teach her early morning yoga class that was a short walk from his place. And then there was Jade- *mmm, Jade.* His Friday night fling. He still had a hard time believing that she was a kindergarten teacher, but had absolutely no complaints about her bedroom performance. She was wild, kinky, and down for *anything.* They only got together every other week because, well, too much of a good thing, right?

Whatever this infatuation with Gabriella the she-demon was, it wasn't anything he hadn't already experienced.

A light knock on his door snapped him out of the various day dreams he was now having. He cleared his throat. "Yeah, come in."

To his surprise, it was Gabriella pushing his door open and setting files on his desk. "These were outside my office, but last I checked, you were doing the Day-Star case, not me."

She was in a skirt. A fucking tight pencil skirt that hugged those sweet curves and showed off her killer legs. Her dusty rose colored button-down shirt hugged her waist, and she'd left more buttons open at the top. And as usual, she was wearing those sexy pumps with the pointed toe. *Dammit* this was not going to help him focus.

"Emmett?" He could hear her voice, but was either unwilling or unable to take his eyes away from the hem of her skirt. "Emerson?"

"Hm?" Finally he blinked up and she was eyeing him curiously. Her eyebrows were pulled together and her mouth was set in what might have been a frown, but on her it just looked like a sexy pout. "Oh, yeah, that's my case. Thanks."

"Everything okay?"

"Yeah, I'm good." His eyes slipped back down to her legs.

"Are you sure?" Her lips tugged up into a playful grin. "If I didn't know better, I'd say you were staring."

Emerson blinked and shook his head, pushing himself away from the desk. Away from her. "What? No, I wasn't..."

She smirked again and crossed her arms over her chest. "You were staring. But I'm sure I should just take it as a compliment, right?"

Damn her. And damn that skirt. Damn her lips and that fucking cute smirk. It all made his brain turn to mush. This wasn't like him. He didn't fall apart in front of women. He didn't turn into a giant mess of stupid words and completely lose control. He cleared his throat and willed himself to gain composure. What the fuck was she doing to him?

"Sorry, you just, um...you look nice today," he said, letting his eyes do one last sweep of her legs before landing- *and staying-* on her face.

"I look nice?" Gabriella repeated. She looked skeptical, arching one eyebrow at him. *Dammit, even her eyebrows were sexy. What. The. Fuck.*

Emerson shrugged. "Sure. I mean, for someone who's going to kidnap puppies and make a coat out of their fur. Yeah, you look nice."

Her laugh was warm and sensual, and it made his dick go semi-hard. He tried not to draw attention to it by adjusting himself again. "So first I was a She-Devil and now I'm Cruella? You know, I actually happen to like dogs."

"Do you have one?"

"No."

"Maybe you should get one," Emerson suggested. "I hear they're great for stress. Or maybe you just need to get laid. That might help with all the *Cruella* vibes you're putting off."

Her jaw dropped as she stared at him indignantly. "Oh, but I thought I already had, with all my potential baby-daddies I have running around."

"Then maybe you just need to get some from someone who knows what they're doing." He gave her his own charming smirk, finally feeling like he was taking back control of the situation.

There was a silent moment that passed before Gabriella leaned both hands on his desk in a way that pushed her perfect tits together, making them front and center of his vision. "Someone...like you?" she asked, then bit her lip.

God dammit. She looked so shy and so fucking hot looking at him like that. His throat went dry and he forced himself to not stare at her cleavage, even though it was *right there.*

Clearing his throat again, he looked right in her big brown eyes. "Ideally, someone like me. I definitely know what I'm doing in that regard."

The corner of her beautiful mouth twitched up just slightly. "Yeah? What would you do?"

The muscles in his lower abdomen clenched and his heart jolted into overdrive. He hoped like fuck she couldn't see it on his face. Were they really doing this?

"You really want to know?" he asked, and watched the little nod of her head. Well, if they were doing this, they were fucking doing this. "Well, for starters, you should know that I always make sure the woman I'm with is fully satisfied before I worry about my own needs." He stood and ran a hand down his tie, tugged at the cuffs of his suit jacket. "I would bring you to my place, take off that blazer, make you comfortable. I'd pull you in close and kiss you, deep and slow, as I unbuttoned your blouse and pushed it off your shoulders. I'd sit you down on my bed...get on my knees in front of you and pull those sexy shoes up onto my shoulder and kiss my way up your legs, one at a time."

He paused, watching the steady rise and fall of Gabriella's chest. She was still biting her perfectly plump bottom lip, and he could see where a pink blush had crept beneath her golden brown complexion.

"What about my skirt?" she asked.

"I would leave it on you," he replied. "I'd push it up over your waist and bury my face between your thighs...Want me to keep going?"

"Yes." It was barely a whisper, and his previously semi-hard cock was now at full attention.

He swallowed before continuing. "I would kiss and lick between your legs, eating you with your panties on until you had your hands in my hair, fucking my face, begging me not to stop. And then I'd pull your panties down with my teeth and finish giving you everything you asked for. With my mouth, my fingers…until you were coming so hard you wouldn't know if you should thank me, or hate me."

Gabriella grinned ruefully. "Why would I hate you?"

"Because you'd know you'd never have an orgasm like that again, and you'd have to keep coming back to me to make you feel good." He leaned toward her over the desk now, and he could smell her perfume. His gaze swept from her mouth, down her neck, over her chest, and landed on the hem of her skirt, wishing he could do everything he'd just described.

"You sound awfully sure of yourself," she said. Her voice was nearly breathless and he thought maybe she was imagining the same thing he was.

He'd completely lost himself in the fantasy, but he was sure she was feeling it, too. Wanting him, too. There was no hiding that her body reacted to him. Responded to his words. He tucked a stray piece of hair behind her ear and lightly traced his fingers along her jaw. "Let me show you how sure I am."

Gabriella straightened abruptly, backing away from him and snapping through whatever trance he'd been in. She smirked playfully at him and it hit him- she was fucking with him. "Not a chance, Emilio."

The witch backed away from his desk and toward the door. Yep, there were those devil horns again, poking through her hair. He would have taken Tuesday's downpour over being left hot and alone in his office with a massive hard-on pushing against his dress pants. A hard-on for this woman who he clearly had no business trying to be anything but enemies with. Who fucking did that? Got a man hard just to tell him no fucking way?

Their score-card was adding up, and she was definitely winning.

Chapter 6

The following week, Emerson did his best to focus on the war. The battles between him and Gabriella. He didn't pay attention to her skirts, or how phenomenal her ass looked in those high-waisted dress pants. He definitely didn't check out her cleavage anymore, and he did his best to avoid staring too long at her mouth. That damn seductive mouth. Her smirk, her silvery, smooth voice that he couldn't get out of his head. Working on the same floor as that woman was fucking torture, but he got his head in the game and focused on what mattered.

On Monday, he discovered that she was terrified of bugs when he heard a scream as he walked by her door. He burst into her office and saw that she was standing on her desk because there was an earwig on the floor. He stepped on it for her and couldn't help his own evil laugh as he walked back out of her office. On Tuesday, he'd left a fake cockroach on the inside of her desk lamp, and when she turned it on that evening and saw its silhouette against the lampshade, he had a hearty laugh at the scream that echoed through their office floor.

All week, Emerson couldn't figure out what the hell was wrong with his desk chair. He'd sat in it Monday morning and it wobbled so bad, he thought he was going to fall over. Finally on Thursday, he'd discovered that she'd replaced one wheel with a much smaller one. Evil genius.

After finding out about her Cuban heritage, he'd put a framed photo of Fidel Castro on her desk. As he'd hoped, she didn't notice until one of the partners stopped in her office and pointed it out. In retaliation, she'd hidden a *Playgirl* magazine in his desk drawer, and Tyler had found it when he'd asked him to grab a folder out of the drawer. Tyler busted out laughing and held it up just in time for Angela, the hot young office intern, to walk in and see it.

"...and this morning, I got to the office and Angela told me how brave I am for finally coming out." Emerson finished off the list of ridiculous pranks he and Gabriella had been throwing at each other all week.

He was sitting at the kitchen island at his best friend, Brody Kalahan's house. His wife, Amira, was throwing pasta into a large pot of boiling water and laughing at each of Gabriella's retaliations. Amira was *not* Emerson's biggest fan, but she tolerated him because of his and Brody's friendship. "She thinks me and Tyler are a couple."

Amira laughed. "That was sweet of her to make you think you could get someone on Tyler's level. He's way too cute for you."

Emerson scoffed as he snapped the top off his second bottle of Heineken. "Tyler would be lucky to get with a guy like me. I'm a very gifted and generous lover."

"Wait, wait," Amira said, practically gasping with laughter. "Tell the story again about how she left your ass in the rain."

Emerson rolled his eyes, unsurprised that Amira loved hearing about him being left, dumb-struck in the rain. Amira was his ex-fiance's best friend, and even though Raelyn had moved on and was getting married in just over a month to the man she'd really been in love with her whole life, Amira still hated him for how their relationship had ended.

"I need something big, you know? Something that will really send her away screaming," Emerson said, then took a long, refreshing pull of beer.

He jumped suddenly when a gray and black ball of fluff hopped up onto the counter next to him, nearly making him tip over his beer bottle.

Fucking Basil.

The previous fall, this cat kept coming around the Kalahans's house, and Amira continued to feed it every day, so of course the creature came back every day around the same time. One night when Emerson had been on his way in for a video game night, he'd overheard her call the cat Basil, so he knew it was only a matter of time before the thing was living inside, despite Brody's severe cat allergies. It was a cute little creature, when it wasn't trying to scratch your eyes out.

Emerson glared at the cat whose bright yellow-green eyes stared back unblinking. "Bro, your cat's doing that creepy stare-down thing again," he said, eyes going dry with the effort to not blink first.

"Better hope Gabriella doesn't find out you're terrified of cats," Brody said, reaching across to pet Basil between his ears. "She'll empty the shelter and put all of Traverse City's stray cats in your office."

"I'm not afraid of cats," Emerson insisted. "This one is just a demon in disguise. Aren't you?" He stretched his hand toward the cat and it hissed, so naturally, he hissed back.

"He doesn't like you because he's a good judge of character," Amira said, for what was probably the hundredth time.

"It's not normal for a cat to target one person like that," Emerson replied, still eyeing the furry demon on the counter. Basil was now in a crouched position, swishing his gray and black striped tail back and forth, not taking his eyes off of Emerson. "There's something wrong with him."

"There's nothing wrong with him. He's a sweetheart." Amira stroked the cat's back, but he still didn't blink or look away.

Emerson lowered his voice to a whisper as he peered at the cat, "You're not fooling me, you little shit. You're not a normal cat. You're a fucking hell beast, and one of these days, I swear I will send you back to where you came from."

Basil hissed again and Emerson flipped the cat off.

"Jesus," Brody laughed into his beer bottle. "You are the only grown-ass man I know who will start a rivalry with a fucking cat."

At the mention of a rivalry, Emerson broke eye contact with the cat and looked back at Brody. "Oh, right, back to the original topic...I need something good. But nothing illegal, you know? I can't risk my job, but I need her to leave."

There was a stretch of silence as Brody studied his friend from where he leaned his back against the counter. His bright red hair was illuminated by the setting sun coming through the kitchen window. "I don't think you actually want her to leave."

Emerson looked taken aback. "What do you mean? Of course I do. She took my fucking case and made me look bad in front of the partners."

"I don't think you need any help making yourself look bad," Amira remarked from the stovetop where she stirred the pasta noodles.

"I don't think *you* need any help being a snotty-" Emerson was cut off by a smack to the back of his head.

Brody looked sternly at him, "Don't talk to my wife like that."

"She started it!" he argued.

"She makes way more money than me and it's her house," Brody replied. Amira stuck her tongue out at Emerson and made a face, but he could only glare back, having to hold his tongue.

"What I was saying," Brody continued, "is that I think you're actually enjoying this little office war. I think you look forward to it. And you like learning new things about her. I think...maybe...you *like* her."

Emerson stared blankly at his lanky, freckled friend. "Is that what you think? Really? You think I'm in fucking third grade and want to tease the girl I have a crush on?"

"Pretty much, yeah."

Emerson scoffed. And then scoffed again, unable to come up with a clever retort right away. "Um, you're delusional. I do not like the She-Devil, okay? She's awful. She's probably in charge of some witch coven where they do seances and burn their ex-boyfriends' belongings and sacrifice the first-born male to their man-hating, tri-horned, bat-winged leader."

Both Amira and Brody stared at him with the slightest looks of concern in their expressions. Finally Brody broke the silence, "Did you just describe the demon thing in Hell Slayer? That game we played last week?"

"Maybe." He shrugged. "The point is I don't like her. As a matter of fact, I completely *dislike* her and want her out of my fucking head."

"Emerson," Amira said, leaning over the island and putting a hand over his. Her straight black hair fell in a sheet over her shoulder as she held his confused gaze. He wasn't used to any sort of eye contact, sincerity, or displays of affection from his best friend's wife. "I've always known you were kind of a left-handed monkey wrench, but are you actually listening to yourself? You're obsessing over her. When was the last time you gave a woman this much thought when you weren't just trying to have sex with her?"

"I'm not obsessed!" he snapped. "I'm focused."

But even he knew over the past week and a half since Gabriella had stormed into his life, he'd been anything but focused. She made his head fuzzy, his thoughts were completely consumed by her, even if it was just trying to figure out ways to destroy her. He liked how relieved she had looked when he got rid of that pesky earwig, and even the playful smack to his arm when he finally came down and showed her the bug under her lampshade was fake. It was like she wanted to be mad, but was so relieved that it was fake that she couldn't help but sigh. That feminine, sexy sigh that made his chest tight and his dick stir in his pants.

"You're not focused, man," Brody said. "It's not like you to let a woman run your life or run around in your head twenty-four-seven."

"It's not because I like her, Bro. It's because she's fucking infuriating." Emerson felt like he could have growled at how infuriating she was.

Yes, she was always in his head, constantly occupying his headspace when he should be putting his time and energy on other things. Other women. His job. Tyler's farewell party from the office. It was the kid's last week at the firm and he'd wanted to throw him a party over the weekend, but had barely put any thought into planning it.

"Why don't you just ask her out?" Amira asked. She spooned a noodle out of the pot of boiling water and offered it to Brody to try. "Instead of fighting the inevitable, just ask her out on a date. Maybe it'll go well. Or maybe it won't, but you'll at least be able to put your mind at ease. You'll know there's nothing there and you can move on. Get your life back."

"I don't want to date her, Amira. I thought I'd made that clear. Besides, I don't *date*. If anything, I might try to fuck her, but I don't date. You of all people should know. You're always the first to remind me how much I suck at it."

"That was two years ago," Amira replied. "You and Rae have been broken up for over two years, she's getting married, and here you are, going on thirty-three, and still convinced there's nothing more to life than your gross little rotation of hoe-bags that you go through every week."

"Wow, thank you for that. The judgment and the reminder that I'm getting old," he grumbled, taking another swig from his beer bottle. "There's nothing wrong with how I live my life. I like my weekly rotation. I like knowing that I can bring home someone new if I want. I like that I can be out late on a fucking Wednesday night and not have to explain why to anybody. I like my life. It's easy. It's comfortable. And most importantly, I don't have to worry about when I'm going to let someone down next. Because all the women I sleep with throughout the week know exactly what to- and what *not* to- expect from me."

The looks on Brody and Amira's faces told him that he'd said too much. He'd opened the door to a conversation he did not want to have, and knowing them, he'd have to leave in order to avoid it.

"You know, you're the only person who is so sure you're only going to let people down," Brody said quietly. "Amira might be right about you being a bit of a headcase sometimes, but you *do* know how to be loyal."

Emerson snorted. "Bro, I've literally cheated on every girlfriend I've ever had since I was fourteen. I wasn't built for relationships...I can't pull off the long-term thing." Angrily picking at the label on his beer bottle now, he mumbled, "I inherited the anti-monogamy gene. Can't fix genetics."

Brody rolled his eyes. "That's in your head. You've made yourself believe it's genetic. Like you can't escape the urge to cheat because it's some curse your dad put on you by making you watch him hook up with all your childhood nannies and housekeepers. Just when you start feeling like you could be happy you let that shit creep up and get the better of you."

Amira nodded in agreement. "Your father has you brainwashed. He wants you to be just like him, doesn't he? Follow in his footsteps? Be the next Senator Yates who lies through his teeth to crowds of people, hypnotizing them with a charming smile and a nice, full head of hair."

Emerson flicked his gaze up to Amira for half a second before focusing back on his beer bottle. Her words twisted uncomfortably in his chest and made his stomach churn, remembering the last conversation he'd had with Rae that officially ended their relationship. She'd said similar things to him, though her delivery had made it twist like a knife.

Three years he was with Raelyn DeRose, and it was the easiest three years of his life. They'd met when she was finishing up her Master's degree in Ann Arbor, and he was interning at the District Attorney's office. Brody and Emerson were living in a townhouse together after college, Amira and Rae were roommates, and Brody had been dating Amira for years.

Law school had kept Emerson busy enough to not be able to meet many people or be very social, but one night there was a storm and the power went out at Amira and Raelyn's apartment, so Brody offered to let them both stay at the townhouse. Emerson had come home from a late night at the gym, and there she was on the couch watching March Madness while Brody and Amira were fooling around in his bedroom.

Their relationship had been easy. Seamless. Sure, they argued from time to time, but Emerson liked to start shit and Rae always challenged him. He thought she was the one. He thought he'd finally found someone who could shut down everything he'd believed about himself before.

Yeah. Apparently, he thought wrong.

Not long after popping the question, he fucked up. For reasons he'd be damned to admit to anyone, including Brody, he reverted back to his old ways. He spiraled, from one mistake to the next, until Rae was walking in on him at the office, not even fully undressed, pounding the flirty legal intern into his desk.

It was low. Lower than low. And he'd hated himself for it. Honestly, two years later, he still hated himself for it. Even more, he hated that everything Rae had said to him when she finally came out of hiding, confronting him at his apartment, eyes welled with tears that she was holding back, was probably true…

"You may be the one who cheated, but I'm the one who's sorry. I'm sorry your father has your head so messed up that you actually think you have to be just like him. I'm sorry that you'll probably spend the next several years pretending that you're happy with countless, meaningless hook-ups, and lying to everyone, telling them that's just who you are. But I know it's not, and so do you."

It was quite the speech, and she'd thrown her engagement ring into his chest before walking away, not giving him a chance to respond.

Not that he had a good response anyway. He'd fucked up and it was over. However, being the obnoxiously self-assured, cocky bastard that he was, he played into it. He acted like everyone should have seen it coming. Like anyone who expected more from him was an idiot and needed a reality check. Emerson Yates wasn't a relationship guy. Emerson Yates didn't need a girlfriend, much less a fiancé or a wife. He was better off being a ladies' man.

So, sure, maybe it was exactly what Rae had predicted he'd do. But really, it's what he was good at. And everyone would be best to just lower their expectations of him in that regard. It was better this way. It helped him remember not to get involved with anyone, which meant that he never let anyone down. It was easier. More comfortable. And he liked his life that way.

And just because he couldn't get Gabriella Cabrera-Perez off his mind didn't mean anything was changing. It didn't mean he liked her or wanted to be with her. Nope, she drove him absolutely nuts. And he knew exactly how to prove it.

Gabby was pacing in her office, going over the notes on her presentation that she would be giving in approximately forty-five minutes. Tom had asked her to give the partners a brief summary on all the work she'd done for the case up to this point. It had only been two weeks, and the case would likely run on for a few months, but they wanted to see what kind of progress she was making. She had always been a very good public speaker, but it didn't change the fact that the anticipation of giving a speech made her nervous.

Tyler came in to ask her if she needed anything else, and assured her she would do great. She was sad that it was his last day at the firm, and couldn't imagine finding another intern who was nearly as thorough with the same attention to detail. He'd been a God-send the past two weeks working on this case.

Right as Tyler left, Emerson found his way into her office and she groaned. "What do you want?"

Emerson put his hand to his chest like he was offended. "I'm coming in to tell you good luck, Gabe. Am I not allowed to do that?"

"I swear if you do anything to screw this up," she said with warning. "If you have like...a jar of bugs you're planning to release or something...Are you even going to be there?"

He grinned, and it was devilish and handsome, and she tried her best not to think about what he'd said a week ago about burying that obnoxiously good-looking face between her legs. His words, his deep voice describing how he would drive her wild had not left her all week. It hadn't been easy to back away from him after he offered to show her just how well he could do those things, but she had to. She could not let him get the upper hand.

"I wouldn't miss it. And you don't have to worry about any bug jars or Castro references. I'm just there to watch."

"Really?" she asked, eyeing him skeptically. She was standing in front of her desk, arms folded over her chest as he approached.

He stopped directly in front of her. He was close. Way too close. She could smell his cologne and maybe his shower gel. It was fresh and enticing. An earthy, manly scent that made her pelvic muscles squeeze. Her lady parts were complete traitors around this man. He tilted his head down to her, and again he was staring at her lips. He always looked at her lips, like he was imagining doing things with them. Kissing them. Biting them. Sucking and tasting them. There was a sudden flare of heat between them and she couldn't help licking her bottom lip.

She almost missed it when he asked, "How about a truce?" His low, gravelly voice took a few beats to register.

"A truce?" Gabby raised a skeptical eyebrow.

"Mhmm."

God, how is he still getting closer? Any closer and our lips are going to touch, and I definitely don't need that. I don't want *that.*

Do I?

She unfolded her arms and braced her hands on the desk behind her. She couldn't back up any further without sitting on her desk. And then it would be far too easy to wrap her legs around his waist and pull him in.

"How do I know you mean it?" she asked. And why was her voice so breathless? She seriously sounded like she *wanted* him to kiss her. But she didn't. Absolutely not.

He grinned again and dipped his head so his mouth was right next to her ear, that deep, seductive voice speaking right into her. "Can't you just trust me?"

She laughed quietly. "No." Letting her eyes flutter shut, she inhaled his scent again, waited for his kiss or his touch, *something* because she knew it was coming. His mouth was a fraction of an inch from her skin, and even though she knew it was a horrible idea, she suddenly wanted it on her. She wanted to feel his mouth on hers, his hands on her skin. Ever since he'd described how good he would make her feel, she couldn't get the image of him between her thighs out of her head.

She hated it, of course. But there it was. Maybe her brother was right, and hate-sex *was* a real thing.

He breathed her in and reached behind her. She thought maybe he was going to wrap an arm around her, pull her close so that her body was pressed against his. And she knew with sudden certainty that she was going to let him.

Emerson cleared his throat abruptly, making her jump. He stood up straight and held a leather coaster in his hand. "Clearly I can't trust you either. Stealing my coasters out of my office...Who told you I hated water rings?"

Gabby's heart was beating a mile a minute and she exhaled sharply. He winked and backed away from her. "Good luck in there, Gabe."

When her office door closed she made a frustrated noise and sat back on her desk. *Dammit!* She should've known better than to get sucked in by his charm!

She shook her head and tried to focus back on her presentation. Tried cooling off. Contemplated a change of panties now that she was decidedly moist between her legs.

Okay, so he got her that time. There was always a chance to even up the score, but it would have to wait. For now, she would have to settle for showing him just how right she was for the case that he thought was his.

In the conference room, Gabby stood at the head of the long table, ready to present. Emerson was sitting near the back, and she couldn't help noticing that he wasn't looking directly at her. His leg was bouncing, and his eyes stayed down. She thought maybe he still felt weird that, at least in his mind, this should have been his presentation.

Tyler looked encouragingly at her from his seat next to Emerson, as did many of the associates and partners she'd met over the past couple of weeks.

Once everyone was seated, she made her introduction and began her presentation. Everything was off to a smooth start; She barely had to look at her notes, her charts were tasteful but appealing, and each part of her case argument was succinct and to the point. It wasn't until about halfway through the presentation that she stumbled over the first typo.

"Alpha-National Bank knew exactly who to put their trust in," Gabby squinted up at the screen, where instead of 'Alpha-National' it read 'Alpha-Dog'. *Weird.* She chuckled and commented on the odd typo, but continued relatively seamlessly. The next slide, however, had her grinding her teeth. There was a crude cartoon picture of a dog wearing a bandana that read *Alpha* doing doggie-style with a person who was supposed to be the plaintiff in the case.

"Um," Gabby cleared her throat as she stared at the image, wondering how the hell it got on her presentation. There were uncomfortable coughs and stifled laughs throughout the room and she tried to make light of the situation. "Okay, looks like someone's still trying to put me through some newby hazing."

On the next slide, various words were replaced with inappropriate words. Words that had absolutely no business being in a professional presentation at a law firm. And to make matters worse, she had no way to explain how it all happened. If Emerson had somehow hacked into her computer, it would still fall back on her. If he'd come into her office while she wasn't there, the partners would have every reason to believe she couldn't keep things confidential.

She was beginning to sweat a little, and her hands shook slightly as she held her notecards. "Okay, I'm clearly having some technical problems here." Gabby snatched the remote off the table and shut off the visual presentation. "No matter; I've got everything I need to report up here." She tapped a finger to her temple and, willing her voice to lose its shaky tone, finished her presentation from memory and her written notes.

She refused to look toward the back of the table where she knew Emerson was likely trying not to laugh until she'd wrapped up her last few words and the room gave their polite applause.

Finally, she raised her eyes to the back of the room where Emerson's mouth was hidden behind his hand. If she didn't know better, she'd say he looked guilty or ashamed, but that would mean he actually knew how to feel empathy for someone else. His stormy blue gaze flicked up to hers and held her piercing stare for a few heavy moments.

Clearing her throat again, she said in a voice far brighter and friendlier than she felt, "Mr. Yates, could I see you in my office, please?"

Fuck.

Fuck, fuck, fuck.

Emerson bit the inside of his cheek as the associates and partners filed out of the conference room. Gabriella was staring daggers at him and he had no idea what to expect. He knew she wasn't his boss and couldn't very well tell on him, exactly. If she told anyone he'd been able to hack her presentation, it would be both their asses.

He wasn't a cyber-nerd by any means, but he knew the ins and outs of the software systems the office used. If the partners knew what kind of shit he pulled on a regular basis, they'd fire his ass without a second look back. But Gabriella might be in trouble, too, if they thought she hadn't been careful enough with confidential information.

The organ in his chest was working in overdrive, but he managed to get out of his seat, ignore Tyler's disapproving glare, and slip out into the hall. Before heading straight to Gabriella's office, he made a quick stop in the bathroom. He leaned over the sink and caught his breath, waited for his heart rate to come down.

Why was he so fucking nervous?

Because what he'd done was low, even for him. Because he was a fucking idiot for wanting to prove he didn't like her. He wanted to do something that he knew he couldn't pull off if he had any sort of lingering feelings for her. Anything that was more than competition. But what he'd done was stupid. It was juvenile, and he'd started to regret it as soon as he'd taken his seat in the conference room.

"Just tell her you're sorry," he breathed, looking at his reflection in the mirror. "Tell her it was stupid and you should've given her a heads up so she could've fixed it. You just got carried away."

Letting out another breath, he straightened. Emerson headed back out into the hall, past his office and into hers, where she was already waiting for him, arms crossed over her chest.

"Lock the door behind you." Her voice was quiet, but demanding, and he did as he was instructed.

"Listen, Gabe, I-"

"No," she cut him off, "No, *you* listen! I get that you aren't used to hearing the word *no* very often and you're used to always getting exactly what you want. I don't know much about you, but it doesn't take a lot to figure out that you're just another entitled asshole trying to make a fucking joke of something that I actually had to work for. This may be hard for you to believe, but not everyone had their careers handed to them because of who their parents are. Not all of us can sit around and fuck off all day because we have a trust fund to fall back on. You could have gotten me fired, Emerson. Do you get that?"

He wanted to correct her. He wanted to say that she had no idea what she was talking about, she didn't know anything about him or his parents or the way he grew up...but she was right. And he fucking hated it. He hated that he'd become this stereotype. The poster-boy for white male privilege, with the rich-boy social status to boot.

"Yes, I know. And I'm sorry," he said, sheepishly. He lowered his head but lifted his gaze to look at her. "I don't know what I was thinking. It was stupid. It was low. Even for me. I really am sorry."

Gabriella gazed back at him for a few silent moments until she shook her head and scoffed, muttered something under her breath in Spanish. "You are so...infuriating, you know that?"

It was Emerson's turn to scoff. "Me? You think *I'm* infuriating? You come in here with your HBIC attitude, your fucking insane body, and *God dammit*, that mouth of yours, I swear I've never been so obsessed with someone's lips in my fucking life. And you look at me like you're bored when you see me. Like I'm just another...trust fund douche who's not worthy of your time." He took a few steps, closing the gap between them like he had before the meeting.

"I can't...I can't stop thinking about you," he said, then laughed hollowly. He didn't want to admit it, but he found it impossible to keep in.

He was now standing in front of her, so close they were almost touching. She couldn't back up any further and he wanted to put his hands on either side of her, closing her in so she couldn't get away from him. But he knew better. He thought for sure, after the stunt he'd just pulled, if he tried touching her she'd smack him across the face. And he would deserve it. So instead he kept his hands at his sides, clenched into fists to keep from reaching for her.

"I went too far today, and I'm sorry. I just...*fuck*, I can't get you off my mind, and I don't...I don't *do* that. Do you get that? I don't let one woman occupy my headspace. My time. I just don't. You're driving me insane without even trying."

"So, you messed with my presentation to, what? Punish me?" she asked, eyeing him cautiously. Skeptically. He couldn't really make out what her eyes were doing, because he was too busy staring at those plump, kissable lips. Wondering what it would be like to trace his tongue along that perfect, pouting bottom lip.

"Yes," he replied, but that wasn't entirely true. "No." He sighed heavily. "I don't know. I just wanted..." he trailed off, unable to figure out how to finish that sentence.

Those almond-shaped brown eyes were fierce and assessing, and he suddenly felt like she could see right through him. "You were trying to make a point. Trying to...prove something."

"All I proved was that I'm a fucking mess and I can't think straight when it comes to you."

Fuck. Why the hell was he saying those things? Because they were fucking true. Because he was obviously a mess. Because she had him under some kind of spell that made him completely forget everything about keeping it cool around a woman.

"Emerson," Gabriella's voice was a sultry whisper, and he couldn't help leaning into her just a little bit further, "Remember how you said you could either make me thank you, or make me hate you?"

It took a moment, but the words registered and he flicked his gaze up to her eyes. Her chest was rising and falling with her forcibly controlled breaths. His cock was growing hard inside his pants as he watched all her signs of arousal. Her quickened breath, the pulse in her neck, her eyes darkening from maple to almost black.

He swallowed hard. "Yeah. And?"

"You're doing a damn good job of making me hate you," she said. She pushed herself up so that she was sitting on the edge of her desk.

"I can change that." Emerson set his hand on her thigh, and kept his gaze there, watching his hand slide beneath the hem of her skirt and back down.

"I think you're all talk."

He flicked his gaze back up to hers and moved between her legs, forcing her to spread her thighs apart to make room for him. Leaning over her, invading her space, he felt the heat radiating between them. Pulsing, like a physical, tangible thing. She dropped her eyes to where his hand still rested and he bent his head low, his lips nearly brushing the skin just beneath her ear as he said, "I promise you I'm not."

Her eyes were somewhere between aroused and incensed, and he fucking drank it in. Her mouth twitched upward slightly and she scooted closer. The move forced her legs apart just a fraction of an inch more, and his hand slid further up her skirt so that his fingertips were almost at her core. He tensed and held his hand in place, forcing himself to maintain control.

"I'm giving you another chance to prove something. Don't disappoint." Gabriella's eyes blazed and in them he could see her fury, her challenge, but also a wild need. Desire. For him.

Yes. Fuck yes. Anything she wants.

Emerson wasn't typically one for taking orders- he was much better at giving them, especially in the bedroom- but seeing her like this, hearing her voice so sexy and demanding, *god dammit,* it made him want to obey. To do exactly as she asked. He'd been fantasizing about this since that first day she'd walked into the conference room. He just never thought it would actually happen.

With a wicked grin, and his heart trying to pound its way out of his chest, he moved his hand slowly up her skirt, feeling her soft skin beneath his palm. He grasped her inner thigh and swiped his thumb gently down her center over the thin fabric of her panties and she was warm. Hot and eager.

Then he lowered himself onto his knees, not letting his eyes drift from her intoxicating stare, and slid one hand down her long, golden-bronze leg before propping it up on his shoulder. That pointy heel dug into his shoulder and he began kissing, from her ankle, up her smooth calf, her knee, her thigh, until he was so close he could feel the heat of her again. He paused, hovering his mouth just over her black panties, enough that he knew she could feel his breath on her. Then he started his trail back down at a slow, torturous pace.

By the time he made it back up her other leg, he could hear her breaths catching. Ragged, needy. She probably wanted to beg, but was holding back, not wanting to give him the satisfaction.

His lips brushed along the inside of her thigh and he pushed her skirt up over her waist, just like he'd described in his fantasy. Teeth and tongue moved over her creamy caramel skin, biting, nibbling as close to her heat as he could get without giving in just yet. A sound like a hiss escaped her and he teased her again.

God, she was fucking perfect between her legs. Nothing but a black g-string with a little pink bow on the front separated his mouth from her pussy. He could feel the heat of her, like it was reaching out to him, asking to be tasted. Ravished.

Holding her thighs apart, he pressed a kiss right over that pretty pink bow, and immediately felt her quick gasp. He groaned, and pressed his mouth over her, licking and sucking through that tiny scrap of fabric. She was so fucking wet already, he couldn't wait to touch her. He slid a finger down where her skin was slick with need, and knowing he'd done that to her was enough to make him curse. When she whimpered, it made his cock throb, and he did it again. Petting her softly as his mouth worked, scraping his teeth against her panties, teasing her clit until she was bucking into him.

"Oh God," she whispered between gasping breaths. "More...*more.*"

As quickly as he could, Emerson caught the string of her panties between his teeth and dragged them down until they were hanging off one stiletto-clad foot. Then he buried his face in her, sucking at her clit, fucking her with his fingers, groaning into her as he devoured her pussy. She was hot and wet all around him, and his dick was about to break free. Fuck, he couldn't believe this was happening.

Reaching down, he unzipped his pants and shoved a hand into his boxer briefs, fisting his rock-solid length as she continued to fuck his face. She was rocking into him, pulling his mouth harder against her, whimpering, whispering in Spanish, and he couldn't fucking wait to feel her go off. He was going to make her come, and then slam into her with a punishing force, fucking her on her desk.

Gabriella's fingers tangled into his hair and pulled him closer. Just like he knew they would. Just like he promised her. Curling his arm around her thigh and anchoring her against him, he listened to her restrained gasps and praises.

...Fuck yes...

...Oh god...

...Yes, don't stop!

Emerson ravished her with his mouth while he fucked his own fist. God dammit, he was hard. He needed to fucking slow down if he wanted to get inside her.

Then she moaned like she didn't care how loud she was being, like she didn't care that they were in her office. At work. Like no one else outside this room existed. "Oh god, *right there*! Yes, yes, *yes!*"

He groaned as he felt her tighten, all the muscles in her thighs, her lower abdomen, her whole body, shook and sputtered as her orgasm coursed through her. He kept his face buried between her thighs as she came, wanting to make sure she got each and every bit she'd asked for.

She released his hair and collapsed back on her desk, catching her breath. Emerson slowly stood, still stroking his cock as he leaned over her. "So, do you still hate me?"

Gabriella pushed up onto her elbows and her gaze drifted down to where he was fisting himself. "What are you doing?"

He paused. He looked at her skirt that was still pushed over her waist, her legs on either side of him that he could so easily pull around himself as he pounded into her. With a devilishly seductive grin, he answered, "I was thinking we'd finish this."

She let out a puff of laughter, but there was no humor in it. Sitting up all the way, forcing him to back up, Gabriella pulled her skirt down so that it was covering her up again. "Yeah, I already finished. We're done here."

Emerson's eyebrows shot up in disbelief. "What? You're not serious."

"I am, actually," she said. She reached for her g-string that was dangling on the pointed toe of her stiletto and stuck her other foot through to pull it up all the way. "You can go now."

Was she serious? This had to be a fucking joke, right?

But the longer he stood there with his dick out, the more he thought she might actually mean it. Finally, he pulled his boxer-briefs and dress pants back up and headed toward the door.

She had fucking dismissed him. What the fuck?

He didn't even bother to tuck his shirt back in and try looking presentable to walk through the hall. With one more look back over his shoulder, he saw that goddamn temptress smirking from behind her desk.

He returned to his own office in a daze, unaware of what exactly had just happened. If it weren't for her taste still lingering on his lips and on his tongue, he'd think he might have dreamt the whole thing.

His phone rang just as he shut his office door behind him, and he thought maybe she was calling him to come back. Looking down at his phone screen, however, he saw that it was Maya Bishop- his younger half-brother's mom. He cleared his throat before answering, "Hi, Maya."

"Emerson, hi, I'm sorry, I know you're at work," Maya said, her cheerful voice cutting through the fog of What The Fuck Just Happened in his brain.

He tried to refocus his thoughts. If there was anything or anyone he could pull his shit together for, it was his little brother, Kolbe. Maya was a single parent and Kolbe wasn't always the easiest kid, but she did her best. They had recently moved up to Traverse City from Romeo. Emerson didn't know if she simply wanted to move for a better job, if she thought being closer to him would make things easier on them, or if she wanted to get away from all the reminders of Johnathan Yates and what a piece of shit human he was. His guess was as good as anybody's.

He was still breathless, panting a little and his heart was a sledgehammer in his chest, but he tried to sound calm. "No, it's fine, I'm not busy. What's up?"

"Kolbe has baseball practice until 5:30 every day next week, and I was wondering if you could pick him up. I picked up some later shifts at the hospital," she explained. "He'll have to stay with you until like eight o'clock, if that's okay."

"Of course, yeah," he replied. "I love hanging out with him. I look forward to it."

"Great, thank you so much. You're a life-saver," Maya said, sounding genuinely relieved.

After hanging up, Emerson shoved his phone back in his pocket and leaned his back against the door. Thinking about the last half-hour, he almost wanted to laugh. He scrubbed both hands down his face, and made his way to his desk, marking in his calendar that he'd be picking his younger half-brother up from ball practice next week before he forgot, losing himself in thoughts of Gabriella.

He thought getting a taste of her would fix his obsession, but he already knew it was only bound to get worse.

Chapter 7

Gabby paced in her living room, glass of chardonnay in hand. She couldn't believe what had happened at work. She couldn't believe Emerson had so immaturely botched her presentation, or that he had so obviously tried to get her fired. Their office war was a real thing, but there had been moments all week that she'd actually thought it was kind of fun. The pranks were funny, and she sort of looked forward to finding new surprises in her office each day. Emerson's new attempts to get under her skin were becoming entertaining, as was the opportunity for retaliation.

But he'd taken it too far. And then...*aye Dios mio...*then she- *she-* had put *him* on his knees and been the recipient of the most heart-pounding, toe-curling, down-and-dirty oral sex of her life. Her heart still hadn't quite calmed down, and each time she thought about his stormy blue eyes fixed on her as he slowly dropped to his knees to worship her, she found herself hot and flustered, her pulse vibrating, just barely contained beneath her skin all over again.

Cocky, arrogant, self-obsessed, and overly self-assured Emerson Yates had been brought to his knees. By *her.* And he'd enjoyed it. He didn't have to admit to it, because she knew. Somehow he'd been the one kneeling before her, making it look as though she had all the control. As if she had all the power. But Gabby had felt anything but in control. It seemed it didn't matter his position, Emerson was a man in charge. A man who knew what the hell he was doing. A man who certainly knew his way around a female orgasm and had proven with absolute certainty that he was *not* all talk. He brought it. He could talk the talk, and walk the walk. Though she could definitively say she enjoyed the "walking" more than the "talking".

She hadn't wanted to moan, but she couldn't help it. She didn't want to squirm and writhe and buck underneath him, but there was no stopping it. She sure as hell didn't want to fist his thick blonde hair between her fingers and grind into him harder, but…it just felt so damn good. Another shiver rippled through her and she felt her lady-muscles clench, as though they, too, were reminiscing on that fantastic orgasm that had happened almost exactly twenty-four hours ago. Gabby dropped into her plush, off-white sofa and fanned herself. She was flushed and it wasn't the wine making her face hot.

Three quick knocks on the front door snapped her attention out of her daydreams and toward the entrance of her condo. Tall, lean-muscled, graceful, handsome Marco swept into the room, followed by the much less dramatic Max, who shut the door quietly behind them.

"Gabs!" Marco sang as he made his way into the living room. He plopped down next to her and surveyed her appearance.

She had barely made any sort of indication that she'd even registered she had guests. Marco narrowed his eyes suspiciously. The telepathic twin thing wasn't entirely true- he obviously couldn't see inside her mind, but he knew her well and therefore he could read her like a book.

"Gabs?" he said her name again and leaned back to swipe his gaze over her. He turned to look at Max who was standing with his arms crossed, legs shoulder width apart. He looked like a beautiful blonde body guard. When Marco turned back to Gabby he gave a wry smile. "What happened? Does this have to do with that sexy lawyer man?"

Gabby opened her mouth, then closed it. Opened it again. "I'm…going to need some more wine before we get into this."

Marco snatched her nearly empty glass from her hands and glided to the kitchen where she heard the cork being pulled back out of the bottle. When he came back, the glass was way past its imaginary fill-line, but she didn't complain. She gladly accepted the cool, crisp white wine, and drank.

Ten minutes later, she was sitting in the same spot on her sofa, with Marco on one side of her and Max sitting in the armchair facing her, both men completely rapt with attention. Marco's jaw had dropped and yet he was still somehow grinning, in complete awe of his twin's complete bad-assery. Max, who was usually much more difficult to read, was leaning back with one arm crossed over his chest while the other hand held his chin and he stared at her in amazement. He almost looked as though he couldn't quite believe what he'd just heard, and was trying to wrap his mind around the whole thing.

"You...are a complete badass. You're like...Lucy Liu," Marco said, striking a dramatic *Charlie's Angels* finger-gun pose. "You're a female James Bond, and he was just another easy-peasy, floozy conquest."

Gabby laughed and pushed her hair back with one hand. "Marco, it's insane. What I did was insane. I mean, part of me wants to like, put on stunner shades and use the hallway at work like my own personal catwalk: Head Bitch In Charge coming through! But then I realize that what I did...it's technically sexual harassment, right? I mean, he wants to get me fired and now he probably can."

"It may not be sexual harassment," Max countered. His low voice sounded smooth and even, always reasonable. Gabby and Marco frequently joked that he should have been a teacher, because something about his voice just makes people want to listen to him. "At the very least it was highly inappropriate workplace behavior. I mean, he consented. He came onto you, too. There was no coercion on your part. You two are of equal station, so to speak. You aren't his boss or his superior." Max took a sip of his wine and eyed Gabby over the glass. "And based on everything you've told us about him, he doesn't exactly seem like the type to want to admit you got the upper hand. I have a feeling your secret is safe."

Gabby groaned and sunk into the couch cushions. "That should make me feel better, but it really doesn't. It makes me feel like I'm using it against him. Like I knew he would never be the type to admit it, and that's why I made him do it."

"You didn't *make* him do anything," said Marco. "If I remember correctly, you said that he offered to do it a week ago. He asked you to *let him show you* how good he was, didn't he? I don't think you have anything to be worried about or feel bad about. Maybe just the fact that you definitely made the man leave your office with blue balls, but other than that, I think you're just a total boss bitch."

"It was a power move," Max added, with an approving nod. "I think he needed to be knocked down a bit, like we talked about last time. Make him question that massive ego of his."

Marco's eyes lit up suddenly. "Speaking of *massive* things...you saw it. How was it? Did it live up to the hype? Does the Herculean *dragon* match the Herculean bod? Or are his good looks and gym muscles compensating for something?"

Gabby felt heat creep into her face and neck and she bit back a grin. "It was...impressive. The guy definitely hit the gene-pool jackpot. I almost didn't want to turn him away."

"No?" Marco questioned. "You were going to let him just take what he wanted?"

"*Almost*," Gabby repeated firmly. "No one is pretty enough to do what he did and still come out on top- literally or figuratively."

"That's my girl." Marco squeezed her in a tight hug around her shoulders. "We need to celebrate. No staying in drinking wine tonight. Let's go out. We'll show you some of our favorite spots. You need to learn the new city you're in. I promise there's more to this town than your stuffy law firm and its beautiful blonde bastard."

They found themselves at a small bar on Union street downtown. There was a live band playing a variety of cover songs ranging from Blink-182 to Matchbox 20 to their own emo-punk versions of Beyonce and Taylor Swift. The eldest Cabrera sibling, Isabel, had suggested the place and met Gabby, Marco and Max outside the bar around 8:30 before the place really started to fill up.

After finding a booth situated near the back of the bar, Marco wasted no time filling Isabel in on Gabby's work drama. The Sexy

Lawyer Man, the high-dollar case, the pranks, and of course the Indecent Incident, as they were now referring to it.

Isabel had an amazing poker face. She was a pediatric psychiatrist at the hospital in Traverse City, and though she was constantly reading others, she was nearly impossible to read herself. Her expression remained intrigued, but otherwise unreadable. She looked pensive as she took a sip from her red wine and pushed back her gorgeous copper-red hair. Isabel's natural hair color was the same dark brown as Gabby's, but she'd been dyeing it the most beautiful shade of copper since some time in high school, and it was always shiny and long, with perfect body waves as if she'd just finished shooting a shampoo commercial.

When Isabel remained silent for a few moments, Gabby blurted, "Okay, what? I know you have thoughts about this, you don't need to shrink me. Just tell me what you're thinking, like normal gossiping sisters."

Isabel's expression didn't falter right away. She observed Gabby for another silent moment- save for the chorus of Tamia's "So Into You" in the background- before her mouth twitched up in a nearly indecipherable gesture. "Do you *like* this man?" Isabel asked finally.

"*No!* No, of course not," Gabby replied, perhaps too quickly. "He's arrogant and immature. He's the poster child for wealthy, white male privilege. He's so cocky, and he thinks he can do whatever he wants without consequence."

"So it's a purely carnal attraction?" Isabel questioned.

Gabby hesitated, though Marco was nodding vigorously next to her. "I...I guess. I don't want to be attracted to him. But he's just...yes, it's a physical attraction. *Carnal* or whatever. He's completely gorgeous. Like if Zeus and Thor had a baby. Or if Abercrombie and Fitch models got on Chris Hemsworth's workout plan. No- if Calvin Klein underwear models mated with Norse Gods and superheroes. That's what he looks like. It's just not fair. And I haven't even seen him with his shirt off yet."

Isabel's eyebrow ticked upward and she felt Marco and Max's eyes flash to her.

"Yet?" Isabel repeated.

Gabby's mouth opened, halted by her slip-up. "I mean...I didn't mean that. I just meant, I hadn't seen him with his shirt off, but I would imagine it's pretty impressive under there."

"Because you think about it?" Marco asked, knowingly. His facial expressions and reactions showed absolutely everything, contrasting dramatically with Isabel's uncanny ability to conceal all emotions. Going from discussing anything with Marco to having the exact conversation with Isabel was sort of like getting whip-lash.

Gabby groaned and admitted reluctantly, "Yes. I think about it. Trust me, if you saw the guy you would think about it, too. But I don't try to. I just can't help it. And now that I've seen how impressive the one-eyed monster between his legs is, it's even more difficult to not think about the rest of it."

"Well, at the risk of sounding too much like a psychiatrist, I say don't overthink it. If you're looking for a serious relationship and a life partner, I think you know it would be best to walk away and avoid sending him on any more *errands downtown,*" Isabel said with a small smirk. "But if you're okay with having fun and think you're capable of a purely carnal relationship, I don't see where the hesitation is. Have you ever had a relationship like that?"

Gabby shook her head. "No, not really. I mean, I've had a few hook-ups, but nothing...recurring. And I really don't think I want a relation-ship. I don't want this to turn into a *thing.* It was a one time thing. I was angry, but aroused all at the same time. I don't see that happening again. I think it's best if I just keep my distance."

"Laaaame," Marco groaned dramatically. "I say you get more action. You have a stressful, exhausting job. You deserve a little sexual release. How convenient that he's right there in your office?"

She was about to argue that that wasn't the point when her attention was drawn to a booth where a group of four were pulling chairs and an extra table to the end to make room for a large party. She recognized two of the four and immediately glanced back down at her drink upon seeing Emerson slide into the booth.

"Oh God," she whispered to herself. She glanced up at her siblings and brother-in-law who all looked at her curiously. "He's here. In that group that's sitting down."

Marco gasped and Gabby quickly put her hand on his arm. "Don't look! I mean, you can look but not all at once."

In the booth, Marco was sitting next to her, Max across from him, and Isabel next to Max. Gabby was facing the new group that had just come in and had the sudden urge to switch places with her sister.

She watched as Marco slowly lifted his gaze up to check out the group. "Which one is-" he began, and then, "oooh. Sweet...Jesus." There wasn't a lot that rendered Marco speechless, but here he was. Staring and slack-jawed. Across the table, Max scowled and snapped his fingers in front of Marco's face. He blinked and looked at his grumpy-looking husband. "Sorry, babe. It's just...be subtle, but take a look."

Max's eyes were still narrowed, but he obliged, taking a look around the small bar space as though looking for their waitress. When he turned back to the table, his eyebrows were raised as he stared at the center of the table where the drink specials menu was placed. "Oh...I get it now."

"Why does he have to be here?" Gabby whined. "Tyler's with him. If Tyler sees me he'll probably wave me over."

"Who's Tyler?" Max asked.

"He's an intern. Really smart, super helpful. Yesterday was his last day though, so I'm kind of sad about that. He's been a huge help," she explained. "He's next to Emerson. The younger looking one with the short beard."

"Oh, you mean Mr. Tall, Milk Chocolate and Handsome?" Marco asked, grinning.

"Yes, that one," she replied with a small laugh. "He's actually really sweet. I didn't realize they were friends outside of work."

Gabby let her eyes briefly drift back up to the table and she saw their waitress who looked to be in her early to mid-twenties with caramel brown hair greeting the table. She watched the exchange of looks between her and Emerson and- oh. No, she didn't like that. Not one bit.

She dropped her gaze back down to the cocktail in front of her and felt her insides simmer and twist.

What the hell was that all about? It's not like I actually like *him.*

Chancing a glance back up, she saw as the waitress combed her long-nailed, manicured fingers through Emerson's hair and he grinned up at her like they were sharing a secret. Although, it really wasn't much of a secret. They had definitely seen each other naked. And something about that bothered Gabby. And then that realization bothered her even more.

Why did she care who he'd been with? She didn't like him. She didn't want him. Not really. This knowledge should be comforting to her. She suspected he was the type to sleep around. He probably went to bars and picked up cute, young waitresses all the time.

But this waitress, who also happened to be *their* waitress, had clearly hooked up with him on more than one occasion. Maybe they had a purely sexual relationship, like the one Isabel had suggested she start up with him. Well, now that was definitely out of the question. Gabby wasn't going to be just another piece for him to play with. Nope, he clearly had enough of those.

Not that she was considering it anyway, of course.

"Oh, looks like our waitress might be able to tell you a thing or two about what Sexy Lawyer Man looks like under all those layers," Marco said, also watching the interaction. "They have definitely seen each other naked. A few times."

Gabby felt her body temperature rise, and then scolded herself inwardly for reacting at all. Then she gasped and her eyes went wide as she had a completely horrible thought cross her mind. "Oh my god! What if that's his girlfriend? I just assumed he was single, but...what if I came onto him when he's already in a relationship?"

"Do you think he's the cheating type?" Max asked, raising a curious eyebrow.

"I don't know. I really don't know anything about his life outside of work. Oh my god, this is a disaster." Gabby put her face in her hands, elbows on the table. "I made a guy go down on me when he was already with someone else."

"You didn't *make* him do anything. And you don't know that she's his girlfriend," Marco said, waving his hand in the air dismissively. "One way to find out though."

Seconds later, their waitress was standing in front of their table again, asking if they needed another drink or wanted to put in a food order.

Marco smiled sweetly at the girl- Taylor, according to her name tag- and brought on his charm that was responsible for him making new friends everywhere he went. "Oh my gosh, Taylor, I'm sorry if this is weird, but I couldn't help noticing you at that table. Is that your boyfriend? He's so handsome- you guys are such a cute couple!"

Taylor smiled brightly, but the brightness dimmed a little as she glanced back at Emerson's table. "Thanks! But, um, no, we're just friends."

"Oh, that's too bad," Marco said, his face falling with disappointment. "You guys would be so cute together."

"Well, thank you." Taylor grinned and looked down at her notepad. "So, did you want any food? Appetizers? Something else to drink?"

Her immediate change of the subject suggested to Gabby that she wished they were more than just friends. Well, more than friends with benefits or fuck buddies, or whatever the arrangement was.

They ordered a couple appetizers to share, but nothing more to drink yet, and Gabby watched as Taylor walked away, her bouncy pony tail swishing along behind her.

"Well, there you go," Max said. "She's not his girlfriend. Are you going to go over there?"

Gabby scoffed. "No. No way. Actually, Isabel, switch places with me. I don't want him seeing me here. I get enough of his obnoxiousness at work, I don't need it here."

"Seriously?" Isabel asked, as though it were a completely ridiculous request. When Gabby stared back intently, Isabel rolled her eyes and stood to switch places.

Once in her new seat, facing away from Emerson, Tyler, and their friends, Gabby sighed, satisfied. "Okay, now let's please talk about anything else."

Max was the first to propose the new topic, which was always a winning choice around the Cabreras: Baseball. "So, how about them Tigers?"

"Tigers?" Gabby said, glad for the abrupt subject change. "How about them Titans? I can't wait to see Robby play on Wednesday!"

Her youngest brother was rumored to be the star player on the team and she hadn't watched him play since he was in tee-ball. Baseball was sort of a big deal in her family. Her dad had played when he was younger, she and all of her sisters played softball, and Marco had played all the way through high school. They all tried to make at least one major league game together during the season, and made a big deal about watching the Tigers play on TV. And no matter who was in the world series, they always threw a huge world series party at the end of the season.

"He's so good," Isabel said, smiling fondly. "And I don't just mean for a fourteen-year-old. He's just good. Like a miniature Miguel Cabrera...or Quinn Casey."

The entire table let out a collective groan-slash-sigh of longing at the mention of the steamy baseball player turned sex icon.

"He's supposed to come back this season," Marco said, tipping his tall beer glass to his lips. "I'm not sure when, but Max and I paid for the all-access MLB channel so we can watch all their games."

Gabby sighed. "Seriously, no one looks as good in a pair of white baseball pants as that man." In her mind, baseball pants were the equivalent of men's lingerie. And *white* baseball pants were like a skimpy lace thong.

"What a shame he's engaged," Isabel said, shaking her head slowly. "I mean, good for him, but there was just something comforting about knowing a man like that was still on the market."

"Good for him?" Gabby questioned. "I think you mean good for *her.*"

"Good for both of them," said Max. "Obviously I don't swing that way, but there's no denying his fiancé is a babe. The girl is gorgeous."

"True." Marco nodded. "And it's super cute how they knew each other as kids."

"It's not surprising he clung to his feelings for her," Isabel chimed in, full psychiatrist voice present. "He had a lot of trauma as a child and she stuck with him through it all. She's likely a very comforting presence. Maybe the only consistency he's ever known."

"Okay, Dr. Freud, thank you for that," Gabby said with a small laugh. "We can't get through a single night without you trying to psycho-analyze someone. And this person isn't even here!"

"I deal with kids who grew up like him every day." Isabel shrugged. "It was difficult to not take an interest when all that came out a few months ago."

Gabby focused her attention back on her drink and took a sip. When she set her glass back down, Marco caught her attention with a gasp and his always-expressive face.

"What?" she asked.

"Sexy Lawyer Man just had new friends join him," he explained. "Wow, hot people really do travel in packs, don't they?"

"Who is it?" Gabby sat up straight and observed her brother's facial expressions.

"He sort of looks like Milk Chocolate McSteamy Pants, but darker, and maybe a little older. And he's got a woman with him- also gorgeous. Where do these people come from?" Marco kept his eye over Max's shoulder and continued to watch. "Oh, that was nice. He let the couple take the booth, and he's sitting in one of the chairs on the end."

"Anyone else?" she pressed.

Marco shook his head. "Not joining them, but he definitely just checked out that girl's ass. Just some brunette chick who walked by. My God, his eyes are intense, and I'm way over here."

The flash of Emerosn's sapphire gaze was front and center in her mind as she once again pictured them locked on hers as he slowly lowered himself between her legs. She was hot all over again, warmth pooling low in her belly and spreading downward, pulsing between her thighs. She tried forcing her lady muscles to not have a reaction, but it was no use. They remembered all too well.

"Oh, who's that?" Marco was now watching the table intently, not being subtle in the least. "Another woman just stopped by their table and is talking to him…"

Gabby and Max watched Marco, waiting for the play-by-play while Isabel made far more discreet glances toward the table behind them.

"She's got her hand on his shoulder…he just turned to face her, and she's like, standing between his legs…*oh my*, that is scandalous. You are in public, sir!" Marco looked back at Gabby and Max who were obviously waiting for further explanation. "She's wearing a really short dress and his hands are on the backs of her thighs, like he's about to put his hands up her dress right here and now." He looked back up and continued, "She's whispering something in his ear…Oh, that's a wicked grin. What did she just tell you, Sexy Lawyer Man?"

"You should see the looks on everyone else's faces," said Isabel. "His friends all look either extremely uncomfortable or annoyed. The one woman sitting next to the red-haired guy looks disgusted, but not at all surprised, like this happens all the time."

Marco gasped again, grasping the edge of the table dramatically. "Oh! Here comes Just Friends Taylor! This should get interesting!"

Gabby couldn't help grinning a little, even though her brother's description of Emerson and the new brunette had her stomach clenching with frustration, annoyance, and another emotion she couldn't quite place- or at least didn't want to give a name. If Emerson was about to get slapped, she wanted to witness it.

"Okay, I have to see this. I'm going up to the bar for a drink and to try spying from a distance," she declared, standing up. "Anyone need anything?"

"I'll take another Two Hearted," said Max.

"Same," Marco added.

Turning on her heel, Gabby took off toward the bar, finding a spot that concealed her well enough but gave her a decent view of Emerson's table. She wondered if she was being a little crazy, but then reminded herself how disappointed she would be if Emerson got slapped in her vicinity and she had actually missed it.

When Taylor approached his table, Gabby was surprised to see that Emerson didn't miss a beat. He grinned at her, and didn't even bother looking guilty about the situation he was caught in. He gestured from one woman to the other, looking comfortable and cool as a cucumber. She couldn't believe it. He was introducing the women, and had a hand on each of them- one hand still resting on the back of the brunette's thigh, and the other holding Taylor's hand.

Emerson was talking casually, as though it were perfectly normal to be in the presence of two women he was sleeping with at the same time. That's what Gabby had determined from his body language; he'd already slept with the brunette, too, but she guessed neither of them knew about the other. But the more Emerson talked, the more the two women seemed to relax. By the end of the exchange, they were both smiling, looking at him adoringly, and seemed to be unfazed and no longer upset about the other woman's presence.

What the actual fuck? Does he have secret powers of hypnosis? Is that why his eyes do that sparkling thing?

Gabby took a moment to read the rest of the people in his party. The woman next to the red-haired man had brown skin, shiny black hair, and a pretty face, though she looked beyond disbelief at what she was witnessing. Gabby could relate. Tyler looked like he also couldn't believe it, but in a far more impressed sort of way than anyone else at the table.

"Can I get you something?" The bartender's voice interrupted her observation of the group, and she turned to face him.

"Yeah, can I get two tall Two Hearted Ales and a Moscow Mule?"

The bartender nodded and dipped away to make her drinks.

She was about to refocus her attention on Emerson's table when a petite woman with wavy brown hair slid onto the bar stool next to her. She wore a short-sleeved white sundress with a small floral pattern and a deep scoop in the back of the dress.

The woman leaned toward the bartender who was squeezing lime slices into a copper mug. "When you get a chance, could I just get a big pitcher of water? And a glass of Sprite?"

The bartender simply responded with a nod, looking otherwise bored at her request. She turned toward Gabby and caught her looking curiously. The woman smiled and looked genuinely friendly. "Sometimes I think my boyfriend got me pregnant just so he could have a DD for nine months."

Gabby found the woman's smile to be contagious and grinned back. "How far along are you?"

"About three months," she replied. "I hope he knows that once the baby comes out, he's driving me to *all* of the wineries in this town."

Gabby laughed. "I've been wanting to go to some of those. I just moved here and I didn't realize how many there were."

"I just moved here in March, but went to a few during the winter. Chateau Delecroix is beautiful, but more expensive. Worth it though. And then there's Bel Lago, which has one of my favorite ciders and a great ice wine. Black Star Farms is a good one, too. There are so many."

"How do you like living here?" Gabby asked, interested to hear from someone else who was fairly new to the area.

"Well, I'm from Southern California, so the weather is definitely an adjustment," the woman replied, pushing her hair back out of her face. "But if you're already used to cold weather, it's an amazing place to live. I love it here."

"I'm Gabriella," Gabby said, offering her hand to shake.

The woman beamed and took her hand, "Zoey. Nice to meet you, fellow new person."

The bartender slid her finished Moscow Mule toward her, along with the first beer before heading to grab the second. Gabby let her eyes wander over to Emerson's table again, where she noticed three more people had joined. A handsome, fair-skinned man with light brown curls was making an unimpressed face at the spectacle of Emerson and his two lady-friends. He was tall and well built. Muscular, but not in an obvious way with sharp cuts and ripples in his muscles. There was some meat on his bones, like he worked out but also liked pizza and tacos.

There was another couple who had joined the group, and they looked a little younger than everyone else. The girl was curvy and adorable, with a ton of long, curly brown hair, and Gabby wondered how much work it took to make it so shiny and tame. Next to her was a lean-muscled guy with short, dark brown hair, small ear gauges, and a flat-billed Yankees hat flipped backward on his head. He had his arm wrapped around the girl's waist with his hand stuck in the back pocket of her high-waisted jeans.

Taylor moved away from the group after appearing to have taken the newcomers' drink orders. Before leaving, however, she'd given Emerson's broad shoulders an affectionate squeeze and took her time removing her lustful gaze from his own.

Gabby scoffed and rolled her eyes, looking back toward the bar where her bill was waiting with all three of her drinks.

Zoey seemed to have noticed her derisive noise and traced her previous line of sight. She then smirked. "Huh...that's not usually the reaction he gets from women."

Gabby blinked to Zoey. "You...know Emerson?"

"Ah, you *know* him. That makes more sense," Zoey said with a nod. "Yes, I know him. I'm actually here with that group. My boyfriend is the delicious hunk of man meat with the curly hair."

"Oh...how do you know Emerson?" Gabby asked.

"Well, it's complicated. But I can assure you I don't know him in the way most women know him," Zoey replied. "Technically I know him because..." she looked upward and chewed on her lip, figuring out the connections in her head, "my client for work is engaged to Emerson's ex. And Jett- my boyfriend- is one of my client's best friends, and Emerson decided he wanted to be Jett's friend...and, well, Emerson gets what he wants. So I guess they're friends now. Although it's a very reluctant friendship, I have to admit."

Doing her best to connect the dots that were just laid out before her, Gabby squinted, then nodded once she'd figured it out. "You know, I hear that a lot. That Emerson always gets what he wants."

"He does," Zoey said simply. "It's his...power of persuasion. I'm not really sure how he does it. I've seen it in action and I still don't understand. He can be a lot to handle at times- he's *very* dramatic- but there's good in there. He has a sweet side to him, believe it or not."

Gabby snorted, clearly not believing it.

"Really, he does," Zoey insisted. "I mean, when I first met him, I thought he was a complete ass. He was unbelievable- like I didn't think he could actually be real. Who is that much of a stereotype? But the more he comes around, the more good I see in him. He just hides it well."

Taking one last look in his direction before paying her bill, Gabby tried to imagine what it would be like to get to know him. What he would be like if they weren't either in constant competition at each other's throats, or a wildly burning ball of lust, heat, and intense attraction in each other's presence. What was he like when he wasn't trying to prove something or impress someone?

These thoughts were swiftly interrupted when the brunette who was still standing between his legs dipped her head to whisper in his ear, and his wicked grin dragged across his lips again.

Ugh. Nope. I don't need that in my life.

Gabby shook her head to clear her thoughts. She had her suspicions about what Emerson might be like when it came to women, but now she was sure. And honestly, it was worse than she thought. The man was combative, selfish, arrogant, and clearly made a sport out of manipulating women. She'd been down that road before and had no interest in making the same mistake twice.

Emerson watched Olivia walk away feeling abundantly satisfied that he would definitely not be going home alone tonight. Olivia had been one of the girls in his weekly rotation previously, but ended their arrangement when she wanted to take her relationship with her boyfriend a little more seriously. He couldn't say he was surprised that the relationship hadn't lasted. But it had been a few months since they'd seen each other last and if she was looking for someone to fuck away the disappointment of a failed relationship, he was her guy.

Having Taylor walk up while they were making plans for later that night hadn't been ideal, but he sweet-talked his way out of that mess. He'd actually impressed himself with that and half-ass thought he might be taking both of them home tonight. If there was ever a night he needed a boost like that, it was this one.

He was still having a hard time comprehending exactly what had happened in Gabby's office the previous evening. She'd wanted him. He could see it in her eyes. Behind the fire of anger there was lust and yearning. The same as he'd been feeling since he'd opened the door for her that first morning just weeks ago. And he knew- *he knew*- he'd brought his A-game. He couldn't get her sounds out of his head. The gasps, the moans, the pleas for more. That feeling of victory when she'd grasped his hair tight between her fingers told him he'd won. She was giving in and wanted him to take her.

But then...she dismissed him. And he had no idea what the fuck to do with that.

Grinding his teeth at the memory again, he made himself relax. He let out a slow breath and leaned back in his chair, reminding himself that he'd get out his frustration later. He'd told Olivia to let him know when she and her friends were leaving and he would take her home with him.

Looking back at the expanding group at his table, he did a double-take when he noticed an unfamiliar face, and another he hadn't seen in a while. Jett's little sister, Lizzie, was there, all long, curly hair, and smooth, delicious curves. She wore high-waisted blue jeans and a black crop top with off-the-shoulder sleeves. Next to her was a douchey looking guy with a backwards hat and an arrogant face.

Lizzie's face lit up as she saw Tyler sitting in the large booth next to his brother. She squeezed between Emerson's chair and the booth, leaning in to pull Tyler into a tight hug.

"Oh my gosh! Tyler, I haven't seen you in forever! Congrats on graduating from law school! That's so exciting!" Lizzie exclaimed.

Emerson didn't miss the uncharacteristic warm, friendly smile on Tyler's face, nor the fact that his hand lingered on Lizzie's arm for a moment after she backed out of their hug.

Interesting.

Lizzie and her new boyfriend took their seats on the other side of the table, and Emerson found himself assessing the guy carefully.

This was the first time Emerson had actually met one of Lizzie's infamous picks of the month, as Jett frequently called them. Sometimes they lasted three or four months, but they all ended with Lizzie on her brother's couch with a pint of Ben and Jerry's, watching *John Tucker Must Die.* He'd witnessed it before, and it was actually how he'd met Lizzie.

As he looked across the table at this new guy, he found himself feeling weirdly protective, wondering exactly what he was going to do to make Lizzie ugly-cry as she shoveled ice cream into her mouth. He didn't know the guy's name, but his face was cocky, he had a possessive sort of hold around Lizzie's waist, and he didn't care to know much else. He didn't like him. Damn, this must be how Jett felt every time she brought one of these jackasses around. How exhausting.

"Everyone, this is Kyle," Lizzie announced, gesturing toward the new boyfriend. "Kyle, this is Brody, Amira, Victoria, Chris, Tyler-" She beamed again as she acknowledged him, "-and that's Emerson."

Kyle nodded to everyone and gave what was almost a polite smile, but it just looked cocky. Emerson must not have been the only one to notice the way Lizzie lit up when she greeted Tyler, or the way Tyler had responded, because Kyle removed his arm from around her waist, and placed his hand on her upper thigh with a pointed look in Tyler's direction. Kyle arched an eyebrow and set his jaw. The move was meant to claim his territory, and it pissed Emerson off more than he ever thought something like that would.

Tyler was taller, broader, and more muscular than this punk. He'd been an athlete back in the day; a star player on the football, basketball, and baseball teams in high school, and he'd even played baseball in college. Tyler had a naturally long and lean build, but since going to the gym with Emerson over the past several months, he'd definitely bulked up. And standing at least six-foot-four, he could be downright intimidating if he wanted to be. But of course, he was Tyler, so he never wanted to be.

Emerson shifted his gaze toward Tyler and was unsurprised yet disappointed to see that he wasn't engaging in a stare-down with Lizzie's new punk-ass boyfriend. Instead, he had dropped his attention to his Heineken bottle, though Emerson guessed he wished it was something stronger now.

Jett sat down in the chair next to Emerson and moments later Zoey found her way back to the table, leaning between her chair and Jett's to set a pitcher of water in the middle.

"I thought you were just going to the bathroom," Jett said, immediately jumping in to do any and everything to make Zoey's life easier-grabbing the pitcher to lighten her load, pulling her chair out for her. Jett was a gentleman. He was traditional and was always there to help anyone who needed it. When it came to Zoey, he went above and beyond. When it came to pregnant Zoey, he was practically her man-servant.

"I did, but then I thought I saw our waitress leave the table as I was coming out. So I stopped at the bar," she explained. She sat down and leaned toward Jett, giving him a quick peck on the lips. Jett smiled and seemed to relax.

Good God, the man was obsessed. Cue whipping sound.

"What did I miss?" Zoey asked, looking around the table at everyone.

"Lizzie was just introducing us to Kyle," Emerson replied. Jett faced Emerson and gave a subtle eye roll, clenching his jaw as if to keep from saying anything he probably shouldn't. But Emerson got the jist.

"Oh, good." Zoey took a sip from her glass of Sprite, and Emerson had the feeling she was also trying not to say anything that might not be particularly friendly. She reached her hand across the table and placed it on Tyler's, snapping him out of his quiet thoughts. "Oh! Tyler! I just met this woman up at the bar. She's super pretty. Actually, she was smoking hot. I thought of you because, well, everyone deserves to find love, right?"

Emerson scowled. "She's smoking hot and you thought of *him*? What about me?"

"Emerson, you literally had your hands full with two girls when we walked in here. What are you possibly going to do with a third?"

"I think you'd be surprised at how creative I can get."

Zoey rolled her eyes and looked back at Tyler. "Anyway, her name is Gabriella, and she's sitting… over there." She gestured toward the back of the bar and Emerson held his breath as he let his eyes wander that way. How many smoking hot Gabriellas could there be in this town?

Certain he was looking at the correct booth, he realized Gabriella was facing away from him, so all he could see was the back of her head. But it was her. He was sure of it. Across from her was a woman with long, copper-red hair that fell in large curls over her shoulders, and there were two men at the booth. The one Gabriella was sitting next to had his arm draped across the back of the booth, and all Emerson could tell was that he had lighter blonde hair than himself, and appeared to be quite tall. The other man facing him had dark hair that looked black in the dim lighting of the bar, and an angular, handsome face.

A swirl of anger picked up in Emerson's chest. Anger, frustration…jealousy, and oddly, possessiveness. That was a new one, and he had no idea what it was doing there. But the feeling that he didn't want either of those men to have their eyes on Gabriella clawed at him from the inside out. There was an unfamiliar pressure in his chest and he clenched his jaw, swallowing his sudden onset of emotions. Emerson didn't have emotions when it came to women. Again, he didn't do feelings, except for the steamy bedroom kind. That was it. That was his limit.

All at once he realized the whole table was observing him with various looks of intrigue.

He blinked and looked back to them, intentionally avoiding Tyler's amused facial expression. "What?"

"I feel like I just pointed out new prey to a starving wolf," Zoey said.

"I really don't think he's starving, but seriously, what was that look for?" Jett asked, nudging his elbow.

Emerson shook his head. "Nothing." Involuntarily, his eyes swept back up to glare at the back of Gabriella's head. He felt the twitch in his jaw and his temple as he remembered the previous evening at work again.

"How do you know her?" Zoey asked, surprising Emerson enough to snap his attention away from the back of Gabriella's head.

Tyler laughed and explained, "She's *Gabriella Cabrera-Perez*...his arch-enemy. The She-Devil, She-Demon, Cruella. The Poison Ivy to his Batman. The Lex Luthor to his Superman."

Amira slapped the table, causing Brody to jump. "Oh. My. God. You mean my hero is here in this bar?" She turned unsubtly in her seat and followed Emerson's line of vision. "Oooh, is she the red-head or the other one facing away?"

"The other one," Emerson replied, though it was more of a growl. He still hadn't taken his eyes off the back of her head and was realizing that he likely looked like a sociopath.

"We should totally ask her to join us!" Amira said, smile bright and voice way too excited.

"No," Emerson growled, still glaring. Jesus, what was his problem? Why couldn't he just look away?

"Please?" Amira asked, barely containing herself. "Oh my gosh, I want to hear all the stories from her point of view. I'm sure you left out something to keep from embarrassing yourself. I need to hear it all."

"I told you everything," he said, reluctantly tearing his eyes away and focusing on the beer bottle in front of him. He rubbed his jaw and looked around for Taylor. "I could use a fucking shot or two right now."

"What happened yesterday?" Tyler asked, eyeing him curiously.

Emerson paused, beer bottle to his lips. He took a drink, swallowed, set his beer down. "Why do you think something happened yesterday?"

"Because you were weirdly quiet," Tyler replied. "You never told me what happened after she asked you to come to her office…" Tyler wiggled his eyebrows suggestively.

"Oooh, step into my office, Mr. Yates," Brody said with a horrible British accent.

"Nothing happened," Emerson stated. He shook his head and looked around the bar again. Taylor was behind the bar talking to the moody looking bartender. The way her body was angled toward him, he wondered if she was sleeping with him, too. When the bartender's gaze lingered over Taylor's tits in her low-cut top, he at least knew the guy wanted to be sleeping with her.

Emerson wasn't surprised to find that it didn't bother him. He got Taylor to himself twice a week, and that was plenty. She was fun, but doubted if he was the only guy she was having fun with. Though he made sure all the girls he slept with knew they weren't exclusive, he always worried about them forming attachments.

"Something definitely happened. You were in there for a while and the door was locked." Tyler leaned back in the booth and raised his eyebrow as if to say *please explain.*

Emerson snapped his head to look at Tyler. "How the fuck did you know the door was locked?"

"Because I stopped by to offer some help and discovered the door was locked."

"Really?" Zoey questioned, leaning forward to look at him around Jett. "She didn't seem like she liked you very much. Like at all."

"Wait, what? You talked about me with her?" Emerson glanced toward the bar where Zoey and Gabriella would have had their conversation then back to Zoey. "What did she say?"

Zoey shrugged. "Not much, really. She just saw you over here with those other girls and kind of rolled her eyes. I said that wasn't how most women reacted to you, she asked how I knew you, I explained. That was about it, other than maybe another eye roll."

Emerson furrowed his brow. *Well what the fuck?* She didn't like him at all? She had just used him to get off and that was it? That seemed unlikely. He couldn't fathom it. Wouldn't accept it. There was more between them, wasn't there? Not relationship, sappy feelings, but surely she was interested in more than just an *oral presentation.*

He let a hot breath out of his nose and glared once again at the back of her head, then at the two men in the booth with her. Who the hell were those guys anyway? What were they to her? Did she actually like them? If she was with the blonde guy next to her, was he going home with her? Would he get to touch her? Taste her? Feel her skin against his as he moved over and inside her?

His inner monologue let out a frustrated grumbling of words and sounds that was certainly not any language he recognized. He was suddenly too hot, too constricted, and he began tugging at his tie. His face contorted into what could only be described as a glower and he clenched his jaw yet again. He needed to get up. To move around. He wanted to walk over to Gabriella's table and cause a scene, shouting and demanding answers for what the hell she was trying to pull.

Instead, however, he shrugged off his suit jacket, rolled up his shirt sleeves and chewed on the inside of his cheek. And he continued to silently fume to himself, not caring that everyone was staring at him again as though he were some curious new creature that had just materialized in front of them.

Hesitantly, Tyler leaned forward, putting his forearms on the table much like Emerson was doing at the moment. "Did something happen between you guys? Did she say something about the whole...you ruining her presentation thing?"

Emerson shook his head. "She called me out, I apologized. She said some things that were perfectly accurate about me, and I apologized again. And I meant it. I fucked up, I went too far, too childish. And then..." he paused, knowing for a fact he was not sharing what had actually happened next. "Then I thought we were on the same page. I thought maybe things would be cool between us, but then out of nowhere she told me to leave. She said 'we're done here, you can go'."

"And that bothered you that much?" Brody questioned. Brody looked truly concerned, though Emerson knew he was fully invested in the idea that he liked Gabriella. He was beginning to think there might be something to that.

Emerson sat up and cleared his throat, shaking off his frustration and the possibility that he wanted anything more from Gabriella than the job she'd snatched out from under him and maybe her body. "No. It's fine. She just confuses the fuck out of me. I'm not going to worry about it."

There was a brief silence at the table before Zoey graciously brought up a new subject. However, had he known what the topic was going to be, he might have tried to break the silence first.

"Are you guys ready for next weekend? Don't be idiots. I don't want you guys making a bunch of work for me to sort out," Zoey said seriously.

Emerson furrowed his brow, confused. "What's next weekend?"

"Oh, I guess it doesn't apply to you. Or Kyle. But it's Quinn's bachelor party in Vegas," Zoey replied. Her face conveyed the same level of enthusiasm Emerson felt at the topic. "It could potentially be a publicity nightmare, so if one of you guys could stay sober-"

"You're not serious," Chris said, laughing. "Our best friend since we were eleven is getting married and you expect us to stay sober at his bachelor party? Oh, no. That ain't happenin'."

"Not a chance," Tyler agreed, shaking his head. "It's going to be a shit show and we're going to love every minute of it. Even if we don't remember it."

Emerson looked to Brody and narrowed his eyes. "Are you going, too?"

Brody averted his eyes, but nodded.

"You. Traitor."

Looking sheepish and a little pleading, Brody threw his head back. "I'm sorry. But come on! It's Vegas. And Quinn Casey's bachelor party? I can't pass that invite up!"

Emerson polished off his bottle of Heineken and slammed it on the table. "Fine. Fuck it. Tell me where it is. I'm coming with you."

"You're not going," Jett said definitively. "No fucking way."

"Why not? All my friends are going. I'm going. Tell me where it is or I'll crash it. I'll make it a publicity nightmare for your pregnant girlfriend."

"If I don't tell you where it is, how will you crash it?" Jett asked.

"I'll just follow Brody out of work on Friday and wait for him to go. It's not hard."

Jett groaned. "You don't even like him. You guys don't get along. Why would you want to go to his bachelor party? He's marrying your ex-fiancé. It's twisted. You can't go."

"You're the best man, right? Isn't that your call?" Emerson pressed. He knew he was being absurd, but he suddenly hated the thought of all of his friends having fun in Vegas without him.

"Yeah, it is my call, and I say you're not going," Jett stated. "It's not personal. Not with me, anyway. But you know you can't go. Case would be fucking furious if you showed up."

Emerson slunk back in his chair and sighed. "Fine. It's fine. I'll plan a different Vegas trip and we'll see whose is better. But I just want you all to know that this isn't fucking fair and I hate all of you just a little bit right now."

They moved on from the bachelor party, to Rae's bachelorette party, to Amira's horrifying tale of how a woman came into her office at the women's center with a small-ish model rocket stuck in her vagina, to sex toys in the bedroom, and so on. An hour and a half had passed before Emerson felt a hand skate over his shoulders and down his arms. He turned his head to see Olivia looking a little more than tipsy as she giggled into his neck where she started peppering him with light kisses.

Olivia sighed and groaned into the spot just below his ear. "God, I've missed you so much." Her hands slid over his shoulders again, but now down his chest, over his stomach. "And I've missed-"

"Okay!" Emerson grabbed her hands just in time before they palmed him over his pants in front of everyone. "Okay, honey, looks like it's time to get you home."

Oh yeah, she was drunk. Way too drunk.

Standing up, he pulled out his wallet and threw some cash on the table. He pulled his jacket back on and tucked Olivia under his arm, close to his body so she wouldn't stumble too much on the way out.

"Have fun tonight!" Brody waved, and did his best to conceal a laugh at the way Olivia was now pawing at Emerson.

"Who knows, maybe tonight's the night we try butt stuff," he replied with a wink.

"Emerson William Yates! You'd better not take advantage of that poor girl!" Amira shouted, pointing a finger accusingly at him.

With his signature wicked grin, he replied, "I would never."

He chuckled at the looks on his friends' faces, but honestly doubted very much that anything at all would happen with Olivia. The most likely scenario with her in such an inebriated state was that he would drive her home and tuck her into bed where she would immediately pass out.

Although earlier in the evening he'd felt a desperate need for a wild night of fucking out every little frustration from the past thirty-six hours, seeing Gabriella and recognizing his jealousy over the two men she was still sitting with a few booths away had thrown a wrench in that plan. All he could think about was her. How to get to her. How to prove she felt more for him, because he knew she did. She had to. How to show her there was more to him than what she thought she knew. He didn't know why it was important that she learned these things about him, but it felt urgent.

As he opened the door with Olivia under his arm, he chanced a glance at the back of the bar again. Gabriella was standing in the aisle and pulling her purse over her shoulder when she looked his way and they locked eyes. She paused, and so did he. Everything for a moment stood still. He didn't know how to react, but waited for her inevitable look of boredom or disinterest. The look she always gave him when he wanted to see something more.

It didn't come.

For a half-second, her eyes dropped to Olivia, then flickered back up to him.

From a distance it was hard to tell, but he could have sworn she looked somewhat dejected. And maybe there was something wrong with him, because the thought, the mere possibility that she was disappointed to see him leaving with someone else made him feel like he was finally on top.

With the quirk of an eyebrow and a small tilt of his lips, he smirked, triumphant, before leading Olivia out the door.

Chapter 8

Monday at work was slightly strained. Maybe a little awkward, even. Emerson never stopped by Gabriella's office to bug her, he didn't initiate any pranks or playful teases. As a matter of fact, the one time he'd seen her that day, he'd kept his mouth uncharacteristically shut.

While refilling his coffee in the break room, he turned around and saw her looking around the room, intentionally not making eye contact. Without thinking, he noticed her empty coffee tumbler in her hands and reached for it, snatching it from her and promptly filled it with coffee- he knew she took it black- and handed it back to her. As if that weren't awkward enough, he then moved around her and out of the break room without a word.

Without any drop-ins from Tyler, since he was no longer an intern at Warren & Blakely, Emerson had been forced to fully focus on work. It had been a productive day, but it dragged on and he was grateful for the excuse to leave early to pick Kolbe up from ball practice. The middle school wasn't too far, but he thought he'd try to get there early so he could actually watch his little brother play.

The small parking lot next to the ball field was already full, so he parked on the street and walked over to the field. He scanned the ball diamond for Kolbe and saw him on third base with a glove, waiting for the batter to swing.

Leaning with his arms folded over the top of the fence, Emerson watched as the batter hit a line drive straight into Kolbe's glove. He was impressed at his brother's speed; a blink and he would've missed it. Kolbe threw the ball back to the catcher as a new player stepped up to bat.

The new batter pulled his batting helmet over his head of thick, black hair. He was thin, naturally tan, and had an intensity about him as he stepped up to the plate. Everything about the kid's posture and stance told Emerson that he took the game seriously. It didn't matter that it was practice, or that he was only scrimmaging against his own teammates. He was in it to win it. Emerson was reminded vaguely of Benny Rodriguez from *The Sandlot* as he watched the kid get in the zone.

There were some hollers and calls of encouragement from his teammates in the dugout, and some playful, taunting chatter from those in the field. The pitcher wound up and sent in a fastball-

Crack!

The ball went flying straight down the center, over the pitcher's head, over the second baseman, into far center field. The kid sprinted, dropping the bat on his way to first. He kicked up dust as he rounded second, and dived, hands reaching for the third base plate as he slid with a *whoosh* past Kolbe, nearly knocking him down. Kolbe caught the ball less than a second after the kid slid into the base.

"Safe!" a coach called from next to third base.

Emerson watched as Kolbe held his hand out to the kid and helped him up. He couldn't hear what they were saying, but saw the smiles on their faces as they shoved playfully at one another the way boys do when they're messing around, teasing.

It made him happy to know that Kolbe had made friends in his short time at a new school. Change of any kind was tough for a kid going through puberty; moving to a new city and starting a new school with only three months left in the school year was bound to be a difficult adjustment. The plus side was that he would at least know some of the kids at his new high school in the fall, even if it was just the kids on his baseball team.

Another boy stepped up to bat. When he swung, he sent the ball high and left. The left-fielder caught the pop-up, but not before the player on third base crossed home.

When the players started coming in from the field, Emerson guessed practice was over and waited, watching as Kolbe and his team huddled and listened to their coach's critiques and compliments before sending them on their way.

"Impressive catch, kid!" Emerson called out as Kolbe slung his bat bag over his shoulder and walked out of the dugout. The kid who'd hit a triple was walking next to him. Kolbe was about two inches taller, but they had similar builds. Lanky, athletic, young teenagers who hadn't quite grown into their limbs yet.

"Will! You're earlier than I thought," Kolbe said, making his way over to him. Ever since the first time they'd met only five years ago, Kolbe had called him Will instead of Emerson. It was weird to think he'd only known his brother for five years, but then again, their father had kept him a secret for nine years. There was a lot of lost time to make up for, and Emerson always tried to make the most of the time he got with the kid.

"Did you really think I'd make you sit around and wait on me?" Emerson asked, feigning offense.

"Not on purpose," Kolbe replied. "I just know you work a lot. And you get stopped by hot chicks everywhere you go." He turned to his friend and said quietly, "You never know what's going to hold this guy up."

The friend gave a reserved smile, as though he almost felt guilty even being amused at the idea that Emerson could have gotten held up by one of many "hot chicks".

"Will, this is Robby." Kolbe gestured to the kid next to him. "Robby, this is my brother, Will. The one I told you about."

Robby met Emerson's eyes for a moment and he gave another reserved smile as he waved. "Hey, it's nice to meet you."

Emerson grinned at the kid's politeness. "You, too. That was one hell of a triple out there."

"Thanks." Robby's smile pulled up farther on one side. It was almost a smirk, but Emerson got the impression he was too polite to get cocky.

"Hey, can you take us to dinner?" Kolbe asked abruptly. "I'm starving."

Emerson raised his eyebrows. "Both of you?"

He was used to taking care of Kolbe. It had been an adjustment, learning how to care for another individual and not feel like he was going to do something horrendously wrong. The idea of taking Kolbe and one of his friends was a little more than daunting, even if the kid seemed like he would pose no problems.

"Yeah." Kolbe shrugged, then turned to Robby. "Who's picking you up today?"

"I don't know. Hopefully not Lola again," Robby said.

"I was kind of hoping it *was* Lola." Kolbe smirked. "She's hot."

Emerson couldn't help laughing as Robby made a face. "Gross, dude. She's my sister. And she just got her license. Being in a car with her is terrifying."

"Don't you have like…three sisters?" Kolbe asked. "Are they all hot?"

Robby rolled his eyes. "Four sisters and one brother. And Elisa is eleven, so if you tell me you think she's hot, we're gonna have a problem."

"Six kids?" Emerson nearly blurted, then let out a low whistle. "That sounds like a full house. Do you ever get time to yourself?"

"It's not so bad," Robby replied. "My three oldest siblings are all adults with jobs and stuff. So it's just me, Lola, and Elisa at home."

Emerson nodded and looked around at the park where kids were getting in their respective cars and heading out. Several of the kids waved and said bye to Kolbe and Robby. He turned back to the two fourteen-year-olds who had already switched the topic back to their ball practice.

"Do you want us to wait for whoever's picking you up?" Emerson asked.

Robby didn't get a chance to answer before a familiar voice called out for him. Robby lifted his head and looked over Emerson's shoulder, smiled and waved. "Hey Gabs!"

 Emerson froze.

What were the fucking chances of this?

He didn't turn around to face the woman he knew was approaching, completely unsure of how to proceed. He caught Kolbe's face, however, and immediately the knot in his chest loosened with the amusement of it. Kolbe was staring, wide-eyed, with his jaw nearly hitting the ground. Emerson was a little worried he'd start drooling so he nudged him.

Kolbe blinked a few times, raised his eyebrows, and leaned toward Emerson, muttering, "Dude, you *have* to work your magic on this one."

Emerson sighed heavily and nodded. "Believe me, kid, I've tried." When Kolbe's face went curious, Emerson subtly held up a finger to his mouth with a silent "shhh". Then he turned around with his crooked grin and mustered his charm yet again. "Hey Gabe."

Gabriella froze now, with her arm around Robby's shoulder, releasing him from a hug, and Emerson took this moment to let his eyes make a slow, intentional sweep of her body from head to toe. Like him, she was still in her work clothes; a pair of black dress pants that were tapered at the ankle, an ivory, long-sleeved blouse that was sheer so that he could see the camisole tank beneath that closely matched her skin tone. And the pointy stilettos.

His gaze slid back up to her face, lingering for a longer-than-was-appropriate moment on her mouth, before meeting her dark brown eyes.

She started forming her words before they came out, "What are you doing here?"

Emerson grinned, satisfied that he'd taken the upper hand so far in their interaction. "Same as you, I think. Just picking up my brother from practice."

Her eyes shifted to Kolbe standing next to him and her brow furrowed in confusion. It was the usual reaction when Emerson introduced Kolbe as his brother to anyone, leaving out the *half* part.

"You guys know each other?" Robby asked, looking back and forth between Emerson and his sister.

"Sure do," Emerson replied. He felt his eyebrow twitch and the smallest whisper of a smile cross his lips.

After having such an uncomfortable day at work, being completely unsure of how to approach Gabriella, he realized he really didn't want their days at work to be like that. He'd been quiet and evasive, and met her only with stony silence. But he didn't want to be overly hesitant around her. He didn't want to keep ignoring her and giving her the silent treatment.

Yes, she had gotten the better of him in a big way on Friday, but he thought he made up for it when she saw him leaving the bar with Olivia the next night. Though he couldn't stop thinking about it, what had happened in Gabriella's office had made him...not exactly mad, but stunned. Stunned, frustrated, and confused. And, if he was being perfectly honest, turned on. He had been completely turned on by her assertiveness and the way she had completely demanded control.

So, he was back to his usual. Or at least, close to his usual. He felt a little more determined now. And he knew it wasn't just about the Alpha case anymore. This was more personal.

Kolbe stood next to Emerson, his eyes darting back and forth from his brother to Gabriella. He let out a slow breath then looked at Robby. "Dude, this is gonna be awkward, but I think your sister slept with my brother."

Gabriella's eyes went wide as saucers and her eyebrows shot up. She practically screeched, "*What?!* No. No, we haven't." She looked down at her little brother whose face was a display of absolute horror. "I- we...We are *not* sleeping together. We have *never* slept together. We...we just know each other from work."

Kolbe nodded, knowingly. "Ah, know each other from *work*. Gotcha." He gave an exaggerated wink. "What kind of work would that be, Will? You're a lawyer, so I can only assume you two were working on an *indecent exposure* case? Did you let her go through your briefs? I'm sure there was some heavy compliance with section *sixty-nine* of that article-"

Emerson cut him off with a swat to the head, though he was struggling to hold in his own laughter. "Will you fucking stop? We're not having sex. We work together."

"Oh." Kolbe's shoulders might have drooped. "Well that's disappointing."

Letting out a quiet laugh, Emerson scrubbed a hand down his face. "Jesus..." He looked up at Gabriella and Robby who were staring in stunned silence. "Sorry. I might've told him too much about...you know, birds and the bees. He asks a lot of questions."

"And he's got all the answers," Kolbe added, enthusiastically. Emerson felt that weird flip-flopping sensation in his chest that he got every time his little brother insinuated that he was actually a good big brother or role model.

Gabriella's eyes flicked between Emerson and Kolbe again. "So, you two are brothers?"

"Yeah. Can't you see the resemblance?" Emerson put his arm around Kolbe's shoulders and pulled him up next to him.

They really did resemble one another in most ways. Kolbe was likely going to be about as tall as Emerson, they had the same mouth shape and square jaw, though Kolbe's was softer yet, having not fully gone through puberty. Even their eyes had the same ability to pierce and hypnotize, though Kolbe had inherited the icy blue shade of their father's.

Really, Kolbe was a darker version of Emerson. Kolbe's skin was the color of an extra frothy mocha and his hair was dark brown, whereas Emerson was fair-skinned with sandy-blonde hair that had a tendency to darken slightly in the winter months.

Gabriella and Robby seemed to survey them and finally she nodded. "Yeah, I can. Especially when you're talking."

In unison, though Kolbe sounded more thoughtful, and Emerson's tone was matter-of-fact, the brothers said, "People say that a lot."

Before too long of a silence could stretch between them, Kolbe asked, "Do you guys want to go to dinner with us? Will's buying."

Emerson narrowed his eyes at his brother.

"Will?" Gabriella questioned.

"That's me. He refuses to call me Emerson."

Kolbe made a face. "Damn right I do. You know what kind of guys are named Emerson?"

"Enlighten me," Emerson said flatly.

"Rich, boring-ass, pretentious, entitled white dudes who drink scotch and smoke pipes," Kolbe explained. "Also, it's too long. Too many syllables. But most importantly, it's too damn white."

Emerson pressed his lips together and nodded, having heard this explanation several times. His eyes lifted to Gabriella who was trying- and failing- to bite back a laugh. "He's got a point," she said, clearly amused.

He liked her smile, especially in this easy, relaxed setting. He found himself wanting to see more of it, so he said, "I'm fine taking them to dinner. I haven't eaten yet, and if we go back to my place, the kid's just feasting on Hot Pockets and mac n' cheese."

Gabriella seemed to hesitate, but Robby looked up at her eagerly. "Um...okay, sure. We'll just follow you."

He couldn't help smiling, and also couldn't help noticing that it was more than just his usual smirk playing across his lips.

"Can we go to that bar your friends own?" Kolbe asked.

"We eat there all the time," Emerson replied. Really, he just didn't want Chris and Jett to see him out with Gabriella. Having dinner. They would give him endless shit, and if Tyler was there he would really never hear the end of it.

"Can we go to Hooters?" his little brother asked, hopefully.

"*No.* Your mom would kill me, and we don't even have one in town."

Kolbe considered some more. "How about that Mexican restaurant on the other side of town? Agave?"

Emerson looked up at Gabriella and Robby. "Do you guys like Mexican food? The portion sizes are massive, and the chips and salsa are endless."

"Yes! They have the best burritos," Robby replied enthusiastically.

Gabriella still looked slightly frozen to the spot, as if she had no idea how she ended up being coerced into spending her evening with Emerson outside of work. He was a little dumbstruck himself, but he was oddly looking forward to it. He couldn't remember the last time he'd had dinner with a woman- other than Amira when he invited himself over, but of course that didn't count.

But this wasn't a date either. This was just two people- work colleagues- taking their brothers, who happened to be teammates, out to dinner. It was definitely *not* a date. Emerson didn't date.

They pulled into the parking lot of Agave, Gabriella and Robby taking the parking spot next to them, and all walked in together. He almost immediately was wondering what everyone else would make of their situation. Two teenagers in their dirty practice clothes, and Gabriella and Emerson in their pristine work attire. He almost laughed at the thought that someone might see them and think they were a family. And then his stomach did a weird dropping thing like when you're falling backward in a chair and aren't sure if it's going to tip all the way over or not.

He shook his head and blinked a few times before realizing the hostess was talking to them.

"Four, please," Gabriella said to the young woman working the hostess stand.

The girl was likely in her early twenties, and Emerson realized with alarm that he would normally be checking her out. Giving her *the look.* But he had no interest in doing so at the moment. There was nothing wrong with her. She was pretty and had a nice smile. Also, her black pants hugged her curves well. But then he looked at Gabriella and couldn't help thinking the young hostess, at least for him, wouldn't satisfy his full, gluttonous appetite.

The hostess led them to a booth where Emerson and Kolbe took one side, and Gabriella and Robby took the other. Gabriella was sitting directly across from him and he had yet another sudden realization that he needed to make sure he didn't stare at her. She hadn't noticed in the conference room her first day, and she was facing the opposite direction the other night at the bar when he couldn't take his eyes off the back of her head. Both times he'd thought of himself and his behavior as a little sociopathic. Tonight he would relax. Act normal. Just be himself. But maybe...*maybe* a more pleasant version of himself.

"So," Kolbe began, always the one to break the silence, "I need to talk to you about girls."

Emerson glanced sideways at his brother. "Oh yeah? What about them?"

"Well, not all of them, but there's one...there's one I'm interested in, I think," Kolbe replied.

"Tell me about her," Emerson said, grinning. He loved this part of being a brother. Imparting knowledge. Sharing stories from his own experiences. Bonding over this kind of stuff was huge. And he had a lot to share on this topic, after all.

"She's in a few of my classes, and it sounds like we're both going to TC Central next year," Kolbe said. "She's kind of shy, but I've made her laugh a few times, so I thought maybe she could be interested. She plays on the volleyball team *and* she does track and field. Legs for days. And she's super hot."

Emerson chuckled. He'd been waiting for that.

"I was going to try one of your moves, but it didn't seem right. With her being shy and all, I just wasn't sure how to approach her in that way," Kolbe explained. "Last month I tried that thing that you did. The move you put on that chick at Trojan. You know...the one where you were just watching her and giving the look. The one where you said you just look at a chick and imagine her naked? And then she just walked over to you and you were like 'sorry if I was staring, I just couldn't take my eyes off you'. And then she giggled and offered to let you get a closer look? Remember that?"

He paused briefly to let Emerson give a slow, disbelieving nod as Gabriella put her hand over her mouth to stifle another laugh.

"I did that to a girl last month and she just got freaked out. She thought she had, like, a pimple on her face or something, and that I was just staring at it."

Emerson gave himself a minute to compose his thoughts- and his mild embarrassment- before continuing. "Right. Well, that only worked on that chick at the bar because I knew she'd been eyeing me since she walked in. I wasn't the only one staring. Also, thirteen and fourteen-year-old girls don't want to be stared at. They're self conscious. They've got all sorts of things going on. They probably just started shaving their legs, they're getting used to having breasts- or not having breasts, while all their friends have them- and stuff like that. You don't want to look at them too intently for too long. They'll start to think something is wrong with them."

Kolbe nodded, considering the advice like Emerson were an ancient wiseman, and Kolbe was the apprentice. "But don't girls like to hear that? That you can't take your eyes off them?"

"That's first or second date stuff," Gabriella chimed in. "You don't want to be too intense too fast."

The three boys at the table all turned and stared at her for a moment with looks of confusion on their faces.

"What? I was a teenage girl once. Don't you think asking a *girl* for girl advice might be a good idea?" she asked defensively.

The boys continued to stare.

"Did you date when you were a teenager?" Robby asked, brow furrowed deeply as if the very idea of his sister as a teenager baffled him.

"Yes, of course I dated," she replied.

"You never date now," her brother said with a shrug. "I don't remember the last time you brought a guy home to meet the family. Wasn't it Ben?"

Her eyes flashed to Emerson for a brief second and he thought maybe she was feeling self-conscious now. "Yeah, it probably was Ben. But I've also not been living in the same state. It's not like I haven't gone on dates, I just haven't found anyone to be serious with."

Robby's furrow deepened as he looked a little disgusted. "So…what's that mean? You just slept with all of them and that was it?"

She gave a nervous laugh. "No, I definitely didn't have sex with all of them."

"Only a select few got that lucky." Kolbe smirked and raised his eyebrows suggestively.

Emerson delivered a swift smack to the back of his head and glared, though again, he had a hard time fully disguising his smirk. The kid was funny. He was like a miniature Emerson clone, but he still wanted to make sure to set a good example for him. Not that he was at all ashamed of the way he lived his life, but he just felt like Kolbe deserved better. Could do better.

Kolbe muttered a quick "sorry" before switching his attention to the waiter who now appeared at their table. The guy introduced himself as David, who had the faintest accent. He read off the food and drink specials, but all Emerson could really pay attention to was the way he kept his eyes on Gabriella.

Really, guy? I'm right here.

Not that they were on a date. Or that he had any claim to her whatsoever. But that's what it looked like, right? How could someone so blatantly undress her with his eyes when another guy was *right there?!*

When Emerson looked back at Gabriella, expecting to see the same look of boredom she always gave him, he scowled even further. She was smiling.

No. Just no.

"*¿De dónde eres?*" Gabriella's voice was so smooth and natural as she spoke Spanish. He loved the way it sounded coming out of her mouth. He did *not*, however, like that she was still smiling and looking at David as she said the words.

"Guatemala, y tú?" David responded, and his attention focused even more heavily on Gabriella. His smile brightened, though it was tinged with mischief. Emerson knew that look. He'd given it plenty of times to plenty of women.

She answered and the two of them continued a small conversation in Spanish, of which Emerson understood nothing. He had taken French in high school, and was severely regretting that decision at this point. His jaw clenched as his eyes flicked back and forth between Gabriella and David, and when she started laughing at something, he cleared his throat abruptly.

Everyone looked at him and he did his best to smile politely, although he felt like he was somewhere between a grimace and an animal bearing its teeth.

David straightened and he looked quickly between Emerson and Gabriella a few times before catching on.

Yeah, that's right, buddy. She's here with me.

Kind of.

"Sorry," David said, though he flashed another smile in Gabriella's direction before addressing Emerson. "What can I get you to drink?"

He ordered a Heineken for himself and Kolbe ordered a Pepsi. After Gabriella and Robby made their drink orders, David finally left them alone, though not before giving Gabriella another sly grin.

"What was so funny?" Emerson asked, eyes fixed intently on the menu.

"Oh, nothing," she replied, with the wave of her hand. "He was just talking about how everyone assumes he's from México just because he speaks Spanish and works at a Mexican restaurant, and then if he tells them he's actually from Guatemala, they seem to get uncomfortable like they're in the presence of an illegal immigrant. He said he can see them deciding if they need to call immigration."

Robby rolled his eyes but didn't look away from his menu. "Yeah, and then he hit on you."

"What? No, he didn't." She shook her head.

"I speak Spanish too, remember? I understood the whole thing."

"He wasn't hitting on me, he was just being friendly."

Emerson let out a derisive snort and Gabriella looked across the table at him, eyes narrowed.

"Trust me, he wasn't just being friendly. Guys aren't *just friendly* to hot women who aren't wearing a ring," he said. He saw her eyebrow raise and the corner of her mouth tug up, and he added, "Yes. You're hot. I think you're hot, my brother thinks you're hot, the waiter, and probably every other person in this room except the kid sitting next to you thinks you're hot. Don't act surprised."

She looked thoughtful for a moment, chewing on her bottom lip. "Why can't guys just be friendly? What are you supposed to do? Be rude?"

"No, not necessarily," he replied, shrugging. "But I guarantee he was hitting on you. I don't even know what he was saying, but he was definitely trying to get in your pants."

Robby's eyes widened and he nodded his agreement. "Trust me, you didn't want to hear what he was saying."

Suddenly, he really did want to know what the guy had said, but also knew that it would likely piss him off and make him overly short with him. Honestly, he couldn't blame David. *Fucking David.* He knew with absolute certainty that if he'd met Gabriella in any other setting or any other way, he would have been pulling out all his best moves.

"Hey," Kolbe snapped. "Can we get back to my problem? Shy girl...make sure I don't stare too much. What's my next move?"

Emerson hummed, considering. He didn't have much experience with the shy ones. "Well, if she's shy, she just needs someone to bring her out of her shell. Keep making her laugh, and maybe ask her out somewhere with your friends. Like a group thing. Maybe that would take the pressure off."

"That's a terrible idea," Gabriella said, shaking her head. She looked at Kolbe and reached across to put her hand on his arm. His eyes widened like he was terrified, staring at Gabriella's manicured hand touching him. She said sincerely, "Don't do that."

"Excuse me, how is that a terrible idea?" Emerson asked, offended.

"She's *shy*, Edward. Why would you think she would enjoy being around a ton of people?"

He stared at her and creased his brow. "Don't give my brother advice. That's my job."

"You're giving him bad advice. I'm saving him from scaring this poor girl away," she argued.

"It's not bad advice." He looked at Kolbe who was still staring at the spot on his arm where Gabriella had touched him. "Ask her to a party. Actually, no, don't ask her. Keep your confidence up and just tell her you're taking her out. Girls love confidence- that's true for all ages. Just tell her there's a party and that she should go with you."

"Okay, are you intentionally sabotaging him now?" Gabriella asked, incredulous. "Kolbe, don't do any of that. Trust me, she will go running the other way."

"Listen to me, Kolbe. You said it yourself, I have all the answers."

Gabriella rolled her eyes. "Seriously? You're going to insist he take your bad advice? You know it's bad, you just don't want to agree with me."

"That's insane. You're the one who started arguing," Emerson pressed. "He should take *my* advice because I know what I'm doing." He smirked suddenly, figuring out how to, once again, take the upper hand. "You saw me in action at the bar the other night."

Kolbe smiled at him with his usual expression, like he was the most impressive and inspiring person he'd ever met. "You scored again? Oh, hell yeah. That's why you're the best."

"Does...does that happen a lot?" Robby asked. He'd been silently watching the conversation, but suddenly his interest had piqued.

Gabriella cut Emerson off before he could say anything, "Don't tell my brother about any of your sexcapades. Tell your brother all you want, but Robby doesn't need to hear it."

"It's okay, I'll tell you later," Kolbe said, nodding toward Robby.

Emerson laughed quietly to himself, then remembered another detail about that night at the bar. The part that had him staring at her all evening like a psycho. "You know what? Now that I think of it, maybe Kolbe should take your advice. I seem to recall you sitting with not one, but *two* guys at the bar."

As expected, Robby made a horrified face. "*Two* guys? Gabby…that's…that's gross. What the hell?"

She delivered what sounded like a quick scolding to Robby in Spanish before turning her attention back to Emerson. Unexpectedly, she laughed at the look on his face. "You mean my twin brother, Marco and his *husband*, Max? Those two guys?"

Emerson paused, mouth open, and Robby breathed a sigh of relief. "Oh…"

There was a sudden light feeling in his chest now, like he was floating a little, and he tried his best to hide the smile that threatened to spread across his face. There was no reason to feel so relieved that she hadn't gone home with another guy. There was no reason to feel a little less threatened, even when the waiter came back to the table with their drinks and to take their food order. He shouldn't have been feeling threatened in the first place.

Maybe she wasn't looking for anyone. She was a busy, independent, hard-working woman with better things on her mind than finding a husband. Maybe in Maryland she'd had guys she could hook up with when she needed a fix. Maybe, as unbelievably good-looking as she was, if she felt like she needed some bedroom action, she would simply walk into a bar, pick a guy, and say "You, come with me".

As he looked up at her, sipping from her sangria, he had the wildest, most absurd thought. Maybe…*maybe* she was already interested in someone. Someone who was just as attractive and independent, yet slightly less hard-working than she was.

He liked the thought. Actually, he *really* liked the thought, but didn't know what good it would do either of them. The only kind of relationship he was capable of providing was a physical one. He wasn't going to change, and he didn't feel like disappointing anyone else. He was no longer in the business of breaking hearts for sport. It wasn't fun. Sure, as a teenager he'd been a little shit who liked to play games, but he'd matured since then. However marginally. He didn't want to hurt someone again, and the very thought of being the reason Gabriella was upset or hurt or broken-hearted already made him feel lower than low.

"So...whose advice do I take?" Kolbe asked after David left the table again.

"Mine." Emerson and Gabriella spoke in unison.

She let out an exasperated huff. "You're going to ruin his chances with that girl. She's going to be overwhelmed in a big group. I guarantee she would prefer something quieter and more intimate so you two can get to know each other."

Kolbe looked to be in deep concentration, then he looked at Emerson hesitantly. "I feel like that's a good point."

"Okay, how about this," Emerson said. "If your intentions are just to get physical with the girl, take my advice. That's my sweet spot. That's what I know how to do. If you want to develop a relationship with her, Gabby's advice is probably what you wanna go with."

She gave a small smile, conceding. "Have you ever had an actual relationship or have you just been this-" she gestured vaguely up and down at him, "-this obnoxious Casanova your entire life? Don't you remember your first crush? How it felt to actually have feelings for someone?"

"Of course I've been in a relationship, I just didn't care for it," he replied with an easy shrug. "And my first crush was Rachel Christy in first grade. She moved the summer before second grade and I was positively heartbroken. I decided then that feelings weren't my thing." His crooked grin conveyed the playful manner of his story, and he was pleased when she smiled back.

"That must've been so hard for you," she teased. "My first crush was also in first grade. His name was Andre Rodriguez, and we held hands and ate lunch together for a whole week."

"Aw, that's adorable," he said, somewhat sardonically.

"I kissed Mallory Daniels behind a tree on the playground in third grade," Robby chimed in.

Gabriella's eyes went wide and she looked at her little brother in shock. "Your first kiss was in third grade? Robby! Does Mom know?"

Robby laughed quietly. "No, but Dad does. And actually, Mallory kissed me. I had no idea it was coming."

"My first kiss was in fourth grade," said Kolbe. "Kylie Benson. I walked her home from school and made my move when I walked her to the door."

"Smooth, kid." Emerson nodded approvingly. "You're a natural."

Their dinners arrived and they continued their talk of first crushes, first kisses, first dates, and so on. Emerson found out that Gabriella's first real boyfriend was the same Ben that Robby had mentioned earlier. They had started dating their sophomore year of high school and were together for quite a few years after that, though she didn't give details on when or why the relationship had ended. Emerson shared minimal details about his first girlfriend, and avoided the manner in which they broke up at all costs. Luckily no one pushed, so he was safe on that front. For the time being, anyway.

"So..." Robby spooned a glob of sour cream on his plate-sized burrito, "when was your last real relationship then? I know Kolbe says you don't *really date*, but...you've had more than just your first girlfriend, right?"

Emerson slid his jaw to the side as he considered his question. He really didn't want to discuss Raelyn right now, or try to skip around the truth of how their relationship ended. Kolbe knew Raelyn, and he'd really liked her. He'd been upset to find out that Emerson wasn't marrying her after all, and had asked a hundred times why they couldn't make it work. If he was sure they couldn't make it work. What had happened? Could they fix it? What if he just tried harder...

Kolbe was to never know that Emerson had cheated on her. Not only because he wanted to be a good role model, but because he knew that if Kolbe ever found out the truth, he'd lump him in with their dad. Kolbe didn't really know Johnathan Yates. He'd met him one time, and that had been by accident. He knew he was their dad, and that he was a politician, and that he paid his mom to keep quiet on the whole thing.

He knew that Johnathan hated Emerson's insistence to be in his life, feeling as though someone would see them together, find out the truth, and ruin his career. He also knew that Johnathan Yates was a serial cheater, and so Kolbe wanted *nothing* to do with cheating or cheaters.

"My last relationship was…about two years ago," Emerson finally said.

"Really?" Gabriella asked, hovering her fork over her plate. She looked truly surprised.

"Yeah. I haven't had a lot of girlfriends though. Miranda in eighth grade, then like two or three others in high school. I didn't have a steady girlfriend at all through college or law school. Then I met my last girlfriend about a year after I graduated from law school."

She slowly bit the piece of enchilada off her fork and appeared to be thinking hard as she chewed, considering his words. "And you broke up two years ago? So you must've been together for…"

"Three years," he answered. He watched as she looked surprised again, and then the surprise turned to curiosity. "Didn't think I had it in me to commit to the same person for that long?"

"No," she said, honestly.

He smirked, then took a drink of his beer. "Yeah, neither did I."

"You're talking about Raelyn, right?" Kolbe asked, eyes brightening. His grin almost looked as mischievous as Emerson's. "Damn, she was fine. I don't know how you let her go."

"Ooh, Raelyn," Robby said. The look on his face nearly mirrored Kolbe's. "Quinn Casey's fiance's name is Raelyn, and she is-" he let out a breath, as though speechless, "-she's like my dream girl. She is why I need to be a major league ball player. Because those guys get girls like her."

Emerson closed his eyes and pinched the bridge of his nose. And then he waited for it.

"Yeah, Raelyn DeRose," Kolbe said. He nodded toward Emerson, who was now leaning onto his elbows, staring down at his plate of food. "That's his *ex*-fiancé."

"Fiancé?" Gabriella repeated, in utter disbelief. "You were *engaged?*"

Yep. There it was.

He sighed and sat back up, then scrubbed a hand down his face. "Yeah. It didn't work out."

Gabriella's jaw hung open slightly, and Robby's eyes were wide and awe-struck.

"And now...now your ex-fiancé is getting married to Quinn Casey? The baseball player?" she asked, separating the questions as though needing to sort out this new information.

"Yeah."

"The one who plays for the Dodgers?" She said the words flatly, as though stating rather than questioning.

"That's the one."

"All-Star swooped right in and stole her from him," Kolbe said, before taking a massive bite of steak quesadilla.

Emerson's head snapped to look at Kolbe, eyebrows steepened, then back to Gabriella. "That's not what happened."

Mouth full, Kolbe countered, "That's exactly what happened."

"*No*, it's not. Me and Rae had been broken up for over a year before they started dating," he corrected.

"You weren't happy about it though," Kolbe pushed. Emerson rolled his eyes, but Kolbe continued, "I don't blame you. I wouldn't be happy losing her either. God, remember all those times you and Raelyn let me go with you to the beach? And she'd wear those sexy bikinis? Mm-mm, she looked like a swimsuit model. You should've made a calendar of her."

Thoroughly mortified, Emerson half-sighed, half-groaned as he put his face in his palm and wished Kolbe's mouth had an off button. He recalled a time when Jett had said the same thing about him, and made a note to apologize for his constant talking.

"Why did you call off your engagement?" Gabriella's voice was soft. Soothing to his ears, and he lifted his head to look at her.

Again, he couldn't tell the full truth. He didn't want to lie to her, though, so he thought of the most vague yet true explanation he could. "She wasn't the one."

"No?"

He shook his head. "I wanted her to be, but no. She wasn't."

After a long pull from his beer, he set the bottle down, and she gazed at him with a new softness in her brown eyes. Nodding, she said, "You were more in love with the *idea* of her than you were with who she actually was?"

"Maybe something like that."

He pulled at his tie and loosened it. He felt constricted and sweaty all of a sudden. He needed to change his clothes or chug his beer or dump a glass of water on his head. It was like being claustrophobic in a wide-open space. Talking about his relationship with Rae- specifically, the *end* of his relationship with Rae- always made him anxious. It made him remember how horrible he'd felt and how senseless it had been. It had nothing to do with wanting to be with her still. He was over her and had been for a while. He'd come to terms months ago with the fact that she had moved on and was both happier and better off without him. And that was fine.

What he hated was the disappointment he felt in himself. The continued proof that he was just like his dad. That he was no better than the man he'd despised since he was a young teenager. And the fear that he never would be better.

"That had to be tough. So, did you break up with her then?" Gabriella asked. She was looking at him with genuine compassion. It's like she was noticing for the first time since they'd met that he was more than just a smooth-talking ladies' man. Unfortunately, the truth of this topic wouldn't exactly work in his favor to prove that.

Again, he hesitated before responding. Emerson hadn't exactly broken up with Raelyn, but he was definitely the reason they'd called off their engagement. Even though he'd known his screw-up was beyond fixable, he'd still tried to talk her into staying with him. Even though he'd known that he no longer wanted to get married and that he was sure he couldn't do the long-term commitment thing, he'd still clung to the idea that maybe he could fix it. Maybe he could make it work somehow. Maybe he could be that guy- the one who could commit.

In the end, Raelyn had been the one to end things. She wasn't going to give him another chance or even consider forgiving him- not that he could blame her- so they'd ended it.

"It was…sort of a mutual decision," he said after a moment's hesitation. Okay, so he hadn't wanted to lie, but with Kolbe sitting next to him, it would have to do.

"Oh." Gabriella looked somewhat surprised. She probably couldn't imagine him being so amicable and cooperative with someone. And honestly, she had the right idea. After taking a small sip from her sangria she added, "Well, that probably made it easier for both of you then."

Not wanting to lie or almost-lie again, he simply replied, "Probably."

She took another bite and chewed slowly, studying him as if seeing him in a new light. He didn't want her feeling sorry for him or thinking he was still heart-broken and pining for his ex, so he narrowed his eyes suspiciously. "What?" His voice was slow, deep, and demanding.

She shook her head and blinked, her expression now turning playful. "I just have a hard time imagining you getting down on one knee and asking someone to marry you."

A slow smirk dragged across his lips. "Which part is more unbelievable? Me asking someone to marry me or getting on my knees?"

Instantly, a heated blush colored her face and she nearly choked on her drink. After a few light coughs, she dabbed at her lips with her napkin, then met his mischievous stare. She smiled a shy, knowing smile. "Definitely the part where you profess your undying love for someone other than yourself."

He tipped his beer bottle up, drank, set it down, and the mischief in his eyes matched that of his grin. "Well, I don't get on my knees for just anyone."

When she dropped her gaze and swallowed, he felt satisfied again. Point- Emerson.

Robby's voice snapped him out of his head and back to realizing he and Gabriella weren't alone at the table. "So, like…if you guys broke up mutually…what are the chances I could meet her? And, I mean, if Quinn Casey is there, too, then that would be a nice bonus."

Gabriella shook her head and laughed. "Oh my god, Robby, you really are a teenager now, aren't you?"

"Well," Robby said with a shrug, "it doesn't hurt to ask."

"I got you, man," Kolbe chimed in. "She may have dumped his sorry ass, but she still loves me. We'll make it happen."

"Think we can get her to take us to the beach?" Robby asked Kolbe, an impish look on his face.

Kolbe's grin reflected Robby's. "I'll take that challenge."

Gabriella looked back and forth between the teenagers, then glared at Emerson. "Your brother is corrupting my brother."

Emerson laughed, then reached across the table to fist-bump Robby. "Welcome to the dark side, kid."

As they continued eating, they tried to focus on the boys and their love interests rather than inspecting the dangerous territory that was their own love lives. If he and Gabriella were going to get into that, he wanted to be honest with her. He didn't want to give her half-truths and lie by omission about everything. Plus, he sensed there was hesitation on her end to discuss whoever that Ben guy was. He wanted to know more about it. More about her.

When they said their goodbyes in the parking lot and went their separate ways, he suddenly felt as though he'd run into a brick wall. Not without alarm, that feeling returned like he was falling backward, hovering on the edge of righting himself or going all the way over. That long-unused muscle in his chest seemed to drop and his stomach did a few flips as he recognized his desire to have *more* with her. More than touch, more than the physical, more than hot, sweaty, good fucking.

In the car, he swallowed hard, tossed his suit jacket and tie behind his seat and let out a long, shaky breath.

No. No, this is not happening.

Not again.

I don't do feelings.

I'm not good at relationships.

I don't want her like that.

"I like her," Kolbe said, his voice cutting through the spiraling panic of Emerson's thoughts. He glanced over at his little brother with a short hum. "Gabby, I mean. I like her. She seems cool."

Pushing the start button of his car, he sighed. Finally, he was going to let himself be honest. "Yeah, kid. I like her, too."

Chapter 9

Gabby was at her computer in her office Thursday, having just finished her lunch when she received an email from Emerson. She narrowed her eyes at it curiously before opening the email to find a detailed scorecard of all their pranks and one-ups over the past two and half weeks. Monday had gone by with no pranks, but he was back in full swing by Tuesday morning after their dinner with Robby and Kolbe.

Like most people at the firm, she parked in the same spot every day, and when she'd pulled into the parking lot Tuesday morning, her parking spot was blocked off. There was caution tape surrounding it and four orange cones in each corner of the space. She had promptly hopped out of her car and moved the tape and cones over to his parking space so that he was now blocked in.

Of course, it hadn't stopped there. On Wednesday, posted on her office door when she arrived was a bright yellow sign that read *Baby on Board*, and her office was filled with light blue and pale pink balloons. When she opened the door, the balloons floated out into the hallway, and she couldn't take a single step in her office without kicking them around. She'd spent at least thirty minutes bagging up the balloons in large trash bags, but a day later, her office still smelled like latex.

Gabby couldn't help smiling as she read through the email.

Emerson: 95 points

- Desk removal service: 5 points
- Who's your Baby Daddy?: 5 points

- Uncle Castro: 5 points
- Bug Lamp: 10 points (That scream was priceless)
- Oral presentation: 50 points
- No parking: 5 points
- Surprise baby shower: 10 points
- Sub Decaf: 5 points (Feeling tired this morning?)

Gabe: 90 points

  ◦ Car-towing + Walk in the rain: 15 points
  ◦ Wobbly chair: 5 points
  ◦ Missing coasters: 5 points
- *Playgirl* surprise: 5 points
- Coming out party: 5 points
- Cock tease: 10 points
- Kicking my ass out of your office after I ate that pussy like you never knew was possible: 50 points (-5 because that was rude)

Gabby laughed as she read the last line, then clicked reply, deciding to add a few marks of her own. Under Emerson's column she made a new bullet point:

- Ruining coworker's presentation with immature doggie-style graphic: -10 points

Next to "oral presentation" she changed his original 50 points to 40, and next to his "sub decaf" bullet point, she typed in a note:

-Dangerous business. This is how serial killers are made.

She then updated the points so that he now had 75 points and she still had 90, and hit send.

Looking into her white tumbler of *decaf* office coffee, she sighed. No wonder she wasn't feeling productive. After staring for several moments, she decided to head back to the break room and brew a new pot of coffee. She wouldn't be getting any work done without it.

In the break room, she made a beeline for the coffee maker, opened the cupboard above and saw two canisters of coffee, one regular, one decaf. She grabbed the regular container and began spooning coffee grounds into a fresh filter.

"How do you know I didn't switch them?" Emerson's deep voice behind her nearly made her jump.

She turned to face him. "Excuse me?"

"The coffee. How do you know I didn't put the decaf grounds in the regular canister, and the regular in the decaf?"

His face was unreadable, but as she stared at him, her slow-moving, uncaffeinated brain working to comprehend what he'd said, the slightest trace of a smirk tugged up one corner of his mouth. The dark sapphire-blue of his eyes twinkled, and she glared in response.

Gabby let out an aggravated huff. "You truly are evil, aren't you?"

He shrugged, clearly pleased with himself.

"I'm calling your bluff," she stated.

"Okay."

"If you swapped them, you would be responsible for the entire floor's lack of productivity for the day."

"True."

Turning back to the coffee maker, she continued, "You might have come in and brewed decaf while no one was in here, but I doubt you had time to actually switch the coffee grounds without anyone catching you."

"Of course. That would be excessive."

She paused. He was now leaning against the counter next to her, watching her intently. She narrowed her eyes at him again, considering.

Everything he'd done up to this point was excessive. It wasn't far-fetched to think he would swap out coffee grounds and she knew it.

She huffed again. "Which one is regular? I have barely gotten any work done today. My coffee I brought from home has long-since worn off, and I still have at least five hours to go."

He smiled, triumphant. "That one's labeled regular."

Her eyes flashed from the canister in her hand then back to him. "Okay, yes, but *is* it regular?"

"That's what it says."

She chewed the inside of her lip, then shoved the canister in his direction. "Fine. You make the coffee."

"I don't need to. I don't drink coffee after noon."

Staring at him and trying her best to read his face, but finding herself only able to pay attention to how frustratingly handsome he was, she sighed. "That's it. I'm walking to Starbucks."

Emerson's laugh rumbled through his chest, and she felt weirdly liquified by the sound of it.

Why? Why did he do this to her? Him, of all people? *Ugh!*

"Want to get me a grande Americano?" he asked, casually.

Gabby glared. "You just said you don't drink coffee after noon."

"It's not coffee, it's espresso. And it's Starbucks, not this office crap."

"You can get your own espresso." She shoved the coffee canisters back in the cupboard and avoided his piercing blue eyes. If it was possible, she could've sworn he was more attractive and alluring than usual. He wore a charcoal gray dress shirt that hugged his shoulders and biceps, and stretched across his deliciously broad chest. His tie was a simple black-on-darker-black pattern, and all the dark hues made him look stunningly dangerous. The kind of dangerous that women can never resist.

"Are you saying I should come with you?" he asked, "So that I can buy my own espresso and you can get your coffee?"

"No," she snapped, too quickly. "No…I'm saying, if you want espresso then get it yourself."

"You're moody today."

"Well, someone gave me decaf coffee. That's what happens." She moved around him, still avoiding his gaze. She could not make eye contact with him right now. Not after their dinner Monday night where she had learned there was more to his life than work and random women. Not after seeing how adorable he was with his little brother. She could criticize the things he taught the kid all she wanted, but it was undeniable how much he cared about Kolbe.

It had been easier to just think of him as a guy who didn't care about anyone else, whose only concern was getting laid on the weekends and making money on the weekdays. But now she knew he was capable of more. He'd been engaged. He'd been in love before, and she could tell he still felt *something* about it. Whether he still missed her or had regrets, she wasn't sure, but the way he'd seemed physically uncomfortable discussing their break-up hadn't gone unnoticed.

She could handle a purely physical attraction to Emerson. What she was less sure of was her ability to handle anything more than that. An attraction to *him.* Who he was. His personality, his charm, his presence.

She didn't want to want him. There might be more to him than she had previously assumed, but that didn't change the fact that falling for him, for someone like him, still felt like a bad idea. A really, *really* bad idea.

As her hand reached for the door handle, Emerson called out, "Hey!"

Gabby's eyes flashed to him. To his face. Those eyes.

Ugh…not the eyes.

She raised an eyebrow curiously at him and waited. His gaze was penetrating, like an X-ray as he scanned her from head to toe. His attention hovered over her mouth, and she self-consciously bit her bottom lip. Flickering his stormy blues back up, he grinned again. "You look really beautiful today."

Her breath stopped. She continued to stare, but ceased to breathe.

Say something.

Remember to breathe and say something!

How was she supposed to respond to that? It was a real compliment. It wasn't a dirty comment, or a suggestive innuendo. It was just…a compliment. And she was tempted to believe he meant it. The words made her feel like melting, like she was a thirteen-year-old school girl and her crush had finally noticed her. The warming sensation that had become familiar in her lower belly and between her legs when she was around Emerson suddenly spread into her chest.

No, no, no.

Nope.

Don't go there, girl.

Don't. Even. Think about it.

"Um…okay," she said, before she could really decide how to respond. Thinking before speaking was a thing for a reason. "I mean, um…thank you."

He was still looking at her with that grin. That adorable, sexy, How Is He Even Real, Why Don't You Just Fuck Me Already grin. It was, in a word, infuriating. She waited for him to say something else, but he didn't. And when she couldn't think of anything to add, she abruptly opened the door and slipped out.

Once out of the break room and down the hallway a few paces, she cringed. How did he do that? She never lost her nerve. Especially over a guy. No matter how absurdly yummy he was. Or probably was. She supposed she wouldn't know.

She cursed herself for thinking about what he did or did not or probably tasted like. Then she imagined ripping open his dress shirt and licking the steel plane of abs and chest that he was undoubtedly hiding beneath his clothes.

I wonder if he has chest hair.

He seems like the type to have everything cleaned up.

Maybe not. I distinctly remember hair when I saw him holding his-

Again, she scolded herself for thinking about it. But then of course she continued to think about it. She practically zoned out in the elevator down to the lobby. Walking down the sidewalk to Starbucks, she tried her best to not think about Emerson. His strikingly handsome face. His muscles. That deep, ovulation-inducing, Made For Bedtime voice. His warm, masculine scent as he leaned over her to whisper in her ear. Standing between her spread legs. His hand sliding up her skirt. His mouth on her heat. His hand on his thick, throbbing-

Clearly, she was doing a great job not thinking about him.

She thought about the email from him and decided she agreed. She deserved to lose five points for sending him away.

Back in her office with a venti black coffee, filled with ever-blessed caffeine, she sat behind her desk and tried to get back to work.

Around 4:30, the familiar two quick knocks on her door prepared her to see Emerson again, pushing his way into her office with his usual greeting. "Hey Gabe."

"Erwin," she responded.

He plopped comfortably into the chair across from her, leaned back, his legs in a wide, casual manspread. "How did I end up with 75 points instead of my original, much-deserved 95?"

Gabby bit back a wide grin. "You lost 20."

"Mhmm. I saw that," he said flatly. "How did that happen?"

"You can read, can't you?"

She was staring intently at her computer screen, clicking and opening different windows, typing in different things to make it seem as though she was actually working. Really, she had just typed *Men's names that start with E* into a new search bar. She was running out.

"I can agree to losing ten points for ruining your presentation," he said, and she guessed he was using his deliberation voice. His lawyer tone; slow, concise, reasonable. "However, the ten-point deduction on my oral presentation is bullshit, and we both know it."

She suppressed her grin and looked up at him, all business. "As the recipient of said oral presentation, I don't know that that's something you can accurately judge."

The truth was it had been a phenomenal *oral presentation* and in her own mind she had already given it a millionty-ten points. But he couldn't know that.

Emerson nodded, his face set in an unreadable, almost stoic expression. "The only inaccuracy on my part was giving it a mere 50 points. To be frank, I think I was being modest."

She leaned back in her chair, folded her arms over her chest, and narrowed her gaze. "Are you capable of such a thing?"

His mouth curved upward on one side and he replied, "I think you'd find I'm capable of a whole lot more than that if you gave me the chance."

They were in a staring contest now. His crooked, sexy grin against her defiant, unyielding glare. She could feel her body betraying her, though. Heat spread up from her chest and into her face. A different kind of heat swirled around in her stomach, dropping lower until there was a dull, pleasant ache between her thighs.

Damn him.

"I say we give it the 60 points it deserves," he said.

Sixty, huh? Modest again. Regardless, Gabby relented, "Forty points."

"Sixty."

"Forty."

"Sixty-five."

She let out an exasperated huff. "*Thirty*-five."

He made a sour, incredulous face. "Like hell, Gabe. That was some top-notch tongue fucking. Maybe if you hadn't wrapped your fingers in my hair and demanded more, I'd let it go with forty."

It had been a task to not react to his filthy words, along with the images and sensations they elicited from her memory. She rolled her eyes. "Fine. Forty-five."

His left eyebrow quirked upward the slightest bit, and when she was expecting him to argue again, he instead surprised the hell out of her by asking, "What are you doing tonight?"

Now she knew her expression faltered. "What?"

"Tonight. Kolbe and Robby have a game. Are you going?"

She blinked. Right. That. "Oh, yeah, I was planning on it. Are you?"

"I am," he said with a short nod. "I've been picking Kolbe up every night this week and he's been staying at my place until his mom gets out of work, but since he has a game, she'll just pick him up from there."

"Oh…okay." She wasn't entirely sure where he was going with this abrupt change of topic.

"Do…" he paused, cleared his throat, "Do you have plans for after the game?"

Gabby was suddenly unaware of what facial expression she was making, but thought she must look confused. Dumbfounded, bewildered, disoriented. Surely…surely he wasn't about to ask her out? Like…on a date, right?

"Um, I don't think so," she said, slowly.

Emerson grinned and she struggled to decipher its meaning. Was it a true smile? Was it his usual wicked, I've Got You Where I Want You smirk? Why was everything so difficult today?

"Good. Um," he paused again. He was looking down at his tie, playing with it, flipping the end of it up and back down. "Tyler's going to the game, too," he blurted suddenly.

Gabby's eyebrows raised at Emerson's sudden, loud volume. "Oh. Okay, cool…"

"I think he misses me," he replied, his voice back to a normal, conversational speaking register. "Anyway, he mentioned going out for drinks afterwards if you…if you think you want to go."

Her chest deflated as she released a breath, and she couldn't tell if she felt relieved or disappointed. She quickly reminded herself that it was silly to think he was going to ask her on a date. Not to mention, a date with Emerson would be…preposterous. Absurd. A really, *really* bad idea.

"That sounds like fun," she finally said. "I haven't been able to get out much since moving here, so, yeah. Drinks sound good."

Emerson's eyes flicked up to hers, almost in surprise. "Yeah?" He grinned, and this one was much more readable. He was pleased. Happy, even. "Okay, good."

He stood and ran a hand down his tie, smoothing it over before pushing the chair back up to her desk. "We can continue our debate over a couple beers."

A small puff of laughter escaped her lips. "With Tyler there? Really?"

"Sure," he said, lifting and lowering one shoulder in a quick movement. "He can mediate."

She stared at him, disbelieving. But then again, maybe she should believe it. There wasn't much she would put past him. With a frustrated grumble, she sighed. "Fine, take your fifty points."

His grin was one of utmost satisfaction. Her uterus may have clenched.

"See you at the game, Gabe." He winked and slipped out the door. And she was once again left wondering whether she should hate him, or if she should thank him for actually giving her something to look forward to.

Chapter 10

Emerson had not been expecting so much excitement at a middle school baseball game. After running home to change out of his suit and into something more casual- a pair of faded blue jeans and a white t-shirt with a shallow v-neck- he'd waited, somewhat impatiently, for Tyler to meet him at his apartment, and then they'd driven to the game together.

Upon arriving at the ball field, Emerson immediately began scanning the crowd for Gabriella. He'd almost missed her, too, because he'd never seen her in anything but her work clothes. Half expecting to see her still in the same curvy hip-hugging dress pants as earlier, he was stopped in his tracks at the sight of her in a sexy black sundress and a pair of black and beige wedge sandals.

His breathing shallowed. His heart raced. His eyes zeroed in on her as they dilated, taking in the sight and cataloging each new reason why sundress season was his favorite season.

The dress was short and flowing with short sleeves and a deep, plunging neckline that came together just between her breasts where it was tied in a small knot. Beneath the knot, a triangle of skin was visible, making the dress look as though it might actually be two separate pieces.

Emerson slid his gaze from the triangle of perfectly bronzed skin down her skirt to her legs. The skirt stopped mid-thigh and gave him a nearly painful, mouth-watering view of her smooth, full thighs. He loved those thighs, and remembered exactly how they'd felt beneath his palms, against his lips and tongue. They were thick, Instagram-model thighs. But better. He suddenly felt it should be illegal for her to wear a dress like that around so many people. So many puberty-addled, adolescent boys. *Him.* That dress made him want to do things.

When Tyler yanked his attention away from where he was staring, a jumble of sexual fantasies flashing around in his head like they were on crack, he had to blink several times. He also had to remember how to move. How to breathe again. How to get a fucking grip.

They walked over to Gabriella, where she promptly introduced them to her brother, Marco, and his husband Max. Then Isabel climbed down from her spot in the bleachers to introduce herself before point-ing to the rest of the family; their parents were sitting near the top wearing matching t-shirts that read *Team Cabrera* on the front, and they sat next to the youngest, Elisa, and the sixteen-year-old Lola.

Emerson could already tell that Lola was going to look much like Gabriella. In the least creepy way possible, he registered that he under-stood Kolbe's attraction to her. Unfortunately for Kolbe, however, she was smiling and flirting with the boy standing next to the row of bleachers, eyeing her with equal interest.

He hadn't expected to meet Gabriella's entire family, nor had he expected to get along so well with everyone. He'd been told a few times he could be a bit abrasive, and was surprised to find himself enjoying Isabel's clinical critiques of everyone, himself included, and Marco's boisterous personality and the way it contrasted with Max's quiet stoi-cism. He hadn't expected simply being next to Gabriella, spending time with her and talking, to be so easy. So natural.

He hadn't expected to get into the game so intensely- he'd never played baseball, and had always thought it was a slow sport to watch. This game, though, seemed to move quickly. There were a lot of great plays, including one in which Kolbe caught the ball thrown in from center field to his position on third base, getting out the player running from second, and swiftly threw the ball over to first, where the batter was then called out. He and Tyler even stood up with Gabriella's family when Robby stole home base during the top of the seventh inning. He jumped and shouted proudly when Kolbe hit a home run, and at the end of the game he ran down to the dugout where the team was celebrating their win to scoop him up in a crushing hug as he told him how great he'd played.

Perhaps most surprising of all was once Emerson had said goodbye to Kolbe when Maya picked him up and the crowd was clearing out. Gabriella stepped up beside him and gave a shy smile.

"I actually rode with my brother and Max, but apparently they changed their minds about going out tonight," she said. She looked down at her hands which, he noted, she didn't seem to know what to with.

It felt as if air had been swiftly punched out of his lungs. She wasn't coming with them. He wasn't going to get to sit with her and get to know her better. He wasn't going to be able to admire her in that dress anymore tonight. His eyes did another sweep of her appearance, greedily drinking her in, knowing he could never get enough of this sight.

He hadn't realized he'd failed to respond at all until she was speaking again. "So, if it's okay with you, I guess we can all just ride to the bar together."

Emerson blinked back up to her face. His mouth hooked up on one side and he nodded. "Yeah, that's not a problem. We'll just shove Tyler in the back seat."

Tyler began to protest, stating that he was the tallest, took up the most space, and the back seat of Emerson's Lexus was tiny. It only had two seats instead of the usual three. But Emerson cut him off with a pointed stare and in the end, Tyler was forced to crawl behind the front seat and scrunch himself up in the back.

"There's a reason sports cars don't have back seats," Tyler grumbled, folding his arms over his chest. Emerson glanced back and had to stifle a laugh at the image of Tyler's long form uncomfortably folded behind the passenger seat. His knees were practically in his chest.

Lucky for Tyler, it wasn't a terribly long drive from the field to Trojan Horse. As soon as he climbed out of the car, he stretched his limbs with a loud, satisfied groan of relief, much like the genie when he floated out of the magic lamp.

The three of them walked toward the bar where there was a short line out the door. Thursday nights were always busy at the sports bar, but Emerson felt like he'd been avoiding the place enough. Not to mention, most other bars were home to waitresses and bartenders he'd had intimate relations with. He hoped drinking at Trojan would reduce the odds that he'd run into a former fuck buddy. At least a little.

"Are we sitting at the bar or do we want a table?" Emerson asked.

Gabriella raised her eyebrows, peering from the line and back to Emerson. "Does it matter? I feel like we'll probably just get what's available."

Emerson smirked down at her and she watched as Tyler moved past the line. They followed, and the bouncer moved aside to let them in when they approached the door.

Gabriella looked up at him in question. "Um…are you famous and I've just never heard of you?"

He laughed. "No, Tyler's brother owns the place. Well, him and his friend, Jett."

"So you can get in whenever you want, too?" she asked.

"We're all friends."

"Wow, that seems dangerous. Do you really need to feel any more self-important and entitled than you already do?" she teased, though she was smiling.

"I do, actually. My ego is the very essence of who I am," he replied, returning her playful smile.

He watched as her eyes moved over the inside space, taking in all the details. The dark wood grains, the beams wrapped in bare-bulb lighting, the sports and beer posters, jerseys, and equipment littering the walls, along with several flat screen televisions airing different games and sports networks. She stopped suddenly as her eyes grazed across the wall behind the bar. There was the usual back-lit liquor display that raised to the ceiling, and a section of wall that even had some local wines displayed. Next to the liquor display, however, was Emerson's least favorite part of the bar: The shrine.

Now that she knew Quinn Casey was with his ex-fiance, he wasn't surprised to see her look curiously at him, one eyebrow raised, then back to the display of Quinn's jersey, signed baseball and bat, along with a few framed pictures beneath of Quinn, Chris, Jett, Rae, and Tyler when they were kids. The pictures weren't clearly visible from where they were standing, but Emerson knew they were there.

He let out a sigh then explained, "Tyler, his brother, Chris, and Jett all grew up with him. They like to brag about it."

She remained quiet but nodded slowly.

"So, do you want to kick someone out of a booth or take a spot at the bar?" he asked, abruptly changing the subject.

"The bar is fine," she replied.

Without thinking, he placed his hand on the small of her back and led her toward the bar. As soon as his hand made contact with that space just above her ass, he wondered what the hell he was doing, but knew it would be too awkward to remove it. Plus, he didn't want to. He'd made the move and now he was committed. At least touching Gabriella was something he knew he could commit to.

When she took her seat on the bar stool and his hand slipped from her back, he immediately missed the contact and was already searching for excuses to put his hands on her again.

"Two Heinekens and…" Alaina Costello's silvery, smooth voice drew his attention reluctantly away from the hem of Gabriella's dress. Alaina was one of the managers Chris and Jett hired in December when they finally had the extra money, and plenty of demand, for a new manager. Before that, the two bar owners had practically worked constantly. Since then, they'd also hired two assistant managers for Alaina to boss around.

Gabriella looked at the liquor display behind Alaina and chewed her bottom lip while she contemplated. "I'll have…a whiskey and ginger."

"Well whiskey?" Alaina asked.

"Jameson, please."

Emerson peered at her curiously. "Jameson, huh?"

"Yeah, and?"

He shrugged. "Nothing. I guess I just figured you'd be more of a tequila girl."

She glared at him as Alaina set a bottle of Heineken in front of him, and one in front of Tyler. "Why? Because I'm Latina?"

Biting back the laugh that threatened to burst out, he chuckled, "I didn't even think about it, but that's probably why, yeah."

"You're such a jerk," she said, poking him in the arm. She was laughing as she said it and rolled her eyes. "Well, I'm not Mexican, I'm Cuban. If anything you should assume I drink Caribbean rum."

"Do you?"

"Sometimes," she replied with a nod, "but usually I just drink wine. Chardonnay, mostly."

Alaina slid a bar coaster in front of Gabriella and set her high-ball glass of Jameson and ginger ale down. Emerson handed the bartender-slash-manager his black card and told her to put all their drinks on his tab. He realized with an inward cringe that pulling out his American Express black card was out of habit; a move he typically reserved for buying a drink for an easy one-night-stand. It was a douchey move, luring women in by flaunting how much money he had, but it worked.

Alaina glanced down at the card in her hand, clearly noting that it was far more weighted than most credit cards. When she looked back up at him, then to Gabriella, she nearly rolled her eyes, but tucked his card away with the rest of the open bar tabs.

"What was that all about?" Tyler asked, watching Alaina walk down the bar to a new customer.

"I don't think she likes me," Emerson replied.

"Did you forget to call her after a romantic evening together?" Gabriella asked, grinning.

He looked for any hint of jealousy in her expression but saw none. Damn.

"Uh, no." He shook his head. "She's never liked me since we met."

"You're kidding!" Gabriella exclaimed. "But you're so pleasant and agreeable! How could someone not like you?"

On his other side, Tyler laughed into his drink. "Don't forget humble, chivalrous, and modest."

"Empathetic," Gabriella added.

"And your compassion for others is just immeasurable," Tyler said.

Emerson pushed his tongue against the inside of his cheek and nodded. "Thanks, guys. It means a lot to hear your true feelings."

Gabriella bit her lip and glanced around Emerson, leaning forward to look at Tyler. In a stage whisper she held her hand to her mouth and said, "I don't think he understands the sarcasm."

Emerson's hand flew to his chest and he gasped, "Ouch! The truth comes out! This hurts. Good job, Gabe. You hurt my one feeling."

"Aw, I'm sorry," she said, placing her hand on his shoulder as he lifted his beer to his lips. "Was that one feeling anywhere near your penis?"

He choked on his beer laughing, and coughed, trying not to let it spray all over the bar in front of him. She and Tyler laughed as he composed himself. He grinned wickedly. "As a matter of fact it was. Now I need someone to kiss it and make it all better."

Gabriella narrowed her eyes at him, and he could tell she was trying not to grin. Her eyes darkened in a seductive, challenging glare, and he felt his breathing change again like it had earlier at the ball field. He looked at the bare skin revealed by the plunging neckline of her dress and could see the swell of her breasts moving. Lifting, then lowering. Rising…and falling.

His heart was tripping and stuttering over itself as he realized with urgency that he wanted her. He wanted her *now.* And not in a gentle way. Not in a cute, Take You Out To Dinner, Let Me Get The Door For You and Hold You In My Arms way like he'd been thinking about at the office or at the game. He wanted her in a needy, desperate way. He wanted her in a Bend You Over, Fuck Til It Hurts kind of way.

His jeans were suddenly tight and uncomfortable where his dick had gone from semi-hard to physically aching with need. There was no way she wouldn't notice if her gaze dropped, but he didn't care. She should know what she was doing to him. What she always did to him. That dress, her gorgeous skin, her fucking lips. Always, the lips.

He replayed her question and then his teasing response in his head and decided to blame her for feeling like this. It was her fault he was imagining her looking up at him from between his legs, pressing her full, soft mouth to his hard, aching erection. Kissing it. Making it so, *so* much better.

"Hey! Gabriella, right?"

The familiar, bright voice saying her name caused Emerson to blink several times and look to the woman standing behind his and Gabriella's stools. Zoey was smiling as she looked at Gabriella, then explained, "We met at the bar the other night. The one on Union."

"Right, yeah," Gabriella nodded. "Zoey?"

Emerson was surprised to see that Jett wasn't with her. "You know, you spend a lot of time in bars for a pregnant woman," he remarked.

"I'm picking Jett up. He must be in the back still," said Zoey.

"He still lets you drive?" he asked, sarcastically. "But Zoey, you're three months pregnant!" He slammed his fist on the bar top. "This is an outrage!"

Zoey looked at him, exasperated. "He's not that bad. He just wants to make my life easier and less stressful. Lord knows I need it this weekend."

"You need to have more faith in us, Zo," Tyler said. "We'll keep it under control; there will be no publicity bullshit. Just trust us."

"I trust *you*," Zoey said. "I trust that *you* won't end up on the front page of *Los Angeles Tea with a Twist* in nothing but a tie and a stripper's g-string. Seriously, Quinn better realize that he needs to keep it together this weekend. I can't believe he's going to Vegas. *Vegas!* You'd think Rae would have vetoed that."

"Now...is it a regular necktie, or a bow tie that you're worried about?" Tyler asked, keeping his expression flat.

Zoey rolled her lips between her front teeth, clearly annoyed. "Make fun of me all you want. It's not *your* job to make sure Quinn Casey stays out of trouble so he can return in July. The manager does not want a big scandal right before he comes back."

"Give me the details," Emerson said, raising his chin to Zoey. "I'll keep him out of trouble. Let me go to Vegas with them and he'll be so pissed, he won't want to have fun all weekend."

Before she could respond, Jett rounded the end of the bar and wrapped his arms around her waist, pulling her against him. He kissed her. And then he kissed her again. And then his hand was cradling her head behind her neck as he kissed her some more. With tongue.

Emerson glanced awkwardly away and caught Gabriella glancing down at her feet, absent-mindedly scratching a spot behind her ear. When he chanced a glance back at the disgustingly love-struck couple caught up in their heated embrace, he felt a pang of…something.

What was that?

Desire? No, he felt that all the time in varying degrees.

Resentment? No, not that. He was happy for them, and was honestly glad it turned out Jett could be smooth when he wanted to be. He was more than a curly-haired, gentlemanly dork. Good for him.

His brow furrowed as he partially studied them, partially studied his own feelings and tried to decipher them.

Envy.

That was it.

Not envy about Zoey. He didn't want Zoey, though she was, admittedly, a hottie with a body, and her pregnancy boobs were hard to look away from at times. No, this was envy about what they had. What they were doing. He was envious of Jett because he had a person. Someone to call his own. Someone who was there at the end of the day and was just as excited to see him as he was to see her.

His eyes drifted to Gabriella again and another daydream clouded his brain: Emerson coming home from work to find her in his apartment. She was sitting at his kitchen island, helping Kolbe with his homework, and when Emerson walked in, she looked at him and smiled. A real smile. Then he smiled back. He closed the gap between them and leaned over her, slipping his fingers through her hair and holding her face steady so he could kiss her. And then she kissed him back. And then Kolbe made a disgusted noise and told them to get a room, but they ignored him and continued kissing. Just kissing. And…it was amazing.

"She doesn't look like a Cruella to me, Emerson," Jett said, seemingly out of nowhere.

Emerson had to physically shake his head this time to snap out of that daydream.

That daydream.

What the hell?

"What?" he asked, blinking.

"You've apparently been talking about me," Gabriella said. "Telling all your friends what a lovely person I am. All those charming nicknames you have for me and the best I've come up with for you is That Obnoxious Guy From Work."

"I love the work stories," said Jett. "Having his car towed, the rumor that he and Tyler are a couple…"

Gabriella gasped. "Oh my God! How could I forget!" She turned back toward the bar and flagged Alaina down. "We need a round of Jameson please, for the happy couple. They recently came out and we are just so proud."

Alaina paused, looking between Emerson and Tyler as if she'd misheard. Nonetheless, she rolled her eyes and poured three shot glasses of Jameson.

Emerson glanced down at the shot glass in front of him, then back to Gabriella who was grinning mischievously. "You know it's a work night, right?" he asked.

"But we need to celebrate this new stage in your life."

"If I didn't know better, Gabe, I'd think you're trying to get me drunk."

The look she gave him brought explicit images back into his mind. Scenes of her kneeling between his legs, taking her roughly from behind, fucking her as she writhed and screamed beneath him were once again playing like a movie reel in his head. A dirty, sweaty, X-rated movie reel.

She smiled wickedly. "Maybe I am."

He tossed the shot back.

Chapter 11

This was dangerous territory. Gabby was sitting in a booth in the back of the bar with Emerson. They hadn't checked their phones to see what time it was, and she honestly had no idea how long they'd been there.

When the bar had begun to clear out, Jett found them a booth. At first, Tyler, Jett, and Zoey were sitting with them, and Tyler's older brother, Chris joined when he clocked out. Jett insisted on hearing about the office war from her perspective, and they had to fill in the new pranks from that week. For obvious reasons, she skipped over the incident on Friday, but Emerson had happily chimed in with the story of them running into each other Monday night.

They all seemed shocked that Emerson had taken everyone to dinner, but that didn't really surprise Gabby. She had already made the assessment that he wasn't the type of guy who took women out to dinner. Not that it had been a date, but...still. She at least liked to think he wouldn't have done it for someone else. One of his many, *many* floozies.

Okay, maybe it wasn't fair to call them that.

After the second round of shots, Tyler got a little loose-lipped about Emerson's very active sex life. The *rotation*, as he apparently called it. All these women were agreeing to the arrangement, and she shouldn't judge them. For all she knew, his Monday-night girl had a Tuesday-night guy. Maybe his Tuesday-Thursday girl had a Monday-Wednesday guy. It was fine. They were all consenting adults, they could do whatever they wanted.

Gabby had expected Emerson to get uncomfortable with the conversation. Other people openly discussing his sex life? Shouldn't he have wanted to keep that quiet?

Instead, he acted like it wasn't a big deal. He was cool and calm. They could've been talking about his weekly dinner schedule, as much as he seemed to care. And that was the part that bugged her. Not that he was boastful about it or acting like he was the hottest piece of ass in the surrounding counties- because he probably was- but he actually didn't seem to care. About any of it. About *them*. These women. Again, he wasn't crude toward them and he didn't go in detail about anything. They were just part of his schedule. Part of his routine. Like...brushing his teeth.

A few women greeted him throughout the evening, but he didn't make an attempt to flirt back. He would just give them a quick smile or a nod of acknowledgement.

All of this should have made her disgusted by him. She should have called him a womanizing man-whore and threw her drink in his face. But after they finished the conversation about his numerous lady-friends, he'd leaned toward her, softly brushed the pad of his thumb just above the arch of her cheekbone, before gently plucking a fallen eyelash off her cheek and sitting back, telling her to make a wish.

Sitting so close, her brain was fogged with his intoxicating, clean-man scent, and she found it difficult to look away from him.

It was the first time she'd seen him in anything but a suit. Sometimes he took off his suit jacket and she was graced with the glorious sight of him in a dress shirt that did its best to make him look modest, covering up all those muscles. If she was really lucky, he'd roll up his sleeves and she was allowed to ogle over his sinfully corded forearms.

Today he was dressed casually. A white t-shirt that stretched over his broad chest and hugged his strong shoulders and biceps. Those arms were, in a word, *juicy*. And to make matters worse, he had a tattoo. She couldn't see the whole thing, but knew it spanned from his right pectoral, over his right shoulder, down his arm, stopping at the elbow. From what she could see, it looked like a knight's armor, and visible beneath the shallow v-neck of his shirt, she could see some kind of script, like an old English blackletter script.

Emerson Yates in blue jeans was a severely underrated sight. They were faded and worn in all the right places. She tried her best to avoid glancing down at his zipper, where the denim was especially faded. As though his jeans didn't *quite* fit him right in that spot. Like they were just a touch too tight to fully accommodate what he was packing.

However, when she did make the mistake of sneaking a peek in his lap, she was instantly hot and flustered. He was hard. He was big. And hard. And he'd made no attempt to conceal it. He sat comfortably in the booth, legs spread wide, but not obnoxiously so. The steel pipe in his pants was pressed against his thigh, straining his jeans, and Gabby felt herself melt just a little.

Her heart rate increased, her breaths were suddenly shallow, and images spun around in her head. Not the same images that had been flashing through her mind since Friday's unbelievable oral presentation, but new ones. Scenes that hadn't happened yet.

She pictured Emerson leaning back on her couch at her condo, just like he was now. Legs spread, arms stretched over the back of the couch, shirt off. She definitely wanted his shirt *off.* She pictured herself on the floor in front of him. *Crawling* to him. To the heavenly space between his legs. Skating her hands up his thighs and grasping that hard length that pressed aggressively against worn denim.

That was when she'd ordered her second Jameson and ginger.

Now they were alone, everyone having dipped out at some point. Tyler had left with Chris, and Gabby suspected that either Jett or Zoey, or perhaps both of them, started to get a little handsy beneath the table because they'd left abruptly. Zoey's face was tinged with pink and she was trying to suppress giggles. She hadn't been drinking obviously, and when they turned to leave, Jett slipped his hand in the back pocket of her jeans to tug her close.

It was kind of annoying and gross how in love they were. But it was at least ten times more adorable.

Gabby wanted that. One day.

She reached for her highball glass that was mostly ice and drank.

"Need another?" Emerson asked, his voice low and impossibly sexy.

She swallowed, then shook her head. "Just some water maybe."

He nodded and flagged down a server, rather than waiting for one to come by or going up to the bar. Gabby had always found that annoying when people just stick their hand up and wave over a waiter or waitress who was probably on a mission to get drinks rung in before they forgot the order. But somehow when Emerson did it, it was so casual and non-demanding. He smiled easily at the waitress whose attention he'd grabbed and she, like most women, was in a clear state of stupefied, flustered wonderment at the sight of him.

"Could we get a couple waters when you get a chance? No rush," he said, coolly. The waitress nodded rather than try to form a verbal response. The crooked grin as he said "Thanks" no doubt sent the girl over the edge. Gabby suspected that even though he'd told her *no rush*, their table would be the absolute first one the girl came back to.

Gabby's elbow rested on the table and she leaned, holding her head up in her hand as she gazed at Emerson, narrow-eyed. "How do you do that?"

He raised an eyebrow. "Do what?"

"Do something that would be obnoxious if anyone else did it, but on you it's…" she trailed off, not wanting to finish the sentence. She wasn't quite tipsy, but she'd be lying if she said she wasn't feeling a light buzz.

"It's…what?" he prompted.

She sighed, letting her lips make a quiet motor-boat sound. Emerson laughed as he watched her, still waiting. Finally she rolled her eyes and said, "Just annoying."

He smiled, amused. "'Annoying' is just another word for obnoxious. And you've already called me obnoxious at least once tonight."

"I don't mean it," she said. She could feel the familiar inhibited mist that came with drinking whiskey. She was always in control, and she liked it that way, but sometimes she needed to loosen the reins.

His piercing blue eyes were sapphire now. Twinkling. He was pleased. "You don't?"

"At work I do," she said, letting out a puff of laughter. "I don't know. I guess Tyler was right. You just…get used to it."

He narrowed his eyes and they lost their twinkle. Then he dropped his gaze, and before she could register what he was doing, she felt his thumb drawing slow, mesmerizing circles on the back of her hand where it rested on the table.

"I know I'm not the easiest person to get along with," he said. "But I would be lying if I said I didn't want you to do more than just *tolerate* me."

Gabby's attention was fixed to their hands. His slow, soft circles tracing around and around. She couldn't look away.

"I know it's a bit like third grade, but I enjoy pranking you," he said. She could hear the grin in his voice and couldn't help giving a small smile in return, though her eyes still didn't move away from their hands.

Her pulse was getting away from her, blood pumping heavy in her ears. She wondered if he could feel it beneath her skin where he was touching her. This was worse than staring at his hard-on. This was physical. His touch was electric, intoxicating. She wanted more.

The perky waitress set their glasses of water down, and she could barely flicker her gaze up and mutter *thank you* before settling her focus back to his touch.

"Listen, Gabe, I…" he paused, as if the words were stuck in his throat, "I was telling the truth on Friday when I said I can't stop thinking about you. It's still true."

It took a moment for the words to find their way into her alcohol-and-Emerson inhibited brain, and when they did, she flashed her gaze up to him. He was looking intently at her. His expression fixed, one eyebrow furrowed slightly more than the other. He looked different. The confidence that always shone so forcefully was diminished slightly. He was nervous about what he was saying. But…he was being sincere. Or so it appeared.

Gabby cleared her throat and retracted her hand, abruptly sliding it out from under his. She took a drink from the fresh water glass in front of her. A long, slow gulp, and she could sense him watching her still. She set the glass back on the table and looked around quickly, assessing the situation.

She was in a bar with Emerson.

Emerson Yates.

Emerson Yates who…had a big ol' steel pipe in his pants.

They were alone. They'd been drinking.

Her decision-making ability was impaired, her judgment was impaired.

He was dangerously sexy.

He was telling her he couldn't stop thinking about her.

He gave phenomenal oral presentations.

But he probably did that for a lot of women.

A lot of women.

Miss Thursday Night Fun Times could be waiting for him at his apartment right now.

For the first time in several hours, she checked her phone. It was past midnight, which meant they'd been in this bar together for about four hours.

Doing her best to blink the haze and whiskey and lady-bit stimulating man scent away, she finally said, "I need to go."

He sighed and scrubbed a hand down his face. "Gabe, this is new for me."

"I know, it's just…it's after midnight and we have to work tomorrow. I need to get home."

His face became hard to read. Was he confused? Frustrated? Angry? All of the above? After a beat, he nodded, resigned. "Okay, I'll go pay my tab and then I'll take you home."

"*No*," she said, her voice ringing with panic as she slid out of the booth after him. "No, I mean, I can just walk. My condo isn't far from here."

Emerson studied her. "I didn't mean *take you home* like, take you home with me, I just meant I can drop you off."

"I know." She nodded and tried to seem casual, but her voice was too high. "I just like the fresh air."

Studying her again with his beautiful X-ray eyes, he swallowed, then stiffened his posture. "Okay. Then just let me walk you home."

"I don't need-"

"I'm walking you home, Gabe," he stated. His deep voice was clipped and demanding, leaving absolutely no room for negotiation. "It's after midnight, you don't know your way around the city yet, and some assholes don't know how to control themselves around a woman who looks like you in a dress like *that*."

She watched as his eyes did a brief survey of her short dress before he turned around and headed toward the bar.

Outside, they walked down the sidewalk, right past Emerson's Lexus. There was a chill in the air, even though it had been sunny and warm earlier that day. It was late May and though it felt like spring and the hint of summer during the daytime, Gabby was surprised by how quickly the cold took over once the sun had gone down. She held her arms crossed over her chest, making a feeble attempt to warm them with her hands.

"If I had a sweatshirt or a jacket I'd give it to you," Emerson said. His hands were in his jeans pockets and he stared ahead as he spoke.

"It's fine," she insisted. "I'm not cold."

She caught him giving her a sideways glance, likely taking in the goosebumps that covered her arms, then looked straight ahead again.

Biting her lip, she tried to figure out how to get their conversation flowing again. In the bar they'd been teasing, flirting even. The words were flowing well and everything was just easy. Really easy. But now she couldn't help feeling like he was upset. Mad, even. And why? Because she hadn't fallen for his line? His move to get her to go home with him, or invite him to come home with her?

Well, that wasn't happening.

Sure, at the time she'd felt like maybe he was being sincere in the bar, talking about not being able to stop thinking about her. But he hadn't specified in what way. Maybe he couldn't stop thinking about her in his bed, or on her office desk. The more she thought about it, the more she was certain he couldn't have meant more than that.

Remembering the conversation of his weeknight gal-pals, she decided to focus on that. It didn't matter that they'd been getting along or that they seemed to have chemistry. That was probably just him. He probably knew exactly what to say to each woman to get what he wanted from her.

Not this girl.

"So," she began, raising her chin in defiance, "exactly what percentage of Traverse City have you slept with?"

His pace slowed for a fraction of a second, but he recovered quickly. "Well, definitely less than half if you consider half the population is probably male."

Letting out a frustrated huff, she corrected, "*Women,* then. How many women have you slept with in this town?"

"Are you looking for an exact number or a percentage? You kind of changed your question." His tone was flat, and he was still looking ahead.

"Never mind." She felt like grinding her teeth. "I don't see why you're not more eager to get back to your place. Don't you have someone waiting for you?"

"Nope."

"Why not?"

He lifted one shoulder. "Made other plans."

Still unwilling to let him get to her, she scoffed. "Like what? Did you think you were going to make me your Saturday night fling? You still have Saturday open."

"It's Thursday," he stated. "How could you be my Saturday girl tonight if it's Thursday?"

"It's not going to happen, Evan. I'm not going to be just another floozy bimbo side dish. Another late night conquest of yours to brag about to your friends."

He stopped now, but still didn't look at her. She hesitated about a step and half ahead of him, watching his expression turn from distant to somber. Of course it was dark, and the streetlights didn't provide near enough light to provide details hidden by the night sky, but she knew his eyes were stormy. That dark, gray-blue color of a sky filled with thunder clouds.

His silence was unusual. Eerie, even. She didn't know what to make of quiet, pensive, perhaps offended Emerson. But she straightened her back, kept her chin up, and showed no signs of backing down.

"I wouldn't ask you to be," he said, finally, and it was almost a whisper.

Her jaw clenched as she swallowed, still defiant. Still refusing to let her guard down or let him pull whatever voo-doo magic he'd done in the bar that made her feel like she actually wanted him. To be with him and spend time with him.

Emerson Yates was not the guy she wanted. She didn't want an emotional, real relationship with him. She *couldn't* want a sexual rela-tionship with him. He was too dangerous. Too tempting. She would end up getting hurt.

She nodded stiffly. "Good."

They resumed walking in silence, but after a few blocks, when Gabby's condo building was in view, he let out a humorless laugh. Or it was kind of like a laugh.

"It didn't bother you when my friends brought it up. Why does it now?"

She gave him a sideways glance and tried not to admire his profile. Seriously, in his casual jeans and t-shirt with nothing but the moon-light and some street lamps illuminating his other-wordly physique, he looked like a Norse God trying to blend in with mere mortals.

He repeated his question, "Why does it bother you?"

"It doesn't." Her tone was far softer than she'd meant it to be, but his expression, this new demeanor was doing weird things to her.

He stopped walking and faced her, grabbing her forearm to make her stop and face him, too. "That's a lie. You wouldn't be giving me shit about it if it didn't bother you."

She scrambled for any reason besides *I don't like picturing a bunch of blonde bimbos using you like an orgas-tastic jungle gym.* She didn't know why she assumed the girls were all blonde, but it seemed like he'd go for the Barbie type.

When a seemingly reasonable response popped into her head, she went with it. "As a woman, it's completely offensive. You just set up a time and place and they're just another part of the routine. It's like going to the gym or taking your car to the carwash. It's just something you do. You don't even care about them. If you miss a scheduled session, it's like 'oops, I missed leg day, oh well!' And then you make up for it next week."

He was quiet, stony, glaring. After what felt like a decade, he said, "It's not offensive to women. All the women I sleep with are on board with it. They know exactly what it is, they know we aren't attached and aren't going to be. They're using me just as much as I'm using them. It's mutual. Isn't that what women were fighting for during the sexual liberation of the sixties and seventies? 'Let us fuck around as much as guys and not get judged for it!' If anything, I'm a feminist. You're welcome."

"A feminist?" she repeated, flatly.

"And as for it being a part of my routine...I would never miss leg day. I might miss a carwash though."

He was trying to be funny and she was not going to go for it. She sighed. "The point is, you see these women as conquests. A way to scratch an itch or-"

"I like sex, okay?" His voice was firm and clear. "I like to have sex, so I make it part of my routine. So what? I'm not ashamed. People can go ahead and try to make me feel ashamed all they want, but it won't work. It's just sex. It's an activity that I am *damn* good at and I've been doing since I was fourteen." When Gabby's eyes widened in surprise, he nodded. "Yeah, fourteen. Same age as our little brothers. So fucking what? You want to know how many women I've fucked in Traverse City? Maybe you should ask how many girls I got with in Romeo. Answer's gonna be the same- it doesn't matter."

She huffed. "Yeah, it doesn't matter. Just like they don't matter." She continued walking and quickened her pace. There was no doubt about it, she was mad now. Furious, enraged, and unbelievably, still jealous. As if the image of four or five lingerie-clad women crawling all over him hadn't set her teeth on edge, now she was picturing a whole crowd, an entire football field of women. They were all reaching for him, trying to take his clothes off and he was in the middle on a spot-lit stage, just soaking up the attention.

It took a moment before she heard Emerson's footsteps jogging to catch up to her. They were just outside her condo now, where the building ended and led into a small, dimly lit alleyway.

"How about you, Gabe?" he asked, feigning casual niceties. "How many guys have you been with?"

"That's none of your business," she growled.

"But you asked me, so it's only fair."

She glared. "You didn't give me an answer."

Shrugging he replied, "A lot, I guess. I don't really know. Maybe six this year. I can give you that much."

It was an answer of sorts, she supposed. Not that it really mattered. She didn't actually want to know the number, she'd just needed a reason to fight with him so she wouldn't feel too tempted to invite him inside. It was a petty move, but she'd felt the need to protect herself against him and his...*everything*.

"Congratulations," she said with mock cheerfulness. "That's just over one new girl a month. You're on a roll."

The muscle in his temple ticked as if he were clenching his jaw. She assumed the muscles beneath his beard were also making similar movements. He let out an aggravated sound, somewhere between a huff and growl, and grabbed her arm, pulling her off the sidewalk and into the narrow alley next to the building. He crowded her so that her back was against the brick wall. Without preamble or any sort of warning, he pressed himself into her and- *there it was.* She gasped. The steel pipe was pressed firmly against her stomach. She was almost literally trapped between a rock- or in this case, a brick wall- and a hard place. *His* hard place.

Emerson gripped her wrists in his hands, holding them against the wall on either side of her head. He bowed his head to her ear and whispered, "Can't you feel what you do to me? How much you drive me crazy? I can't fucking take it."

She was at odds with herself. Her brain and lady business were at war with each other, once again. Consequently, her response was, "I imagine a lot of women do that to you" while hungrily grinding against him. Mixed messages didn't go well with matters of sex and relationships, so she tried her best to keep her composure and still her hips.

"I have my system, my relationships the way I do for a reason. I'm not going to lie to you, I'm not very good at relationships. I told you before, I don't let one woman take up all the space in my head, but you..." he paused, and she felt his hot breath on her neck, "you don't give me much of a choice. You're in my head all day, every fucking day."

"Like this?" she breathed. Her wrists wrestled feebly against his grip. "Pushing your cock into me? Manhandling me and shoving me against walls?"

His mouth was on her neck now.

SOS! Lips on neck!

She felt the slow curve of a grin against her skin and he let out one word in a low, seductive growl, "Sometimes." His mouth traveled lower, finding the nape of her neck, kissing her collarbone, before licking his way back up to her ear. "God, you taste good." It was a whisper and a groan mingled into one.

Her stomach was filled with butterflies. Impatient ones trapped in a box, trying to escape. Heat warmed her lower belly and melted lower until there was a hot, demanding ache between her thighs. Her knees felt suddenly weak and she was grateful he had such a firm grip on her wrists.

"Excuse me!" Someone shouted. A man's voice had caused Gabby's eyes to shoot wide open, and until then she hadn't realized they were closed. "Excuse me, miss, is he bothering you?"

Emerson immediately released her and took a step back. The tension evaporated, and she was both thankful and disappointed. He looked as if he'd just been startled awake. His eyes were heavy-lidded still with lust, and his chest heaved up and down, exhausted from the restraint of not taking her right there in an alleyway. And she'd been about to let him.

What the hell is wrong with me?

"Miss?" the man asked again.

At last, Gabby looked to the man who appeared to be only a little bit older than them. He was relatively fit, but had nothing on Emerson's Gladiator form. "I'm fine. We're good."

"You sure?"

"Mhmm," she said with a nod. "Thanks though."

The man looked from her to Emerson a few more times before seeming satisfied and walking away.

Emerson was still breathing heavily as he gestured toward the building. "Is this your condo?"

"Yes," she replied. She realized that her back was still against the wall, but thought she might need it for support. The stability of her legs was questionable.

"Can we finish this conversation inside before I get accused of harassing you in a dark alley again?"

Conversation? Were they having a conversation? Honestly, she couldn't remember a whole lot after feeling his mouth and tongue on her neck. Was she mad at him? Weren't they arguing? About what?

"Okay, sure," she responded, absent-mindedly.

It wasn't until they were in the stairwell- she hadn't wanted to be alone in an elevator with him- that she recognized what was happening. He was coming upstairs. To her home. To finish their "conversation" that involved her being pushed against the wall and him having his way with her after all his Emerson-isms fogged up her brain and got the better of her. His scent, his touch, his *voice-* his voice alone was something she could easily orgasm to, she was certain.

"You're not coming up to my place," Gabby said suddenly, stopping on the square landing to the third flight of stairs. She faced him and he stopped, stilling on the top step.

"Okay…where do you propose we have this talk?"

"We weren't *talking*, Emerson. You were…" she trailed off, gesturing from him to her neck.

With a devilish grin, he quirked one eyebrow. "Yes?"

"Okay, I get it. You can't stop thinking about me, you want to manhandle me and put your mouth all over me, and have your wicked way with me," she said, letting it all tumble out. "But that's not enough of a reason for me to just do it. To just give in. I know you get what you want all the time, but don't you think that maybe the only reason you're so interested is because I'm *not* interested?"

Stepping onto the landing, he moved toward her slowly. She felt like a deer being stalked by a wolf. She was an antelope, and he was a lion. The alpha lion. The king of the pride.

Another slow, sexy smile curved his lips. "First of all, I don't believe that. I think you're interested, but you wish you weren't."

Okay. Hit that nail right on the head…

"Second, that's not why I'm interested. This isn't some chase where once I've had you, I won't want you anymore. Trust me, I'll still want you."

"How do you know that? Have you ever met a woman who wasn't interested? Anyone who didn't like you, or didn't immediately fall for that stupid, sexy grin?"

He laughed, and it was a low, raspy, seductive sound. His hands were on her hips again and her back was again pressed to the wall. "Alaina," he said, and she blinked. "The chick bartending tonight. She's never liked me. She's attractive, but I won't pursue her just for the chase."

Gabby remembered the look of thinly veiled contempt that the bartender at Trojan had given him. Her first assumption was that Emerson had slept with her, and now they weren't sleeping together anymore. Apparently that was not the case.

Somehow, her hand ended up on Emerson's chest, and she could feel his heart racing like it was going to pound its way out of his rib cage.

"Third, *Gabriella*," he said, dipping his head to make eye contact. "You actually called me Emerson a minute ago."

She smiled in spite of herself, and then he swallowed hard, his face losing all playfulness, all hints of teasing. "And last but not least, because this is fucking terrifying…" His chest was heaving again. Rising and falling slowly, while his heart sped up beneath her palm. Leaning into her, his lips brushed her ear as he spoke, and his hand slid from her hip to the tie of her dress that was situated between her breasts. "I *like* you, Gabby. I really fucking like you."

The only thought flashing front and center in her mind was *He's telling the truth. Believe him.* There was no cyclone of freak outs, no expletives, no terrified shrieks telling her to run the other way. Only the recognition of vulnerability in those gorgeous eyes of his.

And just like that, a spark ignited between them, her brain shut off and her libido was ruling the show. Her hand slipped from its place on his chest down to his jeans. She palmed the rock-hard length of him over the stressed denim and he groaned in her ear, slamming his palm against the wall behind her.

A whoosh of breath escaped her at the sound of his groan. He kissed her neck, her jaw, and hovered for a moment over her lips. Forcing her eyes to open, she peered through her thick lashes up into the deep blue storm behind his eyes. Again, his eyelids were heavy, his gaze focused on her mouth. He leaned just the smallest fraction closer…and she closed the gap. Her free hand curled into his thick hair and pulled his mouth to hers.

And then she was dizzy, lightheaded, blissful. His tongue slipped through his lips and traced hers. He kissed her once, twice, nibbled and pulled at her bottom lip with his teeth, then kissed her again. This time, his tongue swept through her mouth, tasting her, savoring her. She swore she had never been kissed like this before. She never wanted to be kissed any other way.

While her mouth was busy with his, and her fingers tangled in his hair, her other hand busied itself working to unfasten his jeans. Once undone, she plunged her hand beneath the band of his boxer briefs and grasped him. She moaned against his lips as she felt his warm, thick length in her hand. He groaned and cursed as she began stroking him from base to tip. Her fingertips circled the broad head of him before sliding back down his smooth shaft.

Emerson's palm slid up her skirt, as though savoring the feel of her thighs on his way to her center. A finger toyed with the band of her panties and she arched into him. Tormenting her by sliding his finger over the front of her thong, he pulled his mouth away from hers and bent his head to look down her body where one of his hands was teasing her beneath her skirt, and the other was tugging at the knot tied between her now-heaving breasts.

"Fuck, I can't wait to see all of you," he whispered, and she melted further into the wall. She couldn't respond in words, so her feeble attempt to reply came out in a whimper. He kissed her cheek, the sharp arch of her cheekbone. Then she felt his thick finger dip inside her and she gasped. "I'm going to taste this pussy again. I'm going to make you come against my lips, and I promise you won't be able to send me away this time. Got it?"

Again, she couldn't find it in herself to respond. Her breaths were loud, she was wrapped up in every sensation. He cradled her head with both hands and looked deeply, devastatingly, into her eyes and kissed her. He kissed her good and slow and deep. Then his hands slid down her neck, over her breasts which he gave a firm but gentle squeeze, and continued over her hips, down her thighs...and up her skirt.

The image that teased her in her dreams, both sleeping and waking, played itself out in front of her again. He lowered himself to his knees, never breaking eye contact. She whimpered again, not being able to recall a time she ever felt so needy for someone's touch.

One solid palm slid up her left leg from her ankle to her core and back down, where he lifted and draped her leg over his shoulder.

Emerson glanced up at her with a knowing, devilish grin as he gently swiped a finger down her slick crease. "Mmm, all of this, just for me?"

"Shut up, Emmett." It was meant to sound more like her usual bickering tone, but instead came out as a sigh of longing. She should have been embarrassed at how wet she was for him, but instead she sunk back into the wall and let him take control.

A low rumble of amused laughter rolled through his chest before he ducked his head under her skirt. Kissed both her thighs, nibbled, licked, and sucked at her skin. Reliving the sensation of his lips and his tongue between her legs, his short beard against her bare skin, was like falling back into her best fantasy. This time, however, he only gave her one kiss over her panties before pushing them aside and digging in.

He absolutely devoured her. One long stroke of his tongue had her legs shaking, and he grasped her hip to keep her still. His tongue teased her clit, circling, licking, and sucking. She moaned and gasped, whimpered and panted. Simultaneously cursing and praising him as she curled her fingers into his hair and rocked her hips into him.

He groaned, deep and greedy. She loved the sound, so she rocked into him again. He dug his fingers into her skin and continued his work on her body. When he did it, it was fucking art. It was a whole damn masterpiece.

Skin hot and sweaty, she felt her body flush, goosebumps rippled across her skin and she gasped. "Oh my God, yes…yes, yes- Emerson, don't stop-" He definitely didn't stop. He kept moving his tongue in the same deliciously perfect motion. Honestly, she had no idea what it was he was doing down there, but it *worked.*

A white-hot flash erupted from her core and spread outward to her limbs and he buried his mouth deeper, pushed harder against her to draw out her orgasm. She sputtered and shook, trembled and gasped. The waves kept coming and it was almost too much as he kept going. Licking and devouring and digging his fingers into her thighs.

When he pulled away, she tried to catch her breath, heart pounding, lungs exhausted, and head still dizzy with sensation.

Emerson slowly lowered her leg from his shoulder back to the floor and stood, leaving one hand under her dress to keep petting her clit, making her feel like her orgasm was still crashing through her. Maybe it was. She was a little disoriented after the intensity of it. He pinned her with his seductive stare and wiped the back of his hand across his mouth. She was still leaning against the wall for support, his continued strokes of her clit not helping her compose herself. She definitely wasn't shooing him away this time. She wasn't running away either. She couldn't if she wanted to.

Full disclosure: She *definitely* didn't want to.

Then his body was against hers again, and when he rubbed her just right, she groaned and curled her fingers in his shirt. One hand dropped down to his cock again and began stroking. It was thick, hard, and warm. So inviting. So tempting. Tempting, because she'd considered returning the favor after her fantastical, celestial, cosmic experience of oral presentation number two. But as drunk on him as she was, she wasn't *actually* drunk, and there was no way she was giving him the satisfaction of being on her knees. Not just yet.

"Was that still only worth forty-five points?" he asked, nipping at her earlobe.

She grinned. "I gave you the fifty points."

"Was it only worth fifty then?"

"It definitely exceeded expectations."

"So, what's that? Like a hundred points?"

Her hand slid down his shaft, cupped his balls and squeezed gently, making him groan. "Sure. I'll give you a hundred for that one."

"Wow, no negotiation? No argument? You're just…giving it up?"

"I'm both distracted and deliriously satisfied right now. Nothing I say in the next half hour really counts."

He slipped his hands behind her to grip her ass. "Oh, honey, you're not deliriously satisfied yet." He then yanked her up so her legs were wrapped around him, hooked at the ankles behind his back. With his pants still mostly on, he pushed them just far enough down to comfortably have his dick out, then reached into his back pocket for his wallet and produced a condom.

She watched him tear open the packet and roll the latex down his length and found herself feeling surprisingly relaxed. No longer panicky, anxious, and vulnerable like she'd felt earlier. Like he'd played some trick on her to get her there. Whether her brain was still taking a break and her vagina was doing the decision making, she was unsure, but she wanted this. Wanted him. Most of all, she wanted to believe him.

Gabby's arms wrapped around his shoulders and clung tightly to him and she watched where he held the base of his cock, aimed directly at her opening.

The cold wall pressed against her back and he growled in her ear. Similar to his demanding no-nonsense tone from earlier, he ordered, "Tell me you want it."

It was forward, and words caught in her throat at the menacing urgency. Her pulse was skittering and stuttering again, out of control, looking for safety.

"Gabe, I'm not going to fuck you like you want unless you tell me you want it," he said. It still sounded like a command, but she understood now. He was making sure she wanted this. Asking for permission. Consent. In his own Sexy Lawyer Man bossy kind of way.

In a breath, she exhaled, "I want it."

"What do you want?" He inched toward her and the head of his cock was now pushing against her. She could've sworn his shoulders were vibrating with restraint.

"Your thick cock," she whispered in his ear.

He grunted and leaned forward, pressing one hand against the wall next to her head. It appeared he was the one needing support now.

"And what do you want me to do with my thick cock?"

She knew what he wanted her to say, and part of her wanted to drag this whole tease out just to see how long he could hold back. But fortunately for him, she didn't want to wait, either.

She hummed like she was taking her time to make a decision and she felt the wide head of him press further forward until she groaned and whimpered against his neck. "I want you to fuck me with it. Fuck me the way you know I want." She demanded it, and offered it up like a challenge.

A hot breath of relief blew against her neck as he groaned and he slid into her fully. All the way to the base, until she was absolutely full, and held himself there. To refrain from crying out too loudly, she bit his shoulder and he moaned.

That sense that he was vibrating with restraint magnified tenfold as he held himself deep, breathing hot and heavy against the nape of her neck. When he began to move inside her, she grasped his hair, holding tight as she adjusted to him. She let him set the pace, and it was a steady, solid rhythm. Not too slow, and not wild, frantic fucking like she sensed his body wanted.

Her breaths became shallow, and they echoed through the space. His grunts and growls were masculine, and his filthy words in his deep voice might have made her start ovulating right then and there.

...fuck, Gabby, that pussy's so tight...

...oh God, you feel good...

...fucking made for me...

...gonna make me explode...too fucking soon...

...I can't fucking take it, baby, your sweet pussy is so tight, fuck...

She wanted to say something equally dirty, something so filthy it could return the favor and make him feel like a puddle of sweet, sinful satisfaction. But her brain was still off. Thinking was not her forté. The most she could string together was *yes, oh god, yes!* And *fuck, just like that!* But it seemed to do the trick.

He slid in and out of her, sometimes slowing the pace to draw out a long, tormenting stroke. She waited for him to use his fingers, pet her again on her clit while he moved into her. But then, as he started to increase his pace, as she began to sense that he was losing control, about to lose himself and let go of his release, she started to feel it. The slow build. The cresting wave inside her as he pushed deep, hitting just the right spot.

"Don't stop," she panted, gripping behind his shoulders. "Don't stop, oh my god."

"Come for me again, baby."

The build became faster, more prominent, she was approaching the peak…closer, closer…

Gabby felt the tension in his muscles as he did his best to hold back. Emerson slowed his movements, but his breaths were ragged and frantic, losing all control. Then his muscles rippled and shuddered, contracting beneath her palms as he released a moan of pleasure through gritted teeth. With another thrust, he shoved her hard against the wall as he let himself go, and she gasped as the mounting wave crashed and shook through her. Clawing at his shoulders, muffling the sounds of her cries by kissing his neck, his jaw, his mouth, her body clung to him.

For a long moment, he held her in his arms, pressed against his chest, and kissed her. They kissed and tasted each other while he was still inside her as they both came down from an unbelievable high, and she absolutely reveled in it. He brushed back a chunk of her hair, combing his fingers into her thick, dark, wild mane, never letting their mouths part. Lips and tongue and teeth, barely coming up for air.

When he stopped, he let out a shuddering breath, kissed her on the cheek, and slipped out of her before setting her back on the ground. He tied the condom off and shoved it back in the condom packet that had fallen to the floor, then pulled up his pants and boxers. He started adjusting her skirt, but she brushed him off.

Emerson studied her for a second and asked quietly, "Are you okay?"

She blinked up to him, but immediately dropped her gaze and nodded. Her brain had turned back on and was wondering what the hell just happened. They were in a stairwell. In her condo building. She'd told him not to come up to her place because she hadn't wanted this to happen. But it happened anyway. And now she had to deal with the awkwardness of it.

"Hey." Emerson tried slipping an arm behind her back in a sweet, boyfriend-like gesture. Only, he wasn't her boyfriend. He'd made it perfectly clear he wasn't *anyone's* boyfriend and there was a reason he kept it that way. She stepped out of his reach and sensed his posture stiffen again.

"I'll, um...I'll see you at work tomorrow, okay?" Gabby stepped around him and toward the next flight of stairs.

"Gabe...tell me what's wrong. What did I do?"

"Nothing," she replied quickly. "Nothing is wrong. I just...it's late. I should get to bed. You know, in case someone switches the coffee on me again."

She didn't look back at him because clearly she couldn't resist him. His face, his body, his charm. So, instead she quickly ran up the stairs to the fourth floor, slipped inside her condo and promptly locked herself in.

Emerson had told her that he liked her. *Really* liked her. And then...*oh God, what was wrong with her?*

The truth of it was, she liked him too, however much to her dismay. But with everything she knew about him, and everything there still was to learn, she simply didn't trust him.

Chapter 12

Emerson spun his leather coaster absent-mindedly on his desk, staring at nothing in particular. He chewed the inside of his cheek as the image of Gabriella's retreating form flooded his mind again. What was he supposed to make of that? They'd had sex- really good, needy, urgent sex. Hell, he'd fucked her against the wall in a stairwell- It didn't get much more urgent and desperate than that. There wasn't a whole lot he could do to stop it.

Of course, if she'd told him no he would have walked away, but she hadn't. Not only had she not told him to back off, but she'd nearly begged for it. She'd told him she wanted it. Wanted him to fuck her. Every time those words replayed in his ear, he struggled to breathe.

So why had she left?

Why wouldn't she look him in the eye?

Had he done something wrong?

Did she think it was a mistake? A sort of buyer's remorse, but with sex?

He couldn't believe it had happened. He'd needed her so badly, he'd just plunged in, still in his shirt, with his jeans just undone. He hadn't been able to explore her like he'd wanted. She'd kept that dress on. Fuck, he'd left her panties on, just pushing them to the side because he'd been so damn impatient.

After she'd run up the stairs, he'd stood on the stair landing for a while just wondering what his next move should be. He'd contemplated following her, demanding answers.

Maybe that's what he would have done if he was certain he could do more. If he'd been sure he was in it for the real thing, he wouldn't have let her make it all the way up the next flight of stairs. He would have told her she could trust him, that he wouldn't hurt her. He would have promised her she had nothing to worry about.

As it was, however, he couldn't say any of those things. He refused to lie to her. He wanted to be able to say those things. Or at least he thought that's what he wanted. Honestly, it scared the shit out of him to even think he might want those things.

On his walk back to his car, he'd told himself to forget about it. Forget about her. She was too complicated, too temperamental, too hard to read. Gabriella was hot and cold. She pulled him in just to shove him away. She seduced him, whether it was intentional or not, and then left him feeling hollow.

Yes, he realized the irony of all this. The user becomes the used. He'd never felt like he really *used* women. Not anymore. Or if he did, the using was mutual.

Now he glanced down at his phone and wondered if he'd be better off canceling his Friday night plans with Jade, too. He felt like he needed to get some answers before making that decision. If Gabriella was done with him...done with *whatever* this was...maybe he'd be in the mood to use his every-other-Friday night fling for a distraction. The only problem was that he had no idea how to approach it. How to approach *her* after what had happened.

The clock on his phone told him it was just past noon, so he decided to take his lunch break since he was clearly not getting anything done now. He called a bistro around the corner, put in a pick-up order, and slipped out of his office.

The walk and fresh air seemed to help clear his head and ease the tension in his shoulders. The frustration was still present, but at least he was able to focus on something else. By the time he arrived at the bistro, he'd decided that thinking about Gabriella, thinking about Jade or any of the other women who were just *part of his routine* wasn't doing him any favors. For the first time in a long time, he thought maybe he needed to just take a break from women in general. Clear his head. It would be like a body cleanse. A detox.

The idea was oddly calming. No women. Maybe he needed a guys' night. Maybe he could pick Kolbe up and call up the guys and invite them over for some *Call of Duty.* He was in the middle of planning the beer and food menu when he walked into the restaurant, past the wide French doors that led to the outdoor patio seating and saw a familiar sheet of light blonde hair.

The irony, again, did not escape him. Of course he'd been looking forward to a woman-free evening, and a potential woman detox when he ran into Raelyn DeRose.

She was sitting alone, and he noticed her giant, aptly named furry companion, Harry, was lying at her feet next to the chair. Her hair was down as usual, flowing down to the middle of her back, and she was wearing high-waisted blue jean shorts, a white, long-sleeved cropped shirt, and the familiar low-rise Converse on her feet. It didn't matter how pretty or feminine every other part of her was; Raelyn DeRose was a tom-boy at heart.

He was paused in the middle of the doorway, chewing the inside of his cheek. He should just go up to the counter and get his lunch order. There was no reason to stop and talk to her. Even though she was the last person to be in a real relationship with him. Even though she was the *only* person he'd been able to commit to for such a big chunk of his life. Three years might not be a long time for most people, but the longest relationship he'd been in before Raelyn was about three weeks. Maybe. Probably closer to two and a half.

He considered the thought that she could help him or give him advice. What if she could tell him about all the things he'd done right in their relationship? She might be able to tell him what made her fall for him in the first place. What made him boyfriend material in her eyes? Why had she decided he was worth the risk?

Before he could talk himself out of it, he was pulling the French doors open and heading toward her table. Harry picked his fluffy head up and looked at Emerson, and his tail wagged in recognition.

Without announcing himself, he pulled out the chair across from Raelyn and sat down, suddenly unaware of exactly how to approach this topic.

Raelyn's bright blue eyes lifted from her phone and her eyebrows raised in surprise before narrowing in suspicion.

He decided to jump right in. "We were engaged once, right?"

Raelyn's eyes were narrow for a couple beats longer before she snapped her fingers, looking as though a lightbulb just went on in her head. "Oh my God! *That's* where I know you from. I knew you looked familiar."

His mouth tugged up in the smallest smile. Rae had always been funny, though her sense of humor was often dry or dirty. That's probably why they'd gotten along so well.

She resumed her suspicious, guarded expression. "What do you want, Emerson?"

"It's nice to see you, too, Rae. I'm doing well, thanks for asking." He smiled pleasantly, though it held the bite of sarcasm behind it. She didn't respond, and continued to glare at him from across the table. He looked around briefly. "Is All-Star here?"

"No, he left for Vegas this morning with the guys," she replied, reaching for her ice water.

Dammit, that's right. Quinn's bachelor party was this weekend and pretty much all of his friends were going. So much for a guys' night.

"Does that make you nervous?" he asked. Quinn hadn't exactly been a saint before reconnecting with Raelyn. His sex-life and other social exploits had been all over the tabloids and internet for years.

"Not really," Rae said with a simple shrug. "At least, not in the way you would think. I trust him, I just don't always trust his crazed fans. When we were in LA, he got swarmed by like four women and one of them just *groped* him. I mean, full-on, hands to the pants, grab and squeeze."

He raised his eyebrows. "That's actually kind of fucked up." Rae hummed in agreement and a silence hung between them for a few moments while he tried to remember exactly what he wanted to ask her.

"I wanted to talk to you about something," he said, hedging slightly. "About us. Our relationship."

The suspicion in her gaze increased. "Okay...?"

Emerson's knee began bouncing up and down nervously beneath the table and he pulled at his bottom lip. "Why did you like me?"

He should have expected the derisive laugh she responded with. "You know, that is an excellent question. I often find myself wondering the same thing."

Staring blankly at her, he then rolled his eyes. "Thanks. What I mean is...you obviously liked me enough to stay with me for three years. I must have done *something* right...What about me...what did I do that made you want to be with me? What made you think of me as...relationship material?"

She studied him curiously, pursing her lips as she contemplated. "Hmm...Poor judgment?"

He exhaled and leaned back in the chair, defeated. Clearly this had been a bad idea. "Never mind," he sighed, rubbing his brow in aggravation.

Rae's playful smile didn't falter, but she leaned forward, resting her elbows on the table between them. "Why do you ask?"

Sighing heavily again, he replied, "If you're not going to be helpful, Rae..."

"Okaaaay, fine." Rae set her phone down and placed her hands out in front of her, palms down. He couldn't help noticing the massive diamond on her left ring finger and comparing it to the one he'd bought her. The one that had consequently been thrown at his chest before she walked out of his life.

She tilted her head now and looked at him, still smiling. It was an amused, closed-lipped smile that gave him the impression she still wasn't taking this conversation seriously. "It wasn't poor judgment," she said. "There were lots of tequila shots involved, so I believe that's actually called *impaired* judgment."

Rolling his eyes, he pushed himself out of his chair. "Thank you, this has been great. Very helpful and enlightening."

"All right, all right," she laughed, reaching for his jacket sleeve to halt him. "That was the last one, I promise."

He glared at her, silent and stony. His jaw flexed before he resigned himself back into the chair. He decided to just come out with it. "There's this girl- *woman*...whatever. Anyway...Gabriella. She just started working at the firm a few weeks ago and I hated her at first but now...now I can't stop thinking about her. I just don't know how to do this. I forgot what it was like to actually feel something for someone. Be in a relationship...I have no fucking idea where to start, or even if I should. What if I just screw it up? What if I..." he trailed off and shrugged.

"What if you cheat on her?" Rae supplied, finishing his thought. "You know, that's not the only option. That's not the only outcome for a relationship."

"Maybe not for most people," he muttered.

She rolled her eyes then set her gaze on him intently. "Listen, I know you have more daddy issues than a sorority girl at a Spring Break wet t-shirt contest in Cancun-" Emerson frowned but couldn't find it in him to disagree with her- "but you are a good guy, Emerson."

His frown deepened. Actually, he scowled in adamant disagreement.

As if reading his thoughts, she insisted, "You *are.* I know you like to hide it, but deep down beneath all the moodiness and the stubbornness, the combative, manipulative, man-whorish behavior, you're one of the good ones."

He couldn't stop scowling. Nothing she'd said was a compliment- at all. She was not doing a good job of making him believe in his abilities to actually be *one of the good ones.*

"Maybe you need someone who's even more moody and stubborn and combative than you are to bring the good guy out," she said, and the comment grabbed his attention. "Maybe..." She grinned slowly, looking as though she was fighting a laugh. "Maybe someone who will leave your ass stranded in the rain or plant *Playgirl* magazines in your office."

His brow creased for a second before he let a smile show on his face, too. Of course she'd know all about it. His friends were all of her close friends. He wouldn't be surprised if someone had shared the stories he'd been regaling them with each day.

"Amira called me as soon as you left their house a couple weeks ago," she explained through a small laugh. "She and Brody said you were in denial, but I guess you're past that stage now."

Scrubbing a hand down his face he sigh-groaned. "She's just so complicated. One minute she's got her fingers tangled in my hair, fucking my face, and the next she kicks me out of her office. Or she's letting me fuck her up against a wall in a stairwell- *in a fucking stairwell, Rae!-* and then she's not making eye contact with me and rushing up the stairs to get away from me. I don't fucking get it."

Raelyn looked shocked into stunned silence for a few moments, her mouth opening, closing, then pursing her lips, then sliding her jaw to the side, contemplating. "I'm sorry- *what?* You're sleeping with her already? I'm confused. I...You...you went to Chow Town in her office?"

"We're not sleeping together. We had sex once- last night, actually- and yes, I...I went down on her at the office. But then she kicked me out. And last night after we had sex, we kissed for like a solid five minutes. Just kissed. And then she couldn't wait to get away from me."

"Interesting..." And she looked genuinely interested. "Have you told her you like her? Maybe she thinks it's just sex and has never done that kind of relationship. I mean, not everyone's as emotionally dysfunctional as us."

"I don't want it to be just sex. I told her that. I told her I liked her, we had *amazing* sex, and then she just left." Saying it out loud made him feel even more confused than when he was just playing the scene on repeat over and over in his head.

"Hmm…" Rae leaned back and crossed one arm over her body while raising the opposite hand to her chin, as though trying to solve a riddle. That's definitely what Gabriella felt like at this point- a riddle.

"Maybe she's afraid of having feelings for you. I mean, you work with her and I wouldn't be surprised if you have a bit of a reputation around there. Maybe she's heard people talk and just doesn't think you're a relationship kind of guy. "

Emerson considered it for a beat. It wasn't completely out of the question for people at work to talk, and he didn't know who else she interacted with throughout the day. But she'd been letting her guard down last night, he could feel it. So why did she close back up?

"She does know about, you know…my *other* girls. The girls I see during the week," he offered, then added quickly, "But I'd stop seeing them if it was just her."

"I have no idea what you're talking about, but I think I'm okay with that."

Emerson rolled his eyes. "Just the girls I hook up with on a regular basis. We talked about it and she seemed okay at first, but later when I was walking her home she brought it back up and it was pretty clear she wasn't okay with it."

Raelyn's blue eyes stared blankly into his, and he got the distinct feeling he'd said something wrong.

"Emerson William Yates, I thought you were smart."

He looked away briefly, catching Harry's big brown-eyed stare. The dog cocked his head as though equally confused. "What do you-"

"You like this woman and you talk about all your other conquests in front of her? You tell her you're still banging all these other chicks on the side? You like her and you're *still banging other chicks on the side?!*" Rae's voice raised with each question and Emerson glanced around at people sitting within earshot.

"Well, it's not like we're dating," he replied defensively. "And I didn't bring it up- Tyler did. I didn't want to deny it and thought maybe starting off with honesty was a good way to go, given my history."

"You need to end it," Rae stated urgently.

Confused again, he looked at her for clarification.

"With the side pieces. End it with the side pieces before you pursue her seriously. If it doesn't work out, I'm sure you'll be back in business in no time."

He gnawed on his thumbnail as he mulled this over. It made sense, of course, but he didn't want to act too rashly. He had a good thing going and while he enjoyed the idea of being with Gabriella, he didn't want to get ahead of himself. Her actions and behavior toward him were so inconsistent. What if he ended things with his weekday girls just to get a flat-out rejection?

Okay, Rae was probably right. He'd be back in business in no time. He could just call the girls up and pick up where they left off, or if he really wanted, he could probably find all new women.

Unable to give her a direct answer or commitment on whether he would flip his world upside down for the possibility of being with Gabriella, he gave a somewhat noncommittal nod.

Unfortunately, Raelyn saw right through his non-answer. She shrugged and put her hand up in an aloof gesture. "Or don't. Keep doing what you're doing. Keep seeing women you don't really care about while you sit back and watch the girl you really want from a distance. She sounds like a catch, I'm sure she'll find someone else before long."

The thought of Gabriella with someone else instantly heated his insides. He thought back to watching the waiter at the Mexican restaurant flirt shamelessly with her and imagined seeing them out together. Walking down the sidewalk, David's arm wrapped around her shoulders to hold her close as they whispered in Spanish to each other, kissing and smiling.

No, he definitely didn't like that option either.

Again, Rae read his face and brought him out of his unwelcome daydream when she said, "You were a really good boyfriend, Emerson."

His brow creased in confusion and he met her gaze. Her blue eyes were soft and sincere, and he couldn't remember the last time she'd looked at him like that. With a slight shock of surprise he noted that, although it warmed his chest that she wasn't looking at him with outright disdain or annoyance, her eyes on him like that no longer made him feel any amount of possessiveness over her. She wasn't his anymore. He'd burned that bridge, dealt with it, and was ready to move on to his next chapter. The only problem, of course, was that he had no idea how to do that.

The now-familiar narrowed skepticism returned to her eyes as she pointed at him. "I will absolutely deny it if you repeat anything I'm about to say, so don't repeat it. I will personally sneak into your apartment and shred all your suits and put Nair in your beard balm!" she warned, and he put his hands up in surrender, then crossed a finger over his chest as though making a promise.

Her expression softened again before she continued. "You were good at being there when I needed you, and you actually paid attention when I talked. Like that time we were walking downtown in Ann Arbor and passed that jewelry store? I'd made an offhand comment about how I'd always wanted to be the kind of person who actually wears a watch, rather than relying on my phone for time, and you surprised me a week later with a really nice watch from that store. It was such a small comment, but you remembered it."

Emerson's mouth tugged up slightly as he remembered their walk around town. He'd taken her to a football game earlier that day and they were walking around trying to find a place to eat when they passed the small jewelry store.

He also remembered Brody telling him that buying a seven-hundred dollar watch for the girl he'd only been dating for three months was way too much. But he did it anyway.

"You were always really generous with your time. You were one of the busiest people I knew at the time because you'd just started at your first law firm. They had you working on a ton of cases, doing the boring reading part, and you still always made time for me, even if it meant coming to my apartment when I was already asleep. I'd wake up and you'd be there and it was...I don't know, it was really nice. Really sweet."

He smiled a little more, having forgotten all the things he'd done early in their relationship. He'd been consumed by her, and it wasn't something he'd ever felt before. The constant need to be with her, to have her next to him as much as possible had been equally exhilarating and terrifying. He would have done anything to make sure she knew he was thinking about her. That he wanted her, every second of every day.

"Finding someone to connect with is the hard part. After that, it's just being thoughtful with your words, your actions. You're going to fight- knowing you, probably a lot," she added with a small laugh, which he mirrored. "Just let her know you're there. Tell her and *show her* that you think about her and it's not just about the sex. That might be kind of difficult after the whole stairwell incident, but I'm sure you can do it. You're pretty persistent when you want something."

Staring at nothing in particular, he was thinking up ways to show Gabriella he thought about her. A way to show her he listened, that he'd be there for her.

He looked back at Rae with a grin, remembering when they first met. "You thought my persistence was annoying. You told me at least five times a day that nothing was going to happen between us, and that you'd just tolerate me because our roommates were dating."

Raelyn laughed. "Your persistence *was* annoying. You thought you were so smooth and subtle, always making sure you were shirtless in front of me after spending two and a half hours at the gym."

He shrugged, grinning smugly. "It worked, didn't it?"

"Tequila shots. The tequila shots worked."

"And whose idea was it to do shots?"

"*Yours!*" Rae insisted, then leaned back in her chair. "I may have suggested the very clever and creative game of Strip-March Madness, but that's irrelevant."

Emerson laughed, remembering the suggestion that came after three rounds of shots. They were watching *March Madness* and Emerson's bet was that the Blue Devils would win, Rae's bet was on the Hawkeyes. Her clever strip version of simply watching a basketball game was that any time his team made a basket, she had to take something off, and when her team scored, he had to strip. The game did not last long.

It had been a long time since he'd really thought about the beginning of their relationship and how much fun it had been. How much he'd enjoyed being with just one person and having one person to make happy.

Then that familiar sick feeling punched him in the stomach as he thought about how he'd brought it all to an end.

He peered across the table at his ex-fiancé now, curiously. "Why would you want to help me? Isn't it weird giving me advice? Telling me how to make someone else happy based on what I used to do to make you happy?"

Rae's expression was incredulous as she searched his eyes. "Emerson, I know it may seem like I moved on really fast but I did love you once."

The sick feeling churned in his stomach again and he averted his gaze.

"And because I loved you, I want you to be happy. Just because we didn't work, and even though it ended the way it did…that doesn't mean you don't deserve to find someone."

His eyes flicked back up to her, surprised by her words. They reminded him of why he'd been attracted to her when they'd met five years ago. Raelyn had grown up even more privileged than he had, far more wealthy, with a loving home and all the luxuries anyone could imagine and then some, and yet she was so humble. So down to earth. Sure, she could be dramatic from time to time and was definitely a smartass, but she was always empathetic and could show compassion for anyone, whether they deserved it or not.

"Who invited *you?*"

The sudden sound of his best friend's wife's voice made him blink. Amira was standing next to his chair, staring down at him, an obvious look of distaste on her face.

Naturally, he smiled with mock sweetness as he greeted her, "Mrs. Kalahan, so nice of you to join us!"

Amira addressed Rae. "Seriously, what is he doing here?"

Raelyn shrugged. "I'm not really sure. I was minding my own business, sending dirty texts to my fiancé, and he just appeared."

"I was picking up a lunch order and saw Rae sitting out here, so I thought I'd be neighborly and say hi," Emerson explained. "Which reminds me, my food is definitely going to be cold by the time I get back to the office."

Raelyn gasped suddenly and beamed up at Amira. "Girl! You forgot to tell me the story about Emerson getting on his knees to give the office chick the orgasm of a lifetime, before she kicked him out without giving his business so much as a *how do you do!*"

Amira's eyes widened and her jaw dropped. "*What?!*" she shrieked. "Stop! She did not!" Her elated stare met Emerson's horrified face and he groaned, dropping his head into his hands. Amira's delighted laugh made his jaw clench. "Okay, go get your lunch and eat it here. I need to hear this whole story."

"There's more!" Rae interjected, causing Amira to gasp excitedly again.

"*No!* No, don't say anything else!" Emerson pointed a finger at Raelyn. He shook his head and muttered, "I can't believe you told her that."

Amira took the third chair at the table so that she was situated between him and Rae now. She set her large purse on the ground and gave Harry a pat on the head before turning back to him. "Then go get your lunch and tell me yourself. I already can't wait."

He groaned again and scrubbed a hand down his face. Finally he sighed and resigned himself to his fate. "Fine. But I'm only doing this because I don't want to eat alone in my office."

He stood grumpily from the table and stomped toward the door to head inside and get his order from the pick-up counter. Once inside, however, he allowed himself a small smile. He felt better. Lighter even, knowing Raelyn didn't still hate him and actually wanted him to be happy. That she even believed that he could find happiness.

Feeling more confident about his ability to take things forward with Gabriella, he started whirling plans around in his mind. He wasn't going to let up. He'd be persistent and consistent. He'd show her that he meant it when he said he couldn't stop thinking about her, that he could be thoughtful and generous. He could shake up his routine and make drastic changes to show her that he could be someone else. There was more to him than the guy he'd been for the past couple of years...He just had to remember how to be that person again.

Chapter 13

Gabby was holding a fresh cup of dark brew black coffee and staring at the Google screen on her laptop. She had just gotten back to the office after an extended lunch with Marco downtown at some swanky Asian-fusion restaurant. The food was delicious and Marco's cocktail looked spectacular, but all she'd really been able to focus on was the restaurant across the street where Emerson was having lunch with a gorgeous, leggy blonde who Marco swore was Raelyn DeRose. He explained how she was practically royalty in this small town, and she explained how the Traverse City Princess was Emerson's ex-fiancé.

So why were they having lunch together?

Annoyed, ashamed, and yes, fine, a little jealous, Gabby had typed the name *Raelyn DeRose* into the search bar at least six times before erasing it. She was not going to be that girl. The jealous girl who cyber-stalks and conducts social media searches on some guy's ex. Some guy she wasn't even interested in, no less! Or at least, she didn't think she was interested.

Okay, a guy she didn't want to be interested in.

But even from her view across the street, the woman had been intimidating. The long blonde hair, her perfectly tanned skin, her long, crazy-toned legs. Inwardly, Gabby was cringing and growling and throwing her coffee cup across the room. Outwardly, she was glaring at the search bar.

"Okay, just one search. Five minutes and then I'm done," she reasoned with herself. She typed the name of Emerson's ex into Google one more time and pressed enter.

Several articles popped up about Raelyn DeRose and Quinn Casey. Tabloids, paparazzi photos of the two of them doing everyday things, introductory articles about the new Major League physical therapist, and different interviews the couple had done together. After scrolling far enough, she found articles from the previous summer when they had apparently been sighted together for the first time at a wedding.

An article written by a journalist named Regina Todd immediately grabbed her attention when she saw the name Emerson Yates in the small blurb beneath the headline. She clicked aggressively on the headline and waited impatiently for the article to load. Her leg bounced up and down beneath her desk as she began reading, holding her warm Starbucks cup of coffee to her chest, and then suddenly she stopped. Her whole body froze as she saw the first photo attached to the article dated less than a year ago.

Emerson and the blonde-haired, blue-eyed beach babe were standing next to each other; Emerson in a black tuxedo and Raelyn in a cherry red two-piece formal dress. Emerson was looking intently at her while she looked into her glass of champagne. The look Emerson was giving this other woman made Gabby's insides heat up- and not the good kind of heat. The anxious, overwhelming, bitter, jealous kind of heat.

Her eyes narrowed as she chewed the inside of her cheek and continued scrolling through photo after photo of Emerson and his ex. Looking at each other, smiling, laughing together. They *looked* like a couple, even though this was supposedly a month or so after The Ex reconnected with Quinn Casey.

And today, the day Gabby happened to know the baseball player and all of his friends were out of state for his bachelor party, Emerson and The Ex had lunch together. Was that supposed to be a coincidence?

Gabby went back to the Google homepage and typed in a new search: *Raelyn DeRose and Emerson Yates.* This search yielded a whole new slew of articles and pictures that she was not expecting. Whether she was high on her jealous-fueled anger or just a glutton for punishment, she decided to forgo the articles and click on the *Images* icon.

Photos of Emerson and The Ex flooded her computer screen. The same photos from the wedding as well as older ones in which they were both impeccably dressed and attending various fundraisers, charity events, and other galas of some sort. Remembering Marco's comment about The Ex being royalty in town, she assumed these events where they were photographed had to do with her family and whatever they did.

Maybe she was some sort of heiress, or her family owned a chain of hotels or department stores. Maybe they were politicians.

Ugh...politicians.

She clicked through picture after picture of them dressed in designer clothes holding hands, him with his arm around her, the two of them in an intimate embrace, photos of them kissing. *Kissing!*

Glaring particularly hard at the first photo of them in which they were dressed casually, The Ex leaned into Emerson with her hand on his chest and he kissed the top of her head. Her chest felt tight. She wanted that. She wanted him to look at her like that. Hold her and smile at her like that.

She was so wrapped up in the idea of mentally replacing The Ex in each of these photos with herself- much like a psychopath would probably do- she didn't hear her office door open and close.

"Hey Gabe-"

Catastrophe struck.

Gabby gasped and jumped at the sound of his voice and squeezed her paper coffee cup. The instant burn of scalding hot coffee first met her hands, then her chest, and dribbled down her stomach and she stood, dropping the cup to the floor.

Putting priorities first, she slammed her laptop shut before promptly tearing off her coffee-covered blouse and fanning herself. She attempted to mop up the coffee on her chest that was now soaking into her bra.

"Whoa, holy shit- Gabby, hey-" Emerson slipped off his suit jacket as he slid behind her desk, then wrapped it around her shoulders. He pulled the jacket shut and held onto the lapels as he unintentionally- at least she *thought* it was unintentional- brought her close to him.

Again, she felt her breath stop. He had this effect on her. She gazed up at him in surprise through her thick lashes and his eyes met hers. They were a dark, stormy blue, and she could've sworn he was also holding his breath.

Emerson abruptly cleared his throat and stepped back. "Sorry, I um..." He glanced around the office and his eyes fell on the closed laptop. His gaze narrowed and he looked back at her. "Were you watching porn?"

"What?" Her eyebrows shot up and she looked back at her closed computer. "Oh...no," she laughed nervously. "I, uh...I just didn't want to spill coffee on the keyboard."

"Right," he said, then cleared his throat again. His eyes dropped to what was visible of her chest beneath his jacket. "Are you okay? Did you, um...did you burn your skin?"

She looked down and noted that her skin was slightly reddened, but not seriously burned. "No, I'm okay. Thanks, though. And thanks for the jacket."

"Here, let me, uh..." Emerson began loosening his tie and unbuttoning his white dress shirt.

Gabby watched attentively as he unfastened the last button and began shrugging out of his shirt. He wasn't wearing an undershirt, and her eyes went wide at the sight of his muscles. *All* of the muscles.

The man was ripped. His shoulders were stacked and strong, his chest was broad, tattooed, and possibly the most impressive sight she had ever seen. His abs were absolutely cut and shredded. It was like standing in front of a photoshopped *Men's Health* model. Like Hugh Jackman in *Wolverine* or Chris Hemsworth in...anything.

She was staring. She was staring and...still staring.

"Here, why don't you take my shirt? I've got an extra one in my office," he said, snapping her attention back up to his face.

"Oh, thanks." Gabby took the offered shirt and her gaze went immediately to the tattoo of knight's armor on his chest. The chest plate of the armor was intricately detailed as though engraved with a medieval lion and the roman numerals XXVI. The old English blackletter script was above the chest plate and ran just above his collarbone, and she really wished she knew what it said, but couldn't seem to find her voice to ask. The armor continued over his shoulder and ended at his elbow.

It was quite the sight.

It was a sight she couldn't take her eyes off of.

She pulled his dress shirt on and subtly inhaled his scent that now surrounded her. His mahogany-teakwood cologne mingled with his natural musk and her insides burned. The good burn this time. A deep burn. Liquid heat flooded to her core and she could have sworn her breasts involuntarily perked up.

"Here." Her breathless voice barely sounded like her own as she reluctantly handed his suit jacket back to him. His tie still hung loosely around his neck and she honestly thought she could look at him shirtless with just a tie and his dress pants for the rest of the work day.

Unfortunately, however, Emerson pulled his jacket back on, but it helped her regain her thoughts. She could still see his skin and rippling muscles through the gap in his jacket, but he wasn't quite as distracting.

"Listen, Emerson…about last night," she began, having no idea what she was going to say, but knowing she had to address it. She had to let him know it was a mistake and that was all. A mistake they needed to move on from. They could continue their lives the way they were. "Last night shouldn't have happened. It was…it was a mistake. I don't- It's not going to happen again. It was a one time thing, and I think we should just pretend it didn't happen."

Emerson's mischievous eyebrow twitched and he smirked as he looked at her, and she knew he was reimagining the previous night's events. Was it the intimate moment they'd shared in the bar when he'd traced circles on her hand? Was it when he pressed her against the brick wall outside her condo building? Or…was it when he pulled her leg onto his shoulder? The desperate, yearning look they shared before she told him to fuck her?

Ay Dios mio...que estaba pensando?

She must have muttered the question aloud because he gave her a curious look, arching an eyebrow with a brief hum.

He hesitated a moment, scratched his bearded chin, and his gaze swept over her. "Gabe...Gabriella- Gabby? Can I call you Gabby?"

She smiled, eyes glinting. "No."

He laughed and the tension seemed to ease in his shoulders. "Fine then, *Gabe...*" His attention was focused on her chest. Or maybe it was his shirt. His shirt on *her*. "Listen, I was just coming in to ask you...What are you doing tonight?"

She raised her eyebrows. "Um...tonight?"

"Yeah." He nodded. "Do you want to go to dinner?"

"Dinner? Tonight?" She repeated.

He was asking her on a date. A *date* date. This wasn't going out for drinks or meeting each other at a baseball game; it wasn't even getting roped into taking their brothers out to eat just because Emerson was buying. This was a real date.

But...Emerson didn't date.

She opened her mouth, paused, then finally exhaled. "I can't. I'm working late."

"How late?"

"Real late," she replied. "I'll have to eat here. I'll order food or, who knows, maybe I'll just skip a meal. It wouldn't hurt. What's one meal? My thighs could probably use a break from...food."

His brow creased in confusion and his gaze dropped. He took a step toward her so there was barely a gap between them. "I like your thighs."

"Um..." She swallowed, and tried to take a step back, but he halted her by placing his hands on her hips. Her exceptionally curvy hips.

"As a matter of fact, I think about them a lot." His devilish look was easy to read this time. She knew exactly what part of the previous night he was thinking about now.

"Okay, well, sorry I can't have dinner with you. I just have a lot of work to do. I took a long lunch and I've left early twice this week, so…"

"Right." He nodded once and his devilish grin still didn't fade. "Okay. How about tomorrow night? I doubt you're working late on a Saturday?"

"I'm not, but…" Gabby bit her lip, feeling trapped as she tried to come up with another way to weasel out of a date with the man who was incapable of dating and relationships. "We have a family thing. And Sunday…Sunday is another family thing. It's all weekend."

Emerson grinned back at her, clearly not deterred.

"Listen, I don't think it's a good idea anyway," she said. "Like I said, it was a one time thing and it should stay that way. I don't want things to get weird at work."

He nodded once again and put his hands in his pants pockets. "Right." He stepped back, but she felt his hot gaze on her all the way to the door. He pulled the office door open and gave her one last sweeping look. "I'll be back to get my shirt some other time."

When the door closed behind him, Gabby let out a long exhale and sunk back into her chair, but stood up abruptly when she realized it also had a spot of coffee on it. She glanced at her computer and thought about how she'd been cyber-stalking his ex, then shook her head.

What the hell was I thinking?

Though she knew turning down his dinner invitation was the right thing to do, she still hated that she'd done it. She wanted to spend the evening with him. She wanted to get to know him in a new capacity. Fewer drinks would probably be the best option- she could stick to chardonnay.

But it didn't matter. It wasn't going to happen. He didn't date, and she refused to get tangled up in another mess where she had feelings for someone she couldn't have.

Gabby hadn't been lying about needing to work late. She had been productive throughout the week, but felt as though she were a little farther behind than she otherwise could have been if not for all the distractions. She was used to being ahead of the game, and telling Emerson she'd be staying late gave her the motivation to actually stay and get work done. The way the week had gone, if she left early, she knew she was sure to run into him out and about somewhere unless she went straight home and stayed there.

Not that it mattered. She didn't owe Emerson any explanations if she chose not to work late, but she knew she'd be in for some sort of sexy, glowering, eye-twinkling interrogation if she hadn't kept her word and got caught.

As it was, working late wasn't unusual for lawyers, and she wasn't the only one who had stuck around the office after the usual 5 o'clock out time. On her last trip to the break room, she'd noticed three other offices that seemed occupied on her floor, so she knew she wasn't the only one doing overtime on a Friday evening.

Around 7 o'clock she was once again on the floor surrounded by legal documents, briefs, and her own notes when she hit a lull in her progress. With a heavy sigh, she leaned back against her desk, but sat back up almost immediately when there were two sharp knocks on the door.

Though she knew those knocks, and knew who she'd see pushing the door open, she was still surprised to watch Emerson enter her office with two paper bags in his hands.

"Look at that, you are still here," he said with his usual crooked grin. "You almost had me thinking you made up having to work late just to get out of dinner with me."

Gabby stared, brow furrowed, and it took a moment for the scent of grease, cheese, and bacon to reach her. Her stomach growled in response.

"Uh...no," she replied, slightly dumbfounded. Collecting herself, she cleared her throat and resumed her boss-bitch persona- or at least she tried. "Some of us actually work around here. Not everyone has time to litter offices with hundreds of balloons or sneak decaf coffee into the break room just for something to do."

Emerson gasped, mocking a wounded expression with a hand to his chest. "I work, Gabe. I'm so good at my job, I get everything done with time to spare so that I can pull off these great pranks."

"I assume you're using the term *great* lightly?" she teased.

He merely grinned at the familiar banter, pushed the door shut with his foot, and made his way to her desk where he set the bags of food down.

"We didn't eat at Trojan the other night, but you should know that they have a wicked bacon cheeseburger," he said, beginning to pull the deliciously scented food out of one bag.

She stood from her position on the floor and took a moment to appreciate his appearance yet again. He was dressed casually in a navy blue t-shirt that hugged his perfect form, and a pair of light stone-wash jeans with small rips and tears here and there. She couldn't help inhaling his freshly showered, clean-man scent as she watched him empty the contents of each bag onto her desk. Out of one bag he pulled two bacon cheeseburgers, two orders of crinkle-cut fries, and a bunch of condiments. Out of the other, he lifted a six-pack of Heineken and an elegant-looking bottle of Chardonnay that was some brand she'd never tried before.

"What's this?" she asked, eyeing the obvious date-in-a-bag that had been delivered to her office. She chewed the inside of her cheek as she willed herself not to smile.

This man...has never heard the word "no" in his life.

She would be lying, however, if she said she hated that about him at that particular moment.

"It's dinner," he replied. "Since you can't go out until next week."

Gabby narrowed her gaze and crossed her arms. "I never said I could go out with you next week."

His cocky, self-assured grin did new things to her. Where three weeks ago, she wanted to smack it off his face, tonight she wanted to feel those smug lips all over her.

"Well, I guess it's a really good thing I brought our date here then."

She huffed. "This isn't a date- I never agreed to go on a date with you! Besides, you don't date."

The twinkle in his eyes never faltered and his grin grew the slightest bit wider. "But what if I wanted to?"

Her chest threatened to swell and burst at his words, but she internally scolded the reaction and told the quickly beating organ in her chest to hold onto its panties.

"Emerson...you can't just decide that like you're picking out a new suit- 'Well, usually I wear black suits, but I think I want to try charcoal now.' It's not that easy."

His eyebrows lifted. "You think it's that easy to just change what suits I buy? Gabe, that takes weeks of research- months, even."

Letting out a reluctant half-laugh, she groaned. "Stop trying to be funny, I'm being serious. You can't just tell me you don't date, there's a reason you have a system in place, and that you're bad at relationships, and then come in here all cute and thoughtful and tell me you want to go on a date."

His mouth twitched again in that easy, devilish smirk of his. "You think I'm cute?"

Before Gabby could let out any more than another exasperated groan, he took a step closer and made her whole body freeze when he brushed her hair back and let his hand rest on her cheek, cradling her face in his large, warm palm. He gazed down at her intently and her insides betrayed her brain yet again, warming up at his touch, wanting to draw him in and keep him close. Wishing he would wrap his arms around her and pull her body flush against his. *Damn those twinkling, hypnotic blue eyes.*

"Trust me, I've tried talking myself out of this at least a dozen times-"

"That inspires a lot of confidence."

He gave a silent laugh, but continued, "It's just dinner, Gabe."

She was chewing the inside of her cheek again, considering. The scent of Emerson freshly showered was enough to cloud her judgment, but he'd also brought her favorite food, she was hungry, and the burgers were getting cold. If their dinner went awry, she could always blame being manipulated by her two favorite scents: Bacon and man.

"Fine." As soon as the word was out of her mouth, his smile widened, though it wasn't necessarily an overjoyed sort of smile so much as it was a smug I Always Get My Way kind of smile, and she cursed herself inwardly for it. She held up a hand between them and layed out some ground rules, "It's just dinner. Two people talking, getting to know each other, definitely *not* drinking, but I will take the bottle of chardonnay home with me."

Emerson nodded once. "Right, fine, one drink each."

She narrowed her eyes. "No drinking. There are bottles of water in the break room."

"I brought burgers from Trojan Horse; I'm pretty sure it's sacreligious to *not* drink a beer while eating a burger from there."

She glanced at the six-pack of beer on her desk. For some reason her brain was telling her that he was making a good argument. Or maybe her brain was taking a step back again and letting other body parts make decisions for her. "Okay fine, I'll have one, too- *Just one.*"

"Deal."

Gabby realized his hand had fallen from her face and was now easily resting at her hip, so she stepped back. No logical reasoning could be done with this man that close. She walked around her desk to her chair and sat down. Emerson stared curiously.

"Aren't you going to sit?" she asked, gesturing to the chair next to him.

"I just know how much you like the floor, I thought we'd eat picnic style. Sitting across from you like this, I feel like I'm being interviewed."

She arched an eyebrow. "Did you bring a picnic blanket?"

He looked down at the empty paper bags on the desk as if he might have forgotten to pull out a blanket. "Um...no."

"Then we're eating at the desk," she replied. "I promise not to ask you what makes you feel qualified to be on this date, or what your greatest strengths and weaknesses are."

Emerson sat down with a grin and reached for a bottle of Heineken. "Well, I think you already know one of my greatest strengths. You've experienced it twice and gave me a hundred and fifty points total for it."

She felt heat course through her chest and face and was thankful her skin didn't allow her to redden easily. Deciding to not comment, because that was dangerous territory, she instead asked, "How did you know I like bacon cheeseburgers?"

He snapped the top off of a second beer bottle with a bottle opener on his key chain and passed it to her. "Tyler told me. He gave me a lot of information about you, actually."

Halting the beer bottle on the way to her lips, she looked at him curiously. "What do you mean?"

He laughed. "Well, that first week when he was constantly in here helping you, he was only in here that much because I told him to. I mean, he really is great at helping and I figured you could use it, but I told him to, uh...gather intel. I was sizing up my opponent."

Her jaw dropped. "Are you serious? Tyler was in here being nice because he was *spying* on me? For *you?*"

Laughing again, he replied, "Well, not exactly. I mean, he was being nice because he is nice. He's a good guy. Totally not meant for corporate law, even though he'd be really fucking good at it. But yes, I asked him to find out what he could about you. Unfortunately- at least at the time it was unfortunate- he basically brought me back a dating profile. Convenient now though, huh?"

"I feel so violated," she said, though there was a grin on her lips. "That was so manipulative and deceitful...Good for him. Maybe he's more suited to corporate law than he thinks." She took her first drink, then set the bottle down. "What else did he tell you?"

A low laugh rumbled through Emerson's chest and he shook his head. "Oh no, I'm not giving all that up. You'll just have to wait and see."

"You're pretty confident that I'll want a second date, then?"

"No, but I'm pretty confident that I'm persistent enough to keep pushing for one."

With no immediate response, Gabby bit back the grin that threatened to show on her face and dug into her food.

Point Emerson- Trojan Horse bacon cheeseburgers were a solid ten.

An hour later when their food was long gone and Emerson was of course on his second bottle of Heineken, despite the argument that ensued when he reached for it, they had covered several topics. Gabby had explained about her family, her parents' trek from Cuba to Florida when they were teenagers, and their hard work that got them to Michigan where they had three more kids. They talked about how she had graduated early from high school and her full-ride scholarship to Yale, along with her first few jobs after law school that seemed to be preparing her for a career in politics which she had absolutely no interest in.

"My dad is still pushing for me to get into politics," Emerson sighed, setting down his beer. "I didn't really even want to go into law, but it wasn't up for negotiation."

The statement surprised Gabby and she peered at him from across her desk. "What do you mean?"

He scratched his jaw. "My dad's a politician- a senator, actually. He's a complete ass and didn't really give me much of a choice when it came time to think about college. It wasn't really worth the argument. The guy puts the 'dick' in 'dictator'."

Her eyes went wide now. "Your dad is a senator?" She thought for a moment, trying to recall all the names of currently-sitting members of Congress, then nodded. "Right, Senator Johnathan Yates. He's your dad..."

Emerson merely grunted his confirmation.

She remembered the photos she'd looked at earlier during her Google search of him and Raelyn. All the pictures taken of them at charity events, galas, and other public appearances had been for his family, not hers.

Part of being a law student was knowing members of the Supreme Court as well as Congress, their political affiliations and stances on certain issues. It was hard to keep tabs on all of them, but Senator

Johnathan Yates stuck out in Gabby's mind for many reasons, not least of which was his impressive appearance in a suit. Clearly that was genetic.

"So…Senator Yates- your dad, I mean…Isn't he a really strong Family Values kind of guy? What about Kolbe? Didn't you say you had the same dad?"

Emerson's laugh was humorless when he looked up and scrubbed a hand down his face. "Uh, yeah. That's just political bullshit that he spews to keep getting re-elected." He paused, scratching the label on his beer bottle for a few silent beats before continuing, "He has never been faithful to my mom- at least I don't think he has. And my mom puts up with it because of the money and the lifestyle, so it's not like it's a secret."

Gabby remained quiet, waiting for him to decide if he was going to keep going. Inwardly, she was shocked. Having known nothing but a loving family her whole life, she couldn't fathom being part of one in which lying and cheating was just something they had to accept.

"I met Kolbe about five years ago," he said, finally. "My dad kept him a secret for years, but when my friend, Brody was interning at one of his law offices down state, he came across some legal documents that looked suspicious, involving a lot of money transfers. Basically he was sending money to the same account every month for the past nine years. It wasn't a business account, and Brody thought that was odd. He brought it to my attention, we did some digging, and found out he'd been sending Kolbe's mom hush money."

"And you confronted him about it?"

He nodded. "My relationship with my dad has never been great, but that really made the divide even bigger. He tried to act like it wasn't a big deal, and I pointed out that hiding a brother from me was a huge deal. He argued, telling me Kolbe wasn't my brother, that he was just…some accident. A mistake. He said he wished he'd known sooner so that he could have…put a stop to it."

Gabby's brow furrowed, then her eyes widened as she realized what he'd meant. "He would have paid for her to end the pregnancy?"

"Exactly." His jaw clenched and he scratched at the beer label some more. "Don't get me wrong, I'm all for a woman's right to choose what she wants to do, but with my dad...it wouldn't have been much of a choice. I know him too well. He would have found some way to bully her into it, whether she wanted to or not. And the fact that he has a son out there that he cares so little about, that he can so easily say he wishes didn't exist because it creates an inconvenience for him..."

"What made you decide to be involved with Kolbe? I'm sure your dad was furious."

"Still is," he huffed. "But I'm glad I did it. He's a cool kid...I guess I just know how lonely I was for so much of my childhood, I always felt like if I had a sibling it wouldn't have been so bad. So, even though I was in my late twenties by the time I found out about him, I just...I don't know...My family is so fucked up, I thought maybe if I could have a relationship with Kolbe, it would be like I fixed it a little. Like it wasn't such a mess."

Gabby studied him as he looked down, not meeting her gaze. It was weird to think that his life was anything other than perfect. She was sure she had him pegged as some kind of Golden Boy his parents both doted on and spoiled to no end. Sure, he'd grown up surrounded by wealth, but everything else about his childhood sounded so cold...So mechanical and lonely.

"If your dad hadn't forced you into a career in law," she began, leaning forward now and catching his attention enough for him to look up at her, "what would have been your choice? What would you do if you weren't a lawyer?"

The corner of his mouth tugged up just a little and he looked up, contemplating. "Well, being a lawyer isn't that bad. I mean, I'm a really good arguer, and I'm persuasive. Also, I don't think I have to remind you how great I look in a suit-" he paused as he looked pointedly at her, as though waiting for her to agree. She obliged with an eye roll and a reluctant nod, waving him to continue. "But if I could be anything else...hmm...I would have to say...The next Hugh Hefner, for sure. Except I'd wear a suit, not a robe."

Gabby couldn't help laughing, and was glad he'd lightened the mood even though she was pretty sure he wasn't joking at all. She threw a wadded up napkin at him that hit him in the chest. "I should have guessed."

And just like that, another hour passed. They covered more ground: What their college years had been like, where they'd interned, their favorite vacation spots and places they had yet to see but really wanted to. Another hour went by and they talked about high school and what extracurricular activities they'd been involved in. Gabby was unsurprised to discover that Emerson had been a star athlete and captain of the water polo team- It really didn't get any more stereotypical than that. She told him about playing softball and being class president and valedictorian, which he didn't seem shocked by at all, either.

After another hour it was completely dark outside and they had resigned themselves to the floor, surrounded by all her work while they covered their favorite movies, TV shows, and books, favorite music, and concerts they'd been to.

"My first concert was *Fall Out Boy*, my sophomore year of high school," Gabby said.

Emerson chuckled and leaned back into the desk behind him. "You don't strike me as the emo-rocker chick."

"No, I wasn't really. I mean, the show was good, but it was my boyfriend's pick," she replied. She sat with her legs tucked beneath her, leaning against the desk, as well. They were only inches apart and she found herself wanting to lean closer to him, wanting to breathe in his scent, feel the warmth radiating off of him. Their position on the floor somehow felt intimate even though they weren't touching.

His blue eyes flashed when they met hers and she could have sworn they darkened. "Your boyfriend…is this that Ben guy Robby mentioned?"

Suddenly wishing she hadn't limited herself to a one drink maximum, she nodded.

He arched one eyebrow, urging her to continue, but she said nothing. "And…?" he coaxed.

"And what?"

"Were you two together for a long time, or have you not had a serious boyfriend since high school?"

She blew out a reluctant sigh and fiddled with the small buttons of the shirt she was wearing. Emerson's white dress shirt was loosely fitted around her significantly smaller frame, but it was comfortable. She glanced sideways at him. "It's sort of complicated."

"And the story about my family wasn't?" he pressed. "Besides, you know about my ex. Hell, you can do a Google search on her or read about her in the next issue of *Sports Medicine Today* or…whatever."

Pausing to stare at her hands for a brief moment, she schooled her facial expression to give away absolutely nothing at the mention of conducting a Google search on his ex. There was no way he could find out about that. It would make her seem too interested, too invested, and way too jealous.

Finally, she cleared her throat and looked back up to see him waiting patiently. "Okay, fine…" She sighed again, then brushed her hair back out of her face and prepared herself for the exhausting tale of her only real long-term relationship.

"Ben Mendoza was my first serious boyfriend- my only serious boyfriend, I guess. We started dating my sophomore year of high school, but had known each other since middle school. We were friends before, although I think we both knew it was more than that. He knew my dad was pretty strict about me waiting to date until a certain age, so he waited until my fifteenth birthday to really ask me out. So, we went to homecoming together, went on dates, I went to all of his football games, he came to my softball games. At least in high school, things were really great."

She gave herself a break before continuing and allowed herself a glance at Emerson who was still listening intently. "When you're young like that, feelings are so intense. Young love is so strong, but also extremely fragile. You make all these promises of forever but you have no idea just how long forever is. You have no idea what is waiting for you outside the confines of high school…but I hung onto the promises for a long time. Longer than I should have."

"But he didn't?" Emerson's low voice, so close to her ear, nearly sent a shiver down her spine.

She nodded. "But he didn't."

"How long were you together after high school?"

"Well, we went to different universities. I moved to New Haven to go to Yale, and he stayed in Florida to get his pre-law degree. We tried the long distance thing the first year and it was tough, but we did it. I was too focused on school to even think about going out and meeting new guys. When we both came back home for the summer, we spent all of our time together, but decided to break up before going back to school. It just made sense, I guess. But the way he presented it was like a way to stay focused, keep our eyes on the prize, get through school, and then we could be together later. Of course, as young and naive as I was about love back then, I believed it. I really thought we'd be together after college."

Reaching for her bottle of water and really wishing it was instead the bottle of chardonnay that still sat on her desk behind her, she took a slow drink. She hated this part of the story. It bothered her to think of how cute and naive she once was, how easily she had believed Ben because he was supposed to care about her. Sure, it was years ago, but it still stung. It stung and it was embarrassing.

"After undergrad, Ben came to New Haven. He got into Yale Law and I was insanely excited that we were actually going to be together. It was like our four years apart had paid off and everything would be smooth sailing from there. Of course, that's not how life works."

"He came all the way to Yale but didn't want to be with you?" Emerson asked, a deep crease in his brow.

Wavering slightly, she nodded her head from side to side. "Not exactly. Like I said, it's sort of complicated. We were together, but not really. He'd act like we were dating whenever we were around each other. If we had classes together, we'd sit together and it was like having my high school boyfriend back. In front of professors, he liked to stick next to me- probably because I was head of the class and it made him look better. If I saw him out in public, he'd have his arm around me like we were together. We slept together and he'd stay the night, or I'd stay with him."

"Sounds like you were together," Emerson remarked, still watching closely.

"It probably looked like it, too, but I guess we never really talked about it. He was always careful to make sure there wasn't a label. The whole time we were at Yale together, he kept me within reach for the convenience of it, but we were sort of in limbo. I had no idea he was seeing other women...Law school is taxing so I thought maybe he seemed distant because he was busy or tired, or maybe he had his mind on an upcoming exam or something. But when I stopped by his apartment one night and met a particularly disheveled-looking under-grad student on his doorstep...leaving...I put two and two together, the rose-tinted glasses came off and I saw the past two years for what they were."

Emerson still had his brows furrowed deeply and his frown made him look almost menacing, though she sensed his anger wasn't directed at her. "So this guy just strung you along for two years? Or six if you count undergrad..."

"Assuming he was sleeping around that whole first year of college-"

"He was."

"Probably-"

"Not *probably*- he was," Emerson stated. "If he slept around on you while you were on the same college campus, I can guarantee he slept around while you weren't in the same state."

"Right, well, I just hate talking about it. I'm smarter than that, you know? I should've seen it coming or at least questioned why he was so shady about it all," she reasoned, rolling her eyes at the memory of her overly trusting younger self.

He shrugged. "Like you said, feelings are really intense when you're young. Maybe in the stress of law school, you had to cling to memories from a simpler time. High school was easy, he reminded you of high school…it was a comfort."

She nodded slowly, having never thought of her attachment to Ben like that. It was a new perspective, and it made a lot of sense. Everyone else who knew the story also knew Ben, and was a part of Gabby's family. They weren't exactly impartial enough to look at it as an outsider.

"Hey…" he whispered, and his hand slid against the side of her face, tilting her chin upward to meet his gaze. "All of us have things in our past that we wish we could change. You gave your heart to someone who didn't deserve it, but you learned from it. You've turned into this bad-ass boss-bitch who doesn't take shit from anybody, and it's the sexiest thing I've ever seen in my life. I love giving you shit just to have you throw it back ten times better."

She couldn't help smiling at his sweet words.

"Ben Mendoza sounds like a fucking chump and if he could see you today, you would have him crawling on the floor, groveling at your feet, begging for your forgiveness." He lightly brushed the pad of his thumb across her bottom lip and she had to hold in a whimper. "Of course, you would tell him to fuck off and let him know that you've only got time for one asshole at a time to get on his knees and beg for your attention…and that guy's me."

Those dark, glimmering eyes met hers and heat flared through her. It was intense and instant, hot and blazing. The burning need for him came out of nowhere. Over the past few hours, they'd been talking, laughing, sharing, and enjoying each other's company, but now…after talking about something so personal, a piece of her she kept guarded, she couldn't help the flood of emotions that spilled over at his reaction.

The man sitting next to her on the floor was not the man she had expected. The cocky, arrogant, selfish, entitled jerk she thought she'd met on her first day was someone else entirely. It was a shield he wore. Armor he kept in place so no one could see the real him.

She swallowed, and her voice was breathless when she asked, "And what's something in your past that you wish you could change?"

Licking his lips, he stared at her mouth, and his breath hitched slightly. "I...I've been the guy girls shouldn't have given their hearts to. Lots of times."

She searched his eyes and saw that there was a hint of warning in them. The dark flicker of his gaze was still dangerous, it still made her crave things she probably shouldn't, made her want him in ways she should be ashamed of.

Heart pounding, blood rushing in her ears, electricity sparking in her veins, she ignored his warning. All the warning signs, the red flags, the flashing lights and sirens that told her to beware of this man were drowned out in her sudden need for him.

She inched closer.

Emerson let out a shuddering breath and the deep growl of his voice was barely audible as his chest heaved with forcibly controlled breaths. "Gabe...I'm not one of the good guys."

Another warning that her brain, heart, and vagina chose to deflect.

Her fingers wrapped tightly in his shirt and she pulled him closer, crashing her mouth into his.

Chapter 14

Oh god, yes.

His mouth was pressed to hers, hot, wet, eager. Lips sliding over hers, he shoved his fingers through her hair, grasping, clinging onto her like she was the only thing keeping him on the ground.

Wait...no, this wasn't right. This wasn't part of the plan.

It was a painstakingly difficult move, but he separated his mouth from hers. The sounds of her labored breathing made his cock throb beneath the zipper of his jeans, but he willed himself to push out the thoughts of all the hot, sweaty, bad things he wanted to do.

"Gabe," he exhaled, "Gabe, I can't...I don't want-" He stared into her almond-shaped brown eyes and lost all conscious, coherent thought. "Fuck, I want you."

Gabriella kissed him again, her full lips feeling so right against his mouth. His tongue swept out and traced between her lips before plunging inside and tasting her. It was a forceful kiss; clawing, aggressive, and demanding. There was nothing sweet or gentle about it, and she gave it right back. Her tongue wrestled with his, she nipped playfully at his bottom lip before coming back to taste him even deeper.

His hands slid down her ribs, waist, and hips, and fingers dug into her perfectly round curves as he pulled her on top of him so that she straddled his lap. Now her hands curled behind his neck, bringing his mouth closer, the kiss deeper. Pulling him into a beautiful, blissful haze, where only she existed. Her sweet scent of lavender and honey, her soft hands, softer lips, and perfect kisses.

Everything about her was good, *so fucking good.* The way they fit, the way she tasted, the way she moaned into his mouth when he gripped her hair even tighter.

His chest tightened and he felt himself wanting to completely engulf her. Consume her, take her for his own. Hide her away and keep her all to himself.

But he couldn't.

He couldn't have someone like that. Or at least, he couldn't make it last.

The muscle in his chest pumped furiously, protesting avidly against his thought process that was now spiraling down, down, *down,* hitting the pit in his stomach.

Gabriella was amazing. Phenomenal, smart, sexy, gorgeous, witty-everything he could possibly look for in a woman. But that didn't change anything. That didn't change who he was, who he would always be. She was too good for him, and it was best she knew now.

Again, he tore his mouth away from hers, and he felt like his stupid brain was punching himself in the dick as it throbbed and pushed hard against his zipper. "Gabby, I mean it," he breathed. "I'm not one of the good guys. I can't...I can't give you more than this. I can't make you any promises. You deserve someone who can promise you everything."

Her fingers loosened their grip on his shirt and she rested her forehead to his as her chest rose and fell with heavy, gasping breaths. Beneath his shirt that she still wore- *his shirt,* God he loved the sight of her in his shirt, wrapped in his scent, engulfing her like he wanted to do- her full tits were almost level with his mouth and it was nearly impossible to restrain himself from tearing through the buttons and burying his face between her heavenly swells.

After moments of nothing but the sounds of them both trying to catch their breaths, Gabriella kissed him lightly on the mouth. "What makes you think I want more than this?"

It would be a lie to say her words didn't tug painfully at his chest. Yank, rip, or tear might be more accurate verbs, but he swallowed it down. If she didn't want more than this, that was good. Perfect, even. He wasn't good for more than that anyway.

He just...really wished he could give her more. Really wished she wanted more.

This wasn't supposed to just be about sex. The whole point of this evening was to show her that he could be better than that, do more, give more. That he didn't always have to be a playboy who remained completely unattached. He still wanted her to believe that...he still wanted to believe it himself.

"Besides," she breathed, and he couldn't help brushing his lips against hers even for a split second, "I'm sure you're capable of keeping some promises..."

He looked up at her curiously, arching an eyebrow. "Think so?"

Her fingers curled tight in his shirt again and she rocked into his lap, over where he was needy and aching for her so badly. "If you promised to make me come, I bet you could make good on that."

All thinking power in his brain was lost in that moment as he was sure every last bit of his blood rushed into his cock.

*Well fuck...*she was not making this easy on him.

He wanted her to give in to more than just the physical, carnal attraction that pulled them together so fervently.

Tell me you want more...tell me you want me...*tell me you* feel *something here.*

But as she covered his mouth again with more hot, wet kisses, his heavy eyelids shut and he sunk into the sensation. His hands gripped her hips tighter and he thrusted upward as she rocked into him again.

If physical was what she wanted, that's something he could do. That's what he was good at.

Again, he pulled away so their lips were just barely separated. "Is that what you want?" he asked.

"Yes."

His wicked grin flashed, an involuntary reaction when his dick knew it was going to get what it wanted, and he shoved down any thoughts that threatened to intercede on her request. If she wanted him to make her come, he'd do it. Hell, he'd give her so many orgasms she'd beg for him to finally let go.

Their eyes met and his voice came out in a rasp, "Ask nicely."

"Like hell," she replied, with a sardonic yet playful laugh.

He grinned again and nipped at her jaw. "Come on, Gabe…Ask me nicely to fuck you, and I promise I'll make you come. I promise I'll give you what you want."

Sliding her hands beneath his shirt, feeling her way up his stomach to his chest, she returned his playful tease, and as always, did him one better. "I'm not asking, and I don't want it nice."

Emerson swallowed a groan. "Then I'm not *asking* for my shirt back." His hands grasped the soft fabric of the shirt and tore it open, letting the buttons rip off and fly in every direction. Level with his mouth now was the incredible sight of Gabriella's rounded breasts, bronzed and pushed up in a deep plum lace bra. He felt his eyes glaze over and his mouth begin to water as he shoved the shirt the rest of the way down her arms and tossed it away.

His hands skimmed up her ribs while his attention remained focused on the heaving swells of her breasts. He palmed one over her bra and groaned, his erection throbbing harder against the restraint of his blue jeans. Gabriella's tits were magnificent. Full and round, a generous handful in his large hands. He'd seen them in this bra earlier that day when she'd torn her own shirt off after spilling coffee on herself, but hadn't taken the time to appreciate them in the panic of needing to cover her up before someone else walked in and saw her.

Now that he had her up close, he knew that this was a sight only he wanted the privilege of seeing. No one else deserved this view. Honestly, he probably didn't deserve this view but he wasn't about to complain.

With a hand on each breast now, he massaged, squeezed, and expertly caressed them. He worshipped them. They were his God, and he was but a lowly servant.

Her nails scraped down his chest and over his abs from beneath his shirt, sliding lower until she cupped the protruding bulge in his jeans and he practically hissed, raising his hips to press into her palm.

She whispered, her voice thick and silky with need, "Is this what you want?" Her hand rubbed the thick length of his shaft and he throbbed again. It was a fucking miracle he hadn't busted through the denim.

He answered honestly, "It's one of the things I want."

"What else?"

His hands continued their sensual adulation of her tits and he bowed his head to lay wet kisses over her skin. He scraped his teeth over them, kissed, and nipped, then dipped his tongue into the cup of her bra on one side, causing her to gasp and lift her chest into him. He sucked and lapped at her skin, still caressing with his firm hands while he reveled in each sure stroke of his cock that she gave him.

"What else do you want?" she moaned, grasping him harder- making him harder.

"Everything," he rasped. "I want to fuck you, I want to watch you fuck me, riding my cock until you get what need from it." His tongue made a trail back up her neck, and he kissed her jaw, then nipped, and then his mouth found hers and sunk into the sweet relief of her kiss again.

Keeping one hand on her breast, the other gripped her hair, tugging, pulling with just enough tension to control the angle of her head so that he could expose the elegant curve of her neck. Like a vampire going for his kill, he kissed, sucked, and licked a path from her collarbone to her jaw again like he was starving and couldn't get enough.

"I want to make you beg for me, make you moan and shake and fucking feel your tight pussy squeezing my cock, taking me for all I've got. I want to bend you over your own desk and watch my dick as it fucks you, gets covered in you. I want you up against the wall, beneath me on the floor. I want you to dig your nails into me until they leave marks on my legs because you're on your knees with your perfect lips wrapped around my cock. Then I want to come all over your gorgeous tits, lay down on the floor, and let you ride my face until you're screaming my name as you come again and again and again, knowing no one will ever fuck you like I can."

Gabriella's mouth had fallen open just the slightest bit and she looked as though she'd forgotten to breathe and was momentarily speechless. Emerson looked down into his lap where her legs were spread over him and her skirt was pushed up to her upper thighs from straddling him. Her hand lay motionless over the bulge in his pants that threatened to burst at any given second, and he smirked, satisfied that he'd rendered her temporarily stupefied.

Finally she licked her lips and swallowed, then a familiar tug at the corner of her lips told him she had regained her composure.

"Aren't you going to ask nicely for any of that?" she teased.

"No. But you can start by taking my dick out."

She blinked slowly and her eyes flared with wicked heat. "You can take your own pants off- and don't expect me to get on my knees for you. That's *your* job, remember?"

He knew it was a long shot to expect that from her, but she asked, so he answered.

His fingers worked furiously at the button and zipper on his pants, shoving his boxer briefs down with them, and he watched Gabriella strip out of her black nylons and skirt before she settled herself back over him in only her bra and a tiny black g-string. She wasted no time stripping his t-shirt up and over his head.

This was the first time he'd seen this much of her. They'd had two sexual encounters and somehow managed to keep most of their clothes on both times, but now he was naked beneath her and she was barely covered by scraps of lace and silk that could easily be removed. They were bare and exposed. In her office, at their mutual place of employ-ment. But it was after 10:30, so there likely wasn't anyone else around to walk in on them.

Both of his hands skimmed up her thighs, hips, waist, tugged at her bra that remained and gave her tits another slow caress before contin-uing their way up her body and cupping her face. His eyes were greedy and didn't want to look away. Thick thighs, a round ass, nearly flawless bronze skin that was smooth as silk beneath his palms. She narrowed at the waist and her mouthwatering tits could make a man weep. Her body could make a lost soul find Jesus- then turn around and sell his soul to the Devil just for the chance to touch her.

"You...should never wear clothes," he said slowly, as his eyes did a third or fourth, maybe ninth sweep of her body.

"I was thinking the same thing about you." Her almond-shaped eyes met his gaze again, and his sudden slow burn that had taken over ignited into a roaring, full-tilt wildfire again.

Their lips met, mouths tasting and devouring each other in desperate kisses. It was all hot kisses, whimpers, shameless moans, primal grunts, and heavy, gasping breaths. Gabriella's hand slid over his cock, pumping him with impatient, thirsty strokes. Emerson dipped his fingers into the small fabric covering her hot, wet sex, and swiped over her clit. A finger slid down her slick crease and he felt his inner caveman pound his chest with pride at how wet and needy she was for him.

For at least three seconds longer than he should have, he allowed himself to imagine what it would be like to pull aside the meager piece of silk that separated her warm, wanting pussy from his cock and dive into her bare. He wouldn't be able to do it for just a few pumps. Once inside, he thought he'd settle into that new home nicely.

Blinking that savage daydream out of his head, he began blindly reaching and grasping for his discarded jeans. He didn't intend for their hand-play to last long. He wanted to be inside her. If all she wanted from him was to fuck, he was going to fuck. And he was going to make every second count.

There were three condoms in his wallet, still attached in the row, and he pulled them all out, tearing one off and tearing it open. He mentally high-fived his morning self for putting more than one condom in his wallet- he had a feeling they might use them all tonight.

Gabriella watched as he rolled the condom down his hard thickness, licking her lips, all too eager to climb aboard. Emerson grabbed the black string of her thong, but instead of pushing it down, he used his other hand to help twist and snap the damn thing off. It fell to the floor and her eyes were ablaze with lust. Her soft hands slid up his arms and held his shoulders as she placed herself over his waiting cock, fisted at the base by Emerson's firm hand. She slid down onto him and they both moaned, mouths coming together again, feeling the vibrations of each other's pleasured sounds deep inside.

He dug his fingers into her ass as he watched her move in a slow, sensual motion. Her gasps and moans fell in time with her body rocking against his and he fought the urge to close his eyes. It felt so fucking good. Her pussy was wrapped so tight around him, sliding up and down, taking him in and out. Instead, he watched her face, where her eyes were closed in pure bliss. Her lips were parted ever so slightly and he couldn't fight the urge to suck her bottom lip between his teeth.

Tracing his hand up her spine, his mouth trailed wet and hot over her neck again. He found the clasp of her bra and snapped it open, hungrily pulling her bra off and slipping it under her desk, determined to hide it from her. With her breasts freed, they had his full attention. His mouth, hands, tongue, teeth.

"*Fuck*...oh fuck, Gabby, fuck me harder. Ride that fucking cock," he groaned. "Ride it like it's yours, baby, no one else's."

He nearly expected her to tease him or laugh, or even tell him to fuck off and let her do him how she wanted, but he was delightfully surprised when she obliged. She increased her pace, she rode him like she was using him, fucking him for her pleasure and hers alone. He loved it. Loved seeing her let go of some of that control. He even loved that he could be there for her to use. How fucked up was that? He wanted her, wanted more than sex, more than a casual orgasm once or twice a week, but he was more than happy to let her use him if that's all she wanted.

With both hands, he gripped her ass tight, pulling, yanking her down onto him harder. Her tits bounced and he covered a nipple with his mouth, circling his tongue around it and feeling it grow taut and tight in his mouth.

"Oh *god*...Oh *god, yes,*" Gabriella panted. He set his hooded gaze on her intently, watching her get off on him.

"Yeah, baby, that's it," he whispered. "Use me, fucking use me."

"Emerson," she moaned. *"Lo quiero, papi- Aye Dios mio, lo quiero mucho."*

Okay, so Emerson didn't understand a whole lot of Spanish, but he was pretty sure "papi" en español was the equivalent to "daddy" in English. Hearing those pleading words out of Gabriella's sexy mouth, he could've sworn his cock felt at least twice its normal size.

"Fuck yes," he breathed. He was sweating as he thrust into her. "Holy fuck, yeah baby, keep talking to me like that."

"Lo quiero, papi, por favor! Por favor, dámelo! Dura, papi, dura!"

His eyes rolled back as he lost all control, lost in her and everything she was doing to him.

Gabriella leaned into him, pressed her mouth to his temple and cried out through pleasured moans; a euphoric agony as she clamped tightly around him. Waves crashing and spilling over. As she rode out her orgasm, Emerson felt the compression of her sex milking him, taking him for all he was worth, just as he'd told her he wanted. While she was trying to come down from her bliss, he thrust into her, hard and fast, with primitive grunts before white light danced behind his eyes and he released. His low groan vibrated into her breast, his legs shook beneath her, and he came so goddamn hard he saw stars.

As if acting on their own, his arms enveloped her, holding her body close to his as he struggled to catch his breath. His head lay against her chest and he listened to her rapid heartbeat. It was beating fast, but he was willing to bet it had nothing on his. His heart was threatening to pound right out of his chest, and his lungs felt like they'd shriveled up and were no longer accepting new oxygen.

It was panic. The feeling engulfing his chest in an ice bath was panic. He barely recognized the emotion, but that's what it was, and he was freaking the fuck out.

He had feelings. Real ones. Real, immediate, insatiable feelings that threatened to chip away at the hard, metal armor that surrounded the stubborn organ beneath his ribs.

Great…he was forming attachments, and the sex was making those attachments more intense, more real…a lot harder to ignore.

His breathing increased in speed and intensity, and the only way he knew to calm down was to keep holding her. The very source of his problem.

Unaware of just how loudly he was breathing- panting or perhaps hyperventilating- he startled when he realized Gabriella was talking to him.

Both her hands were cupping his jaw, tilting his face up to hers where her brows were pinched together with concern. "Hey…hey, Emeril, are you okay?"

The random *E* name made him chuckle a small breath of laughter. He looked into her beautiful brown eyes and offered a half-hearted smile. "Emeril? Like that guy on the cooking channel?"

She smirked and her eyebrow twitched. "Bam."

He laughed quietly again. "Yeah, I'm okay." He slid his hand behind her neck and pulled her mouth to his, kissing gently. This was new to him, all this kissing on the mouth and kissing after sex, but it soothed him. It grounded him and pulled him out of his spiraling panic.

Taking a slow, steadying breath in and out, he focused his energy on the task at hand. He slipped off his spent condom, tied and tossed it into the wastebasket in the corner before reaching for the two remaining foil packets on the floor next to him.

"I was just worried that…we only crossed the first thing off our list and I only brought three condoms."

Armor back in place, he flashed his devilish grin, letting Gabriella know he'd make sure she got exactly what she came for and then some before flipping her onto her back and making deep-crazy-good on the one promise he knew how to keep.

Chapter 15

For the next couple weeks as May transitioned into June, Emerson continued making good on his promise whenever and wherever Gabriella wanted him. She was adamant about never going to his place and never hooking up in a bed. He'd learned to get creative and was now skilled at scouting out different secluded hallways and quiet spaces for them to be alone so that he was ready when she was.

They'd driven out to a quiet spot overlooking the lake and steamed up his Lexus, frantically fucking in the front seat like horny teenagers, or in the back seat of her Lincoln. The office library after regular working hours, the second floor storage closet during a lunch break, any room on the top floor which was currently abandoned due to a remodel was typically fair game, though they'd had a few close calls. The closest they'd come to getting discovered was by a construction worker on the top floor, but either he hadn't been particularly observant as he walked by the plastic tarp that was working as a temporary door, or he'd chosen to pretend not to see anything.

There had been one time Gabriella had invited him to her place for wine and gossip night with Marco and Max- okay, he'd overheard them talking about it on the phone and invited himself. As soon as her brother and brother-in-law had left her condo, she gave him *the look* and he fucked her on the kitchen island, the couch, up against the wall. Anywhere but the bedroom.

The sex was fucking incredible. Amazing, euphoric, phenomenal. Each time was a celestial experience that made him swear he was getting closer to God. Or maybe he'd just gotten so used to worshiping every inch of her body he'd somehow convinced himself that she *was* God.

It was also turning him into the very type of man he always took pity on. He was like a loyal, overly-eager puppy, waiting for his master to get home and play with him. She had him wrapped around her little finger and he would bend to her will. All she had to do was give him the slightest quirk of her eyebrow, the smallest tug of her grin, even the beckoning crook of her finger and he was there. Panting, on all fours, ready to fucking please her.

He was pussy-whipped. And that wasn't even the worst part.

Pleasing Gabriella, fucking her, making her come, learning her body, memorizing each curve and the way she liked to be touched was one thing. One sultry, alluring, heavenly thing...but each time was more intense. Each time he let loose inside her, he felt more. He wanted more, craved more. His armor wasn't just being chipped away, it was being melted. With each explosion of liquid heat, the fire burned stronger, the yearning for her grew more and more insatiable. But he shoved it down, because that was all she wanted. He shoved it down because, even if she did want more, he didn't trust himself to give her everything she deserved.

It was a Thursday afternoon and Emerson was at the gym working out the lingering frustration that the previous night's fuck-fest hadn't relieved. His weight training regimen was strict and intense, and it operated on a five day split. Five days on, each one targeting a different muscle group or set, followed by two days of rest. Mondays and Tuesdays were his rest days; he felt it helped him ease into his work week if he didn't have anything pressing to do as soon as he got home on those days.

On Thursdays, he worked his shoulders and lats, and as he finished his final set of negative pull ups- an exercise that focuses on the downward motion of a pull up, done slowly for best results- he heard a shrill commotion from the other side of the gym, even with his headphones blaring Rage Against the Machine into his ears. He turned his head and narrowed his eyes, thinking for a second that he recognized the arguing couple.

The man stood in front of the military press bench and wore a backward Yankees ball cap, a classic 80's style muscle tank, and gray shorts that were a little shorter than anything Emerson might feel comfortable wearing in public. The young woman next to him wore black jogging shorts with turquoise compression shorts underneath, and a cropped white t-shirt. With one hand on her hip and the other flying all around as she yelled, Emerson knew that thick, caramel-brown mane of curls was familiar. Recognition dawned just as Emerson lip-read the words "Fuck you" on the guy's mouth in perfect time with Zach de la Rocha's aggressive chant of the same two words through his eardrum-splitting headphones.

Emerson's eyes went wide and white hot rage ignited in his chest, and before he could make a conscious decision to make any sort of move he was stomping down the center of the gym, fists clenched, chest out, and muscles tensed from the previous hour and a half of physical exertion. He didn't care that his muscles were fatigued. Something about Lizzie Miller's sweet, naive innocence made him feel protective like he assumed a big brother would. And seeing that asshole, *Kyle*, yell at her like that, disrespect her and cause a scene in fucking public? That shit wasn't okay.

He yanked his headphones off and let them rest around his neck, and as he got closer to the little punk, he was feeling pretty damn good about how this was going to go.

"Is there a problem over here?" Emerson asked, causing Kyle to turn and look at him. Outwardly, his expression remained stoic, though on the inside he was chest thumping and grunting like a neanderthal at the obvious fear in the kid's face.

"Oh, hey Emerson," Lizzie said, and he could see the tension dissolve slightly in her demeanor. Her brow furrowed and she appeared to be sucking on the inside of her cheek when she offered Kyle a brief sideways glance."We're fine."

Emerson trained his gaze back on Kyle, piercing him with a steely glare. "Didn't look fine from where I was standing."

Kyle stood up straighter and collected some of the cockiness Emerson remembered observing at the bar several weeks ago when they'd met. "She said she's fine," Kyle insisted, lifting his chin and looking like a total douchebag.

Emerson stepped closer, deliberately getting in Kyle's space and peering down at him. "You'd better hope that's true."

Emerson wasn't one for fighting- not physically, at least. But he knew how he looked, he knew his muscles and tattoos probably made it look like he was used to kicking ass and taking names, even though all of his best fights were won with head games and manipulation. He also knew that if he had to throw a punch, he could put this scrawny shit to the floor easily.

Kyle's jaw clenched as he looked Emerson up and down, then looked at Lizzie. "Who is this guy, Liz? Here you are worried about me going to Brock's party tonight and you've got men all over wanting to defend your honor."

Lizzie put her hands on her hips and narrowed her eyes. "I don't trust Brock. I know what you guys are like when you all get together and I think it's weird that you won't even bother to ask me to go with you."

"Babe, I told you it's a guys' night."

"Don't *babe* me right now," Lizzie snapped. "I overheard Brock on the phone talking about the girls coming up from Mount Pleasant to be there, so don't tell me it's just a guys' night."

Kyle clenched his jaw again, clearly caught- and clearly not smart enough to talk his way out of it, so he abruptly switched lanes. "Still doesn't explain who this guy is. Jesus, Liz, we can barely go anywhere without running into a guy you've fucked."

Emerson raised his eyebrows before blowing out a humorless laugh. "I'm not one of Lizzie's exes, *bro*. I'm a friend of her brother's."

Kyle scoffed and took a step back. "Whatever man, doesn't make her any less of a slut."

Instantly, his fists clenched as the rage he'd felt only minutes ago boiled over. He didn't have time to think before his arm cocked back, and he'd never punched anyone before, but it seemed like his body knew what to do.

But then he stopped. He watched a much smaller fist than his own connect with Kyle's jaw and send him staggering backward.

Eyes wide, Emerson watched as Lizzie stood up straight again and shook out her hand. She was heaving, and her eyes were set in a furrowed glower. "Fuck you, Kyle."

Kyle held his jaw and slid it as if setting it back in place before moving toward Lizzie again. "You fucking bitch-"

Emerson stuck his arm out, practically clothes-lining the fucker, and stepped between them. "You might want to quit while you're ahead, kid."

"I'm not fucking afraid of your gym muscles, bro," he sneered. "This is between me and my girlfriend, so you need to get the fuck out of the way."

Lizzie laughed humorlessly behind Emerson. She stepped around him to look at Kyle. "You don't actually think I'm still your girlfriend after this, do you?"

He watched as Kyle's expression changed from a brief look of shock back into his standard douchebag glare. "Fine, that's fine. I was about done with your whoring ass anyway."

This time Emerson reached him first. He grabbed Kyle's muscleless muscle shirt and walked him backwards until his back was shoved-hard- against the mirrored wall. "Listen Kyle, I know it's not your fault your parents gave you a name that destined you to be a raging dick-bag, but you need to learn when enough is e-fucking-nough. I knew you weren't good enough for her when I met you a month ago, but I figured, hey, Lizzie's a big girl, she can make her own decisions. That being said, I swear to God, if you are ever within a ten-foot radius of Lizzie Miller ever again, I will find out. And then I will find you and use my *gym muscles* to rip your goddamn dick off through your throat. Got it?"

Kyle's eyes were wide and terrified, and rather than being on Emerson's face, they were on his hands where he gripped his shirt, possibly realizing how big his hands were and imagining them making good on that threat. Kyle swallowed and nodded.

Emerson held the kid there for a few more beats before releasing him and taking a few steps back, turning toward Lizzie. Her back was turned and he thought he saw her swiping at her eyes. So, feeling wildly out of his league, he placed a gentle hand on her back. "You okay, Lizz?"

She nodded and sniffled. "I'm fine. I just…need some ice."

His voice was low and, he hoped, calming, "Why don't you go get your stuff out of the locker room and meet me out here? We can go get you some ice for that hand."

Lizzie nodded again, but avoided his gaze before walking toward the women's locker rooms with her head down. Emerson let a slow breath out through his nose and turned to glare at Kyle again. His hands clenched into fists at his sides and he wished he'd punched him when he had the chance.

He grabbed his black and lime green Nike bag off the floor on the other side of the gym where he'd been working out and headed into the locker room to change. He conceded to shower at his own place, thinking that Lizzie needed someone at the moment more than he needed to smell decent. After mixing two scoops of protein powder into his Blender Bottle, he walked out to meet Lizzie by the front desk.

Lizzie sighed heavily, and he hated that her eyes and nose were both red from holding back tears. "I didn't even get my workout in…I was supposed to do cardio today."

He grinned, then put his arm around her shoulders, leading her toward the exit. "Don't worry, Baby Miller, I've got a great cardio workout we can do at my place."

"Oh my God, it's so hard!" Lizzie exclaimed, sweat dripping down her face as she struggled to keep up.

"You're overthinking it. Just let your body take over," Emerson said, coaching her through it. "Up, down, up, down."

"You're really good at this."

"I can't believe this is your first time."

Lizzie's face was set in concentration, breathing heavy, drenched in sweat in the middle of his living room.

"Yes! Just like that!"

She threw her hands up and her head back shouting, "Oh my God, yes! That was so good!" Dropping her hands, she staggered back and flopped onto the leather couch. "Let's take a break."

Emerson used his PS4 remote to click back to the home screen where electronica music continued to play on a loop. He kicked the dance pads out of the way and joined Lizzie on the couch, equally sweaty from their many rounds of Dance Dance Revolution.

"Please tell me you play this when you're home alone," Lizzie said, laughing a little. "It would be a little sad and make me feel a lot better about my life right now."

"Baby Miller, I do a lot of things by myself. The joys of living alone," he replied.

"Do you enjoy it?" she asked.

He shrugged. "It has its perks."

"I would be so bored without a roommate," she said. "I would probably drive Jett crazy with how often I'd be at his house just for some company."

"I do that anyway, and I think I only go over there like once a week." Emerson smiled and Lizzie returned it. He reached over to the end of the couch where his t-shirt lay discarded and used it to wipe the sweat off his face.

"How do you do it?" Lizzie asked suddenly after several beats of nothing but Cascada's *Everytime We Touch* filled the room.

Emerson reached for his remote and muted the television. "Do what?" he asked, then gestured toward the silent game on the screen. "I've been playing DDR since middle school. Kolbe kicks my ass though-"

"No, not that," Lizzie said, shaking her head. "How do you...keep sex casual? Just not get attached? I can't do it, so I have this laundry list of ex-boyfriends who all stick around for a couple weeks or a couple months."

"Are you trying to keep it casual?" he questioned. "I was under the impression that you actually liked these guys and wanted it to work out."

"I'm not, and I do. I don't want to do the casual sex thing, but maybe it would be easier. Or maybe I just need to become a nun. Nuns don't need boys."

Emerson laughed. "You don't need a boy either. First of all, you're good enough by yourself. You shouldn't ever feel like you *need* someone else. But if you *want* someone to be with, then you should want a *man*, not a boy. There's a big difference."

She chewed the inside of her cheek, considering his advice for a moment. "I blame Jett," she declared finally. "And Gavin. If Jett and Gavin hadn't given me such unrealistic expectations of what real men were like, then I wouldn't constantly feel like my relationships were doomed from the start."

He laughed again. "You feel like they're doomed from the start, but you go into them anyway?"

"When you have men like Jett and Gavin in your life, and then you get out into the world and realize that guys just aren't like that, you know no one is going to measure up so you just pick one and think, 'hey, maybe this one will be okay', and you go for it."

"Jett is a pretty good guy," he said, nodding. "A little grumpy sometimes, but he's good."

Lizzie sat up and stretched, then grabbed her Hydroflask off the end table. "Mind if I refill my water bottle?"

"There's water and ice in the door of the fridge."

She got up and he followed her into the kitchen, seating himself on one of the bar stools around the kitchen island. The clang of ice dropping into stainless steel echoed through the room and Emerson checked his phone. Nothing from Gabriella. His heart sank a little. He hadn't seen her much at work that day because she was out with clients. Not for the first time he wished he'd asked Tom to name him as her partner in the Alpha case. He didn't like the idea of Gabriella out wining and dining clients, charming them, and getting checked out by pervy old men.

"Shit!" Lizzie exclaimed suddenly. "Oh crap...this sucks." She sunk into the bar stool next to him and put her head in her hands.

"What's wrong?"

"Quinn and Raelyn's wedding is Saturday and now I don't have a date! How am I supposed to find a date in two days?"

"Oh shit, that is this weekend, isn't it?" he said, wondering how he should feel about it. He wondered if he was supposed to feel weird or anxious or moody. His ex-fiancé, the woman he called *his* girl for three whole years, the one woman who'd even come close to proving himself wrong about who he was...In just two days, she was getting married to someone else. Being married off to another man.

Lizzie gasped and sat up straight. "Oh, I'm sorry. I forgot- or at least I wasn't thinking about- Is that weird for you? I'm sorry, I'm such an idiot-"

"No, no, you're good. It's fine. I'm fine," he assured her. And funny enough, he was fine. Sure, he liked to give All-Star a hard time and pretend like he was going to steal Rae back for a crazy, reminiscent night of wild sex, but he didn't mean it. At least, not anymore.

"Really?" Lizzie questioned.

"Yeah, I'm...I'm happy for her." He swore he meant them, but that didn't make the words any less sour on their way out.

Lizzie laughed, and he assumed he was making some sort of face. "You sound like it."

"I am," he insisted. "I'm glad she's happy, even if it's with an arrogant asshole like All-Star. I guess I just...I don't know, it still feels like I lost. And I don't like to lose."

"But if what you lost wasn't what you wanted...aren't you still winning?" she challenged.

Emerson hummed and tilted his head to the side. "I like the way you think, Baby Miller."

Lizzie took a long chug from her ice water and then eyed him curiously. "So...what's your lady situation like these days? Still got Olivia and Jessica and Monica and whoever else coming and going like a revolving porn-door of orgasms?"

He choked on his laugh. "That sounds fucking awesome, actually, but sadly no."

"No?" She grinned at him in a way that suggested she already knew. "Tyler said you've been spending a lot of time with a certain Gabriella Cabrera-Perez...sounds like one hot mamacita."

Nodding, he answered, "Yeah, she is. I mean, the other girls are still there kind of. I...well, I kind of told them that I'd be working nights and weekends for the foreseeable future and I'd let them know when I'd be available again."

Lizzie straightened and her eyes went wide as she smiled. "Oooh reallyyyy?"

He shrugged. "Sex with Gabby is good. Really good. I don't mind focusing my energy on that."

"Mhmm...but it's not just sex, is it?"

He narrowed his eyes. "Yes. It is."

"Aw love, you're usually such a good liar, but you're off today."

"Rae told you," he stated, then pressed his lips together, annoyed.

"You may have been mentioned at her bachelorette party last weekend."

Arching an eyebrow, he thought about Rae and her friends all drinking, getting crazy and acting single again, dressed in little black dresses and other skimpy outfits...talking about him. He didn't hate the thought.

"You girls all sat around talking about me, huh?" he asked, grinning slyly. "Why? Was the stripper not doing it for you and Rae thought, 'man, if only Emerson were here, I wouldn't feel so disappointed'?"

Lizzie scoffed. "Oh please. She's marrying a hunky, multi-millionaire professional athlete. His muscles are sculpted by professionals and from what I hear, it's not just his *baseball* bat that he's skilled with."

Emerson made a face. "Gross."

"She said you actually liiiike someone," she cooed, sounding like a schoolgirl.

"I don't want to talk about it."

Lizzie laced her fingers together, placed her elbows on the kitchen island, and set her chin on top of her hands, batting and fluttering her eyelashes with a smile.

"It's just sex," he insisted. "That's all she wants from me and that works because…it's all I can give her anyway."

"But you want more from her?" she queried. "That must be an interesting change for you."

Emerson shook his head. "None of the women I'm with want anything more either. They know the deal. We hook up, no attachments, no relationships come of it. It's an efficient system."

"You mean the women you *were* with. Doesn't sound like you're with them anymore."

"I already told you-"

"That you told them you're unavailable until further notice, yeah. Because you, Emerson Yates, are a one-woman man. Even if it is *just sex*." Lizzie used air-quotes on the last two words.

He laughed. "No I'm not."

Lizzie stared back, unyielding with a smug smirk on her face. He broke eye contact first, feeling his palms go clammy. He swallowed and tried to focus on something else, and was mercifully saved by his phone ringing.

Perhaps too eagerly, he snatched it off the counter and read the name flashing across the screen: Tyler Watson. He swiped to answer, "Hey Ty, what's up?"

"Hey man, I was just trying to see what you're up to. I had a few missed calls from you this week, and since I'm going to be busy this weekend with all the wedding stuff...I thought maybe you'd want to get a drink? Or I could stop by for some Halo? We could go to Brody's and hang out in the pub...whatever."

Emerson smiled, appreciating the fact that he'd attained yet another thoughtful friend. It had been a while since the guys had all sat around in the garden shed Brody had converted into an Irish pub in his backyard, and it sounded like a great way to spend his night if Gabriella wasn't going to hit him up.

He glanced up at Lizzie's questioning eyes and a stroke of fucking genius flared in his mind. It was about a month or so ago when Lizzie brought Kyle to the bar on Union street, and he could have sworn there was a spark, a flicker...*something* like chemistry or attraction between Tyler and Lizzie. Grinning wider and more mischievously now, he spoke into the phone, "Yeah, Ty, that sounds like a good time. I'm not alone right now, but-"

"Oooh, well if Gabby doesn't want to let you go for the night-"

"No, it's not Gabby," he interrupted. Lizzie's eyes went wide with warning and she shook her head vigorously and began silently mouthing *"No! Don't you dare!"*

"Oh?" Tyler sounded curious, and maybe a little disappointed. All of Emerson's friends were currently enjoying the fact that he'd been catering to Gabriella so consistently. He hadn't given them all the details, but apparently it was still obvious. "Well, that lasted like...two and a half weeks, right? Longer than usual."

Emerson resisted the urge to grind his teeth. Yep. That was exactly why he wouldn't give Gabriella more. He wasn't capable of it, and everyone knew it.

The sudden frustration made him bite out his response. "It's Lizzie, actually. Lizzie Miller."

Lizzie gasped silently and began smacking his arm repeatedly. "My brother is going to kill you!" she whisper-yelled.

Having to take the phone away from his ear to deflect Lizzie's slaps and punches, he finally grabbed her forearm and held her away at arm's length. He put his phone back to his ear and couldn't disguise his laugh entirely as he said, "Sorry Ty, what was that? She is just all over me right now."

The other end of the line was silent.

"Ty, you there?"

More silence.

Finally the sound of a throat clearing came through the phone followed by Tyler's hushed, low voice. "Emerson, are you fucking serious right now? Jett is going to murder you. Twice."

"Nonsense," he replied. "I ran into her this morning and she looked tense, so I offered a little cardio workout to relieve the stress. We were just taking a water break before we get back at it."

Tyler let out a long sigh. "Dude, you better hope this doesn't get back to her brother. This is…this is low, man."

"How's he going to find out?" he asked. "I mean, you wouldn't tell him, would you? Unless…you are upset about it…"

Lizzie's brow pinched together, confused.

"You know, I might. I've known Jett my whole life and he's your friend, too! You…he's made it pretty damn clear that he doesn't want you near her. He knows what you're like, and Liz…she has enough assholes swarming her as it is. You don't need to add to it. Dammit, man, I thought you at least knew how to set some kind of boundaries-"

"Are you mad on Jett's behalf, or yours?"

There was a pause and he heard the struggle as Tyler tried to figure out the correct answer. "Both, I guess! Fuck, man! Maybe I should beat your ass for Jett…it would be the kinder thing to do."

Emerson hummed, pleased at Tyler's reaction.

"All right, Ty. Do what you need to do. I should get back to Baby Miller. I'll see you tonight at Brody's. Five o'clock? That should give us enough time to shower off all the sweat we've worked up," he said with every ounce of cocky pride he could muster. "The girl is in shape- *whoo!* See ya, Ty!"

Lizzie stared at him, jaw dropped and completely furious. "I can't believe you just did that."

He waved his hand dismissively, "Eh, you'll explain when you see him at the wedding."

"You just made Tyler think we were hooking up!" she screeched. "*Tyler Watson!* What the hell is wrong with you?"

"Is that bad?" he asked, curiously. "If it makes you feel better he sounded a little jealous. Definitely pissed, but also jealous."

Her eyebrows raised. "Really?" Then she shook her head. "If he tells my brother-"

"Hey! Why don't you ask Tyler to be your date? Last I checked he was flying solo," he cut her off with his brilliant idea, bringing the plan full circle.

Lizzie scoffed and took another sip of water. "Yeah, I'll get right on that."

"Why not?"

She spun the cap back onto her water bottle and he sensed she was stalling. Finally she shook her head. "Tyler...he wouldn't...I'm not really his type, I don't think."

"What's his type? I've never seen him with anyone."

She stuttered and fidgeted some more. "I don't know, just...not me. He wouldn't ever think of me that way, that's all."

He watched her for a few beats, observing. Did she like him but think he was out of her league? Was there history there that he didn't know about? Eventually, he broke the silence. "Fine, if Tyler doesn't want to go with you, I'll be your date."

She laughed at this. "Not a chance. My brother would kill you even more, and Quinn would finally have the excuse to punch you that he's been looking for since you two met. Not to mention, I don't need to get on the bride's bad side."

"You make a solid case." He sighed and heaved himself off the stool. "Don't worry, I'll clear everything up when I see him later. You wanna do a few more rounds or...are you ready to hit the showers?"

Receiving yet another well-deserved punch to his arm, he laughed and followed Lizzie back into the living room. Teasing was just in his nature, but as they settled back on his couch after another few songs, he knew without a doubt he would never subject Lizzie to his…well, him-ness. He'd never had a little sister, nor had he ever really had any girlfriends who were just friends, no one he ever felt particularly protective of other than Kolbe. He'd also never had a relationship with a woman in which she didn't find him exceptionally more interesting with his clothes off.

Emerson let Lizzie take a shower first and said that when he was done, he'd take her out to lunch before dropping her back off at her house. She'd tried to talk him into Ben & Jerry's and watching *John Tucker Must Die*, but he felt he'd filled his brotherly duties for the day. Maybe next time. Baby steps.

They were both dressed and getting ready to leave when there was a knock on his door. He hadn't been expecting anyone, but his apartment complex had a doorman and a security guard at the desk, so anyone coming up now would have to be someone whose name he'd given to the desk already. Just last week he'd written Gabriella's name down, even though she had never been there before, but for a second he was hopeful.

But when he opened the door to see Jett standing in the hallway, Tyler, Chris, and All-Star flanking him, he deflated a little.

"Hey man! What's-"

That's all he was able to get out before Jett's fist connected with his jaw and sent him staggering back into the wall.

"What the *fuck?!*" Emerson yelled, groaning through the pain. His hand instinctively cradled his jaw and when it came away from his face, there was blood on it. His lip was bleeding.

"Jett!" Lizzie shrieked from somewhere in the apartment. He was slightly disoriented.

"I thought we agreed I got to do that!" All-Star's voice shouted over the ringing in Emerson's ears.

Jett was coming at him again and he put a hand up as Lizzie jumped between them. "Jett, *stop!* Nothing even happened! He was just messing with you guys!"

Jett's brow was furrowed, eyes glaring as he looked back and forth between Emerson and his little sister. "So why are you here?" he demanded.

"He saw me at the gym with Kyle, we got in a fight and broke up. I said I didn't even get my cardio in, so he brought me back here. We were actually working out," Lizzie explained.

"You were?" Tyler asked, stepping up behind Jett.

"Yes," Emerson confirmed. "Damn, you were quick to tell on me...and really quick to assemble the fucking A-Team, *Jesus*."

"Oh...well, then...sorry about that," said Jett. He clapped his hand on Emerson's shoulder and tilted his head. "You okay?"

"I'm fine," Emerson sighed, straightening. "You know I'd never been in a fight before today and now I've been part of two. I gotta stay away from you Millers. *Fuck*."

"Two?" Jett questioned, eyeing his youngest sister.

"You've *never* been in a fight before?" Quinn asked, as though he were accusing him of never having eaten an Oreo before.

"No, never. And Kyle was being a dick. He said some things that I didn't like all that much," he replied. "Lizzie punched him and I shoved his scrawny ass against the wall and told him to stay away from Lizz if he doesn't want his dick ripped off through his throat."

"Nice," All-Star laughed as the others nodded approvingly.

"You did that? For her?" Jett asked.

Emerson shrugged. "Of course."

Jett was quiet for a moment, then the corner of his mouth tugged up. "Thanks. And sorry again for punching you. It's just what big brothers do."

"You're forgiven," Emerson said, shaking Jett's hand.

"So..." Chris, who had been silently observing behind everyone, stepped in. "Does that mean you and Gabriella are still a thing?"

"Um..." he hesitated. "Yeah, it's still...there's something there."

"How about we all talk about it over lunch?" Lizzie suggested. "Emerson was about to take me to get some food, but I think it's only fair that Jett buys Emerson's lunch."

Jett looked disapprovingly at Lizzie for a second, but caved. All of them went out to lunch together and Emerson gave another update of what was going on between him and Gabriella. The guys all chimed in with their advice, and Lizzie gave hers.

She insisted that they needed to help each other since they were both lost when it came to the whole dating thing. Emerson agreed to coach her and give her advice whenever she needed it, including but not limited to what to wear on dates, whether a guy was worth a first or second date, and ironically to let her know when the time was right to get physical in relationships. He promised to let her know when he thought a guy was only interested in sex and even offered to be there to break it off if need be.

In return, Lizzie and everyone else gave Emerson one major piece of advice: Tell Gabriella the truth about how he feels. He needed to tell her that he wasn't seeing anyone else and that their fuck buddies situation wasn't enough.

Emerson laughed. "You guys are insane. Why would I ruin a great thing? We can enjoy each other's company and have great sex, and she still doesn't expect anything else from me. Why would I want to change that?"

Of course he knew why he wanted to change it. It wasn't a situation he was particularly familiar with- or at least he wasn't familiar with this side of the situation- but he knew exactly why it wasn't as perfect as it seemed. He could laugh it off all he wanted, but he knew they were right. He had to tell her the truth before someone…before *he*…got hurt.

Chapter 16

"Marco!"

"Polo!" Her brother's enthusiastic voice came through the speaker of her phone on her vanity dresser.

"Help," Gabby pleaded. She was standing in front of the full-length mirror in her bedroom, turning side to side to check out her fourth outfit.

"What's wrong, sis?" Marco asked.

"I'm getting ready for my date and I don't know what to do!"

Marco gasped. "Did Sexy Lawyer Man finally ask you on a real date? It's about damn time. I know you've been having fun, but you two can't keep ignoring your chemistry."

She sighed, frustrated, as the uncomfortable knot twisted in her gut. "No, it's not Emerson. It's that guy, Jesse…You know, the one Mom was going on about last week at dinner? She set us up and I couldn't very well tell her that I have regular, steamy, animalistic sex with a guy from work."

"Not to mention *at* work," Marco chuckled.

Visions of Emerson with his shirt unbuttoned, tie loosened, and his pants slung sinfully low swirled in her mind. The memory of her ankles hooked behind his back, skirt hiked up and her legs pulling him closer, urging him to go deeper clouded her brain and her knees wobbled. Her vaginal walls clenched remembering the rough slide of his cock as he entered from behind and the sensation of his hands on her hips.

One of her desk drawers was now a collection of ripped black nylons because he was always so urgent to get her out of them. It worked out though- They covered the discrete package of condoms she'd stashed in the same drawer quite nicely.

"Right, well," Gabby blew out a long breath before continuing, "*Sexy Lawyer Man* has made it perfectly clear that he doesn't date. Even the time he asked me on a date and then brought the date to me...I don't know. It was like he was turning into someone else. He was sweet and we just talked all night. I told him about Ben, and he told me that he liked me. He said he'd bug me for a second date...and then I kissed him and it was like a switch flipped...Just like that, he was adamant that he couldn't give me more."

"But you jumped his bones anyway," Marco so eloquently pointed out.

She laughed. "I can't say I regret it. I mean, sure, I was starting to like him, but...the sex is *really* good. I guess I just wanted whatever he'd give me at that point."

It was true; their sex was *amazing*. The fervent grasping at each other's clothing, the taste of his mouth against hers, the way he felt on top of her, below, and behind her...*inside* her. And the orgasms- *the orgasms!* Plural. As in multiple. Each time, without fail! She hadn't told him yet, but he was the first man to ever give her orgasms- again, *plural!-* from vaginal stimulation alone. She'd always relied on her trusty clitoris to bring her over the edge, but with Emerson nothing seemed to fail. His touch, his mouth, his magnificently large penis. It. All. Worked.

What didn't work, unfortunately, was her ability to woo him in some other way. She didn't understand why he felt so certain that he couldn't be in a relationship. He clearly knew how to be generous, and he was thoughtful. Despite their sex-only situation, he never failed to show her that he thought about her. He'd bring her coffee from Starbucks, ask her to join him for lunch which he frequently bought. The previous week when she was stuck with clients and couldn't make it out in time to pick Robby up from practice, Emerson had mentioned that he was getting Kolbe anyway, so he'd offered to drop Robby off, too.

But...somehow, all he was capable of was sex. So, she reminded herself- at least ten times a day- that their arrangement was purely physical. Any other attraction, any feelings she developed were futile. She would swallow them down and put on her big girl panties- figuratively, since they were more literally being stripped off- and accept the no-strings-attached arrangement because it was absolutely the best sex she'd ever experienced. He wasn't lying when he said he could make her want to hate him and thank him at the same time.

"You deserve it," Marco insisted. "Casual sex is a blast and I'm glad you're having fun. But you also deserve to have a man take you out and treat you like a lady. Where's this Jesse guy taking you?"

"Chateau Delecroix up on the peninsula. I guess it's a winery with a fantastic French restaurant."

"Oooh!" Marco exclaimed. "I've heard it's beautiful, but pricey. Max and I have been meaning to make it up there. Let me know if it lives up to the hype and maybe we can do a double date next weekend."

"So it's fancy?" she asked. "Should I wear a dress?"

"Wear your red wrap dress with the long sleeves and the deep V," her brother stated. "No nylons, this is not a work function. Bare legs, and your sexy, strappy Louis Vuitton heels. Have you had a pedicure recently?"

Gabby went back to her closet and began sliding through her dress rack. "How do you know my closet this well?"

"I'm nosey," he replied. "I snooped in your closet. I wanted to make sure you had more than just pencil skirts and silk blouses- Don't get me wrong, you look amazing in those, but in the chance you ever got a date, such as now, I wanted to know you had something that brought on more than sexy office secretary fantasies."

She found the correct dress and heels and stood in front of the mirror once again. "Marco, this is a really deep V...but I do look good. Maybe I look too good for a first date. Is that a thing? Too sexy? Too...va-va-voom?"

"Absolutely not! This is your first impression you're giving him. The first date is the time to show him just how good it can be. Go shave those legs, girl! Paint your toenails, and call me when you get home!" Leaving no room for debate, Marco hung up and Gabby was left with nothing to do but get ready for her date.

At 7 o'clock, Jesse Park, a tall and handsome black-haired, olive-skinned high school science teacher knocked on her door. They smiled politely and introduced themselves before setting off in his silver Ford Fusion up the Leelanau Peninsula to Chateau Delecroix.

Apparently Gabby's mother had met him at Lola's last parent-teacher conference and had basically asked him every question that would go on a dating profile: Are you single? Do you have kids? How old are you? Do you want kids? What are some of your hobbies? Would you date a woman who makes more money than you? Do you like baseball?

Having checked off enough boxes, Evelyn then started spilling all sorts of information about her daughter who just needed to meet people since she was new in town.

"I hope she didn't make me sound too desperate," Gabby said. "I've barely been here two months and I already have a heavy caseload at work."

Jesse laughed. "Not at all, no. Besides, my own mom can be brutal at times. I know it sounds like a Korean stereotype, but she is constantly trying to find me a 'nice girl' to 'settle down' with. She tries setting me up with someone about twice a month."

"I haven't lived in the same state as my family for years…I wonder if that's my mom's plan, too." She took a sip from one of the three tasting glasses in front of her. She and Jesse had each ordered a flight of wine to try while they waited on dinner, and she had three dry to semi-dry whites to choose from, while Jesse had opted for reds.

The first glass she tasted was an oak-aged chardonnay made with grapes picked from a 38-year-old vine. It was exquisite.

Gabby then wondered if she enjoyed the chardonnay more than Jesse's company.

They continued talking, covering basic first date topics like favorite movies and books, hobbies, and what their favorite thing about their jobs were. It was a similar conversation to the one she'd had with

Emerson in her office over bacon cheeseburgers and beer, but it felt completely different. Jesse was nice. He was polite and charming, though not in a devilish way. She felt like he may truly be One of the Good Ones that Emerson had so persistently insisted he was not.

Jesse gave all the right responses to her questions, was thoughtful and intelligent, but there was something missing. By the time she'd finished her flight and ordered a full glass of the first chardonnay, she realized that she wanted him to say something that she could argue with. She wanted him to say something cocky or arrogant so she could roll her eyes and knock him down a peg or two. She wanted him to say something shocking or blunt or wildly inappropriate so she could pretend to be mad at him about it. But he didn't. He just kept being pleasant. Completely reasonable and non-combative.

About halfway through their meal she excused herself to go to the ladies' room and was surprised to run into a familiar face when she came out of the stall.

"Zoey? What are you doing here? Jett didn't drag you here to be his DD, did he?" Gabby asked. Zoey was wearing a beautiful flowing white sundress with small pink flowers printed on it.

Her eyes widened with recognition and she smiled her happy, welcoming smile. "Gabby! Hey! Oh my gosh, you look amazing! Wait, are you here with Emerson? I know he joked about crashing, but I didn't think he was serious. It's always so hard to tell with him."

"Crashing what?" Gabby questioned.

"Quinn and Rae are having their rehearsal dinner here. They're in the ballroom though, so it's closed off, and I think the security is pretty intense, so tell Emerson good luck getting through."

"Wait- they're here? Now?" Her years-old fantasies of meeting Quinn Casey in the flesh spun around in her head and she had to focus. She blinked magazine-cover photos of Quinn Casey shirtless in baseball pants away. Of course that's not what he would wear to his own wedding rehearsal…though she didn't see why not. "Um, never mind. And actually, no, I'm not here with Emerson. I'm on a date."

Zoey blinked. "A date?"

Nodding, Gabby hummed her confirmation.

"But not with Emerson?" Zoey asked, seeming confused. "Are you guys not- Is everything okay? I thought...As much as he talks about you, I figured..." she trailed off, leaving Gabby at a loss for words.

"Um..." Gabby searched for a way to explain the situation. What had Emerson told his friends? Did he really talk about her all the time? About what? Did he go into detail about their inappropriate yet deeply satisfying and steamy hookups? Was he talking about her like he was just another one of his weekday girls? *Was* she just another one of his weekday girls?

"I'm sorry," Zoey said, waving a hand around her head. "It's really none of my business and I'm starting to get that whole pregnancy brain thing. I just thought you two were really getting along and I was excited for him. I haven't known him that long, but lately he's been different. Good different. Happier, I think. And a lot more bearable because he's not constantly hitting on anything that walks. He likes you...I've never known him to actually *like* a girl before."

"Did he say he likes me?"

"Well, yeah," Zoey replied. "Hasn't he told you?"

Gabby swallowed, suddenly feeling hot and sweaty. Her wrap dress felt too tight and her heels were too high, hurting her ankles. "He's mentioned it, but...I mean, it's Emerson, right? He doesn't do relationships. That's what he says."

"Maybe he hasn't done a lot of them, but that doesn't mean he can't change his mind because he wants to be with you," said Zoey. She lifted one shoulder and lowered it. "All I know is that if he's around, he's talking about you. I get that he's made a lot of mistakes and some questionable choices, but I promise you there's a good guy under there, and I think you bring it out even more. I think you make him want to be the good guy we all know he can be. And if he's told you that he *likes* you- out loud- that's a really big deal. It's honestly kind of monumental."

The bathroom door swung open and a tall, gorgeous blonde walked in wearing a long, dark blue dress with a high slit in the skirt. Her hair was in waves over her shoulder and she looked about as glamorous in person as she did on a magazine cover.

Zoey gasped and reached for Raelyn DeRose's arm. "Rae! This is Gabby- Gabriella..." she looked meaningfully at Emerson's ex-fiancé, with wide, excited eyes.

Raelyn turned toward Gabby and her blue eyes were stunningly bright as she smiled, her red lips curving with a knowing expression. "As in Emerson's Gabriella?" Raelyn looked back at Zoey and laughed. "He's actually trying to crash the rehearsal? For fuck's sake, if it means that much to him, I'll tell the guards to just let him in."

Gabby wasn't sure what to make of her response. Was Raelyn happy for them? Had Emerson talked to his ex- *The Ex*- about her? What would he have said? She stood, contemplating for a moment, trying not to be too obvious in her observation of the last woman Emerson had real feelings for. Gabby wasn't easily intimidated, but it was hard not to feel a little out of her depth compared to Raelyn DeRose.

"She's not here with Emerson," Zoey explained, bringing Gabby back to the present.

Raelyn frowned. "Why not? Did you guys break up? What did he do? He probably did something really stupid-"

"No, no...It's not like that between us. We aren't dating. We haven't been dating, it's just..." she paused, feeling thoroughly embarrassed now to admit the truth to these girls who seemed to know Emerson so well. "I guess it's complicated."

"Complicated how?" Raelyn asked, genuinely curious.

"Honestly...he's really sweet and thoughtful most of the time, but he seems to think he can't do real relationships. I don't really understand why- it seems like he'd actually be pretty good at it..." she trailed off, thinking again about all the romantic gestures Emerson so often made.

Raelyn sighed. "He's in denial. He'll come around. He wouldn't have crashed my lunch with Amira to ask my advice on how to proceed if he didn't plan on doing something eventually."

Gabby's eyebrows pinched together as she remembered spotting the former couple across the street during her own lunch three weeks ago.

He'd been asking about *her?* He'd gone to his ex-fiancé to get advice on how to be in a relationship with *her?*

She couldn't help smiling now. "That explains the dinner he brought me that night…"

Raelyn and Zoey each gave her questioning looks and she went on to explain how Emerson had asked her out, but she'd turned him down, so he brought the date to her. And then the switch that was flipped later in the evening when he insisted that he couldn't give her more.

Then, blushing, she told them that for the past few weeks they'd just been hooking up. She knew it wasn't the smart choice, but she felt like she'd done her best to make sure he knew- or at least thought- they were on the same page.

"So…" Raelyn said, concealing a laugh, "you two have been having sex and you're both pretending that it's just sex, when you both want it to be more?"

Gabby paused. No, that didn't sound right. Sure, she may have wanted it to be more, but Emerson was insistent. He was absolutely, 100 percent crystal clear that he only wanted it to be sex.

Wasn't he?

Emerson's sinfully deep, sexy bedroom voice was in her head, repeating a stream of words he'd said, groaned, and whispered in her ear:

"I can't get you off my mind…you're driving me insane without even trying."

"…I'm a fucking mess and I can't think straight when it comes to you."

"Trust me, I'll still want you."

"I like you, Gabby. I really fucking like you."

And when she challenged him about how he didn't date, his confidence when he replied, *"But what if I wanted to?"*

Well…dammit.

She brought herself back to the present and remembered where she was, or more importantly *who* she was currently with. It wasn't Emerson…but it should be.

"Shit," she muttered and shook her head, tucking a chunk of hair behind her ear. "I need to get back to my date. Umm…it was nice meeting you." She stepped around Raelyn and headed for the door that swung open again just before she reached for the handle.

"Oh, sorry," the person entering said as he- yes *he*- nearly hit her with the door. The man was dressed in a navy blue suit that somehow brought out the flecks of deep auburn in his signature messy brown hair.

Quinn Casey. It was Quinn Casey. Right there. Tall and handsome and every bit the delicious man he appeared to be on magazine covers.

She tried not to freak out and go full fan-girl on him as her eyes wandered up and down. He looked damn good in a suit…but maybe not as good as someone else who she was trying her best to push out of her thoughts. Though she couldn't help noticing that baseball pants suited Quinn Casey better. He should definitely consider wearing baseball pants to his wedding.

She probably shouldn't suggest that though.

"It's fine," she managed, her hand to her chest like a freaking damsel in distress.

Quinn smiled at her briefly before his gaze zeroed in on his target behind her. "Rae…there are people in here."

Raelyn narrowed her eyes, confused. "Quinn, what the hell are you doing in the women's bathroom?"

Clearing his throat, the baseball player tugged at the lapels of his jacket. He fidgeted with his tie and brushed a hand through his hair. "You, uh…you gave me *the look*. I thought you wanted me to follow you."

"Aw, sweetie, that was the *I have to pee- please entertain these people* look," Raelyn replied.

"Oh." Quinn's shoulders dropped. "Were those your cousins from France? Baby, you know I suck at French. I know like three phrases and a few random words.…*Parlez lentement, s'il vous plait..Je ne comprends pas...Ma femme est parfaite...Tu veux baiser maintenant?*"

Raelyn placed a hand over her mouth to stifle a look of shock that quickly turned into a laugh. "Okay, please- *please*- do not use that last one on any of my family members. Or anyone, period. Save that for when we get home. Now get out and let me pee."

Quinn gave a curt nod, then held the door open and waved his hand, gesturing Gabby through. "Madame."

She couldn't help the giddyness that welled inside her as her celebrity crush held the door open for her. Who knew the Bad Boy of Baseball was chivalrous?

"Thank you," she said, grinning on her way out.

He followed her out of the bathroom, earning them a few curious glances from people walking by.

"Don't worry," Quinn said, and she couldn't help appreciating that he also had a very nice voice. Low and gravely by nature, a quality most men's voices only take on in the bedroom. "We made sure no paparazzi could get in here tonight, so we won't end up on the cover of *Stars* or *People* leaving a bathroom together."

Gabby giggled- yeah, she giggled. "The night before your wedding, no less."

Quinn nodded. "Yeah, Zoey would be thrilled. Rae probably wouldn't love it either. The guys would probably find it fucking hilarious though."

"I wonder how Emerson would take it," she mumbled, not fully meaning to say it out loud.

"Emerson?" Quinn questioned, halting his long strides abruptly. "Emerson Yates?" He whipped his head around, a whole new air to his posture, a new expression in his eyes. "That fucker's not here, is he?"

"No, no he's not. I work with him," she said quickly. "I've heard he's not your biggest fan."

Quinn grunted. "The feeling is mutual." He glanced down at her curiously, as though piecing together a puzzle. "You work with him? Are you...you're not Gabriella, are you? The one he's got the prank war with that he can't stop talking about?"

"I am, actually," she said, smiling at the mention of their pranks. They were still teasing and pranking each other, but on a much smaller scale.

"But you're here with someone else?" he questioned, raising a curious eyebrow.

"Yeah, I'm on a date…" she confirmed. "Because, as I'm sure you've heard, Emerson doesn't date. So why would I wait around on something that's never going to happen?"

He grinned then. "Yeah, I used to not date, too. I was fully against relationships and swore up and down that I'd never been in love and never would be. Of course, that was all bullshit."

"That's different. You and Raelyn have history. You've known each other your whole lives, haven't you?"

He nodded from side to side. "Yeah, well not everyone can meet their soulmate when they're seven, but my point is that men will say a lot of things to avoid something they're terrified of. When I was a teenager, I was terrified that if Rae ever found out how I felt, she'd reject me. Then I was terrified that if she felt the same, I'd find a way to fuck it up and I'd lose her. Then I *did* fuck it up and I *did* lose her…but even though I knew she was worth fighting for, worth going after…I was fucking scared. So I pretended my feelings for her weren't that strong, and then I pretended I'd never felt anything for anyone.

"Emerson's the same way. He fucked it up before with Rae and now he's terrified to do that again with someone else- *you*, in this case, if that wasn't clear- so he's trying to tell himself he doesn't feel anything."

Gabby was standing just outside the ornate, high-ceilinged dining room talking about relationships and deep emotions with Quinn-freaking-Casey. What the hell was happening?

She noticed that Jesse was still sitting alone at their table. He caught her eye and waved, then looked curiously at the tall hunk of man next to her. She forced a smile his way, then turned back to Quinn.

"Well, I really do have to get back to my date. Thank you, *Quinn Casey* for the dating and feelings advice. It's been fun. Super weird, but fun. Memorable," she said with a laugh.

To her relief, he also laughed, apparently recognizing the irony of the situation.

"Oh!" she gasped suddenly as Quinn began to turn back to his rehearsal dinner. He spun back around. "Shoot, um...never mind. I was just thinking...my little brother is a big fan. He's a really good ball player, too. I don't have anything for you to sign, but he'd freak out if I got your autograph for him."

Quinn's smile was friendly, with just the slightest hint of mischief. "Well, whether I like it or not, Emerson is sort of part of my friend circle now, so...I'll be sure to get you an autograph next time." He winked-*Oh my God, Quinn Casey winked at me!*- and turned around, disappearing through the massive archway that separated the dining room from the tasting room.

Sitting back down at her table, she apologized to Jesse. "I ran into a few people in the bathroom of all places. And then I met Quinn Casey," she said, gesturing to the direction Quinn had gone.

Jesse's face lit up with surprise as he looked over at the archway. "That's who that was? The ball player?"

"Yeah, and well, you already know what baseball fans my family is. And now I can tell everyone how I met Quinn Casey in a women's bathroom!"

Her date laughed. "*In* the bathroom? What was he doing in there?"

"There was some miscommunication between him and his bride-to-be."

She and Jesse finished their meals, and though they continued talking and there wasn't anything particularly unpleasant about him, she couldn't shake the feeling that she needed to be on this date with someone else. Someone more blonde and bearded who knew exactly how to drive her crazy, knew all the right buttons to push. Someone who challenged her and brought out her argumentative lawyer side.

After dinner, Jesse drove her back to her condo, rode up the four floors in the elevator with her, and walked her to her door. She made up her mind in the elevator that she would tell Jesse she had a nice time and would get ahold of him later, which she would. Of course, she wasn't planning on telling him outright that she would be contacting him to say that she was *not* interested in a second date, but it seemed to be the best option. The easy way out.

As they stood outside her door and Gabby dug in her purse for her keys, she heard the elevator door ding behind them and someone else was step onto the floor. She let her attention wander toward the noise, grateful for the distraction- until she saw Emerson's face. He looked from Jesse to her and his usual poker face was gone. Those eyes swirled the darkest gray-blue, an entire deadly, waves-crashing-in-the-ocean storm behind them.

"Emerson-" she said, her voice breathless as he continued to stand and stare at her and Jesse.

"What- Who the hell is this?" he demanded.

She straightened her posture and tried to use a level, even tone. Her insides twisted at the pain across his face, but she hadn't done anything wrong.

"Emerson, this is Jesse," she replied simply.

He stared, incredulous, and waited for her to fill in more blanks. She didn't.

"Okay, so what the fuck is that supposed to mean?" he snapped.

"It means we went on a date and we're just getting back," she said. "You know what a date is, right? That thing you said you don't do?"

Emerson stepped back as though she'd thrown a physical punch. "I asked you out! I asked you to dinner. I brought you dinner- I told you, Gabe, I fucking told you I liked you. *You* are the one who made it about sex. *You're* the one who said that's all you wanted from me! I gave you what you wanted because I thought if I could spend more time with you, if I could be there to cater to your every fucking need that maybe you'd start wanting more."

Completely abandoning Jesse in front of the door, she took a step toward Emerson. "Yeah, you said you liked me. You also said that you can't give me more! So, what am I supposed to do? Just sit around and expect you to change when you've done everything in your power to make me understand that will never happen? I've done nothing wrong here!"

All at once, the anger disappeared from his expression and was replaced with the truth. His emotions lay bare and she knew instantly that everything his friends had said, that The Ex had said about him having real feelings for her was true. It was as if everything they'd shared, each moment, each touch, all their tender kisses, his sweet words and thoughtful gestures all came into focus.

Beneath his insistence that he *couldn't* be more, she now knew it was followed by a yearning, *but I really want to.* All of the times he'd said he wasn't one of the good guys, there was a pleading, *but I wish you'd let me try.*

"Right, you've done nothing wrong. I'm the fucking idiot who let you use me in hopes that it could be more than that," he said, lowering his voice a notch. He pushed his hand into his hair and scrubbed it down his face. "Fucking ironic, right? Of course the first woman I actually want, I can't have. The woman I want only finds me interesting when my dick is out." He laughed, but there was no humor in it. "Fuck, I probably deserve that."

"Emerson," she said, taking another step closer and reaching toward him. "That's not-"

"It's fine, Gabe. It's fine." He backed up toward the elevator again and pressed the down button. "I came over here because I couldn't stop thinking about you. I barely saw you the past couple days and...I just wanted to see you. Even if it was just to talk or...see your face or start a stupid argument because I...*missed* you. I work with you, I just saw you this morning, and I missed you. How pathetic is that?"

"It's not pathetic-"

The elevator door opened and his eyes met hers again. Her heart clenched at the pain in his face and she wanted to soothe it, wipe away every bit of doubt he had with a slow, earth-shattering kiss. One that would let him know exactly how wrong he was.

He took in a breath, exhaled and said, "Listen, I can't do this. The sex-only thing…it's not working for me anymore. I'm done with…whatever this was."

Gabby was stunned, stuck in place as she watched Emerson step back into the elevator. Her heart was pounding and felt like it was pulling, yanking itself out of her chest, begging her to say something, *do* anything. She wanted to stop the door from closing, jump in with him and wrap herself around him, but she couldn't.

The door closed…and she watched him go.

Chapter 17

After apologizing to Jesse, there really wasn't a whole lot else she had to say to let him know that it probably wasn't going to work out between them. He seemed grateful to leave after Emerson's outburst, and she couldn't blame him. She shoved her way into her condo and to her bedroom where she paced back and forth, debating her next move.

She wanted to chase after him. She should have pulled him out of that elevator and told him the truth. That she had only made it about sex to protect herself. He was so convinced that was all he could promise her, and she only wanted to be close to him, so she was willing to take what she could get, convinced that if she let it be casual she wouldn't get hurt.

The revelation Raelyn had pointed out earlier in the evening popped into her head:

"...you're both pretending that it's just sex when you both want it to be more?"

Apparently that was exactly it. They'd both been pretending not to feel anything for the other, except he'd caved first. He'd given in to his building emotions and seemed ready to jump in.

Now it was her turn.

Gabby dug her phone out of her purse and began scrolling through her texts with Emerson. A little over a week ago he'd sent her his address just in case she changed her mind about not wanting to hook up at his place.

Her chest felt like it could cave in. She had put up so many walls and boundaries, certain that it would keep her feelings at bay. If she didn't let him breach the walls of her bedroom and kept their intimacy in the living room, he wouldn't be able to breach the walls of her heart. *Ridiculous. Such stupid rules. And for what?*

She thought if she could stay away from his place, she would maintain control. She would have the upper-hand. As if going to his place would give him some kind of home-team advantage and he'd be able to break down all the walls and boundaries she was trying so hard to keep in place.

Not anymore.

Gabby found his address and punched it into her maps app on her way back down to the parking lot. Still in her red wrap-dress and high heels, she slid into the driver's seat of her Lincoln and was ready to let him in. All she could think about was the pain in his eyes when he saw her with someone else, and she wanted to do whatever it would take to make it better. If she was going to do this, she had to release the chokehold she had on control and show him that she was willing to trust him.

Emerson snapped off the top of his first bottle of Heineken. He guessed the six-pack would be gone before the night was over, but after his first sip he knew beer wasn't enough. He reached into the cupboard over the refrigerator and pulled out a bottle of Jameson and a shot glass.

He threw back the first ounce of amber liquid and it burned on the way down, but it didn't ease the ache in his chest. It didn't settle the feeling in his stomach like he was completely hollow.

This feeling fucking sucked, whatever it was.

He wasn't familiar with it. He felt angry and restless. He was mad at Gabriella for not telling him she was seeing other people, he was mad at himself for getting attached in the first place. He was disappointed in himself for not keeping his cool when he saw her, and knew that work was going to be super fucking awkward on Monday. He'd have to get his shit together by then.

There was only one dim light on in his apartment, and the bit of illumination that came from his backlit shelves in the living room. He didn't want light. He wanted to sit in a den of darkness and drink until he passed out. Until he didn't feel like this anymore.

They weren't even dating. He knew the deal. He knew it was just sex- so why the fuck was he this upset? Why did he feel like he was being ripped in two?

A crack of thunder and a flash of lightning lit up the sky outside the glass doors of his balcony.

Good. The weather was cooperating with his mood.

He sat on the couch in his dimly lit living room, his open bottle of Heineken in one hand and Jameson in the other. Yeah, he looked like a real fucking winner. Why wouldn't Gabriella want him?

There was more thunder, but he also thought it sounded like someone was knocking on his door. He waited and heard the knocking again.

He leaned forward and set his drinks on the coffee table, got up and pulled the door open.

His heart expanded in his chest at the sight of her. "Gabe-"

She cut him off, reaching for him, tangling her fingers in his hair and crushing her mouth to his. He easily melted into her warm, familiar shape. Holding her body to his, he slid his tongue between her lips, breathed her in, hands feeling down her sides, grasping the curve of her ass and pressing his pelvis against hers.

He was breathless when they parted and he stared down at her as if he couldn't believe she was actually there. He noticed her hair and clothes were wet and wondered how far she'd had to walk in the rain to come to him.

"What are you doing here?" he asked.

"I'm sorry," she breathed. "Emerson, I...I don't want to just be another one of your flings. Another number-"

"You're not. You never were," he said, holding her head in both hands now.

"If you feel the way I think you do...then stop seeing those other women. I want it to just be me."

"It is just you. It has been for weeks, I promise. Gabe, I want this. I want *you.*" He pressed his lips to hers and backed her against the door. "But I want you to myself. I won't see anyone else, you won't see anyone else. Got it? You'll break it off with whoever that was tonight..." He trailed his mouth down her jaw and along her neck. "*I* want you, Gabe. *Me*, no one else."

"Yes," she breathed, eyes closed. "Yes, okay, you can have me."

It was like an electric shock to his chest to hear those words. He slid his hands down and around her ass, hitching her up so she could wrap her legs around his waist and carry her to the closest surface- the kitchen island- and set her down.

"This fucking dress," he groaned, tracing the deep V with one hand while the other skated up her thigh. "I can't believe you wore this for someone else...he must've wanted to fuck you so bad. Too bad he didn't know that's my fucking job." He buried his face between her tits where her bare skin was on display, licking beads of raindrops off her skin. He had a love-hate relationship with the dress she was wearing. Loved how she looked in it, loved how it left little to the imagination and showed off every sultry bit of her. Hated the thought of someone else seeing her in it, *really* hated knowing some guy had been gawking at her all night in it.

"Yes, it's your job, and you do it so fucking well," Gabriella moaned, thrusting her fingers into his hair. "Only you know how to fuck me like you do...only you know how to give me exactly what I want."

He came up to whisper in her ear, "And what do you want right now?"

She pulled his mouth to hers, kissing him, tasting him so deep. His head was spinning, he was dizzy and hard and his heart was a marching band in his chest, he was sure she could hear it.

"Everything," she answered finally. "I want everything. I want to feel you all over, on top of me, inside me. I want you to make me come until I can't see straight. Make me come with your tongue, your mouth, your big cock. I want to feel you move inside me, so deep it hurts."

"Fuck yes, baby, I can do that. I'll give you all of it," he rasped, unbuckling his belt. "Where do you want me first?"

She put a finger to his mouth, tracing his lips. His tongue snaked out and licked her finger before playfully biting it.

"And then," she continued, locking eyes with him, "when you think you're done and you've come inside me-" She dipped her hand into his boxer briefs and grasped his hard flesh- "I'm going to make you hard again and let you come wherever you want."

"Anywhere?" he asked, eyebrow arching, pulse skittering.

"Anywhere."

He knew right away he wanted to come on her tits. He wanted to claim them, mark his territory, even though he was already certain they had more of a claim on him.

"We better get started then." He gave her a mischievous grin before slipping down her body, getting on his knees as he'd done so many times. His hands slid up her dress and pulled her panties down, and he stuffed them in his pocket for later.

Her dress was pushed up over her hips and he pulled her to the edge of the counter, kissing a trail up the insides of her thighs, his palms rubbing the smooth skin of her legs. He paused before burying his mouth inside her and slowly swiped a finger down her slick crease with a groan. Looking up, he saw that she was biting her lip, holding her breath as she looked back at him.

"Before I do this," he said, his thumb now circling her clit in a slow, rhythmic motion, "I need to know it's going to be different. I need you to promise me something."

"Okay," she whispered as her eyes threatened to drift shut.

"Promise me you'll stay this time. Promise you won't take off, you won't push me away. You'll stay with me tonight...please."

Her gorgeous lips pulled into a slow grin and she nodded. "Okay, I promise."

His chest threatened to burst open and he allowed a genuine smile of relief before getting back to business. He moved his fingers down, pushed one inside and covered her clit with his mouth and she gasped.

In seconds she was moaning and writhing against him, fisting his hair, pulling him close, begging for more...*more.*

In minutes, her legs were wrapped around him, pleading with him and God, begging for release, screaming his name like she never had before as he did his best to worship and praise her with his mouth, his lips, tongue, teeth, and fingers. When she finally reached that peak, she fell back onto the counter, unable to hold herself up as she bucked beneath him, screaming, gasping, and panting until her body let her relax.

He didn't give her much recovery time- about as much time as it took for him to push off his pants and boxer briefs and yank his t-shirt over his head- before he scooped her off the kitchen island and carried her past the living room, down the hall to his bedroom. Part of him wanted to fuck her on every surface of his apartment- the floor, the living room, the walls, up against the sliding glass door- but a more urgent part of him needed her in his room. In his bed. The rest could wait.

He set her on her feet and kicked the door shut behind them. She leaned into him for support and he wrapped a hand around her back, holding her upright.

"Holy fuck, that was good," she sighed, eyes closed. She looked like aftershock orgasms were still coursing through her, and he couldn't help congratulating himself on a job well-done.

"What was next on your list?" he asked. "Something about...wanting me on top of you? Moving inside you, so deep it hurts? Or was it...making you come so hard you can't see straight?"

She laughed. "You can check that one off the list."

"Doesn't mean I can't do it again," he replied, now moving her toward his king-size platform bed.

"Oh, I'm sure you will."

His fingers reached the zipper on the back of her dress and he undid it, shoving her dress down off her shoulders and letting it pool on the floor. He groaned as his mouth gravitated toward her breasts. "You weren't even wearing a bra? *Goddamn*, what were you thinking? Trying to give someone a heart attack going out like this?"

He sucked in a nipple, teasing with his teeth and licking wet circles around it with his tongue. She moaned and arched her back, pressing into him as his hand teased the other. Her soft hands roamed over his back and shoulders, into his hair, and back down. She slid her palm around his cock that was jutting out, throbbing hard, the tip already wet. He growled at her touch and forced himself to hold back. He wanted to come right now, wanted to jerk off onto her, cover her skin with hot cum. But he needed to slow down. Savor her. Enjoy this. Make her glad she chose him, make her want to stay.

"Come here," she whispered, tugging his hair gently. He slid up her body and covered her mouth with his, devouring her as she pulled him onto the bed with her.

He leaned over her, bracketing her head with his forearms, kissing her so deeply. She reached between them and began stroking him, pumping her hand along his length, and he groaned, flexing his lower muscles to hold back.

"Gabe, you can't make me come yet," he rasped into her neck. "But I fucking want to. God, you've got me so fucking hard, I want to come all over you."

"Not yet." She angled his dick between her legs, tracing the tip down her crease and back up. Teasing him like this was torture. He wanted to dive right in. *Fuck*, he could only hold back so much for so long. He was so hard it hurt, needed her so badly he was considering making very rash decisions.

"You're so fucking bad, baby," he whispered, his voice thick and gravelly. "I should punish you for teasing me like this. Should tie you up and fuck you hard...fuck that pretty mouth of yours that you never let me in."

He was weakened by need, all his energy focused on holding back, so he didn't see it coming when she pushed and rolled him onto his back. Now straddling him with her hand fisted around his shaft, the other caressing and teasing his balls, he strained even harder to hold back.

"Fuuuuck," he groaned, drawing it out as if it pained him. His hips started moving, thrusting upward, fucking her hand. "If you're not careful, baby, you'll have a full on white-wash before long."

"Do you want me to be careful?" she asked.

"I want you to stop teasing me and let me fuck you."

"You already fucked me with your mouth," she said, trailing a finger around the head of his cock. "I think it's my turn."

He was pretty damn sure his heart literally stopped. His eyes bulged out of his head and his muscles and brain ceased to work. He blinked. Several times.

"Your turn to- Oh! *Oh...God,* okay." His body sunk into the mattress as he watched Gabriella lower her head to his lap. Her tongue licked a warm, wet path from base to tip where she swirled her tongue, then covered with her lips. He propped himself up on his elbows to get a better view and gritted his teeth with restraint as she locked eyes with him before taking him fully in her mouth. All...the...way.

His cock touched the back of her throat and she groaned around him, sending a shiver through his entire body. Her mouth was hot and wet, and she sucked him just right. Not too hard, but not tentative. She knew what the fuck she was doing. She pulled him out, then took him deep again, and swirled her tongue around him on the way back up. Her lips sucked gently on the head and her tongue licked up the pre-cum that had started to accumulate. She devoured him like he was her favorite treat. Like she'd been waiting for this. Like she enjoyed it as much as he did. But there was no fucking way that was possible.

He grabbed a handful of her hair and began thrusting into her mouth, and she made the most perfect sounds. Her whimpers and moans ran deep inside him and he couldn't get enough. Didn't want this to stop, but knew it wouldn't last long.

"Fuck, it's so good," he panted. "It's too good...*too* good."

He tried pulling her off him, bringing her up so that he didn't come already. He wasn't ready. But it only made her work harder. Her hands joined her mouth and she worked his cock like a fucking porn star.

"Oh fuck-fuck-fuck, I'm coming- *fuck!*" His legs literally started shaking as he let go, his release filling her mouth. She took him deep, letting him come all the way to the back of her mouth, and swallowed. He collapsed back on the bed, breathing hard, having no idea how he was so out of breath when she'd done all the work.

"I'm dead. Am I dead? I think I died." His right hand covered his chest, feeling his heartbeat race faster than ever beneath his palm.

Gabriella slid back up his body and straddled his hips. "You okay?"

He shook his head vigorously. "No. I think you sucked out my soul."

She laughed, still stroking his mostly-hard cock in her hands. "Do you think you need a break?"

"Give me two minutes," he said, holding up two fingers. "Get back to that list of yours. Then I've got one of my own."

"Oh yeah?" she raised one eyebrow. "What's on your list?"

"Just…a lot of what you just did, but in various rooms. I'll probably need a snack when we get done with your list, so maybe you can do it again while I make us something to eat. And then we'll need a shower, so I figure you can do it in there, too."

"Oh boy," she sighed. "I started something, didn't I? You're going to want that every day now."

He scoffed. "Every day? Every hour, on the hour."

Laughing, she replied, "Yeah, good luck getting me to sign that contract."

"I'm persuasive as hell. It could happen."

"Are you?" She trailed a finger lightly down his shaft, cupped his balls and massaged them gently.

He let out a tortured groan and his leg twitched. "Usually." Looking up at her, he cupped her cheek in his hand and rubbed his thumb over her cheekbone. "Did you mean it when you said you'd stay?"

"I promised, didn't I?"

He swallowed. "Did you promise because I made you promise, or because you want to stay?"

She dipped her head and pressed her lips to his. "I want to stay. I promise."

"Good," he said, smiling. Then he grabbed her by the wrists and flipped her onto her back. "Two minutes is up. I'm taking my time with you now."

She smiled back. "We've got time."

Oh yes...oh yes...fuck yes.

Gabby's vocabulary for the night was reduced to about three or four words. Emerson was moving over her again, deep and slow and taking his time, and she felt completely at his mercy. And she was okay with it. Better than that, she was enjoying it. Letting go, letting Emerson take some control from her. He knew what he was doing and he wasn't going to hurt her. Definitely not in bed.

Well, not in a bad way in bed. She had made the special request for him to fuck her "so deep it hurts" but it was a good pain. The kind of pain that made her gasp at first when he plunged his whole length into her, but softened and blurred into pleasure the more he moved. His hips rocked against her, their bodies pressed together, sweaty and slick and warm. Heated and so in tune. Connected, but more than just physically.

It was far from their first time together, and while the bed felt more intimate, there was something different about this time. Their connection ran deeper, their bodies moved as one, and it was so much more than just a race to the finish. It was more than just getting to the relief of an orgasm. The chase was just as good. The climb was fueled by passion. It was intense and left her yearning for more, never wanting it to end. He had her hanging just on the brink of climax and she wanted to stay there...just a little longer.

They came together in a blissful, dizzying explosion, pulsing, moaning, grasping for each other, and it nearly left her breathless. His weight blanketed over her and his breath was hot and heavy on her neck as he tried to catch it. She splayed her palm over his chest and felt his heart pounding, his cock twitched inside her and she tightened around him in response. She had never felt so close to him before…or anyone.

When he asked her to promise to stay, she felt it. She felt her heart take a leap of faith, jumping in with both feet, letting herself want this. Letting herself believe he did, too. She was trusting him and it felt right.

There was a rumbling noise and she felt a small vibration against her stomach. Emerson laughed and the sound warmed her.

"Told you I'd need a snack eventually," he said, pushing himself up so his chest was no longer draped over her.

She wrapped her arms behind his neck and pulled him back down, missing his body and his warmth. "Five more minutes."

He kissed her, softly at first. Then her tongue parted his lips and they were locked in a deep, devouring kiss. Hard, tasting, consuming. She craved him so much, and now that she'd let herself jump in, she didn't want to hold back anymore. After seeing how hurt he'd been, she wanted him to know she was all in.

"Five more minutes is about to turn into thirty-five minutes," he cautioned, rocking himself into her. She could feel him thickening inside her again. God, he had stamina. *Virility.* He could literally go all night if she wanted him to.

"That's okay," she sighed as he kissed her neck.

They moved together again, familiar and easy. Emerson tore his mouth away. "Hang on…let me change condoms."

She watched his muscles stretch and contract as he reached over to his night stand where they'd left the box of condoms, and her whole body hummed and prickled pleasantly with admiration. Having sex in the dark with this man and not being able to see and fawn over the absolute perfection of him would be a sin. A tragedy. There weren't a lot of men she could say this about, but he was *beautiful.* And he was hers.

He pulled out long enough to take off the used condom and put on a new one. She bent her legs up to his sides as he eased back into her. Grabbing her wrists and holding them above her head, he pushed her into the bed, grinding down on her, into her, already moving hard, but slow.

She wanted to trace the dips and crevices of his muscles but he was holding her down, pinning her to the mattress. God, he was strong. He probably couldn't even tell she was trying to move her hands at all, and she was completely in awe of him. His body, his strength, his unbelievable good looks...His stubbornness, his determination, the intensity with which he did absolutely everything. Emerson Yates didn't do anything half-assed.

Why should he treat being a boyfriend any differently?

His large hands slid down to her hips and flipped her onto her stomach with ease. He dragged his palms over her shoulders, around to feel and tease her breasts, down her sides to her hips. One hand held steady, fingers digging into her curves, while the other slipped down between her legs. She gasped and moaned when he rubbed her clit in soft circles.

"Spread your legs for me baby," he instructed. "Just a little more."

She obliged and was rewarded with the slightest pressure of his cock pushing into her from behind. But he didn't push all the way.

"Please," she begged, rocking her hips back. He held her firm with one hand.

"Please what?" He trailed his lips down her spine, and his tongue moved along her skin in ways that made her tingle.

"Please...fuck me. Hard. Please make me come again." She tried moving her hips back again, needing to feel him inside her.

He hummed against her skin, bit her ass-cheek enough to sting and she whimpered. "Details, baby."

"Emerson, *please*...I want you inside me. I want you to fill me up with your cock...fuck me until I'm screaming. Move inside me and make me come all over your big, hard cock. *Please,* I need it."

He gave her a little more. Another inch as he continued to swipe the pad of his thumb over her clit. She gasped and held her breath.

"You like this big, hard cock?"

"Yes."

"You want it?"

"*Yes.*"

"All of it?"

"*Yes!* I want all of it, *please!*" Her body was humming. There was a knot of hot, aching tension between her legs and she needed him to relieve it. Needed him to stop teasing.

"Good, you're gonna get all of it. Over and over again until I decide to stop." He grabbed her wrists and held them pinned behind her back before shoving the rest of the way inside.

He pounded into her, slick and hot, and she moaned into the mattress, loving every filthy second. Every hard inch of him reached so deep, and the knot of tension began to unravel. So many dirty thoughts, wants, needs, wishes, swarmed around in her head. She wanted to tell him to bite her again, spank her, pull her hair, but she couldn't find the words. She could only gasp and moan, cry for more, plead with him not to stop.

He held her wrists together at the small of her back and she listened to his grunts and growls he gave with each hard thrust, making her toes curl.

"Goddamn, I love seeing you like this," he rasped. "You like giving me control, don't you baby?"

"Yes," she moaned. "Me encántalo. Sabes que yo quiero, papi- Oh *God...*"

He groaned, loud and deep. "Fuck, I don't know what you just said, but keep talking to me, mami."

Her lips nearly curved into a smile before he released her wrists and slid a hand into her hair, making her gasp again. Pulling her hair, he leaned over her and bit her shoulder, still thrusting deep, rocking in and out, never letting up.

It was so good.

So deep.

He reached everywhere, filling her, rubbing that perfect spot that made that knot of pleasure tighten. The pressure between her thighs was blissful, delectable agony, increasing...higher...*higher*...more- *more, yes more!* It was a wonder her body could withstand it. Sparks ignited, white lights flickered behind her eyelids as she squeezed them shut against the waves of pleasure coursing and crashing through her.

"Ay Dios mío...te quiero, papi, te quiero...más! Más, por favor! No te pares!" She grasped the comforter, screamed into the mattress as she came completely undone. Her muscles tensed and shook, she shivered and writhed beneath him. He halted his thrusts, holding himself all the way inside as she rode out her orgasm, feeling her walls clench and squeeze him, latching on and refusing to let go. She wasn't sure her orgasm would ever stop as she lay panting into his comforter, willing her body to relax.

"You're so goddamn tight," he breathed behind her. He sounded like he was in pain with restraint, and she wondered why he was still holding back.

His voice was low and strained as he gave his command, "On your back."

She rolled over and her eyes flickered with lust as she watched him kneeling between her legs. He removed the condom and fisted his length, moving his hand up and down his shaft in a furious rhythm. She felt her eyes darken, mesmerized by the sight of him. As if that perfect dick weren't enough, the way his shoulder muscles rippled, his abs flexed, his forearms corded and contracted as he jerked himself off over her...she never wanted to stop seeing this. She wanted this image imprinted on her retinas, to make a GIF of it and set it as his contact photo on her phone.

Licking her lips, she met his heated gaze, letting her eyebrow quirk up. "Are you gonna come on me, papi?"

He tried biting back his groan, but she heard it deep in his chest. *"Fuck,* I love when you call me that." His hand moved faster over his shaft and she began sliding her hands up her body, feeling herself sensually, putting on a show for him. He leaned over her, angled his cock down to her tits, fucking his hand faster. "Yes...fuck, oh God-"

Moving her hands up and into her hair, she felt thick, liquid heat cover her stomach, her breasts, her neck. When Emerson finished, he braced himself above her, hands on either side of her head, before crushing his mouth over hers again. Holding his face in her hands, she stroked his tongue with hers as they melted into each other.

Ever since their first time in the stairwell, they always kissed like this after sex. There was something so intimate about these moments between them, like they weren't ready to let go so quickly, like they wanted to be together just a little longer.

"There…another thing crossed off the list," he panted.

"I'm surprised you didn't change your mind," she said. "I told you to come wherever you wanted…I thought for sure you'd pick my mouth again."

His mouth opened slightly, seeming stunned. "Fuck…that was a missed opportunity."

She giggled, brushing her fingers over his cheek and into his hair. "Don't worry, you'll get more chances." Looking between their bodies, she realized just how much of a mess he'd made on her. "Was it everything you dreamed it would be?"

He looked at his handywork and grinned. "Sí, mami. Me gusta mucho."

"Is that all the Spanish you know?" she laughed.

"Sí, mami," he said with a wink.

She kissed him again. "Let's go get you that snack, papi."

In the kitchen, Gabriella was sitting on the kitchen counter while Emerson rummaged in the fridge and cupboards for a snack. She wore one of his faded blue University of Michigan t-shirts and he loved everything about it. Her messy bed-head, her satiated grin, her body covered in his scent, and most of all, the fact that she was here. That she'd stayed.

"That is, without a doubt, the biggest jar of peanut butter I have ever seen!" she exclaimed as he grabbed his favorite food item out of the cupboard.

"I basically put it on everything," he replied. "Toast, apples, celery, protein shakes, English muffins, a spoon."

"Protein shakes?" she asked. "How often do you work out?"

He took a spoon out of the silverware drawer. "Five days a week." Feeling her scrutinizing gaze on him, he looked up. "What? Well, I lift five days a week, and then I try to at least do some physical activity other days. Going for a walk or a light jog…Why?"

"How long have you been doing that?"

Digging a spoon into the peanut butter jar and handing it to her, he replied, "Since college, I guess. After high school, I didn't have water polo to keep me in shape anymore so I got into lifting. I enjoy it though, so it's not like work to me."

Gabriella took a long lick of peanut butter off the spoon and he watched intently. "Do you want anything with that? An apple or…celery stick?"

She shook her head. "Is your diet as strict as your workout regimen? Is this all you eat?"

He laughed. "Nah, it's not that strict. I drink a lot of beer, and I'll have a bar burger every now and then. But usually it's steak and vegetables, chicken and rice…whatever peanut butter snack I can get my hands on." Slipping his hands up the sides of her thighs, beneath his shirt that she wore, he gripped her hips, loving the curves there. Loving how his fingers felt digging into her, like he was marking her. "Why? What do you eat to keep this bangin' body?" He kissed her neck, her jaw, the tip of her nose.

She groaned, but it wasn't the sexual kind of groan. It was the kind accompanied by an eye-roll. "You mean how do I make my thighs jiggle like Aunt Betty's Christmas gelatin?"

He scowled. "Whoa- what? Nuh-uh, you take that back!"

"Okay fine, I don't have an Aunt Betty."

His glare narrowed and the furrow in his brow deepened.

"And does anyone really bring a Jell-O mold to Christmas anymore?"

Tightening his grip on her hips, he tugged her to the edge of the counter, stepping between her thighs so she had to spread them for him. He shook his head and squatted down in front of her, pressing his lips to the inside of each thigh, licking and tasting her skin that was salty with sweat and sex.

"I happen to love your thighs," he said, rubbing his lips back and forth over her skin. "And I don't like you saying anything bad about them." He pressed his mouth to them again, sneaking his tongue out and tasting her again. "I like that I can do this-" He sunk his teeth gently into her flesh just hard enough to make her gasp. He brushed his lips over where his teeth had just been. "They're thick-" *kiss-* "sexy-" *kiss-* "and juicy-" *kiss.* "And you know I like you *juicy.*"

"Well that's good, because I like bacon cheeseburgers, Chardonnay, ice cream, and I don't remember the last time I had a workout routine. I used to run, and I'll take a random group fitness class when an interesting one pops up, but I suck at forcing myself to go to the gym."

He stood back up and grabbed his own spoon out of the extra large peanut butter jar. "What kinds of classes do you take?"

"I like cycling, except for the sore butt the next day. And Zumba- I actually love dancing."

He grinned, picturing her out on a dance floor. She'd probably have all eyes on her. "I need to take you dancing then. I just want to watch you. I bet you look so sexy moving your body the way you do."

"I bet I could get you on the dance floor, too," she said, grinning. "We probably wouldn't be there for long once you got your hands on me...felt me move against you."

"My guess is that I would be out there for exactly three seconds, and then I would drag you off to some dark corner and show you my moves."

Emerson turned around and grabbed an apple out of the fridge and a small knife out of the knife block and began slicing up a large honeycrisp apple.

"Would you..." Gabriella hesitated for a beat. "Would you want me to start going to the gym with you?"

He lifted his gaze and an eyebrow. "Do you want to?"

She shrugged and he wasn't sure what to make of the look on her face. It was still dark in the kitchen, with only the dim lights beneath the cabinets on, but he almost thought she looked nervous. Insecure, even. It was adorable, but totally wrong on her.

"Did you and Raelyn workout together?" As soon as the words were out, she bit her lip.

He furrowed his brow, confused. "Does it matter what me and Rae did together?"

"No, it's just…she obviously works out. She's really fit and…tall and blonde and gorgeous."

"Gabe-"

"I'm sure her thighs don't-"

"*Do not* say jiggle. I swear, Gabe, if you criticize your *bangin'* bod or your juicy thighs one more time-" He stopped, realizing he was pointing at her with the small knife. He put it down and laughed. "Sorry, that was a lot more threatening than I meant it to be. But seriously, I don't want you comparing yourself to her or anyone else. You're fucking gorgeous, your body is amazing," he said, grabbing her hand and pulling it to feel his dick over his sweatpants, "and you make me so unbelievably hard when all you're doing is sitting there eating peanut butter off a spoon. If you don't know how sexy you are, baby, I need to do my job better."

Her smile looked reluctant and she dropped her attention back to her spoon. "Sorry, I know. It's just…between everyone else telling me what a babe she is and then seeing all those pictures of you guys together-" She stopped and snapped her mouth shut.

"Pictures?" he asked. "What pictures?"

"Um…" Her eyes flicked around for a distraction and he couldn't help grinning a little.

He couldn't contain the joy this brought him. Had she done a Google search on his ex? Had she been so curious, even *jealous*, about her? After their night at the office, he'd definitely gone to Facebook in search of *Ben Mendoza* to see what kind of guy he was up against. It's only natural to wonder, though he'd felt completely ridiculous.

But now he felt a lot better. Now he felt like they might actually be on the same page. This fucking gorgeous, sexy, confident woman had been jealous at the thought of him with someone else.

"You looked her up, didn't you?" His grin was too wide, but he couldn't help it.

Quickly, Gabriella dipped her spoon back into the peanut butter jar, then swiped a streak of the sticky, sweet snack across his chest. "Oops." She grinned innocently.

His eyes dropped to the glob of peanut butter on his chest. "Excuse you…What was that all about?"

She slipped her fingers into the band of his sweatpants and tugged him forward. Her mouth was hot and wet as she licked the peanut butter off his chest and he groaned, bracing his hands on the counter where she sat.

"Stop trying to distract me," he said, nuzzling the curve of her neck. "What pictures are you talking about?"

Her mouth traced down his tattooed pec, sending shivers down his spine and all sorts of signals to his cock. It was now fully awake, standing at attention, and ready for action. The slow, circling wetness of her tongue trailed around his nipple before she scraped her teeth over it. He hissed and his body shuddered.

Quite frankly, at the moment he didn't give a damn about any pictures she had found or Google searches she may or may not have conducted, but he wasn't going to let it go that easily. He was going to make her admit that she'd been jealous. Make her admit that whatever she'd seen made her want him more. Just to hear her say the words again…*I want you.*

"Tell me, Gabe…" he whispered into her hair. "Do you really think I can't get a confession out of you?" One hand made the familiar path up her leg, beneath the t-shirt that just covered her thighs.

Her soft hands slid up his torso, splayed on his licked-clean chest and she pushed him back gently. He grasped for the hem of her t-shirt, but she raised her foot, pressing it to the center of his chest and forcing him back still, shaking her head with a devilish little smirk.

"You're going to keep me from touching you?" he asked, lightly skating his fingertips from her knee down to her ankle. He pulled her foot up so that it rested over his shoulder and pressed his lips to her skin. Feathering her calf with kisses, tastes, and nibbles. "Come on, honey, just tell me."

Silently, she shook her head again, keeping her lips together in a wry grin. She snatched her foot out of his grasp and hopped down from her seat on the island. He expected her to try to move out of his reach, but instead she stepped toward him. Still holding the spoonful of peanut butter in one hand, she smeared it from the middle of his chest, down the center of his abs, stopping just above the waistband of his sweatpants.

He watched intently, forcing patience, as she swiped a finger over the spoon to scoop up the rest of its contents and held it to his lips. His eager mouth sucked every last bit from her finger and he leaned back against the refrigerator, waiting for whatever came next.

She reached up on tip-toe and licked his bottom lip, but pulled away before he could catch her full lips in a kiss. Instead, her head dipped to his chest and she began licking and sucking her way down the trail she'd made, lowering herself in front of him until she was on her knees and her tongue was teasing the skin above his waistband.

His chest rose and fell slowly, shuddering as she worked his sweatpants down and took his achingly hard cock in her hand. Willing himself not to come at the very sight of her on her knees in front of him, he clenched his jaw and balled his hands into fists at his sides. He was too tempted to grab her hair and fuck her mouth with absolutely no restraint, but somehow he refrained.

Her eyes flashed up to his as she rubbed her lips over the head of his cock. He knew the tip was already wet. Fuck, she made him hard. And when she swiped her tongue over the wet crown and sighed like it was the first taste of an ice cream cone on a hot day, he wanted to come. Right there. All over her mouth and neck and tits. But again, he refrained.

Those perfect, plump lips wrapped around the head of him, sucking lightly as her tongue continued to tease him. He wished his phone was handy so he could take a picture.

Her fingers danced over his balls, up his shaft and back down, cupping him firmly and his groan was low and biting as he held back.

"Fuck, Gabby, you're killing me."

Her gorgeous, brown, almond-shaped eyes flashed back to him and she moved her mouth over his cock. He watched as his hard shaft disappeared inside her mouth, her eyes fluttered shut and he listened to her moan as he reached the back of her throat. Her lips...those fucking lips looked so goddamn good wrapped around his thick length. Like they were fucking made for him.

He wanted to keep watching, but the more she moved and sucked, pumped with her soft fist, grasped at his legs, and whimpered like she was begging for him, his eyes rolled back. He allowed himself to just feel it. Feel her. Enjoy and revel in all that she was giving him.

Throbbing and aching tightness gathered and knotted, growing wilder and harder to contain. He was so hard...*so fucking hard.* No holding back now. He grabbed a fistful of her hair and began fucking her mouth. Sliding himself in and out of her, listening to her sounds as he thrusted between her pretty lips.

At what felt like the last second, he changed course. He pulled out and guided her up to her feet, kissed her mouth hard. She was panting and her lips were swollen and puffy from sucking him so good. God he could really fucking get used to that.

"You have no idea how bad I wanted to come in your mouth again," he said, nipping at her jaw. "But you have a confession to make, and I'll fuck it right out of you if I have to."

He gripped both her forearms in his hands and held them at her sides when she tried to reach for him. "No touching me, baby. Not until I get what I want from you."

Her eyebrow ticked upward. "And what do you want?"

"The truth," he replied. "What pictures did you see? How did you see them?"

She grinned and bit her bottom lip.

So fucking sexy.

Since she refused to confess, he spun her around and pressed his hard body against her warm, soft back and walked her to the glass door to the balcony.

"Put your hands on the glass," he demanded, his voice low and cold. When he released her arms, she did as she was asked. He pressed one hand to the center of her back so that it arched just right, then slid a foot between her legs and kicked her feet out wider. He pushed the t-shirt up so that her bare ass was exposed and he began rubbing smooth circles over her silky skin with his palms. "Tell me, baby…what pictures did you see?"

She stuck her ass out further, as if she knew what was coming next and said coolly, "I don't know what you're talking about."

Smack!

He delivered a sharp slap to one side of her perfectly round ass and she gasped. "Don't lie to me." Now he slipped his other hand down her ass and between her legs, sliding a finger along her crease that was wet and craving him. "Let's try this again, honey. What pictures did you find? And how did you find them?"

"I'm not telling."

Smack!

She moaned, and in her reflection, he saw her bite her bottom lip.

"I'll get my answer one way or another, baby," he said, scraping his teeth over her shoulder. "Maybe you're just being stubborn because you want my cock instead of my hand." He slipped a finger inside her and she gasped, moaned, and shivered. When he pet her sensitive clit with two fingers on his other hand, her legs quivered and he leaned into her to hold her up, his hard flesh pressing against her ass.

"No," she moaned.

"No I won't get my answer, or no you don't want my cock?"

"Both." She snapped her response, but bucked her hips back into his lap so he knew she was playing his game. Drawing it out until they were both shaking with need.

"I think you're lying to me, Gabe," he whispered into the nape of her neck. "I don't think your pussy would be this wet if you didn't want me."

"Well, I don't," she persisted.

He slid a second finger inside her and she bucked against him, grinding into his hand, moaning through clenched teeth as she tried to hold back.

"All right, honey, I'll give you one more chance to come clean." He rubbed her clit, slid his throbbing cock against her backside, and moved his fingers slowly in and out of her wet heat. He wanted to tease her more, but damn, he was going to end up losing his load all over her back without even fucking her. "Tell me the truth. Did you get curious? Did the thought of me with someone else drive you crazy? Did you wonder how the hell I could ever be with anyone else when what we have is so fucking good?"

She hesitated this time, whimpering at the sensations between her legs. "I'm...not telling."

The growl that ripped through his chest was animalistic and raw. He was a fucking caveman and he was about to be anything but a gentleman with her body. On the floor by their feet were his discarded pants from earlier, and he dragged them over with one foot, bent down and snatched a condom out of his wallet. He slid it on and braced himself, holding her by the hips as he plunged into her.

He fucked her hard and rough. She was soft and wet and warm, and he needed her.

"You're so wet, baby. God, I know you say you don't want me, but I think we both know that's a lie. You want me. You want me *bad*, don't you?"

"Oh God, *yes!*"

"Fuck yes," he groaned. "I know you hate the thought of me with someone else just as much as I hate the thought of someone even looking at you thinking he's got a chance." He pumped into her, thrusted harder, faster. "You want this, baby? You want me to fuck you to sleep at night? To give this body what it needs? What it deserves?"

"Yes, yes, yes! Oh my God, *yes!* I want it. I want it so bad."

His movements became jagged as he started to reach the top of that celestial peak. He was climbing...climbing. Sweat dripped down his chest and he watched himself pound into her so hard he thought it must hurt, but she was screaming and crying out, pleading for more, telling him not to stop.

He saw the moment Gabriella's explosion went off just before it happened. Every muscle in her smooth, sexy back tensed. The reflection of her face in the glass was an expression of pure, carnal pleasure, with her eyes squeezed shut, her head thrown back, and her mouth open in a cry of euphoria. Her tight pussy contracted hard around him and he came, shaking and sputtering, leaning one hand on the glass in front of them to hold himself up, and the other wrapped around her body.

This time when he felt the chink in his armor, the hot flames licking at the cage around his heart and melting it away, he welcomed it. Something inside him was tearing down...falling apart, like a wall crumbling into dust and debris.

But with his arms around this woman, he felt better. With her, he felt...whole.

Chapter 18

After an extra long, extra steamy shower, Gabby and Emerson tumbled back into bed, tangled in sheets and limbs. She lay wrapped in his thick, strong arms and she swore there was nothing like it. He held her close, brushing a hand through her hair and the other on her hip as she lay her head on his chest with one leg draped over his body. She traced the Roman numerals of his tattoo and listened to his steady breathing in the dark.

"Why twenty-six?" she asked, letting her finger slide along the V for the third time.

"It's the number of women whose virginity I've taken."

She playfully bit his chest. "Seriously?"

"No." He laughed and tugged her hair lightly. "It's how old I was when I started the tattoo and I just liked how it looked."

"Why the armor?"

"Because it's badass, why else?"

Lifting her head, she rested her chin on his chest and looked up at him. "A lot of things are badass. Why'd you choose a knight's armor?"

Emerson hummed and she felt his chest deflate with a sigh. "I guess because I've always felt like I wear armor- figuratively, of course. I've always deflected the negative, stayed strong and pushed through whatever I had to in order to get where I wanted to be. I never let anything deter me from what I want. I try to think of myself as untouchable…impenetrable. It probably sounds arrogant, but it's worked for me."

Gabby touched her lips to the center of his tattoo. "It suits you. I thought you were going to say it's because you're like a knight in shining armor- every girl's fairytale prince come to life."

He let out a quiet, dry laugh. "Baby, I think you know I'm no one's white knight."

"I don't know...I think you could be."

Though she couldn't make them out in the darkness of his bedroom, she knew his eyes were a dark stormy blue when he looked down at her, twinkling in a way that made her feel like she's being hypnotized. "I'm starting to wonder if you really know what you're getting yourself into."

"You've given me plenty of warnings, but I think you underestimate yourself," she said. "I trust you, Emerson. I don't think you'd ask me to stick around if you weren't sure."

Suddenly, his palm cupped the side of her cheek and he brought her lips up to his, kissing her fiercely. It wasn't intended to start yet another round, but he kissed her deeply, intently. She could feel him giving over to her, surrendering and laying it all out on the table for her. Perhaps the kiss was to let her know how right she was. She got the impression that he was grateful. Grateful for her staying, for coming back for him at all...for trusting him.

When their lips parted, he gently caressed the side of her face with his thumb and rested his forehead against hers. "I'm really glad you're here," he whispered.

"I'm glad, too."

He folded her back up in his arms and they fell asleep, wrapped and tangled in each other's embrace for the rest of the night.

When morning dawned, Gabby rolled over and squinted into the bright sunlight that shone through large windows and she blinked several times, reorienting herself and remembering where she was. After scenes from the previous night flashed in her head- her date, Emerson showing up looking furious, their first kiss at the door and the many, *many* kisses that followed- she looked on either side of her to find that she was in bed alone. Naked, and alone.

She yawned as she sat up and her eyes took in the bedroom. It was very modern, decorated in blacks, whites, and grays. The king-sized platform bed was in the middle of a long wall adjacent to the windows overlooking downtown Traverse City to Lake Michigan. Crisp white sheets contrasted starkly with the black upholstered headboard and dark gray accent wall. The rest of the walls in the room were painted in a feather light gray that nearly looked white. The bed was placed over a wolf-gray and white faux-fur area rug on top of dark gray wood floors. The walls were bare except for some black and white artwork, and there was a door closest to her side of the bed that led to the en suite bathroom that housed a fully tiled shower encased on two sides with floor-to-ceiling glass.

The whole place was modern, elegant, and overtly masculine, but the bedroom in particular was even more so than the rest of the apartment. It wasn't hard to imagine that Emerson used this room for two things: Sleeping and screwing.

Next to the bed she noticed floating nightstands on either side, and on the nightstand closest to her was a small notepad and a pen that was flipped open. A short note was written on the page in neat, efficient, no-nonsense handwriting: *Went to get coffee and breakfast. Stay in bed- I'll bring it to you.*

Smiling, she read the note again. It didn't surprise her that he didn't even have coffee on hand; clearly, he was not the type to ask a woman to stick around long after sharing a night together, but the fact that he'd gotten up early just to be able to bring her breakfast in bed made her insides warm and her stomach fluttered giddily.

She sunk back into the pillows and rolled onto her stomach, inhaling the scent of his sheets. His body wash, his cologne, his natural all-male musk ignited her senses and she rubbed her bare legs through the clean sheets, replaying some of the steamier parts of the previous night's events in her head. It didn't take long for her to get impatient and wish Emerson would just hurry up and get back, breakfast or not.

Then there was a knock on the door and Gabby stilled. Emerson wouldn't be knocking on his own door…unless he locked himself out?

She wondered if he'd walked to get breakfast since he lived right down-town, so she decided to slip out of bed and pull on one of Emerson's shirts and a pair of his boxers before wandering to the door.

Peeking through the peep-hole, she was disappointed to see that it wasn't Emerson, but instead a woman.

Of course...I should have prepared for this.

She chewed her lip for a few seconds before deciding to confront this demon head-on. She was nothing if not an intimidating boss bitch who could tell some former side piece to take a hike, right? Touseling her hair, hoping it looked like that sexy kind of freshly-fucked hair and not a rat's nest of bed head, she swung the door open and stared down her opponent.

The woman was certainly attractive, and noticeably young. She had thick, curly hair that nearly fell to her waist and it was a beautiful shade of dark caramel brown with natural-looking honey highlights. Her heart-shaped face and bright green eyes appeared surprised to see Gabby standing in the doorway instead of the hunk she was probably looking to get jiggy with at nine in the morning.

"Can I help you?" Gabby asked casually.

"Oh...hi," the woman said. She hesitated for a few beats and shifted the items she was holding awkwardly. Gabby's eyes swept down to the heap of what appeared to be clothing in the woman's arms. "I'm so sorry to interrupt...is Emerson...home?"

"Not at the moment, no. He went to get us some breakfast," Gabby replied. Assuming he didn't do breakfast in bed for any of those regular hookups- *hadn't he said he ended things with them?*- she wanted to throw that in this girl's face. A show of dominance. Superiority. Favoritism.

"He did?" The girl looked confused and then her eyes widened and she smiled. "Oh! Are you Gabby?"

"What?" She was genuinely confused. Had he told the girls he used to hook up with about her, too? "Um...yes...I am."

"Oh, thank God!" The woman sighed. "I heard about how you were on a date with some other guy last night, so when I opened the door and there's a woman in Emerson's underwear I'm thinking *oh great, he's back down the rabbit hole!* But it's you! This is so great!"

Thoroughly confused and at a loss for words now, Gabby simply stood with her mouth hanging half open.

The girl shook her head and her shiny curls bounced. "Sorry, I'm Lizzie- Lizzie Miller. I think you've met my brother, Jett?"

"Oh...yeah, I know Jett. You're his sister?" She squinted and furrowed her brow, trying to work out the puzzle as to why this woman was here at all. "So you and Emerson are...just friends?"

"Oh God, yes," Lizzie said, laughing. "Do you mind if I come in? These are getting heavy." She lifted the heap of clothing in her arms and Gabby stepped aside.

Lizzie moved into the apartment as though she'd been there before and flung the pile of clothes onto the kitchen island.

"So...Emerson really told all of his friends about me?" Gabby couldn't help the smile that curved the corners of her lips.

"Yeah. We're a big group, but word gets around fast. We're all sort of like nosey, co-dependent, gossipping weirdos, but I love it. You'll figure it out soon enough." Lizzie began dividing the clothes, grabbing them by their hangers and laying them out separately. Gabby saw that they were all dresses, though it didn't really answer all of her questions.

"What's...with all the dresses?"

"The other day at lunch Emerson promised to be, like...my dating coach," Lizzie explained, but Gabby only raised an eyebrow, even more curious. "I have this tendency to date really shitty guys. Just the other day, Emerson witnessed one of the breakups. He interfered and threatened to tear Kyle's penis off because he called me a slut, then he brought me back here and we played video games. Then Tyler called and, Emerson being his usual self, was joking around and made it sound like we were doing the dance with no pants, when really it was just *Dance Dance Revolution* on the Playstation. Then my brother showed up, punched Emerson in the face, and then we all went to lunch and Emerson promised to help me make better choices."

Again, Gabby's mouth hung open as she tried to figure out a response. Lizzie spoke quickly and in a tone that suggested everything she said was the most important and most exciting thing in the world. It made her feel like she was in high school again, but there was something oddly charming and endearing about the girl.

"So the dresses-" Lizzie began to answer the original question when the door to the apartment swung open again and Emerson stepped through with a drink tray with two large Starbucks coffees and a large brown paper bag emitting a fantastic smell. He stopped short when he spotted the unexpected guest and when his gaze flickered to Gabby, she recognized the look of confusion on his face.

Smiling, she greeted him, "Hey you...Lizzie here was just telling me all about your...adventures the other day." She glanced at Lizzie and asked, "Did you say something about Jett punching him?"

The tension released from Emerson's posture and he continued into the apartment, setting the drink tray and food bag on the counter, away from Lizzie's dresses.

"Right in the mouth!" Lizzie confirmed.

Eyes wide with both shock and amusement, Gabby looked at Emerson. "I thought your lip was a little puffy."

He grunted and handed her one of the coffees, then sipped the other before asking, "Lizzie, why are you here?"

"You're my dating coach, remember?"

Sighing and taking another large swallow of coffee, he seemed to prepare himself. "Okay...and is this like a full time job, or...?"

"You know it's Quinn and Raelyn's wedding today and I don't have a date!" Lizzie replied.

Emerson grabbed two plates out of a cupboard and silverware from a drawer, then began unpacking the contents of the large bag. "I told you to go with Tyler. He's nothing like the guys you usually date- he's a good guy."

"I know he's a good guy, but I also told you that there's no way Tyler would ever think of me that way," Lizzie said, and Gabby thought she might have sensed a little bit of bite to her words. Everything about

Lizzie seemed so friendly, like she lived in a world of sunshine, rainbows, and unicorns, so it was hard to tell.

"Tyler...like *our* Tyler?" she asked, looking at Emerson and he nodded. She turned back to Lizzie. "He's so nice, and if he's single, why not?"

Lizzie rolled her eyes as she laid out a long, dusty rose, strapless dress. "You don't get it. Tyler is my brother's best friend's brother. We've known each other since we were kids. He's a few years older than me so he just remembers me as the annoying little girl who was there when he got to hang out with Chris and Jett. When they were in high school, I was still in elementary school, obsessing over One Direction. They used to steal my diary and read it out loud to each other. It was mortifying."

Emerson and Gabby exchanged a small laugh. "What kind of things did you write in your diary?" he asked, then mocked a gossipy teenage voices, "*Like OMG, today my crush complimented my lip gloss- I'm totally going to let him take my V card at the Spring Fling.*"

"I wrote *QC + LM* with little hearts all over one page, and I even practiced my *Lizzie Casey* signature on a few of them," she said. "God, I had the biggest crush on Quinn. I even wrote a poem about his eyes! His face got so red when they found that page- I wanted to die."

"Well, I know things were different back then, but I guarantee there are plenty of girls today who practice the same thing," Gabby assured her.

"One time in middle school I even wrote different sex-ed questions down and Jett found those, too. He read them to Chris, Quinn, Tyler, and Rae, and then threatened to tell our dad."

"What kinds of questions?" Emerson asked, seeming more amused now by this intrusion than annoyed.

"I distinctly remember wanting to know how fingering worked. Like...*does a boy actually just put his fingers in there and wiggle them around? And what if I have to pee?*"

Emerson bursted out into one of his rare, full, booming laughs. "Oh God, that's awesome!"

Gabby bit back her laugh, feeling for the girl and thinking that must have been absolutely mortifying. Lizzie sighed and leaned back on the counter. "Rae told the boys to stop being mean and then stopped by my room to actually answer the questions, so that was nice at least. But yeah…that's why I'm not asking Tyler, anyway."

"So…you want Emerson to pick your outfit for the wedding then?" Gabby guessed, looking at the display of seven different dresses now laying out in the kitchen and dining room.

"Dean Bennett is going to be there!" Lizzie squealed. "And Weston Bell, *and* Parker Preston! All eligible bachelors, all professional baseball players. I think I could totally be an MLB wife, don't you?"

Immediately intrigued, Gabby asked, "Where is this now?" Emerson cleared his throat loudly and glared when she turned her attention back to him.

"Wow, poor timing to get a boyfriend," said Lizzie, eyeing them. "You could have been my plus one."

"Boyfriend?" Gabby repeated, though she hadn't meant to say it out loud. She locked eyes with Emerson who looked equally confused-surprised-curious.

"That's what this is, right?" Lizzie asked. "I mean, you both like each other…you want to be together and not with anyone else. Maybe you should have this talk."

"Right," Emerson said, now looking at the food between them on the kitchen island.

"So…" Lizzie prompted. Both Emerson and Gabby looked from her to each other.

Oh, so we're doing this now. With an audience. Cool.

"Well," said Emerson, clearing his throat again. He scratched his stomach over his thin t-shirt and raised his eyes from the food to Gabby. "I mean, you know how I feel. I…I want to be with you."

"Yaaaay!" Lizzie clapped her hands quietly and continued to watch eagerly for Gabby's response.

She felt immensely awkward standing there in nothing but a t-shirt and boxers with this girl whom she had just met, but who apparently knew all about her. But when she met Emerson's blue eyes, it was like calming water. She trusted him. She was ready to jump in.

"Yeah, I want to be with you, too." Her shy grin widened at the sight of his beaming smile.

Lizzie gasped excitedly. "Oh, yay! I now pronounce you boyfriend and girlfriend- Now kiss!" Emerson glared at her and she *almost* looked apologetic. "Sorry, I'm just getting into the wedding spirit. Now help me pick a dress and I'll get out of your hair!"

As Emerson made up his and Gabby's plates filled with French toast, bacon, and eggs from the large take-out bag, Lizzie grabbed her first dress choice and ran into the bathroom down the hall. They sat together at the kitchen island and dug in.

"I'm sorry about Lizzie," he said with a playful smirk. "I feel a little bit like I fed a stray cat and she's just going to keep showing up."

"Because you were nice to her and helped her with her douchey ex-boyfriend?" she asked, quirking an eyebrow and unable to conceal a grin. "That was actually really sweet of you."

He shrugged and shoveled a large bite of French toast into his mouth. "I figured it's what her brother would have done, although he still punched me in the face for bringing her back here."

Gabby scoffed. "You brought that on yourself, didn't you? She said you told Tyler you guys were hooking up!"

"No, no- That's not true. I told him I brought her back here for a *cardio workout*. He filled in the blanks. Besides, I was just trying to see if he felt anything for her, and I think I was right about that. Why else would he have run straight to Jett to tattle on me?"

"Well, I don't blame her for not wanting to go with Tyler, I guess. It kind of sounds like they tormented her when she was little."

Emerson waved a dismissive hand. "Nah, she says Jett was the best brother ever. That's probably the only time he was ever mean, and if Rae told them to stop, I bet they never did it again." Gabby raised an eyebrow curiously, so he continued, "It's like a crime in their world to upset Princess Rae. Back in December, Jett almost didn't hire a new manager because he knew Rae didn't like her. The first year I moved up here, Chris and Jett used to get together to play football with different teams in the area, just for something to do, I guess. Anyway, Rae somehow convinced them to kick a guy off their team and put me in his place. Don't get me wrong, I enjoy football, but I never would've asked them to do that."

"Sounds like she just wanted them to like you," she offered. "Or she wanted you to see that she had two friends big enough to kick your ass who would do anything for her." An unsettling feeling rolled in her gut as she remembered how beautiful Raelyn had been in person. It didn't surprise her that a girl like that could make all sorts of men do exactly what she wanted. Did she still have that kind of hold on Emerson? Did she ever? If they were going to be in the same social circle, Gabby knew she'd come across The Ex more than a few times. Maybe she would just have to get used to her. Maybe they'd even get along. Though the thought of Emerson being as devoted to making his ex happy as all the other men in her life seemed to be was adamantly working against that conclusion.

"I met her last night," she blurted out suddenly. "Raelyn, I mean...your ex."

Emerson's brows furrowed in confusion. "How?"

"My date took me to Chateau Delecroix and they were having their rehearsal dinner in a separate ballroom." She added sardonically, "Looks like *Princess Rae* really wants to live up to her name, getting married in a place like that."

She had never been the catty type, and honestly, remembering the brief interaction with Raelyn DeRose, she'd actually thought she seemed like a nice person. But the reminder of who she once was to Emerson...that he had moved away from home to be with her, uprooted his life and picked his place of employment in a town where *she* wanted to live made her feel hot and anxious with jealousy. Would he do the same for her if she decided she wanted to move later down the road?

"The reason she has that nickname- which she hates, by the way- is because her parents own that place. Along with a few others in France, but still..." He put his fork down and brushed his fingers along her cheek. "There's absolutely no reason for you to feel jealous or intimidated by her. We broke up over two years ago and I chose not to be with her. I know I said the breakup was mutual, but..." He hesitated for a few beats and Gabby watched as a stream of unsteady emotions passed over his face and behind his eyes. "I'm responsible for...I'm the reason we broke up."

Gabby was still formulating her question, unsure of what to make of Emerson's comment, when Lizzie's voice broke across the room. "What do we think of this one?"

Emerson held Gabby's gaze for another fraction of a second before blinking away and turning his attention on Lizzie. He made a face. "No. Not that one."

"Seriously?" Lizzie asked, looking down at the buttercup yellow tea-length dress. "What's wrong with it?"

"Are you going to a goddamn tea party, or are you trying to seduce some millionaires?" Emerson replied harshly. "No yellow. And don't bother trying that pink one on either. Think sexy. Got anything black or dark blue...maybe red?" He looked at the array of dresses spread throughout the space before pointing to a floor length emerald silk gown draped over a chair. "That one. If the wedding is at the Chateau, you know it's gonna be fancy."

"The ceremony is on the beach. I don't know about silk on the beach, and the reception is the outdoor venue, not the ballroom," Lizzie replied uncertainly, but she strode over to the green dress and picked it up anyway.

"Just go try it on," he insisted. When Lizzie made her way back down the hall, his attention went back to Gabby. He took her hand in his and pulled it to his mouth and feathering a kiss over her knuckles. "Listen, Gabe...I want you and no one else. I know I'm a big chance to take, but I won't let you down."

She stared back into the gray-blue sea of his eyes, certain that he'd been about to say something important before Lizzie had come out in her yellow atrocity.

He was hers now. Her *boyfriend.* Emerson Yates…was her boyfriend.

She felt the flutter of her pulse beneath her skin as Emerson's lips grazed her hand, then he leaned closer and melted his mouth over hers. She sunk into it, breathing him in as his scent, his touch, his very presence soothed and eased every last bit of lingering doubt out of her thoughts.

Chapter 19

It was the first week of July and Emerson was looking forward to a long weekend of spending time at the beach with Gabriella and whoever else wanted to join. Usually he spent the fourth of July weekend with a big group of people out on the water, but this year he didn't care who else was around as long as she was with him. The past three weeks had been complete and utter perfection. He was in a relationship. He had a girlfriend, and things were actually fucking fantastic. He wasn't freaking out anymore about his feelings, but welcoming them, delving deeper into his relationship with every passing day.

Being with her was everything he didn't know he was missing. Robby and Kolbe had both transitioned into summer travel baseball leagues, and Emerson loved joining Gabriella and her whole family on the days they could make games. Her family was warm and inviting, the complete opposite of what he was used to. He'd developed friendships with Marco and Max, and had a similar relationship with Robby now as he did with Kolbe. Since the two were inseparable, he now hosted both Kolbe and Robby at his place on the weekends that Kolbe stayed over. They played video games, talked about girls and sports, and every bit of it was fucking awesome. He never imagined himself actually enjoying the crazy chaos of a big family, but he was now a little envious of Gabriella and the way she'd grown up.

As expected, Jett, Chris, and Tyler all had animated reactions when he'd shown up at Jett and Zoey's house the weekend after everything was made official with Gabriella under his arm. He'd walked in with a big fat grin on his face and gestured to the stunning woman next to him, saying, "You've all met my *girlfriend,* Gabriella, right?"

Jett had dropped the giant plate of nachos he was preparing, then yelled "Fuck!" at the mess he'd made all over the kitchen floor. Chris's jaw had fallen open as he was rendered speechless, but Tyler beamed, claiming that he'd known all along that this would happen. Zoey must have heard from the other room and she came running and squealing from somewhere else in the house and wrapped Emerson in a tight hug around his waist before pulling Gabriella off onto the porch where Victoria and Lizzie were hanging out.

Now it was the Wednesday before the long-awaited four-day week-end and Emerson was wrapping up a brief on a smaller client, almost giddy thinking about his upcoming lunch date with Gabriella. It was a simple thing, and they'd been having lunch together at work every day since officially declaring their relationship status, but he looked for-ward to it just as much. There was a knock on his door and he smiled, expecting to see his new girlfriend walk through the door, but instead it was his favorite ginger coming to visit from the third floor.

"Brody, what's up?" he greeted. His voice was abundantly more cheerful than what he was used to, but that seemed to be his new tone over the last few weeks.

"You seem chipper," Brody noted, closing the door behind him. "What are you doing this weekend? I thought maybe you and the new lady could come over. I feel bad, I've been working so much I've really only been able to hang out with you guys a couple times."

"This weekend?" Emerson glanced at his computer screen where he clicked open his calendar which he already knew would show he had the whole weekend open. "We don't have plans yet, but..." He hesi-tated then, not knowing how to put into words what he was thinking. Sure, things were different now that he had Gabriella and he'd stopped trying to sleep with every woman in the bay area, but something told him Amira's opinion of him hadn't changed much.

"But what?" Brody asked. "I feel like Jett and Tyler know you better now than I do. I know I've been working a lot, and Amira-" He stopped, an amused grin breaking out across his face as he nodded. "Amira. That's what this is about."

"She *hates* me. And I'm not saying I didn't do anything to deserve that from her, but…I don't want her talking to Gabby about all the things that make me a bad person. I just think it could be a bad idea," he explained. "Unless you think she's over it. I mean, Rae doesn't even hate me anymore, so why should your wife? Don't you think she's overreacting a bit? It's been over two years."

Brody sauntered his lanky frame over to the chair in front of Emerson's desk and sat down. "She hasn't always hated you, and I think she could set aside her…unfavorable opinion of you for a night. I think she'd even be open to trying to see that you've changed. That you're not the same guy who cheated on her best friend."

"Yeah, her best friend, not her. I don't get why she's still mad when Rae's over it."

Brody pinned him with a challenging stare. "What if I told you Amira cheated on me? I got home and found her in bed with some other dude. How would you respond?"

"I'd say fuck that bitch," he replied immediately.

"Even if I told you I was over it down the road?"

"Well yeah, I mean…I guess I wouldn't be able to see her as anything else. Just the woman who broke your heart when you did absolutely nothing to deserve it," he said, his volume and intensity increasing as he completely forgot how they'd arrived at such a topic. "Wait- this isn't your way of breaking this to me, right? Is she fucking around?"

Laughing, Brody shook his head. "No, I'm pointing out that it's easier to be mad and stay mad when someone hurts someone you care about. Yeah, she's reluctant to be your friend again as easily as everyone else, but you have to start somewhere. So, why don't you start with dinner? We'll provide food and drinks and we can all hang out. She can get to know Gabriella, and maybe she'll feel better about things. Now that Rae's happily married to the man of her dreams, maybe Amira can see that all of this happened for a reason."

Emerson considered it for a minute, chewing the inside of his cheek. "Okay, but I don't want to put Gabby in a weird spot either. I don't want Amira treating her like she's the enemy just because she and Rae are still friends."

"She wouldn't do that," Brody said. "She knows her problem is with you, not your girlfriend. Give her some credit here."

As Emerson nodded, his phone began buzzing on his desk. It was closer to Brody, and when his friend looked down at the screen he cringed. Brody picked up the phone like it was covered in something toxic as he handed it over to Emerson. "Might wanna get that…or not."

Taking the phone, his stomach plummeted as he read the name *Johnathan* lighting up the screen. What the fuck did his dad want? He closed his eyes and braced himself before swiping to answer. "Dad."

"Son," the equally cold voice greeted him from the other line. "Where the hell have you been? I haven't seen you in ages."

Confused, though not entirely convinced that his father was concerned about his well-being, he furrowed his brow and responded, "I've been working, Dad. In Traverse City, remember?"

"Of course I remember," Johnathan snapped. "Why you would waste your time and money- not to mention *my* money that paid for your education- on a firm like that is beyond me. You should be back down state. You need to work at one of my offices so you can start working your way up through the ranks. You don't want to be a damn bank lawyer for the rest of your life, do you?"

He was tempted to point out that he hadn't wanted to be a lawyer at all, but knew that would only open a new argument that he wasn't prepared to get into. "There's nothing wrong with the firm I work at. It's a corporate law office, the money is good-"

"Oh, I have no doubt it's a decent firm, but doling out home loans to people who can't handle their own finances isn't going to get you on track to becoming a senator."

Closing his eyes again, he leaned back in his chair and pinched the bridge of his nose. He counted to three before responding, teeth gritted, "I don't want to be a senator."

Across from him, Brody shook his head in disbelief, having been witness to this argument on several occasions.

"Sure you do," Johnathan replied. "That's actually why I called. Listen, there's a fundraiser this weekend in Detroit for my campaign. I want you to be there. I'll introduce you to the right people, you can charm them and their wives and they'll be eating out of the palm of your hand, getting ready to set up your first campaign. We'll figure out the details-"

"Dad, I have no interest-"

"I don't give a damn what you are or aren't interested in, Emerson." There was a thick layer of ice in Johnathan's words, and Emerson reflexively snapped his mouth shut and straightened his back. He wanted to tell him to fuck off, he wanted to hang up, he wanted to tell his own father that he could go to Hell, but instead, he sat quietly and waited for his dad to give him his orders.

"The fundraiser starts at seven o'clock, you will be there early so we can discuss what we'll be telling these donors. *My* donors, Emerson. You understand I'm giving up money that could go into my own campaign to get yours started. Do you realize how many people would kill for this opportunity?"

Again, he wanted to tell his dad that he could take his campaign money and shove it up his ass, or tell him to find someone who actually wanted the opportunity if it's such a good one. Instead, however, he bit his tongue. "Yeah, Dad, I get it."

"Bring a date, too," Johnathan clipped. "Someone respectable, attractive. If she can't keep a conversation with the guests, at least make sure we have something interesting to look at. Got it?"

Jaw clenched, Emerson fumed now. The thought of subjecting Gabriella to his dad's scrutiny gnawed at him. He didn't want to bring her within five miles of that man, let alone bring her to a party he'd set up just to pressure him into a new career path. One that he found astonishingly less appealing than the one he'd already been pushed into.

Not only did he feel an innate need to protect her from him, but he also didn't want her to meet Johnathan for selfish reasons. He didn't want her to see that side of him. The side that his dad brought out. The quiet, submissive, obedient robot that did as he was asked to avoid further criticism.

He swallowed hard. "Got it."

"Good. I'll have my assistant send over the details. Saturday at the Masonic Temple. Black tie, of course."

The sound of his office door opening caught his attention again and he looked up to see Gabriella walking in and shutting the door quietly behind her. She smiled at Brody when he waved, but remained quiet as he wrapped up his conversation.

"Of course. I have to go, though, I have a client," he lied. "See you this weekend." He hung up, feeling sick, but tried to hold it together for the woman who took his breath away when she walked in.

"Everything okay?" she asked. "You look a little pale."

"I'm fine," he replied, forcing a smile. "You look amazing today, have I told you that yet?"

"You tell me every day," she said, smiling. "Who was that? You seriously look like you're going to throw up."

He stood up and made his way over to greet her, pulling her to his chest. He tilted her chin up and planted a kiss on her full lips. "Is that not the usual reaction when speaking with your dad? Because that's how I always feel when I talk to mine."

"That was your dad on the phone?" Her eyes widened. "Wow, what did he want?"

"The usual. Trying to push me into a career in politics. Although this time he went a step further and is having a big fundraising event in Detroit. He wants me to go and pimp myself out to donors and lobbyists so we can start discussing my first campaign."

Brody snorted and shook his head. "Seriously?"

"You told him you don't want to be a politician, right?" Gabriella asked. The sweetness and concern in her voice warmed through his chest. "I mean, he can't force you to run for office if you don't want to."

"Have you learned nothing from dating a Yates man?" Brody asked. "They're head-strong, obnoxiously persistent, and they never take no for an answer." He looked at Emerson. "You're putting on a tux and dancing when he tells you to dance, aren't you?"

Emerson grimaced. "I agreed to go." He swept a hand through Gabriella's hair and cupped her cheek. "He also wants me to bring a date."

Seeming unphased and having no idea what it meant that she would be meeting his father, she simply shrugged. "Okay, sure. When is this thing? And can I be the one to tell him there's no way in hell you're going to be a politician?"

He sighed. "I've told him countless times, but he refuses to hear me or simply doesn't care. Probably the latter."

"Why don't you just tell him to fuck off?" she suggested.

Ah, if only it were that simple. Emerson and Brody both laughed. "I would love to, but that wouldn't get me anywhere. It's hard to explain. My relationship with my dad has never been a good one, and he's always…intimidated me, I guess. He's the only person I feel like I can't just tell off. He's an asshole and I can't fucking stand the guy, but he's my dad. That seems to mean something for some reason."

"Okay, well I'll be there. Just let me know when and where and give me enough time to find something to wear." She grabbed his tie and pulled him down to her mouth.

Her kiss was warm and wet, and was already making his body react in ways that told him he needed to find a private place ASAP. Somehow able to pull away from her, he said, "It's this weekend. Saturday at seven in Detroit." Looking at Brody who was averting his gaze and scrolling through his phone, he got his attention again. "We'll have to take a rain check on that double date, then."

Brody nodded and stood from his chair. "Sure thing. I'll let Amira know we can plan for the following weekend then. Friday night?"

"Sounds good," Emerson agreed. "Tell Amira I look forward to seeing her."

Brody rolled his eyes. "Yeah, I'll make sure she knows you can't wait. And good luck this weekend." He shook Emerson's hand. "You've got my vote, whatever the fuck you're running for."

As Brody made his way out of the office, Emerson laugh-slash-groaned. "I can't fucking believe this. My dad is...unbelievable. What if he makes me go through with it? What if I end up in the fucking mayor's office or something because of this goddamn fundraiser?"

Gabriella hummed, her face buried in his neck. "That might be kind of fun...Mister Mayor." She kissed his neck and up to his jaw. "Watching you make all sorts of executive decisions all day might be...kind of hot."

"Well, no one has ever put it that way before..." Emerson's eyebrow twitched as his body warmed against hers, his dress pants feeling increasingly tighter by the second.

"Really?" she teased. "You're so good at making executive decisions in other areas. One area in particular seems to stand out..." She slid her hand down his stomach and over his pants, palming his growing erection.

He groaned and pushed against her hand. "That's true...I'm quite the executor of my own bedroom."

"Doesn't have to be the bedroom if I remember correctly."

"Fuck." He smoothed his hands up her sides to her breasts, kneading them through the light cotton fabric of her fitted button-up. "Babe, I'm supposed to take you to lunch. You're making it hard to leave this room."

"Oh, I'm perfectly aware of how hard I'm making it." She nipped at his jaw and rubbed the length of his hardened flesh through his pants again. "Maybe I thought I'd bring lunch to you."

His hooded eyes dropped down to her thighs, visible beneath her black pencil skirt. Hands skimming down her sides before trailing back up, bringing her skirt with them, he groaned when he caught sight of the tops of her sexy black thigh-high stockings being held in place with garter straps. Without a second's hesitation, he grabbed her hand and pulled her out of the office.

"Where are we going?" Gabriella's voice rang over the sound of blood rushing from every extremity in his body to his dick.

"My place," he grumbled in response, trying his hardest to focus on anything other than what he'd just seen. He wanted her spread out on his bed in nothing but those thigh-highs and garter. Forget lunch, he was ravenous for something else.

"Your place?" she half-giggled.

"Yep, for a quick fuck. And then we'll pick up lunch on the way back."

True to his word, he drove the short distance to his place, somehow kept himself from tearing her clothes off on the elevator ride up, but once inside his apartment, it was on. He shoved her pencil skirt down, fumbled with the buttons of her blouse, careful not to tear them off even though he wanted to. He carried her back to his bedroom and tossed her onto his bed and completely ravished her.

His shirt hung open with his tie loosened around his neck and he barely took the time to shove his pants all the way down before rolling a condom on and sinking himself into her. This woman was his complete undoing. He lost his fucking mind over her, had no way of reining in his urges around her, and the worst part was that he loved every unhinged minute of it. It terrified him to no end to think of how desperately he needed her, how intensely he craved her, and how fucking impossible it was to say no to her. She completely owned him.

Gabriella's fingers tangled and pulled at his hair, she clawed at his neck and shoulders as she came and screamed his name, her stocking-covered legs wrapped around his waist. Emerson plunged deeper, determined to reach every piece of her, to embed himself into her the way he felt she had done to him. When the tightening sensation in his balls released, his whole body shook as he came hard, collapsing his weight on top of her, his pants still trapping his ankles.

"Sorry," he breathed into her neck. "That was a lot faster than it probably should have been."

She giggled and kissed his cheek. "You did promise me a quick fuck."

"I don't know how you do this to me," he confessed. "Drive me so fucking wild I don't even get my pants all the way off before I come."

"I'll take it as a compliment," she said as he rolled off of her and lay next to her.

He took her hand and brought it to his lips. "Are you sure you're okay with the whole fundraiser thing? It's short notice, and my dad is not a fun person to deal with. Meeting him is something most people should really put off as long as possible."

She traced his jaw with her fingertips and rolled to face him. "I know your relationship with him is…strained…but I want to be there for you. I know the whole night is kind of a joke and you have no plans to ever go through with whatever he's got set up for you, but I still want to be there to support you. Whatever happens, I want you to know I'm in your corner."

He appreciated her words and the gesture more than she may ever know. The fact that she just wanted to be there for him meant the world. Maybe she could bring him some strength and he'd actually be able to stand up to Johnathan for a change. It was a long shot, but with Gabriella by his side, anything felt possible.

It was Saturday afternoon and Gabby was waiting for Emerson to pick her up for their four hour drive to Detroit. Emerson was planning on getting to their hotel to get settled in before getting dressed for the big event. She, however, was planning on making him as relaxed as possible once arriving at the hotel. The tension was practically visible in his shoulders all week, and she was trying to stay strong for him, though she would be lying if she said she weren't a little anxious, too.

The day after Emerson got the phone call from his dad, she'd snuck down to the third floor and asked Brody for information. She knew the father and son didn't get along, and she knew that Johnathan Yates was a power-hungry dictator, but she wanted to know more about Emerson's relationship with him. Why did the thought of him stress him out? Why was Emerson intimidated by him? She couldn't fathom Emerson being intimidated by anyone.

Brody had reluctantly filled in some of the blanks, explaining that Johnathan was a very powerful man, and he'd ruled his household with an iron fist. Emerson realized at a young age that it was just easier to go along with whatever his dad wanted than to upset him. As he got older, he learned Johnathan had his hands in every facet of the government and knew all the right people to provide one-of-a-kind opportunities for his son, as well as the people who could tear his son's life apart if Emerson chose to defy him.

She left Brody's office with an unsettled feeling in her stomach, but felt even more determined to have Emerson's back on Saturday when he needed her. Making a good impression on Johnathan Yates was the least of her worries; she needed to make sure Emerson was at ease, that he wasn't anxious around his father, and even hoped that she could help him feel confident throughout the night. She hated the thought of someone being able to strike out his sexy, cocky demeanor. Well, except for her. But that was different.

Standing in the lobby of her condominium with two luggage bags and a garment bag, she got the text that Emerson was there. Looking out the door, she didn't see his black Lexus at the curb, but instead there was an all-black luxury limousine waiting for her. A driver pulled the door open and Emerson stepped out looking absolutely gorgeous. He'd taken off his suit jacket, but stood in a pair of gray dress pants and a white dress shirt with the sleeves rolled up, showcasing his corded, muscular forearms. A patterned blue and silver tie hung loose from his neck, giving him the most perfect intentionally-disheveled look. And if that weren't enough, his Wayfarer sunglasses and the sexy smirk he gave her when he saw her checking him out made her want to slip out of her panties right there on the sidewalk. She wouldn't need them anyway, right?

She was completely unashamed that he'd caught her staring, possibly with her mouth hanging open and drool pooling at her feet, as he approached her and offered to take her bags.

"You know we're only going for one night, right?" he asked, taking one of the luggage bags by the handle, while his other hand cupped her face and brought her to his lips.

Her heart pounded and butterflies tingled in her stomach as her eyes grazed over him again from head to toe. God, she just wanted to take a bite out of him. Finding her voice, though it didn't entirely sound like her own voice, she replied, "Always best to be prepared."

The driver who'd opened the door took Gabby's other luggage and garment bag and carried them over to the limousine, storing them in the trunk. Emerson led her to the car and motioned for her to get in ahead of him. She slid along the long bench seat that faced a glowing, fully stocked mini bar and Emerson slid in next to her.

"You're staring," he said, a sexy, crooked grin still plastered to his face. He kissed her and pulled her legs across his lap.

"You just look so...sexy...confident...in your element," she replied between kisses. "Are you sure you don't want to be the mayor or something?"

"I'm pretty sure." He skated his hands up her legs. She was wearing a short, sleeveless, rust orange romper, with a pair of strappy black sandals and was glad she'd picked something that showed so much skin now that she had four hours in the back of a limousine with him. She loved the feel of his hands on her and was sure she'd get her fill on their way south. With his lips brushing against the nape of her neck, he pointed out, "I thought you hated politicians."

"I do," she agreed. "Maybe the idea of calling you Mister Mayor is getting to me. I think you'd wear the title well. But I obviously just want what's going to make you happy. If you decide to go along with your dad's whole charade to get you into politics, I'll support you. If you want to tell him to eat a bag of dicks, I support that, too."

He laughed and his breath breezed across her bare skin. "We can definitely role-play the Mister Mayor thing if you want."

"Role-play, huh?" she asked, leaning back. "Is that something you're into?"

"I can be into whatever you want me to be."

"You would wear a full costume if I wanted?" she challenged, brow arched.

"Sure." He shrugged. "I have costumes."

"You do? How did I not know this yet?"

"I'm just easing you into my wicked ways, one little step at a time. You've still got a lot to learn about me."

"What costumes do you have?" she pressed.

He scratched his jaw and hesitated. "Well, I have three costumes. And they're all...Thor."

"Thor?" She looked at him, incredulous. "Like the Avenger?"

"Like the best Avenger, yeah," he replied defensively.

"Oh my God...You're a nerd," she said slowly, a wide grin dragging its way across her face.

"Oh my God," he repeated in the exact same tone. "How did you not have that figured out yet? Video game nights with the guys, my Avengers Blu-ray collection is separated from all my other movies, and I have a shit ton of comic books- although, I guess those are in Kolbe's room, so you might not have realized those are all mine. But seriously, how many superhero discussions have you listened to over the past few weeks?"

She laughed now that the discussions were resurfacing in her mind. "I think you mean arguments." Emerson had gotten into various heated conversations with Jett, Tyler, Brody, Kolbe, and even Robby about superheroes and their movies.

"See? So if you hadn't figured that out yet, that's on you."

"So, what's that mean? I need to get myself a Valkyrie costume to go with your Thor?"

Emerson's mouth dropped open. "That would be so hot. Yes."

Shaking her head, she curled her fingers under his jaw and brought him toward her. "What am I going to do with you Mr. Yates?"

He moved so that he was now holding himself above her and she was lying beneath him on the cushioned bench. "I think you mean Mr. Mayor, and I'm sure I can come up with a few things for today's agenda." His mouth covered hers and heat instantly flooded her entire body as she felt his hard ridge pressing between her legs. Gabby wasn't usually a fan of long car rides, but suddenly four hours didn't seem nearly long enough.

The limo pulled up in front of the MGM Grand just after four o'clock. The driver, Ted, opened the door for them and got their bags loaded up onto a cart. At the check-in desk, Gabby was surprised and admittedly a little turned on when Emerson was greeted by the hotel employees as Mr. Yates. Their backs stood a little straighter, their smiles a little wider as they tried to make a good impression for their special guest. Every male employee wanted to be him, and the female employees made no effort to hide their desire to be with him. No wonder he carried himself the way he did, as if the whole world would stop on a dime to make him happy, if this is the kind of treatment he'd grown accustomed to his whole life.

An attractive blonde showed them to their sixteenth-floor room, pointing out and listing all the accommodations on the way. Gabby didn't miss the way her eyes remained focused on Emerson, speaking solely to him as though pretending Gabby wasn't even there. Upon arriving at their door, the woman leaned in and said with a wry, seductive smile, "If there's *anything* at all I can help you with, anything you need, please let me know." Her gaze lingered on Emerson for what felt like several long seconds.

Gabby felt Emerson's arm snake its way around her waist and pull her in close. "Thank you, Jenna, but I think I've got everything I need right here."

For the first time, Jenna's eyes flicked to Gabby and narrowed just the slightest bit. She straightened, leaning out of his space and offered what was supposed to be a friendly smile. "Of course," she said. "Enjoy your stay."

Once in the room, Emerson closed the door behind them and practically yanked Gabby into his chest. With one arm still wrapped around her waist, his other hand slid behind her neck and brought her mouth to his. The kiss was slow, deep, and heated. Suddenly it didn't feel like the air conditioning was on at all in this place and they were back outside in the July heat.

"You're pretty popular around here," Gabby commented as their lips parted for just a few seconds.

"Am I?" he asked. His hand moved from her neck into her hair and pulled her mouth back over his.

She moaned into his kiss, leaned into his large, muscular frame and soaked it in. His scent, his hands on her, his lips, firm and demanding, his tongue plunging to explore her mouth, the prickle of his neatly trimmed beard against her skin.

"Every woman on our way up here looked at you like it was shark week and you were their last piece of chocolate."

"Shark week?" he questioned, dipping his head to trail over her neck and collar bone.

"You know..." she said, loving the feel of his lips on her, but still concentrating on all the women she suddenly felt competitive against. "Mother Nature's monthly gift."

The low rumble of his laughter vibrated against her skin as he made his way back up her throat. "You're talking about periods right now? That's how you're going to dirty talk me?"

She laughed, too. "You know what I mean. There must have been a dozen women who stared at you like they were going to drop their panties right then and there."

"Hmm...Did they?"

"Jenna practically propositioned you."

He hummed again and tugged her earlobe between his teeth. "I hadn't noticed."

"Seriously?"

With his hands both firmly grabbing her hips, he walked her backward and further into their hotel suite which she now recognized was immaculate. "Seriously," he replied. "I did, however, notice *you* giving me the panty-dropping look when I picked you up." He gently pushed her back onto the king size bed with its bright white comforter and mirrored headboard and climbed over her. His hands grasped her wrists and he pushed them up over her head, pinning her beneath him. "You know, it's kind of sexy when you get jealous."

"Is it?"

"Mhmm." He nuzzled her neck and began placing hot, wet kisses over her skin. "I've got the hottest-"

Kiss.

"Sexiest-"

Kiss.

"Most gorgeous, badass woman in the entire fucking universe-"
Kiss.

"And she still wants everyone else to know they need to back the fuck off what's hers."

She smiled and arched her back away from the mattress as his head dipped lower, trailing his tongue over the sweetheart neckline of her strapless romper. "What about you? Do you ever get jealous?"

"No," he stated, tugging her romper down with his teeth.

"No?" She hadn't expected that response.

He shook his head, now burying his face between her breasts. "When I'm with you, Gabe, I don't take my eyes off you long enough to notice other guys looking."

Oh...well...okay then.

Warmth spread from her belly and chest, down between her thighs where there was a dull, throbbing ache leftover from their four hour car ride. They'd filled the time with role-play, slow, sensual love making, as well as hard and fast fucking. She was sore, but that didn't stop her body from reacting to him.

"But if I did happen to catch someone looking," he continued, now pulling her romper all the way off and letting it pool on the floor, "I would tell him to get a damn good look, because there's no way in hell I'm letting you go." As he slid down her body, she brushed her fingers through his hair and savored the gentle tease of his teeth playing with her panties. "And that's exactly how you should feel when other women look at me. I'm not going anywhere and neither are you."

"So sure of yourself," she teased, though her restless body beneath him wasn't fooling anyone.

He hummed and brushed his lips right between her thighs where her panties still covered her hot, yearning center. She moaned and he pressed his mouth right over her clit. The deep timbre of his voice probably made her start ovulating right then and there. Actually, though she wasn't sure it worked quite like that, she may already have gotten pregnant from it. "Baby, I think we both know I've got my wicked ways of making you stay."

And like the gentleman he was- *sort of-* he didn't even make her beg before slipping off the silky fabric and devouring her. His tongue flicked around her clit before making a long, slow stroke of his tongue over her crease. He moaned like he couldn't get enough and did it again…and again…and *again.* He pulled her legs over his shoulders and flattened his palms over her thighs, pushing them into the mattress and spreading her wide. His strong fingers dug into the soft flesh of her thighs and he pulled her against his mouth. The gentle scrape of his teeth over her clit made her shiver and bite out a loud, shameless moan and she urged him on, bucking her hips up.

One arm curled around her leg and she felt his finger slide inside her, then two. Soft, slow strokes that made her moan and whimper and beg for more. The soreness from earlier made her even more sensitive, and she cried out in dizzy, blinding bliss as he refused to let up.

"Now," she panted, "*God*, Emerson, I want you inside me now."

He stood up abruptly and began unbuckling his belt and snatched a condom out of his back pocket before shoving his pants down along with his boxer briefs. Gabby sat up and reached for him, pulling his shirt free and unbuttoning it with practiced fingers as he rolled on the condom. His tie was already loose, never having fully tightened it from their back seat sexcapades. She began pulling it over his head, but he held his hands over hers, not letting her discard it on the bed. Instead he slid the silky fabric out of her fingers and quickly looped it around both her wrists, tying them together and pushing her arms over her head again.

Holding onto the long end of the tie like a handle, Emerson kept her arms above her head and leaned over her, slowly easing the warm, broad, head of his cock inside her.

"Wrap your legs around my waist," he said roughly, still standing between her legs as he eased back out. She caught her bottom lip between her teeth, immediately missing the pressure between her thighs, but did as he instructed, and used her new position to draw him back in. He growled from deep within his chest as he held back and the sound made her pulse flutter beneath her skin.

"Please," she whimpered, squeezing her legs tighter around his waist. "Please...I need you." He tugged on the tie, causing it to tighten around her wrists and she gasped.

"You didn't get enough of me on the way over here?" He nipped at her jaw and pushed inside, giving her just a little pressure before taking it away again.

"No," she breathed. "Please...I need more."

"Mmm, that's what I like to hear." He gave her a little more. "That good enough?"

She let out a frustrated, tortured groan. "No...please, Emerson. I need you to fuck me."

"Oh is that all?" he asked. "Why didn't you just say so?" His hips snapped into her and she gasped, her mouth open in a silent cry as her head pressed into the mattress. One large hand wrapped around her waist and held her still as he thrusted into her over and over.

Her legs held tight around his waist and she bucked up to meet each and every hard thrust, wishing she could reach out and touch him. Wanting to scrape her fingernails down his chest, claw at his shoulders, slide her hands up the backs of his arms and feel his hard muscles ripple and flex as he moved over her. His mouth covered hers, tongue spearing between her lips and tasting her mouth. He sucked her bottom lip between his teeth and moaned, savoring it like a ripe, juicy piece of fruit on a hot summer day.

Suddenly his movements slowed and his body slid against hers in a sinuous, fluid motion that made the heat inside her ignite, taking off like gasoline to a match. She held on to the sensation of each slow inch in and out, making her body climb to new peaks, new highs. A shudder flared through her and she felt herself squeezing him, clamping down on his cock like a vice as she fell apart around him.

She wasn't even aware of what she was saying, if they were words or just desperate sounds and pleas sliding through her lips. As she came, he returned to his hard and fast jabs before his body shivered and quaked as he bit out a guttural groan. He rocked into her hard and buried his face in her neck, sliding his chest against hers as his cock continued to surge inside her.

The room held nothing but their slowing breaths and steadying heartbeats for several long moments. Emerson released her hands and lifted his head to kiss her. He pressed his forehead against hers and swiped the pad of his thumb beneath her bottom lip, his eyes following its path. Her eyes caught his for a brief moment, mesmerized in the gray-blue sea that was now nothing but calm, peaceful waters. She felt her breath hitch inexplicably as she stared into the depths of them before he abruptly swallowed, cleared his throat, and sat up.

He untied the knot binding her wrists together and she watched his face carefully as he did so. She wasn't sure what it was, but she had sensed a shift, a change in his mood and his demeanor. Sitting next to her, he scrubbed a hand down his face and stared ahead, seemingly at nothing.

She placed a hand on the back of his neck and trailed her fingers lightly back and forth. "Are you okay?"

Clearing his throat again, he nodded. "I'm just…not looking forward to tonight."

"I'm sure it won't be that bad," she said, trying to sound reassuring. "And if it sucks we can totally ditch it. There are probably lots of better parties going on in downtown Detroit on the fourth of July weekend."

He let out a small puff of laughter and shook his head. "My dad's fundraiser isn't really some party I can just ditch, as much as I would love to."

"Well, whatever happens you know I'm just here to support you."

Heaving himself off the bed, he let out a heavy sigh and made his way over to his luggage bag. Gabby admired his naked form from behind, finding herself thinking she didn't get to appreciate that view enough. He held himself with such confidence, even walking completely naked in front of a wide-open window. There was no doubt he was comfortable in his own skin and knew he had absolutely every right to be. She wanted to claw her nails down his hard back and grab his firm ass so she could pull him right back into bed.

"I should probably give you a heads up..." he began. Flipping open his bag, he took out two different ties that were rolled up neatly. "This fundraiser is going to have a lot of people I know...a lot of guys I went to school with, guys I've known for a long time because their parents have been working alongside my dad since I was a kid."

"Okay..." She watched him become tense; he scratched his jaw and fidgeted uncomfortably.

"These people aren't really...They don't live in what many of us would consider *reality*. They're all about money, business, career success...trophy wives. A lot of them are married, but their marriages are more like business arrangements. The joining of families for the purpose of...I don't know...creating an empire...securing success in their endeavors."

Gabby nodded slowly as she listened. She'd heard of people who'd grown up like that, and she'd met a few while attending Yale. They cared about labels, brands, family names and their reputations, and money, money, money. They weren't the kinds of people she'd wanted to surround herself with, but at an ivy league school, they were impossible to avoid.

"I don't remember if I told you that the high school I went to was a private prep academy...but there will be a lot of people here tonight that knew me in high school."

"So, it's like a reunion?" she asked, wondering where he was going with all of this.

He palmed the back of his neck and hesitated. "Kind of, I guess. But I just want you to be aware that you're probably going to…hear some stuff…about me. People like to talk, and some things just never get old."

"What kind of stuff?"

"Just…stuff about what I was like when I was a dumb teenager. Lazy, entitled, and thinking that my dad's money would always be there to bail me out. I was…I was an arrogant little prick, to be honest. I thought I was untouchable and didn't really care how my actions affected others," he explained.

After grabbing a fresh pair of boxer briefs, socks, and settling on a solid black tie, he walked back over to where Gabby still sat. Standing in front of her, he swept his hand down her cheek, traced her jaw with the brush of his knuckles. "You're going to hear a lot of shit that makes me sound like…exactly what I was. I don't want you knowing that side of me, but it's what it is. I can't change it. I can only change who I am now…and I hope the man I am now, at least when I'm with you, is enough to make up for the little shit that I once was."

Gabby took a few moments to digest what he was telling her. She stood up, standing chest to still-naked chest with him and let a wry smile pull up the curve of her lips. "I appreciate the warning, but I kind of had that all figured out within the first ten minutes of knowing you."

His jaw hung open as he tried to look appalled. "Well that…is just…*rude*, Miss Cabrera. I should bend you over and give you spankings for each one of my feelings you just hurt."

She giggled. "I thought you only had one feeling."

"That's right, I do," he said. "Guess I better make it a good spanking." He reached for her and she squealed as she ducked around him and toward the bathroom. She had approximately two seconds to appreciate how luxurious and enormous the room was before Emerson slipped in, wrapped an arm around her waist, and buried his face in the back of her neck, biting playfully.

He held her back pressed up against his chest and spoke low, "Apologize, Miss Cabrera."

"This isn't fair," she argued through her fit of laughter. "You're so much bigger than me!"

"I *am* pretty big, huh?" he asked suggestively, grinding his semi-erection against her bare ass. "God, what kinds of things could I do to you?" His hands gripped her hips firmly and began tilting her forward.

"Okay! Okay, I'm sorry! I apologize, I didn't mean it!" She laughed some more as he pulled her back up to standing.

"You didn't?" He bit her ear and licked behind it.

"No, not at all," she replied. "I didn't think you were like that because you had a rich dad." He waited for her to finish. "I figured you were that way because you're so good looking and knew it."

Humming against her neck, he seemed to consider her response. "That's sort of a back-handed compliment."

She twisted around to face him and slung her arms around the back of his neck. "Ethan, I really do appreciate you giving me a heads up, but I also am very aware of the man you are now. The one I'm lucky enough to call mine. Unless you are a serial killer or did something truly heinous in your past, nothing I hear tonight is going to change how I feel about you now."

His smile looked relieved and he kissed her softly on the lips. "Good. I just needed to hear that." He then glanced down at his watch- the only item he was still wearing- and sighed. "No time for shower sex. Just a regular shower and we need to get ready."

Emerson hopped into the shower and she followed. It was true that she knew who he was now and that she wouldn't think any less of him for his past transgressions, but that didn't make her feel particularly at ease about the upcoming evening. She knew she would feel immensely out of place, and she wasn't looking forward to hearing stories about what an arrogant little shit he'd been so long ago. Then add meeting Emerson's dad on top of all that, knowing she was not the kind of woman who was typically accepted into these social circles. Someone who'd built herself from the ground up, rather than someone who'd been born into a life of wealth and luxury.

But that was nothing she would ever be ashamed of. It was time to put on her boss-girl panties and show everyone exactly who they were dealing with.

Chapter 20

Emerson stepped out of the bathroom fully dressed in his black Tom Ford tuxedo, going with his own style and wearing a slim necktie rather than a bowtie. He'd styled his hair, trimmed up his beard, and sprayed on his favorite cologne, and even he had to admit he was looking pretty damn irresistible. He was ready to see Gabriella's eyes turn dark and lustful when she got her first glimpse of him dressed to the nines, but he was an idiot to think he wasn't the one who would be rendered speechless.

Standing in front of the full length mirror in the bedroom portion of their hotel suite, Gabriella was putting on a pair of shining, dangly, gold earrings, but the earrings were the last thing he was interested in. She was wearing a long, silk gown in a deep burnt orange color. The dress had spaghetti straps that criss-crossed in the back- and *the back. God. Damn.* With the exception of the thin straps, her back was bare, the fabric dipping sinfully low to just cover the first round curves of her ass. When she turned around he felt his jaw drop open as he devoured the sight of the deep, plunging neckline, the way the silk hugged and clung to her mouthwatering, hourglass shape. Her trim waist, the luscious curves of her hips, the high off-center slit that threatened to expose his favorite part of her- those perfectly juicy thighs. The skirt of the dress pooled at her feet and his mind swam with visions of him and Gabriella tangled up in satin sheets, ditching his dad's stuffy fundraiser and having a party of their own right here.

Her smile lit up her face and she took a step toward him, but he held out a hand to stop her. "Hold on." His eyes traveled back up the savory, silky path, stuck for a few extra seconds on her hips, and again at her excruciatingly perfect cleavage.

He was lost for words, which really didn't happen a lot. He had to clear his throat and adjust his tie before speaking again. "Okay, I know what I said about other guys staring at you...but I'm going to have to request that you stay by my side all night."

"Oh yeah?" Her sexy eyebrow arched playfully.

Emerson nodded slowly as his eyes continued their exploration and admiration of the woman before him. "I may even have to follow you into the bathroom."

She closed the gap between them, sliding her hands up his chest and hooking them around the back of his neck. "I guess we're on the same page then. I'm not letting you out of my sight, *Mr. Yates.*"

His laugh melted into a deep groan and his arms looped around her waist, hands on her ass, thumbs trailing the bare skin just above it. "Believe me, Gabe, I'm not even going to notice anyone else. We'll be in a room with two hundred people and I'll only see you."

Their limo was waiting for them downstairs and Ted held the door open as they slid into the back seat. Gabriella was quick to tell him there would be no steamy business on the way to the fundraiser, insisting that her hair and makeup were perfect and she couldn't risk messing that up.

The fundraiser was held in one of three ballrooms at the Masonic Temple, where they'd arrived an hour early, as his dad had requested. Entering the luxurious space, they saw that staff were still scrambling around with their final touches for the evening.

Johnathan and Corrine were both waiting for him. His mother, Corrine, was talking to a man in a black dress shirt, black dress pants, and a gray bow tie. Emerson assumed he was a server for the party, and figured his mom was giving him tedious instructions on how and when to serve hors d'oeuvres and champagne. It was pointless, of course. At events like these, servers typically streamed through the crowd all night with full trays, never running out of food, but more importantly, never running out of alcohol.

Johnathan was talking to a colleague Emerson recognized as Henry Sullivan, who was a state representative. Henry had known the Yates family for years, and his own son who was a few years older than Emerson was enjoying his first term as mayor in Sterling Heights. There was an uncomfortably hollow feeling in the center of his stomach as he saw the familiar faces from his past, and his dad's eyes lit up with recognition before waving to Henry and making his way toward them.

Placing a hand on the small of her back, Emerson held Gabriella close as he walked toward his father. "Dad." He nodded his greeting before gesturing to the woman at his side. "I'd like you to meet Gabriella...my girlfriend."

Johnathan's eyebrows raised, clearly intrigued. Emerson tried not to audibly grind his teeth as he watched his dad's eyes rake over Gabriella a little too appreciatively. He tightened his grip around her waist and narrowed his gaze at his father with a piercing, steely intensity.

"Girlfriend?" Johnathan questioned, his icy blue eyes flashing back to Emerson with a smirk. "You didn't tell me you had a girlfriend. I expected you'd bring some last-minute bar skank."

Well...that didn't take long. We're starting the night strong.

Emerson tucked his tongue inside his cheek and dropped his gaze to the floor. He felt Gabriella's hand slide inside his suit jacket and skate her nails along his lower back and he was immediately grateful for her touch, though the hollow pit in his stomach was still present.

He reminded himself that Gabriella knew what he was, knew how he'd lived before her, and she still chose him. Regaining his confidence and clearing his throat, he met the face that was like a mirror with a twenty-year fast forward. "Well, I guess I'm just full of surprises then, aren't I?"

Johnathan smiled, and it was the closest thing he probably ever got to a genuine show of happiness. With another look at Gabriella he said, "Indeed. She's absolutely beautiful, son. Wherever did you find this one?"

Listening to his dad talk about her like she was a shiny new car or a boat or some luxury item had a new ball of emotions swirling around in his stomach and chest. Now, along with the pit of anxiety, there was a steaming, curling ball of anger, distaste, and protectiveness. He nearly felt guilty for bringing Gabriella along. He'd known his dad was going to act like this, that he'd say things to make them both uncomfortable.

Nearly forgetting that Johnathan had asked him a question, he was glad when Gabriella jumped in and answered casually, "We met at work."

"Ah, I see," Johnathan said, nodding. "Paralegal? Legal assistant?"

The swirl of steam now felt as if it were spitting fire. "She's an associate at the firm," he snapped, with more venom than he'd meant, but he wasn't sorry.

"Really?"

"She graduated top of her class at Yale Law," he added, now feeling the need to brag and lift her up.

There wasn't anything wrong with being a paralegal or assistant, of course, but he knew his dad would never choose a woman who was on the same level career wise, and he definitely wouldn't be with one who could potentially show him up. No, Johnathan Yates liked to make sure he held all the cards and all the power in a relationship, whether it be his marriage, his many mistresses, or simply business. And Emerson was determined to define all their differences, outline them in bold sharpie, underline them in red, and make sure it was clearly stated that he was *not* his father.

Twisting the blade further he added, "She had a full-ride scholarship to attend Yale, too."

Johnathan's smile diminished just the slightest bit, but Emerson noticed it. "Did she? That's good. Maybe she can teach you a thing or two about actual hard work and convince you to stop dicking around."

The familiar charm washed over his face now as he drew his attention back to Gabriella. "What do you think? Can we persuade my stubborn son to take his career to the next level? If you're with him I'm sure you know his potential reaches far beyond a stuffy law office."

Gabriella looked up at Emerson and grinned. "I suppose I would agree...his potential both in and out of the *stuffy* law office frequently exceeds my expectations." She subtly squeezed his ass, and he had to bite back a grin. "But ultimately, he's a grown man and can make his career choices for himself." The piercing, boss-bitch, no-backing-down stare she then gave his father was like fire meeting ice. Plenty of grown men with money and power far exceeding Gabriella's wouldn't dare challenge Johnathan the way she was right now, and *fuck* if it wasn't the biggest turn on in the world.

Johnathan's smirk never left his face, but Emerson swore he could hear the icy shell that must encompass the man's heart solidify further. Though he relaxed his posture and gave a lazy, crooked grin, his tone was still threatening when he replied, "Perhaps you haven't known him long enough, Miss- I'm sorry, I didn't catch your last name?"

"Cabrera-Perez." The words rolled off her tongue like a purr and Emerson was certain he'd never been so simultaneously turned on and intimidated.

"Cabrera-Perez," Johnathan repeated slowly. His crooked grin lingered on his handsome face as he no doubt made calculations and assumptions about Gabriella. "My son may look and dress like a grown man, but I assure you he would not be in the successful position he is now without me, my money, and my ability to pull strings to get him exactly where he needed to be."

While Emerson was rooted to the spot, fully embarrassed and ready to lean back on his default setting of shutting up and doing exactly what his father asked of him, Gabriella was on a whole different page. Rather than back down, she was ready to fight harder.

"Of course, Senator, I would imagine all parents want what's best for their kids and would be willing to go through any means necessary to provide them with the same, if not even better, opportunities than they were afforded," Gabriella reasoned smoothly. "Parents should be willing to provide their kids everything they can with what they're given. For example, my own parents emigrated from Cuba, learned a new language, became citizens, and worked their way from the ground up to be able to provide for me and my siblings. Though I know which accomplishments are my own, I wouldn't begin to claim I couldn't do it without them and their sacrifices."

Oh snap.

Emerson felt like he needed to give Gabriella a microphone just so she could drop it.

Johnathan's grin slowly turned wicked as he eyed her, likely formulating his response, but his mouth snapped shut when she made it known that she wasn't finished. "That being said, I can't imagine my parents ever forcing me down a career path when I've made it perfectly clear that I'm capable of my own successes."

Chewing the inside of his cheek, Johnathan assessed the opponent he'd clearly underestimated. "Well, Miss *Cabrera-Perez*, your parents don't have the power or the money to make those decisions for you, do they? They aren't sitting on five generations of influence in this country and the pressure to keep that influence going. It was quite the charming story though. Perhaps *you* should run for office if we can't get my son on board. I know just the campaign manager to sell that rags-to-*somewhat* riches story to the right demographic. They'd eat it right up, don't you think?"

Anger. Anger and fury and spite welled inside Emerson hotter than anything he'd ever experienced. His dad had no fucking right to talk to Gabriella like that. Sure, he could insult and put down his own son as much as he wanted, but there was no way he'd get away with talking to her like that. No. Fucking. Way. He swallowed hard, unrooting himself from the temporary freeze of his father's presence- but he was cut off.

"I'd be careful with this one, Emerson," Johnathan said, his glacial stare sliding from Gabriella and back to him. "I suspect she's smart enough to take you for everything you're worth." He started to walk away as a few other men in tuxedos and women in evening gowns swept into the ballroom. With one last derisive smirk, he turned back to his son. "Of course, if you're not really careful I suppose I could do that, too."

Well, it was official. Emerson's dad was the biggest asshole in the state of Michigan. Perhaps in the Senate, or the sitting government—and that said a lot. Gabby wasn't fond of politicians in general, but the fact that Johnathan Yates had somehow charmed people into voting for him time and time again frankly astounded her. Sure, he was handsome and had the same ability to charm the panties off ladies that his own son possessed, but how could people not see through him?

Shortly after their encounter with Johnathan, Emerson had led her over to a tall, blonde woman who looked to be in her forties, though Gabby suspected she'd simply aged well. Emerson introduced the woman as Corrine Yates, his mother. She was beautiful, and her silvery light blonde hair was pulled up in an elegant bun. Gabby quickly recognized where Emerson got his eyes. Though Johnathan also had striking blue eyes, they were a cold, glacial pale blue, rather than the deep gray stormy blue she was now so familiar with.

Emerson pulled his mother into a hug and kissed each cheek before introducing Gabby as his girlfriend. Corrine was friendly enough, though she held herself in a similar fashion as Johnathan, as if the money and luxury that surrounded her was enough to make her better than everyone else. Gabby noticed the way she spoke to the servers wasn't exactly rude, but it wasn't friendly. It was cold and impersonal. She was quiet, and though she didn't say it outright, Gabby couldn't shake the feeling that she was being assessed and not quite measuring up to whatever expectation she'd created in her head as the woman her son should date.

Throughout the evening, Gabby was introduced to several of Emerson's old classmates and people with whom he'd grown up. They were standing in a circle with four other guests; One of the men was a defense attorney living in Warren, another was the Assistant District Attorney overseeing cities in Macomb County, and the other was a first-term mayor of Sterling Heights, along with his wife who was an attorney who practiced family law.

Emerson had stuck to his earlier statement of making sure he stuck right by her all night. His arm rarely left its place wrapped around her waist, a comforting hand resting on her hip. When the subject of Emerson as a young, obnoxiously arrogant teenager came up, he would tighten his grip or begin tracing circles over her hip with his thumb. She was surprised at how uneasy he was around these people whom he'd known for so long.

The grip on her waist tightened a little when the ADA, Vincent Gibbs, spoke up again. "Do you remember our senior year when you got a B+ on your AP government final?"

Emerson grimaced. "Oh God, don't remind me." He brushed a hand over his face and shook his head. "That was all sorts of fucked up."

"The teacher, Miss Thomas, was new. Well, it was her second year, so she was relatively new," Vincent began. "She was *smoking* hot, too. All of us had a crush on her...or at least fantasized about her in various ways."

"I couldn't believe I got a B+ in that class. I needed an A, or I thought my dad would beat my ass or who knows what," Emerson explained.

"I feel like I know where this is going," Gabby said, cringing at the thought.

"Miss Thomas had been eyeing your man all school year," Vincent said. "She wasn't old, and Emerson had just turned eighteen anyway. She was probably, what? Twenty-three? Twenty-four? Anyway, he went to her classroom after hours and started...bargaining."

"In my defense," Emerson said, holding up a hand. "It was ultimately her decision. Yes, I went with the intention of perhaps seducing my teacher, but *she* was the one who told me that if I gave her an O, then she'd give me an A."

"And you delivered?" she asked.

"Of course he delivered!" A new female voice joined the circle. A woman with strawberry blonde hair and porcelain skin slid between Vincent and his wife, Hannah. "Have you seen this guy in action? We used to get it on almost every weekend during the summer." She turned her green eyes on Gabby and smiled, swirling her glass of champagne.

"I'm Kate, Emerson's summertime fling from back in the day. Isn't that right, Emerson?"

Gabby could feel the tension build in his posture as he swallowed and cleared his throat. "Right, well, that was a long time ago, wasn't it?"

Kate smiled like a cat playing with a mouse. "Too long." She glanced back at Gabby and her eyes rested on where Emerson's hand lay over her hip before meeting her face again. "We didn't go to the same school, but our families were close. We vacationed together all over; Greece, Italy, France, even Cancun or Jamaica for just a fun little trip sometimes."

"My family vacationed with a lot of colleagues," Emerson said. "It was how they did business."

Ignoring Emerson's clear attempt to tamp down the significance of their various out-of-the-country trips, Kate continued, "I always *loved* going to the beaches, but it was also kind of sad sometimes. I mean, sure the resorts we stayed at were beautiful, but so many of the people who actually *lived* in those places? It was just heartbreaking the conditions they were in. I mean, could you imagine having to actually live in the Dominican or Cabo, or *Cuba?* Tragic."

Though Emerson tensed next to her, Gabby let out a puff of laughter. "Yeah, I would imagine it was hard to have to visit a place that actually made you consider how fortunate and privileged you are."

Emerson grinned as though her win were also his own as Kate hesitated to come up with a response. "Well, we've all had our trials and hard times."

"Of course, but I would imagine it was a difficult thing to come to terms with, realizing that even though you've had everything handed to you in excess and luxury, you've only ever managed to climb so far on the social ladder. I'm sure you're a very successful- I'm sorry, what was your profession?" Gabby waited for the woman to say exactly what she expected to hear.

"I...I organize charitable events. I'm the chairperson of the Macomb Area Ladies' Club-"

"A volunteer organization?" Gabby questioned. She placed a hand to her chest. "Oh, I'm so sorry, I didn't realize you were unemployed." At her side, she suspected Emerson was literally biting his tongue to keep from laughing. "Well, as I was saying, it must be hard to witness people making the most of their situations when you've been given every opportunity this world can offer and, well…you still can't figure out what you want to be when you grow up."

After an icy cold glare that contrasted with the way her cheeks burned crimson, Kate cleared her throat and excused herself from the group.

Emerson finally let out his laugh and hugged her to his chest. "Gabe, I have no idea how you do it, but you are a fucking badass."

She shrugged. "All lawyers enjoy a bit of healthy competition."

Calvin Sullivan, the Sterling Heights mayor, grinned as he shook his head. "Emerson, I think you've met your match with this one."

Never letting his gaze drift away from hers, he smiled and agreed, "You know, I think you're right."

Later in the evening, Gabby made small talk with several politicians, lawyers, judges, business owners, and the like. They were talking to Calvin and his wife, Breanna, when Johnathan asked to "borrow" Emerson for a few minutes. After assuring him that she would be fine with his friends, he followed his dad and she was left to talk about her experience at Yale and her career that followed. She was actually getting along well with Breanna who worked for the district attorney in Sterling Heights, but after a while they were whisked away by other guests who wanted to enjoy their company.

Left alone, Gabby made her way to the bar for a drink. Though servers had been wandering around with trays of what she imagined was at least 500 dollar champagne, she was craving something a little stronger. "Could I get Makers and ginger ale, please?" The bartender nodded and got to work on a heavy pour of Makers with a splash of Canada Dry. Perfect. "Thank you," she said. Plucking the rocks glass from the glossy bar top and turning around, she nearly ran right into a tall, solid figure.

"Oh my gosh, I'm so sorry-" She cut herself off when she realized it was Johnathan Yates who she'd nearly spilled her drink all over.

"No worries, Miss Cabrera-Perez." He drawled her name in the same slow, taunting way he'd said it earlier. "It's only a four-thousand dollar tuxedo. Easily replaceable."

She was careful to not roll her eyes at his conceitedness, though her reply was still doused in sardonicism. "Lucky me."

Jonathan grinned, and she hated how much his mouth went crooked in the same easy way as his son's. She hated the low timbre of his voice and the natural confidence with which he carried himself. "You don't like me, do you?" he asked.

"I barely know you," she replied. It wasn't a lie. It wasn't a direct answer, but it would suffice.

He nodded slowly and his eyes scanned the large ballroom. "I'm not the bad guy in the dramatic motion picture of my only son's life. I only want what's best for him, as you earlier agreed all parents should."

"What if what you think is best for him won't make him happy?"

Johnathan scoffed. "Happy? What's best for him isn't what makes him happy, it's what makes him successful. Powerful. If he wants happiness along the way, I'm sure he'll have no problem finding it." Gabby didn't like the grin that teased the corner of his mouth, but she didn't ask for further details, she merely arched an eyebrow. "Women, Miss Cabrera-Perez, I'm talking about women. He can find and be with and screw as many women as he wants to bring him happiness if that's what he wants, but he's going to play by my rules."

She wanted to be careful. She knew Johnathan's affairs were supposed to be a secret, though somehow she suspected they were well-known, but ignored. Trying to not fire back with the obvious retort that Emerson didn't want to marry a woman just to cheat on her for the rest of his days, she took an extra moment to respond. "How do you think that would look? Your son running for office with different women bouncing in and out of his life? The public wouldn't go for that."

He laughed. "No, of course not. He needs to get married. He needs to find someone from…the right stock, if you will. Cut from the same cloth. Someone who will look good on his arm and, sure, if he wants other female companions, someone who'd be willing to keep it quiet to protect his reputation. Someone who won't expect him to pass up a willing opportunity given the many nights they'll spend apart and the stresses of the job."

"Someone he can walk all over, you mean?" Her blood was boiling, and it took everything in her to not cause a scene and start shouting right there about this man's many affairs and his secret, fourteen-year-old illegitimate love child. "He would never be happy with someone like that. He likes a challenge."

Johnathan's glacial blue eyes met her dark brown ones and she focused on the contrasts, rather than the similarities, between his face and his son's. "I'm not saying you can't be part of his life. Someone there to *challenge* him behind closed doors…but something tells me you wouldn't be satisfied as a mistress."

She took a deep drink from her glass. "I can't imagine how you'd think that of me," she said sarcastically.

He faced her then, and took a step closer, clearly invading her personal bubble. Her initial reaction was to take a step back, but he curled his large hand around her arm, just above her elbow. For a moment, her breath was caught in her throat. She glanced at his hand gripping her bicep, then back into his pale blue eyes, refusing to appear intimidated.

"My son and I are one in the same, Miss Cabrera-Perez. I don't know how long you've known him, but the sooner you figure that out, the better it will be for both of you. He might be hypnotized by you right now, and I suppose I can't say I blame him." He released her arm and slid his hand up to her shoulder. In a move that brought goosebumps to every inch of her body, he slipped a finger beneath the thin strap of her dress and his eyes lingered heavily on the V that so elegantly outlined the curve of her breasts. She swallowed, feet frozen in place. Her lips parted as if to say something, but she couldn't find words. He blinked slowly back up to her face. "You have a lot to be admired… but I bet it's your lips that caught his attention first. It's the first thing I noticed."

Gabby's heart was racing, thundering through her chest, but the room was too full for anyone to hear it. The room was full and yet no one seemed to notice- no one seemed to care- what was going on. A sick, knotted feeling twisted in her gut at his comment about her lips. Emerson *did* love her lips.

They are not the same. Emerson is not his father. They are completely different people. Do not let him get to you.

"Gabe!" Emerson's familiar voice floated to her ears and she felt a flood of relief wash over her. "There you are, baby-" He stopped short as he watched his dad slowly, brazenly remove his hand from where it hovered over her collarbone. He practically snatched Gabby back, as if she were a kid about to wander into a busy street, and held her against his chest. "What the hell do you think you're doing?" he snapped, and his voice was laced with venom.

Johnathan put his hands up. "Whoa, son. I was just admiring your date here. We Yates men can't let such a beautiful woman go unappreciated."

Gabby had seen Emerson angry before. She remembered telling her brother about feeling like he was melting her with Superman laser eye-beams after her first day of work. This…this was different. This was a whole new level. Storm clouds swirled behind his eyes, mixed with thunder and lightning and crashing waves. A whole damn tsunami was brewing. Behind his eyes…and in her panties. It shouldn't surprise her that she thought he was hot when he was angry. Their whole relationship had been built on the ability to piss each other off more than the other.

His voice was low and calm, but the threat was palpable. "Dad, you crossed a fucking line."

When Johnathan laughed derisively, Gabby was almost certain Emerson was going to throttle him, but he kept his cool. She sensed him vibrating with anger, conflicted with the constant intimidation he'd always felt around his father and the fact that this time he *knew* he had the right to blow up at him.

"Oh please," Johnathan said, waving a dismissive hand. "You and I both know how this is going to end. You're going to realize that someone with her background isn't fit for you. You're not cut from the same cloth, son. You can't honestly think you have a future with her."

"Someone with her background?" Emerson repeated slowly, in a dangerous simmering tone. Gabby's vaginal walls clenched involuntarily.

"You know what I mean," said Johnathan. "Go on and have your fun with her, by all means, but you're going to realize I'm right."

Emerson was irate. His jaw was set, fists clenched, his eyes set in a steely, unyielding glower, nostrils flared. "You're un-fucking-believable."

Rolling his eyes and ignoring his son's fury, Johnathan replied, "You know I'm right. You're me, son. We're exactly the same. It's how I know exactly how this is going to play out. You'll have your fun with this one, but she's got an expiration date. They all do. That's how we operate." He flicked his gaze from Emerson's to Gabby's. "And when he's done with you...once you've gotten a taste of what it's like to be with the *boy*, you can let me know when you're ready to be with the *man*."

Somehow she caught Emerson's arm and held it back before he could throw his punch. Sure, she wanted to see Johnathan Yates get what he deserved just as much as...well, probably a lot of people, but she couldn't let Emerson take the inevitable fallout for such an action.

Chest heaving, he glanced down at Gabby, confused as she kept both hands curled around his forearm. She lifted her chin and stared Johnathan directly in the eyes, prepared to stare him down. "Maybe we haven't been together very long, but you and your son, Senator, are *not* the same. I can assure you of that. And maybe we won't be together forever, but I promise you if our relationship does come to an end, it won't be because of some imaginary *expiration* date, it won't be because someone peppier and blonder came along, and it sure as hell won't be because *that's just how Yates men operate.*" Emerson's breathing had slowed marginally and he wasn't quite as visibly pissed off as he'd been seconds before. "And as for your lovely proposition, I already have *the man.* The *real* man."

Emerson snaked his arm around her waist again and the grin beaming on his face was worth every uncomfortable second at that god forsaken fundraiser. "You wanna get out of here?" he asked.

"Hell yeah."

He gave his dad a curt nod. "We're leaving." Snatching Gabby's drink from her hand, he chugged it and dropped it on the tray of a passing server before breezing by the stunned senator. "Thanks for the free drinks!" he called over his shoulder as they made their way to the exit.

Two men were waiting by the large, opulent doors and pulled them open. Emerson stopped and turned around again, shouting over the crowd, "Cabrera-Perez for Senate- Fuck yeah!" Then they ran hand-in-hand out of the ballroom and into the July night now full of possibilities.

Chapter 21

Laughing and stumbling back into the hotel room, Emerson was completely high on the gorgeous, incredible, so-goddamn-sexy-it-fucking-hurt woman next to him. Ted the limo driver had taken them to a few bars downtown where they were way fucking overdressed, but of course neither of them cared. They took a few shots and danced. Emerson bought a round for a random group of people they met up at the bar because *why the fuck not*, and then they got back to their hotel suite in time to watch the many fireworks shows in the city from their sixteenth story view. It had sounded like a nice romantic evening, but as soon as the door clicked closed behind them, a fire was ignited and they began tearing at each other's clothes, letting them fall to the floor creating a trail past the entryway and into the living area.

As horribly as that fundraiser had gone, Emerson couldn't have asked for a better outcome. Watching his woman stare down his dad without hesitation and listening to her rip apart his fears that he was destined to turn out just like the guy he'd resented for so long, was the biggest fucking turn-on, and he felt forever indebted to her. It would take years, maybe a lifetime, to show her how much it meant to him that she believed in him, stood by him, and was willing to shoot down all his demons, but he was going to start right now. Tonight was all about her. Whatever she wanted, whatever she needed, he was here to give her just that.

Her gown fell to the floor at her feet and she stepped out of it, now wearing nothing but a beige and black lace thong and her strappy gold heels. *Fucking hell*, how was this woman his? Mouth watering as he stared at the sight in front of him, he completely inhaled everything about this moment. They hadn't turned the lights on, but the large floor-to-ceiling window allowed for the light of the city to illuminate the room enough to see everything he needed, and still keep her hidden from anyone hoping to look in.

"God, you're fucking beautiful," he said on an exhale, then stepped toward her. Cupping his hand around her neck he crushed his mouth over hers, tongue swiping impatiently through her lips and tasting her. He wanted to kiss her so fiercely, so thoroughly, so passionately that no other man would even dare come near her mouth. He wanted his mark stamped across her perfect plump lips: *Property of Emerson Yates: All others can fuck right off.*

Gabriella moaned into his kiss as her fingers swiftly unbuttoned his shirt. His jacket was already on the floor somewhere and she shoved his dress shirt off his shoulders and arms before raking her nails down his heaving bare chest, making him groan. He palmed her breast, teasing the tight nipple with the tip of his thumb as her fingers worked their way to his pants.

"Tell me what you want," he whispered. "Anything baby, I want to give you anything you want."

With her eyes closed and her head back as his lips brushed along the curve of her neck, she breathed out her answer, "Your mouth. I love your mouth on me."

Emerson let out a deep throaty noise. "I was hoping you'd say that." He backed her up to a wall, skated his fingers lightly up her sides, over her shoulders, her neck, into her hair. His tongue swiped over her bottom lip before sucking it between his teeth.

Slowly, he let his hands glide their way back down her body, taking their time to feel the tick of her pulse as they brushed over her throat, indulge in the swell of her breasts, get lost in every curve her body had to offer. Dipping a hand into the thin lace of her panties, he felt how much she wanted him. Hot and slick with need, he teased her clit with sensual circles. She gasped and whimpered as her body jerked, hips bucking into his touch.

"Shhh…patience, honey," he whispered against her neck. "Let me take my time with you. I'm going to give this gorgeous body everything she deserves."

Her breath was shaky as she exhaled, her body relaxing against the wall as she relinquished control and handed it over to him. His cock throbbed, hard as a rock and straight as a fucking arrow in his boxer briefs, but he ignored it. He wasn't planning on giving it what it wanted for a while yet. No, he'd have Gabriella begging for him to come before he gave into his own desires.

His mouth and tongue made the same leisurely trail down her body, tasting her neck, licking and sucking over the heavenly swell of her breasts, kissing along her ribs, down her stomach, until they finally reached their destination. His fingers still teased, swirling around her clit, dipping inside her two at a time. With his other hand, he stripped the tiny scrap of fabric covering her down her legs and pressed his mouth over her bare mound. She whimpered again and he watched her fingers flex at her sides as she refrained from grabbing his hair and guiding him to her.

It was torture for him to go this slow, to tease this much, so he could only imagine how excruciating the wait was for her. But he wouldn't give in. He wanted her hot and sweaty with need, begging for him to give her what she craved. And then he'd do it again.

He kissed lower…lower still, until his mouth was over her clit. He listened to her ragged breathing and brushed his mouth over the swollen bud again. Finally, he went in for the kill. Dipping his head, he licked one long, slow stroke with the flat of his tongue, and he felt the shiver that coursed up her spine. The moan that burst free from her lips had his dick straining even harder against the thin fabric of his boxer briefs. He took another long lick, and then another. His tongue swirled around her clit…around and around and around again before sucking it into his mouth. She gasped and her hips jerked forward again, but he placed a firm hand over her thigh and pressed her to the wall and continued worshiping her.

It wasn't until her fingers were buried in his hair and she was giving her desperate pleas for *more* and *don't stop* that he finally picked up his pace, using fingers, tongue, and teeth to make her shudder and rock against his mouth as she cried out his name. Her pussy squeezed around his fingers and he felt the hot pulses of her orgasm rush against his mouth.

It was perfect. So fucking perfect and so hot that he almost gave into the throbbing ache in his own pants and fucked her for his own release. Almost. But she deserved more. Way more.

"Has anyone ever given you back-to-back orgasms with their mouth?" Emerson asked, flashing his darkened blue gaze up to Gabriella as he kissed the inside of her thigh. Her breaths were still coming in heavy, not fully recovered from that first orgasm as she shook her head in response. He grinned devilishly. "I didn't think so." Then he pulled one shaking leg over his shoulder, opening her up for him, and started his slow licks, devouring her all over again.

Even before her second orgasm, her legs were shaking so badly that he had to carry her over to the bed to finish. He had her pulled to the edge of the bed with both legs wrapped around his head. They squeezed and vibrated as she came against his mouth again.

With the third, she cried out in bilingual praises and curses before going limp beneath him with the exception of sudden aftershocks as she caught her breath.

He watched her, feeling immensely satisfied at his handiwork, as he peeled off his final piece of clothing. His cock sprang free and was ready for action as he climbed over her.

"Need a little break, Gabe?" he asked. He knew he sounded like a cocky son of a bitch, and his shit-eating grin surely made him look like one, too. But at that moment, he kind of felt like he had that right.

Gabriella pushed a hand through her hair and sighed. "Un minuto, por favor."

He lowered his mouth to her breasts and licked between them. Gabriella shivered and let out a small whimper. "Was that 'pound me now, papi?' I don't speak Spanish," he teased.

She laughed. "Oh that's right, you only speak Smartass."

Sucking a hardened nipple into his mouth, he hummed and laughed. "That is my first language."

Gabriella gently slid her hands down the sculpted plane of his chest and abs, then she grasped his hard, steely flesh and began a slow stroking rhythm that made him shudder. "I love how much you love giving me what I want."

"I love that you let me give you what you want," he said. His hips flexed and he moved his shaft through her hand. "Just think of how many more orgasms you would've had if you'd taken me up on my offer the first day we met?"

"You mean when you told me to give you a call if I got lonely working late?" she asked, raising an eyebrow in challenge. "You were being an ass."

He nodded. "Yeah, but an ass who knows what the fuck he's doing. You still would've gotten the orgasms."

"And lost my dignity with each one," she replied, still grasping him. "No, I much prefer the way I brought you to your knees and slowly made you become obsessed with me."

"That's nothing compared to what you do to me now." He looked between their bodies and watched his cock glide through her hand. "Fuck, I'm about to come all over you and you just started touching me."

"So do it," she said, breathlessly.

He swallowed a groan, along with the urge to do just that and shook his head. "Not yet." He dipped a hand between her legs and stroked a finger down her center. Still wet. Still swollen. Fuck, he wanted to bury himself deep. Spotting the box of condoms on the nightstand, he stretched over her and reached for it. "Shit, only three left. This was a new box...how many did we use on the drive down here?"

"Several." Gabriella stroked his cheek with her fingers and spoke softly, "It's okay though. We'll use what's there and then we can rely on the pill if we need to."

"You're on the pill?" he asked, and she nodded. He chewed his lip and considered. It was reasonable enough, though he liked to feel absolutely certain that there was no chance of a kid happening. That was the last fucking thing he needed. "Okay, but I'll pull out just to be sure."

"So cautious," she said, her lips pulling into a teasing smirk.

"Can you blame me?" he asked, taking one of the remaining condoms out of the box. "You saw what my dad was like. I don't need to be putting my own kid through that."

Gabriella's teasing smile disappeared and she cupped his cheek, forcing him to look in her eyes. Her beautiful, brown, almond-shaped eyes, full of sincerity and complete belief in him. "Emerson, you're not your father. I don't know how long he's had you believing that you are, but you're not. You are so much better than him. So much more. I know I give you shit about being a cocky jackass- and you totally can be one sometimes- but you're sweet, you're thoughtful, you're a good, loyal friend, and an *extremely* generous lover." She pulled him to her mouth, kissing him deeply as he inhaled her and every word she spoke about him. "Not to mention you're handsome-" *kiss* "-dangerously sexy-" *kiss* "-and have the biggest-" *kiss* "-most talented cock, and I can't wait to have it buried inside me."

Emerson had the foil packet ripped open and the condom rolled on in record time. As he leaned over her, she pulled her legs up so they bracketed his sides and he pushed inside her wet, wanting pussy, buried to the hilt. Gabriella arched her back off the mattress and dug her nails into his shoulders. Holding himself above her body, he watched the way she reacted to him. He wasn't even moving yet, and her body was practically writhing beneath him, the swell of those gorgeous tits rising and falling, her beautiful face a picture of pure bliss and carnal desire. Complete perfection.

He dropped down to his forearms and kissed her again as he began moving. Thrusting deep and slow, her hips raised to meet his movements. His skin glided over her silky bronze skin, hot and sweaty, a fire flickering deep in his lower abdomen. He wanted to touch her everywhere, feel her, consume her. Every inch of him craved each and every centimeter from her. With one hand sliding down her sides, palming and massaging her breasts, resting and digging into her hips, he listened to her gasps and moans. He felt her hands all over his back and arms and shoulders, feeling each contracting muscle as he worked to give her all he had.

"Emerson, please…faster. More…" She was unraveling beneath him and he only wanted to make it last. His hips flexed harder, moving faster, fucking her deeper. Her hands slid down his back and grabbed his firm ass, pulling him deeper with each thrust.

He whispered into the skin just below her ear, "You're perfect…so fucking perfect. So beautiful. *Fuck* me, Gabby. Give me everything." Her head pressed into the pillow, her neck arched and he licked and sucked and devoured her skin there.

"Oh God," she moaned. "God, Emerson, you're so hard. So big…fuck me. Take me and never stop."

"*Fuck yes,*" he bit out. His cock was aching, his balls tightening. He was going to explode. He was going to let go of every worry, every insecurity, every piece of him that he kept to himself and give it over to her. She owned him now. He was fucking terrified, but he was conquering his fears with her. She made him want to be better. She made him believe that he actually could be. *She* believed he could be. And he would do anything to be the man she saw in him.

Breathing hard against her skin, his sinuous movements above and inside her became wild. Losing control. Losing himself.

"Yes…yes, oh God, *yes!*" Gabriella panted and gasped. Her body went rigid, her mouth opened in a cry of pleasure, and her pussy tightened around him. He felt her whole body shake and quiver beneath him, her legs gripping harder around his waist, felt the squeeze of her warm, wet flesh around his cock.

With quick, hard, impatient thrusts, he came undone. He cursed and moaned, the fireworks outside their window matching the sparks flying behind his eyes. He shuddered and felt his body release everything as he collapsed on top of her. "Oh…God…" Groaning, he didn't stop the flexing of his hips until he was empty. One last, heavy exhale nearly made him lay limp over her body. He struggled to catch his breath as he felt Gabriella's breasts heave and sigh under his own chest.

Emerson rolled to his side and pulled Gabriella flush against him. One of her legs draped over him and she nestled her head beneath his chin. He held her tight and let his breathing even out, unable to tell the difference between the thunderous boom of the fireworks display outside and the deafening pounding of his heart.

He knew without a doubt that he didn't deserve the amazing woman in his arms. He knew she saw things in him that he wasn't sure were there. He knew he had a bad track record and that maybe if she knew the full truth about him, she wouldn't believe in him so strongly.

His heart clenched painfully and his stomach churned.

Remembering what she'd said about not judging him or changing her opinion about him because of things that happened in his past, he assured himself that he could still be someone who could make her happy. He would do everything he could to hold onto her. He'd put the past in the past. He'd bury it and not let it scare him away from what could be an incredible future.

Funny thing about the past, though…It doesn't always like to stay buried.

Chapter 22

Their drive back home was filled with a lot more talking and cuddling and keeping most of their clothes on than the drive down had been. Gabby wasn't entirely sure what it was, but she'd sensed some sort of shift in Emerson that night after their first round of Fuck Each Other into Oblivion. It was a fun game, but the next round was slower, and then he fell asleep with her enveloped in his arms. They only used two out of their final three condoms, but she was pretty sure he bought a new box as soon as they got back to Traverse City.

The work weeks following were busy, and Gabby had several meetings with clients nearly every afternoon, which meant she didn't see Emerson much at work, but they'd eventually meet up at his place or hers and spend the evenings together. Sometimes those evenings involved hanging out with her siblings or picking Kolbe and Robby up from practice, and sometimes it was just the two of them. They'd go out for dinner or, since neither of them were particularly good cooks, they would try recipes together. Only two so far had turned out well, but they were making progress. Sort of.

Marco and Max held a party at their house the evening of Quinn Casey's first game back after a year off. Gabby's sister, Isabel, was there, along with the guy she'd just started seeing. Robby, Lola, and Kolbe showed up together, the boys both looking particularly thrilled to have made it in one piece. How Lola had passed her driver's test was a mystery to them all.

Everyone was decked out in royal blue except for Emerson, of course. He wore a black and orange jersey and matching hat with the signature SF emblazoned on the front for the San Francisco team. He wasn't exactly a fan of any particular baseball team, but he was insistent on cheering for whoever the opposing team happened to be. When Quinn stepped up to bat, Emerson booed, though he was the only one. The stadium on the TV was filled with cheering fans, signs and banners welcoming the star hitter back to the game.

"Aren't you supposed to cheer for the same team as your woman?" Kolbe asked, eyeing Emerson's attire.

"It's more fun this way," Emerson replied with a shrug. "Besides, we like a little healthy competition."

"It'll be even more fun when his team loses," said Gabby, grinning. "Your team's going down, babe."

"Why do you hate Quinn Casey again?" Max asked curiously from his spot on the couch. He held a paper plate filled with buffalo chicken dip, chips, and celery.

"Because All-Star stole his last girlfriend from him. It was a huge thing," Kolbe replied. Emerson could have swatted him.

"Okay, let's set this straight: First of all, All-Star didn't steal anyone from me; Our relationship ended more than a year before theirs started. Second, I'm currently dating the hottest woman in the fucking universe, I have no reason to be jealous about that situation. Third- and last- I don't *hate* him. He annoys me because he's a cocky SOB who thinks he's hot shit."

Gabby, Marco, and Max all exchanged silent glances. "I'm sorry, are you the pot or the kettle in this situation?" she asked, trying and failing to hold in her laughter.

Emerson sighed. "You sound just like Jett when I tried explaining it to him."

"Sometimes people who are too much alike won't get along *because* they're too much alike," Isabel chimed in, her psychiatrist voice in full force. "Especially when they both have strong personalities. For example, if two people are extremely stubborn, they're unlikely to sway the other or ever come to a compromise."

"Ah, I bet that's it," Marco said, nodding. "You're hot and he's hot and you both know it, so you're both unwilling to concede that the other might be better looking. Neither one of you wants to take second place, so you're in a constant battle trying to prove who's better."

Emerson chewed the inside of his cheek and looked contemplative. "Hmm…well, that's easy. It's me. I'm better."

Gabby laughed and circled her arms around his shoulders. "You're the winner in my book." She kissed his cheek and then turned her attention back to the TV where Quinn hit a triple. "But your team is definitely going to lose."

The rest of July went by with ease and their relationship blossomed from something brand new and delicate into something comfortable and stable. Something with a sturdy foundation that was only getting better with time. Emerson's friend Brody invited them over for dinner with him and his wife at least once a week and Gabby was excited to find a new friend in Amira. She was funny and friendly and really liked to give Emerson shit. Amira and Emerson sort of bickered like brother and sister, and it always provided delightful entertainment for the evening. Not to mention Emerson's rivalry with their cat, Basil. It was actually hilarious how much that cat truly seemed to target him, and even better when Emerson would get in a full-on argument with the creature.

It was the second weekend in August and Gabby and Emerson were leaving Brody and Amira's house after another fun night of drinking, laughing, bickering, and watching Basil try to pounce on Emerson from the top of the refrigerator.

"Hey, next weekend we're having a girls' night here," Amira said as they made their way toward the front door. "Zoey, Victoria, Lizzie, and I were going to hang out here while the guys all go do their thing downtown. We'd usually bar hop, but since two of the ladies are preggers, we figured we'd just stay in. Gossip, watch movies…talk shit about the guys. You should definitely join."

"Sounds like my wine and gossip nights with my brother and his husband," Gabby replied, smiling. "Yeah, of course I'll come."

"Invite them, too. You're always talking about them! I mean, they could go bar hopping with the men folk, I suppose, but I want to meet them."

"I'll let them know they have options," said Gabby. They said their goodbyes and Emerson ushered her out of the house with a warm hand on the small of her back.

"I'm glad you get along with all my friends so well," Emerson said, holding the car door open for her.

"Were you worried that I wouldn't?" she asked once he got into the driver's seat.

"Well, Amira and Rae are best friends. I just wasn't sure if she was going to be weird about it."

"Why would she? You said your breakup was mutual, didn't you?"

Emerson was quiet as he checked both sides of the street before backing out onto it. "Yeah, I did." She watched him carefully and thought she saw him swallow hard. "Gabe, remember how you said-"

The sound of her phone ringing cut him off. Checking it, her brow furrowed in confusion as she saw the number of a senior lawyer at the firm lighting up the screen. She apologized to Emerson and asked him to hang on before swiping to answer. "Hello?"

"Miss Cabrera, this is Dave Wilmot."

Dave Wilmot had been at one of her meetings the previous week, but he was rarely in office. He had an air about him that stated he always had more important things to do with more important people. "Mr. Wilmot, hi. How can I help you?"

Emerson glanced curiously in her direction. Clearly, he knew exactly who Mr. Wilmot was.

"Listen, I'm just going to make this quick. No need to drag it out." His voice was clipped and matter-of-fact, as if this phone call were just another thing to check off his to-do list before reaching retirement. "We're letting you go from Warren & Blakely. You will be given a severance package and may collect your things out of your office tomorrow. I'm sorry, Miss Cabrera, but it had to be done."

Gabby's thoughts were stuck. *Letting me go? I'm fired?* "I'm sorry, I'm afraid I don't understand. Why? When did this happen? What about my cases?"

"Tom will explain tomorrow when you go collect your things. Make sure you stop in the top office and get all your severance information. Again, I'm sorry. We had no choice. Have a good evening, Miss. Cabrera."

Before she could get another word out, he was gone. She stared at the phone in her lap for several silent moments.

"What's wrong? Was that Dave Wilmot? Why was he calling?" Emerson asked. When she didn't respond right away, he put his hand over hers. "Baby, is everything okay?"

She slid her gaze from his hand on hers to his concerned face. "I just got let go."

Emerson's brows pinched together. "Let go? What do you-"

"He called to tell me that they were letting me go and I can collect my things tomorrow. I don't understand. He wouldn't even offer an explanation. He can't do that. You have to give a reason for letting someone go...he said Tom would explain everything tomorrow."

"They can't do that," said Emerson, his voice completely in defense of her. "Who the hell do they think they are? They have no reason to fire you. Who's going to take your case? You're halfway through that thing, they can't just slide someone new in to take over! Baby, this is so wrong. They can't do this to you. I'm going with you when you ask Tom what the fuck his excuse is. He's afraid of me anyway."

"Why would they do this?" she asked. "I've been doing great with this case- everyone at the meetings has been really impressed and keeps talking about how glad they are that I'm the one working the case. What the hell?" It made no sense that they would just fire her like this. She hadn't done anything wrong. Had she made an error that she hadn't seen? Wouldn't they have brought that to her attention first? Something in her gut was telling her that it wasn't right. Whatever she was being fired for was a mistake. Either that, or it was personal.

She'd heard of people taking their issues out on partners and associates. People they had personal issues with- kind of like Emerson's attempt to get her fired or make her quit their first couple weeks working together. Not that she was still worried about that. Since getting together, he'd been nothing but supportive, and was constantly telling her how amazing she was at her job.

"This has to be a mistake, baby. There's no way they have a real reason to fire you. Want me to make a call? I can try to figure out what the hell's going on," he offered.

"No, I can't have you making calls for me, or going to Tom for me," she replied. "I have to do it on my own or they won't take me seriously."

"I just wish there was something I could do to fix it, baby." He brought her hand to his lips and kissed it gently. "Tell me everything Tom says. If there's something I can do to change it or if I can find a loophole or..." he trailed off and she just nodded, her mind spinning.

When they arrived at her condo, Emerson walked inside with her and they talked over all potential possibilities of why she was getting laid off. Still nothing made sense, and she wished they'd planned ahead so that he could stay with her that night. He offered to go back to his place and grab a set of work clothes and an overnight bag, but she shook her head, telling him she likely wouldn't be getting sleep anyway and that she'd stop by his office in the morning.

He left her place around 10:30, and when she got to bed an hour later, all she could do was stare at the ceiling, her mind still reeling. Anger and confusion simmered at the surface and she hoped to be getting answers when she went to the top floor at 8 o'clock sharp the next morning.

At quarter past midnight, there was a knock on her door. Still wide awake, she quietly and cautiously slipped out of bed and down the hall, out to the front door. She sighed and her chest filled with warmth when she saw Emerson through the peephole with a travel bag and a garment bag for his suit. A small smile pulled up the corners of her lips as she opened the door.

"I told you I'd see you in the morning." She tried to sound like she was scolding him, but couldn't keep the happiness out of her voice.

"I knew you wouldn't be able to sleep, and I couldn't sleep knowing that," he said, stepping into the small entryway and closing the door behind him. "So, seeing as we're both wide awake, I thought maybe we could do something fun." He wiggled his eyebrows mischievously, making her laugh.

"Your solution to my insomnia is to keep me up?" she questioned. She tugged on his Detroit Lions t-shirt to pull him close.

"I'm such a genius, sometimes I surprise myself." Emerson bent down and brushed his lips over hers gently. "Why don't you show me to my room?"

He left his bags in the entryway and she led him down the hall to her bedroom where he stripped her down and made her forget, at least for a moment, that she had something to be upset about. He was over her, beneath her, behind her, *inside* her…the world, at least through her eyes, was completely consumed by this man. And she could've sworn she was the luckiest girl in the world. How Emerson could have ever thought he wasn't built for relationships was beyond her comprehension. In this moment, he was perfect, and she was so glad that she had something worth holding onto.

Lying on top of her, chest-to-chest, he sent his final thrust that had them both toppling over the edge, waves crashing together as he surged into her and she held on tight. She had to hold in the words that threatened to escape. Her whole body wrapped around him in every way and he dropped his mouth to hers, kissing, consuming, eliminating everything that wasn't him or them or this moment.

"Emerson, I-" she stopped herself and was grateful for the aftershock of pleasure that cut her off. She looped her arms around his neck, grinding into him and taking every little piece he had to give.

His lips met hers again, over and over, becoming soft and tender. His gorgeous, twinkling blue eyes met hers and for a split second she thought she saw fear in them before he blinked it away. "Gabby," he whispered, brushing his knuckles lightly over her cheekbone, tracing the swell of her bottom lip with his thumb. "Gabby, I love you."

She let out a contented breath of laughter as she smiled up at him. "I love you, too."

When he smiled, his eyes twinkled even brighter. It was a rare smile, one that she'd only seen on a few occasions, but it lit up his face and made all his handsome features that much more inviting. "I mean it, Gabe. I love you so much. And whatever happens tomorrow, we'll figure it out...together. I want you to know I'm here for you, 100 percent. If you need to find a new job, I'll help you. There's not a firm in this whole fucking state that wouldn't be lucky to have you, baby. I just...fuck, I just need you to know that I love you and I'm here for you. Whatever you need."

She laughed at his rambling, his smile completely contagious. Inhaling every word, she knew it to be true. He wanted to be there for her. That's why he came back tonight. He would help her and support her and they would get through it all together. "How did I get so lucky?" she asked, meeting his striking gaze again.

He shook his head. "No baby, *I'm* the lucky one. I don't even deserve you, but I'm trying. And I'm not going to stop trying because that's what you deserve. You need someone who will never stop showing you how lucky they are to have you. How lucky they are that you even let them be part of your life. You're my fucking queen, baby, and I'm just some guy doing his best to measure up."

Another broad smile broke out across her face and she tangled her fingers in his hair and kissed him again. Words as beautiful as his failed her, but she was familiar with a whole other kind of language that he happened to respond to *very* well. After he got out of bed and discarded his spent condom, he fell back onto the covers where they lay tangled, making love, showering each other in kisses and whispered promises of love and a future and countless tomorrows.

Unfortunately this particular tomorrow still sucked. Gabby got ready as if she were heading into work like she would any other day, although most days she wasn't up to her eyeballs in anxiety while Emerson gave her pep-talks over their morning coffee. He whisked together some eggs and made some toast on hearty 12-grain bread. Most mornings, she would have laughed that he'd brought his own fancy health-food bread, but today her mind was too distracted to make jokes.

They had spent work nights together before, so it felt weird when they got down to the parking lot and realized they'd be driving in separate cars. Obviously, Gabby would be leaving work a lot sooner than Emerson.

He took her face in his hands, his voice filled with confidence and assuranc, and it soothed her to the core. "You are going to march into Tom's fancy-ass office, demand to know why the fuck they're letting you go, and if it turns out that it's not some mix-up or misunder-standing, you're going to tell them what idiots they are. You're going to flaunt those sexy boss-lady panties- *figuratively*, of course- and tell them that they fucked up because there's not a single fucking place in this city that isn't already on their knees begging you to come work for them."

Gabby smiled and tried to commit as much of that to memory as she could. She gave him a quick peck on the lips before turning to get into her car, but he hooked his arm around her waist and brought her back for a slower, deeper kiss that made her knees tremble- although that could partially be due to lack of sleep. "Make sure you tell me everything. If there's something funny going on, they'll hear from me. No one messes with my queen and gets away with it."

She agreed to come down to his office as soon as she finished up with Tom and they slipped into their separate cars and headed to work.

Standing in Tom's office half an hour later, she stared down the bespectacled balding man with her arms crossed over her chest.

"The request came from higher up, Miss Cabrera," Tom explained. "I'm afraid there's not much I can do. It really is out of my hands."

"Higher up?" she questioned. "Higher than you and Mr. Wilmot? I haven't met with anyone higher up. How can someone who hasn't been in the office decide to fire me?"

"Again Miss Cabrera, I wish I could tell you something different. I wish we could keep you on; you've been a spectacular asset here, and we hate to let you go, but unfortunately, our hands are tied on this one."

"But what's the *reason?*" she asked for maybe the fifth time. "We have lawyers here, I believe on the second floor, who work in employment law. Surely one of them would be able to tell you that you can't fire someone without providing a reasonable explanation."

Tom looked immensely uncomfortable for a moment. He had a terrible poker face for a lawyer. "Well, this person claims that there have been instances of…inappropriate workplace behavior."

Gabby swallowed, sure she must have heard incorrectly. "I'm sorry, *inappropriate behavior?*"

Tom nodded. He then proceeded to list off things involving their pranks, both hers and Emerson's, but she couldn't help noticing only she was getting punished for them. Placing unnecessary maintenance orders, blocking off spaces in the parking lot, filling rooms with balloons, ruining office furniture, pornographic magazines, and so on.

"Additionally, we had a construction worker from a couple months back while this floor was being renovated say that you were up here frequently during construction." Tom's face went beet red and she thought he might burst out sweating. "He claims there was…again, *inappropriate* behavior taking place."

"Two months ago?" she questioned. "I'm being let go because of things that *allegedly* occurred two months ago. Why? Why now?"

"It has taken time for this to all come to light," said Tom. "But I think you understand that we can't have that kind of thing happening here."

"Harmless pranks between coworkers? Or…?" She stared at him, daring him to say it. Daring him to speak the words out loud and acknowledge she wasn't engaging in this behavior on her own. Not that she wanted to throw Emerson under the bus, and she wouldn't even if she was given the chance, but she did want to know why she was the only one getting fired.

Tom fidgeted with a dark blue folder on his desk before picking it up and handing it over to her. "Your severance information is all in here, along with a detailed account of why Warren & Blakely has decided to let you go."

Gabby took the folder from him and looked curiously at it. "Can I at least know the name of this mysterious person higher up who decided to have me fired?"

"I'm afraid that's confidential," Tom said. He clasped his hands in front of himself and stood awkwardly as a simmering, angry silence settled over the large office.

Finally Gabby nodded and cleared her throat. "Well, I'm sorry for your loss then. I am a damn good lawyer, Mr. Bowman, and I think you're making a huge mistake letting me go." She moved for the door and turned back as she pulled it open. "Have a great day, Mr. Bowman." With that, she slammed the door shut behind her and made her way down to the sixth floor where she needed to pack up her things and let Emerson know how her meeting with Tom went.

Emerson's office was empty when she stopped by, so she decided to start packing up her office and get it over with. She still felt like she had a reason to fight being let go, and she would run it by Emerson to see what kind of case he thought she had. The only problem was that she didn't want to point out that she wasn't the only one engaging in "inappropriate workplace behavior" and wind up getting him fired, too.

Fury ignited her insides again when she saw her office door already open. They weren't even leaving her the ability to clean out her own office before kicking her to the curb? Gabby let out a huff and stomped up the hallway to the open doorway, ready to give whoever was going through her stuff a piece of her mind when she spotted Emerson at her desk with empty copy-paper boxes. She stopped short in the doorway. "Hey...what's going on?"

He glanced up at her with those gorgeous sapphire eyes. "Hey baby," he said. "I caught some maintenance guys coming in here to start cleaning up before you even had a chance to do it yourself. I know someone else gave them the order, but I chewed their asses out and told them to shove the work order up their supervisor's ass."

"That sounds like you." Gabby stepped into her office and shut the door behind her. "Well, I just got back from my meeting with Tom and honestly, I feel like I have more questions than answers."

Emerson's eyebrows pinched together. "What do you mean?"

"He said the request to let me go came from someone higher up and then proceeded to list off a series of workplace transgressions that I've apparently committed in the last two months or so."

The crease between his eyebrows deepened and he took a step toward her, extending his arm out for the blue folder tucked under her arm. "Is everything listed in there?"

"Yeah," she said, hesitating. Again, she didn't want him to see that not all of the transgressions were hers or hers alone. She didn't want him doing something stupid and getting himself fired.

"Can I see?" he asked. "I mean…are they valid transgressions? Or did someone make shit up?" Sighing, she pulled the folder out and flipped to the top page where the ridiculous transgressions were listed. She handed the page over to him and watched his face turn angrier with each line. "Gabe, this is bullshit. I mean, sure we could get fired for getting caught screwing around here but that claim was hearsay, it would never hold up. Did he say anything about anyone else getting fired? Do they think the construction worker on the top floor caught you having sex by yourself?"

"I know it wasn't all me, but I don't want you going up to Tom and confessing being part of this. You don't need to lose your job, too."

He shook his head. "I can't let you take the blame for all of this. I can find a job somewhere else and so can you. I can practice other types of law or find a bank to work for or something. We have options."

She knew everything he said was true, and she was starting to think she didn't want to work for a firm that was so unfair. "I guess I'm just confused…You know this place and the people in it better than I do. Is there anyone who has it out for me but doesn't want to get you in trouble?" She narrowed her eyes at him. "Did you hook up with Angela or someone before we were together and now she wants me out of the way?"

Emerson's jaw dropped and he looked offended, though he still grinned. "I can't believe you'd think that!"

"Seriously?"

He laughed. "I mean, I can't believe you'd think I'd be so careless and sleep with someone I work with if I didn't think it was going to last. That would be awkward when it ended."

Gabby raised an eyebrow skeptically. "You had sex with me before we were actually together." She gasped and playfully put a hand to her chest, teasing, "It's you, isn't it? You're having me fired so it won't be awkward when we break up!"

He let out a booming, evil stage laugh. "Ah, yes. My master plan has come full circle. I've wanted you out since day one and the only way to do it was to make you fall in love with me so I could crush you when things got good." He snaked his arm around her waist and pulled her close. "I thought I made it perfectly clear that you're not going anywhere, mami." With a wink, he kissed her on the forehead before turning his attention back to the paper in his hand.

"Careful with your workplace displays of affection or you'll be the one getting booted next," Gabby said, leaning into his warmth as they both looked at the list.

"They've got to know I was behind half of these anyway, which is why it doesn't make any sense. Why keep me but get rid of you?"

Gabby let her eyes wander down the list of transgressions again and thought hard about who would want her fired, assuming this was personal. It almost seemed as if whoever was responsible for it didn't care how ridiculous it seemed to pin everything on her. Maybe they even wanted them to make the connection...as if protecting Emerson while getting rid of her was the whole point...

She let out a slow breath and closed her eyes as it hit her, counting to five before letting the anger get the best of her.

"What is it?" Emerson asked.

"Think about it...Who do we know who has enough power and influence to have Warren & Blakely fire me with no questions asked? Someone who would like nothing more than to see me gone, all while protecting you and your image?" She looked up at him and his jaw set, a flash of anger darkening his eyes.

"Because my image can't be compromised if I ever decide to run for office," he stated. His voice was cold and hard as stone. "My fucking father, ladies and gentlemen..."

"Why would he make it so obvious? So easy for us to figure out?"

"It's his way of sending a message. He likely bribed or blackmailed someone into firing you and is fully prepared to back them if you try to sue for unlawful termination of employment." Emerson pinched the bridge of his nose and let out a heavy sigh, his hands falling to his sides. "Fuck...Gabe, I feel like this is my fault. I'll call him."

"What's the point? He's not going to change his mind, Emerson. The guy's at least as stubborn as you are. All a phone call would do is show him that whatever he was trying to do worked."

"This isn't right." He shook his head. "You shouldn't have to deal with this. What if I go and tell Tom that it was all me? Everything you're getting fired for was actually me and-"

"It won't matter. Like you said, if your dad is bribing or blackmailing them, they won't waver. Maybe they aren't allowed to fire you...who knows, maybe he made that part of the agreement?"

"I can quit. I can tell them if they're firing you then I'm gone, too," he said stubbornly. "They won't change their minds, but it'll serve them right for doing this to you."

"And then we'll both be unemployed," Gabby pointed out.

"Now that's an idea." He grinned and wrapped his arms around her waist again. Facing her, he pressed their bodies together. "We can sleep in together, eat breakfast, then have sex all morning. Take a break for lunch and continue lying around in bed all day- no clothes allowed, of course."

Though it sounded amazing, she knew she couldn't give up working. She needed an income. She needed purpose, something to do during the day. "Okay, but how would we make our money?"

Emerson shrugged. "I've got some professional grade camera equipment we could put in the bedroom."

Gabby stared at him, unimpressed. "Try again."

He laughed. "Well, this might come as a shock, but I actually have quite the fortune stashed away. My trust fund is distributed a quarter at a time, and I got my first quarter when I turned twenty. I may have been an idiot back then, but I was financially smart and put it in various bank accounts that helped grow it over time. I think we'd be secure for a while."

She wasn't surprised by this information, and maybe he thought it was a valid solution, but she still couldn't fathom just sitting around all day. Not to mention sitting around and living off someone else's money. It didn't matter that he was her boyfriend, she wanted to be independent. She didn't want to have to rely on him to support her financially. Sure, if she needed a little help while she looked for a new job it wouldn't bother her so much, but to simply live off his trust fund and whatever other responsible investments he'd made just didn't sit well with her.

"I'm sure we'd be more than comfortable, but I think you know I can't do that," she said definitively.

"I thought you might say that, but hear me out." He paused dramatically. "What if...you could loosen the reins on the whole independent chick thing and, I don't know...let me spoil you. It would be fun for both of us."

"You want me to give up my independence so you can spoil me?" she questioned skeptically.

"You wouldn't actually be giving it up," he explained. "You would still have everything you do now, but you might...oh, maybe...let me buy you stuff, let me pay for dinner when I take you out without insisting on getting the next one, let me take you shopping or pay for a driver to take us to all the wineries in town- whatever you want. I want to take care of you. I know you don't need it, but it'll make me happy and you deserve it."

Gabby worried her bottom lip as she looked into his eyes that were doing that damn, hypnotic twinkling thing again. "Don't do that!" She pushed against his chest but he barely swayed.

"Don't do what?"

"That thing with your eyes when they get all deep sapphire blue and they twinkle and make it impossible to say no!"

He grinned smugly and his eyebrow twitched upward. "I can't control the twinkle."

Ugh, and now he's being cute, too.

She shook her head and tried her best to bite back a grin. "You're not playing fair."

He scrunched his face curiously. "Let's think about this...I'm offering to spoil you senseless- and that's *on top* of my God-like bedroom skills that you already receive- and I'm not being fair to you? Please explain..."

"*God-like?*" she asked, giggling.

"Would you like to argue that point?"

Okay, she supposed he had her there. She sighed reluctantly. "No..."

"So how is my offer unfair?"

She bit her bottom lip again and considered a way for them to both be happy. "Okay, how about we compromise? You keep your job-"

"Do I have to?"

She stared pointedly at him to let her continue. "You keep your job, but until I find a new one you can spoil the crap out of me. But once I'm back to work, everything goes back to normal."

"Deal," he said, quickly.

"Really?"

"Hell yeah. I honestly didn't think you'd budge on that one. I'll take it." His enthusiasm and excitement over getting to spoil her was completely adorable and she was almost thinking it was a great idea. Except for the fact that she hated having people do stuff for her when she was perfectly capable of handling things on her own.

Then again, Emerson had said that whatever happened they'd get through it together. There would be times he would have to lean on her and other times when she would have to release some of the control and let him take the wheel. Two months ago, she would've thought this was absolutely crazy. Incomprehensible. A no-go. But she trusted him. She loved him. And it was only fair to let him show her how much he loved her, too.

Chapter 23

"What the hell do you think you're doing?" Gabriella asked from her place on her bed. She was wearing a pair of comfy black lounge shorts and a faded blue Miami Marlins t-shirt. Her laptop was on the bed in front of her where she sat with her legs crossed beneath her.

Emerson had made a quick stop at his place before booking it over to her condo after work, grabbing a few different bags to pack her things in. "Well, doll, part of our agreement involves you staying at my place so I can ensure maximum spoiling opportunities." He winked at her as he unzipped a medium sized luggage bag.

"I never said anything about moving in with you!" she protested, as he knew she would.

"Neither did I," he said. "I promise it's temporary, but it'll be so much easier for me to spoil you if you're there in my apartment rather than hiding out here avoiding me so I don't get to do things for you."

"Hm…you saw through my plan, huh?"

"Sure did, dollface." He winked again.

Gabriella scrunched her face up like she always did when she was trying not to be charmed by him. "Doll and dollface? Are you a 1940's gangster from the Bronx?"

Putting his weight on his hands on the bed, he leaned over her laptop to give her a quick kiss. "What can I say? I'm excited and feeling kind of old school…I get to take my babydoll home and show her how a real man takes care of his woman."

She rolled her eyes at him but didn't move away when he went in for another kiss, slower this time. "You're going to have way too much fun torturing me like this, aren't you?"

"My desire to take care of you isn't torture," Emerson said, leaning over her now, making her fall back on her pillows. He pushed her laptop closed and moved it to the nightstand. "Now, looking at your legs in those shorts, knowing exactly how they would feel wrapped around my head...*that's* torture."

"You better hope my resume saved already." She hooked her arms behind his neck and pulled him onto her.

"I hope it didn't. The longer it takes for you to find a job, the more times I get to come back to my place and find you like this." Emerson slid his palms up and down her thighs before pulling them around his waist. He kissed her hard, his tongue plunging into her mouth as he rocked over her.

It didn't take long for their moans to morph into desperate gasping and panting, for their clothes to get tossed onto the floor, for Gabriella to beg and plead for more as he fumbled with the box of condoms on the nightstand.

He could feel her heart pounding to the rhythm of his own as he pumped into her. Impossible to know where she started and where he began, he rolled onto his back and pulled her on top of him, never taking his eyes off her as she rode him.

"Goddamn, it's so sexy to watch you like this," Emerson groaned. He palmed her breast with one hand and squeezed her ass with the other, using his grip on her deliciously round ass to help her fuck him. "So fucking sexy...you own me, baby. You fucking own me."

Gabriella's eyes closed and her head fell lazily back as her mouth opened, ready to cry out. Her whole body tightened and squeezed around him, her tight pussy clenching in a vice grip around him and he lost his battle to keep his eyes open. His other hand dropped to her ass and he lifted his hips, thrusting into her from below, fucking those sexy moans and whimpers out of her lips. His cock throbbed, his balls ached as he tried so hard to hold back, but his efforts were futile. He let loose, eyes rolling back, head pressing into the pillow as a deep growl ripped through his chest.

He was done. Dead. Gone. Coming so hard he saw stars behind his eyelids, gripping her so tight he was sure to leave marks. His legs shook, reflecting the earthquake that was happening inside his chest. Walls crumbling, armor melting fully away as this woman completely and utterly ruined him. Broke him down and claimed him as her own. And he was done fighting it.

Gabriella bent low and covered his mouth with hers. His hands tangled in her hair and he let her kiss soothe him. He might've thought he'd just run a marathon or done five-hundred burpees, the way his heart was pounding and his lungs were gasping for air. Her hands slid delicately up his chest and her lips became softer, their urgency fading into tenderness.

"I love you…I love you so…much," he said between breaths.

Her lips smiled against his. "I love you, too."

Opening his eyes, he peered up at her, letting his gaze travel over her face. "Why?" he asked.

"Many reasons," she replied. "But mostly…because you have a really-" she kissed him- "big-" another kiss, and a playful nip at his lip- "heart." She kissed him again and smiled at his skeptically raised eyebrow, then added, "Even if you don't want people to see it, I know it's there."

"If you say so," he said, brushing her hair behind her ear. "Although, I think you're just determined to see the best in me so you don't have to go back to getting mediocre dick every once in a while."

She giggled and the sound made him smile. "Big heart, big ego, big cock…you're just the whole package, aren't you?"

"That I am, *dollface*," he said with a crooked grin and a wink. "Now let's get you packed up and moved over to papa's." She made another exasperated face at him and he gave her a quick smack on the ass before playfully tossing her onto the bed and picking out her clothes for the next week. Sure, he'd probably get in trouble for "forgetting" to throw any panties in the bag, but it was a chance he was willing to take.

The week that followed was one of the best of his life. Emerson came home to Gabriella every day...in his home...and he *liked* it. Loved it, actually. She pretended to be annoyed with the way he was spoiling her, but he could tell she was enjoying it; she just didn't want to let herself get used to it. Tuesday evening he'd come home to her sitting on the couch submitting resumes and making phone calls to any and all hiring law firms in the area. Emerson had closed her laptop and moved it to the coffee table, cutting off her verbal protest with a heated kiss. They'd had a quick but steamy fuck on the couch in which Gabriella battled him to be on top, rolling onto the floor and around the rug as their power struggle only fueled the intensity between them. In the end, he let her finish on top because, *well...come on,* he couldn't help submitting to his queen and giving her exactly what she wanted.

On Wednesday he'd told her he was going to the gym after work and she'd insisted on going with him. He gave her a tour of the equipment and showed her proper lifting technique. After demonstrating how to properly do squats and deadlifts, his own workout was fairly unproductive. Her form was amazing and he couldn't take his eyes away from her ass in those spandex leggings. An hour and a half later, they were stumbling into the shower back at his place, peeling off their sweat-soaked clothes for a soapy, naked cardio session. Typically, Emerson hated cardio, but by Friday it was becoming one of his favorite hobbies.

Saturday arrived and while he always went to the gym early on the weekends, Gabriella refused to get out of bed, claiming that she was easing into the gym-rat life. Apparently six o'clock workouts were for the more seasoned gym vets, but she said that she'd be in bed waiting for him when he got back.

Walking through the door at 8:15 after pounding a peanut butter protein shake, he was ready to be pounding something sweeter. As promised, Gabriella was still in bed, but she was sitting up with her computer in her lap again, a small crease in her brow.

"Aw, I was hoping to wake you up," Emerson said, hoping the disappointment in his voice would offer him a little extra lovin'. He crawled onto the bed and kissed her cheek, then moved his mouth lower along her jaw and buried his head in her neck.

Gabriella pulled away with a giggle, pressing a hand to his chest. "Babe, you're soaked!"

Emerson wiggled his eyebrows. "Hey, that's my line."

She rolled her eyes. "Take your sweaty self to the shower. You're dripping all over me."

"Again, that's *my* line." Emerson stood up and studied her again. Her eyes hadn't moved from her computer, and that small crease in her brow was getting deeper. "Everything okay?"

Gabriella let out a sigh, but she didn't relax. Her face was still set in concern as she read her laptop screen. "I've heard back from three of the law firms I applied to this week already, but they're all turning me down without much explanation. Just a simple 'thanks for applying, but you're not what we're looking for'. I don't get it." Finally, her eyes drifted to him and slid over his face. "You don't think...I mean...I understand why your dad would have me fired from Warren & Blakely-he wanted me away from you. He probably thinks if you don't see me every day, you'll forget about me."

Emerson nodded his agreement. His dad was sure they were one in the same. Like father, like son. Take a woman out of Johnathan's line of sight, she'd be out of his thoughts just as easily. Clearly, he was hoping his son operated the same way.

"But what if he wants me...out of town all together? Nowhere near you?" she questioned. "Does he have the power to completely...blackball me from practicing law here? In Traverse City or, hell, maybe the surrounding areas. What if he's made it so there's not a firm in northern Michigan that would hire me?"

Emerson's jaw ticked at the thought. He wanted to tell her no, absolutely not. He wanted to tell her that it would be completely excessive and overreaching and there was no way Johnathan would do something that extreme...but he wasn't going to lie to her.

He dragged a hand down his face and scratched his beard- she was right, he *was* really sweaty. "It's only been a week. Less than that. I'm sure something will come up."

Gabriella's eyebrow arched as she looked at him skeptically. "Objection- Dodging the question."

He sighed. "Sustained." Easing onto the edge of the bed he did his best not to sweat all over the comforter or his girlfriend. "It's possible that he would go that far." He watched as she looked helplessly at the rejection email and his heart squeezed painfully. "I'm sorry, honey. Are you sure you don't want me to call him?"

"And do what?" she asked. "Tell him to call it off? Beg him to stop being an ass? Surrender and tell him you'll do whatever he wants if he just gets me my job back? I don't want that. I don't want him to feel like he's won and I sure as hell don't want him manipulating both of us just to get what he wants."

"I'll do it," Emerson said, and she glanced up at him curiously. "You know that, right? I would go through with whatever ridiculous plan he has if it meant making you happy. I'd become the fucking mayor, I'd work at one of his firms, I'd be a goddamn rodeo clown if that's what it took to make him forget all this bullshit and let you have whatever job you wanted."

Her smile was sad, but the look in her big brown eyes still warmed him. "I know you would, but seeing you miserable, playing as your domineering father's puppet wouldn't make me happy." She placed her hand gently over his, apparently ignoring the sweat for now. "We'll figure it out. Maybe I'm jumping to conclusions. Like you said, it hasn't even been a week. Most firms take longer to get back to a potential hire."

Emerson nodded, though he had no doubt in his mind his father was behind this, and he thought Gabriella knew it, too. "Their loss anyway, baby. You'll find something. And if all else fails," he said, giving her a shit-eating grin, "we've still got that camera equipment I can set up."

"Go shower, sweaty!" Gabriella laughed and gave him a playful shove.

He knew he hadn't fixed the problem, but was glad he'd made her smile. She had a way of making him celebrate the small victories. He was still determined to find a solution since he really felt like this whole mess was all his fault anyway, but if he could make her laugh and smile in the meantime, he could at least trick himself into thinking he was worthy of her.

Gabriella joined him about halfway through his shower. He pressed his chest to her back as she braced her hands on the tile in front of them, thrusting into her from behind as he held onto her hips. He went slow, knowing her muscles were sore from her new workout routine, but it was still so intense. She had a way of breaking him down to his barest self, leaving him completely exposed and unguarded. He watched her round ass bounce with each push of his cock, and when she gasped, reaching behind with one hand to curl her fingers in his hair, pressing his mouth to her neck, biting her smooth, wet skin, he could barely stay buried long enough to feel her clench around him. He pulled out after two tight squeezes of her pussy with no time to spare before he was jerking himself off and spraying hot white cum all over her ass and lower back.

His hand slid to her chin, bringing her mouth to his as he groaned and shuddered, kissing her like it was his sole purpose. "I love you, baby," he breathed. "I think you swooping in and stealing my job was the best thing that's ever happened to me."

She smiled against his lips. "Well, I guess now that you finally got what you wanted, it's only fair that you take care of me now."

They dried and got dressed, making their way out to the kitchen to make breakfast. Eggs and toast were really the extent of his culinary talents, but she didn't seem to mind. He diced up a tomato and threw in some green onion for extra flavor and even cut up some mixed fruit. He felt like quite the damn chef.

About three-quarters of the way through their meal as they talked about Gabriella's upcoming girls' night in and Emerson's guys' night out, there was a knock on the door. Emerson tried to remember if he'd pissed anyone off recently, and while he couldn't think of anything in particular, he still took a step back as he opened the door, just in case there was a flying fist waiting for him on the other side.

Nope. Worse.

"Olivia?" Surely this was some sort of nightmare. Standing in the doorway with clear intent in her green eyes was his old fling- well, *one* of his old flings- Olivia. The woman Gabriella witnessed flirting with him as he slid his hands up the backs of her bare thighs in her too-short dress. The woman Gabriella watched him leave a bar with, tucked under his arm as she ran her hands all over his body.

His stomach bottomed out and he started to sweat. He wasn't sure why. He hadn't done anything wrong, but he couldn't help the reaction like he'd been caught.

You're overreacting, dude. You've done nothing wrong. You haven't even seen Olivia in months. Just breathe.

"Hey you," Olivia greeted with a cat-like grin. She reached out for him, but he caught her wrist before she could touch his chest like he knew she was going to do. "It's been a while. Are you still working those long hours?"

"Uhm," he kind of choked as he cleared his throat. "Liv, I'm not...I haven't actually been working long hours. I'm seeing someone."

"What?" She laughed and the disbelief in her tone and expression made Emerson clench his jaw.

"I have a girlfriend," he stated. "And she's here right now, so..."

"Oh." She was disappointed, and she peeked around his shoulder as if she had to see it to believe it. Her eyes went wide as she saw Gabriella at the kitchen table. Emerson didn't dare look. He was rooted to the spot and his one goal was getting Olivia back out the door. When she looked back up at him, she took a step back. "Well, that's too bad. I was really hoping we could have some fun."

Emerson said nothing. One hand was on the door and his body was a shield, blocking his old sleazy life out of his new amazing one.

Olivia did her best to look indifferent, though Emerson could tell she definitely felt put out. And annoyed. "Okay, well...good luck,

Emerson. If it doesn't work out…you have my number." She gave him a sly, seductive grin that, once upon a time, would have had him opening the door and showing her to his room. All it did now was reassure him of his decision to be with Gabriella and absolutely no one else.

"Bye, Liv."

When he shut the door, he took a deep breath and let out a long exhale before turning around to face the only woman he wanted in his bed. His apartment. His life.

"What did she want?" Gabriella asked. The grin and the teasing spark in her eye told him she knew exactly what Olivia was looking for. And the fact that she trusted him enough to joke about it might have made him fall in love with her all over again.

"Sorry about that…" He cringed and made his way back to the table. "Honestly, I'm surprised it took her this long to stop by. She's…sort of difficult to get rid of."

"I bet I could find a way." Gabriella gave him a wicked grin and aggressively stabbed her fork into a chunk of watermelon.

Emerson laughed, knowing with absolute certainty that he was the luckiest man on earth.

Chapter 24

The tires of Emerson's Lexus squealed and screeched to a stop at the curb outside Brody and Amira's house. Emerson was panting, his face pale, eyes wide with fear. Gabby was also panting, but she was grinning and wide-eyed with exhilaration.

"Now *that's* how you drive a car like this!" Gabby exclaimed. She pressed the push-button to turn the vehicle off and unbuckled her seatbelt.

"I'm gonna be sick," Emerson stated. He sat still in the passenger seat with a hand over his stomach.

Gabby laughed and leaned over the console to give him a kiss on the cheek. "Oh, come on. We made it, didn't we?"

"I'm not sure that kid on the BMX bike back there did," Emerson replied, still staring ahead, watching his life flash before his eyes. "This must be where Lola gets it. Kolbe and Robby swear she's fucking terrifying to ride in a car with."

Emerson had lost a bet- well, it was sort of a win-win. Gabby had bet him she could get him off with her mouth in under three minutes, and if she won, she got to drive his car. If he won, well, he'd still get blowie and he'd drive as usual. It was totally worth it.

They wandered up the driveway to the house. The guys were all meeting there and the driveway was full of cars already. It looked like they were the last ones there- even Marco's SUV was there already. For a second she felt bad that she hadn't been there to introduce him and Max to everyone, but then she remembered...this was Marco. He didn't need anyone there to help him make new friends. He was a natural social butterfly, and Gabby had no doubt when she walked inside, he'd have all the attention on him as he entertained them all with his beguiling charm and wit.

And she was right.

As soon as they walked through the door, they heard booming laughter coming from the living room followed by Marco's voice above the noise.

"...wasn't even sure at first if he was gay, but I wasn't stepping away from the challenge either way."

Gabby laughed quietly and shook her head, recognizing the familiar story of how Marco and Max met. They kicked their shoes off and Emerson paused before venturing into the house much further. His eyes darted around the entryway and what they could see of the stairs, then the kitchen. As always, he was on high-alert searching for his furry nemesis. With no Basil to be found, they followed the noise until they were standing just outside the living room.

Marco was standing in front of the fireplace and television with all eyes on him. Brody sat in a gray, overstuffed recliner with Amira sitting on the arm next to him, Zoey sat on Jett's lap on the couch, her adorable baby bump protruding beneath her sundress. Chris was next to Jett, and Victoria had her feet in his lap where he was now massaging them. She was due in two months and looked like the summer heat was getting to her, even in the cool, air conditioned house. Tyler and Lizzie were sitting awkwardly distanced from each other on the loveseat and Gabby remembered Emerson's attempt at setting them up. Max was sitting in a chair with his feet propped on an ottoman, his eyes trained adoringly on his charismatic husband, and a furry black and gray striped cat purring in his lap.

Basil hissed as soon as he saw Emerson enter the living room and Gabby couldn't help laughing.

"Gabs!" Marco gasped excitedly. The room briefly shifted its attention toward her and Emerson and she smiled in greeting at everyone before Marco continued with his story. "So, he asked me if I knew where the sociology section was- I didn't. It was my first day working at the customer service desk, but again, I wasn't going to pass him off to someone else."

"He took me around the entire bookstore," Max chimed in. "I saw the sociology section twice, but didn't say anything because I was having too much fun following him around and seeing where he was going with it."

"He just wanted to stare at my ass a little longer, and I can't say I blame him," Marco said. "So finally, he says to me 'You have no idea where the sociology section is, do you?' And I gave him my best shy grin, at least pretending to be completely innocent-"

"Didn't buy it for a second," Max added.

"Well, it didn't stop you from coming back into the store at least once a week for the next month and a half."

"That's so adorable!" Amira cooed, clasping her hands together. "A real meet-cute. Brody and I just met at a frat party. He helped me and Rae escape out a bathroom window when the cops came looking for underage drinkers."

"That's still cute!" Marco replied. "He rescued you!"

"It was really cute when she threw up on my shoes," Brody remarked.

Amira held up her hand. "I blame Rae for that. She made me be her partner in beer pong and, while we won, she completely carried the team and I drank *way* too much Bud Light Lime in celebration."

"Well, following Rae's lead in anything back then was a pretty solid way to land your ass in trouble," said Chris.

"I resent that, Chris Watson!" A female voice shouted from behind Gabby and Emerson, and she heard the front door close as more people joined the party. Footsteps rounded the corner and there were Quinn Casey and Raelyn DeRose. Or was it Quinn and Raelyn Casey now? The blonde bombshell spotted Chris on the couch with his wife. "I have no idea what I'm getting blamed for, but it's not polite to talk shit about people who aren't there to defend themselves."

"We're talking about how I threw up all over Brody's shoes after he got us out the second-story bathroom window of that frat house," Amira supplied.

"Oh…well then, yeah, that was probably my fault," Raelyn surrendered. Her bright blue eyes trained on Emerson then swung to Gabby and she smiled brightly. "Hey! You might not remember, but we met in the women's bathroom a couple months ago at Chateau Delecroix."

"Yeah, I remember," Gabby said. *How could I forget?* She did a brief, hopefully subtle once-over, taking in Raelyn's bare feet, high-waisted, ripped blue jean shorts, cropped Dodgers t-shirt, and white baseball cap with a silver-gray LA emblem. It was far from the images she'd seen in her shameful Google search or the gorgeous navy blue evening gown she'd worn for her rehearsal dinner. She just looked like a regular person. A very pretty regular person, but a regular person nonetheless.

Emerson lifted his chin and acknowledged Quinn who was standing with his arm around Raelyn's shoulders. "All-Star."

Quinn narrowed his eyes at Emerson. "Asshole," he greeted. Raelyn swatted his chest and whispered a hushed *"Be nice!"* before turning back and smiling again at Gabby.

Unsurprisingly, Emerson grinned. He always enjoyed conflict. "We didn't know you guys would be here." He looked briefly back at Brody for explanation. Brody shrugged, appearing equally taken by surprise.

Amira stood and walked over to Raelyn, enveloping her in a big hug. "I thought you were going to be in LA!"

"We took a detour," Raelyn replied. "We have to head back in the morning, but I needed a night with the girls. I know I've always been just another one of the guys, but traveling with twenty-six baseball players, plus the rest of the staff who are all men…it's a lot to ask of any woman."

"Sounds like a dream come true," Marco said. His eyes were wide and glued to Quinn. Max might have admonished him, but he was also staring at the professional ball player.

"That's my brother, Marco," Gabby said, "and his husband, Max."

"Great season so far," said Max, finding his voice. "That was an awesome first game back."

"Thanks," Quinn replied, smiling. "It feels awesome to be back."

That one-dimpled grin was even sexier in person.

You have a super hot boyfriend. Snap out of it, woman!

Gabby cleared her throat and tried to keep herself in check, making sure she wasn't obviously ogling the baseball stud who her *actual boyfriend* seemed to have a real problem with. Still, a sense of giddyness washed over her when Quinn's golden-brown gaze swept over her and he got a mischievous look on his face. His eyes flicked to Emerson then his grin became even more devilish.

"I'll be right back, baby," Quinn said to Raelyn. "I left something in the car."

As soon as the front door closed again, Emerson shot Raelyn a look. "What's he doing?"

Raelyn shrugged. "I don't know, he said he forgot something."

"He's up to something." Emerson's tone was accusatory and it made Gabby laugh.

"Wow, this rivalry is no joke, huh?" Gabby asked.

Raelyn waved a hand dismissively and stepped further into the living room, squeezing herself between Tyler and Lizzie on the loveseat. "Men are idiots," Raelyn said. She rubbed Tyler's head playfully, as if ruffling his hair- though it was cut too short to make a difference. "Except for you, Ty. You're a sweetheart." Tyler smiled like a proud puppy and puffed out his chest.

"So, Mrs. Casey…tell me more about traveling with twenty-six professional baseball players," Marco said, sitting on the raised stone hearth in front of the fireplace. "Do you get to see them all naked? Do you get drunk together? Do you all sleep in one bed?"

Emerson and Gabby found seats in the living room and listened to Marco play twenty questions with Raelyn about her time on the road. When the front door opened and closed again, Quinn's voice came from the far end of the kitchen as he made his way back into the living room. "So Gabriella…I hear you like baseball…"

She glanced up at the sound of her name and her eyes went wide. Staring. She hoped for both her sake and Emerson's that she wasn't drooling because Quinn Casey was fully dressed in his uniform. Blue jersey, blue baseball cap…*white baseball pants.*

From the couch, Jett muttered, "Oh shit, someone break out the popcorn."

Chris grinned and glanced from Quinn to Emerson and back. "This is about to be one hell of a show."

Ignoring the comments, Quinn stretched, twisting from one side to the other, teasing a side-display of that famous baseball booty before turning around. Marco squeaked. Max cleared his throat and crossed his legs.

"I think I'm due for some new pants soon," Quinn said, squatting low and standing back up a few times. "My trainer has really been focusing on sprints and I feel like these are getting a little tight around the thighs and ass."

"All I heard was *tight* and *ass*," Marco mumbled.

"Get the fuck out!" Emerson roared, pointing toward the door.

"Why?" Quinn asked, crooked grin in place as he turned back to face the room.

"You know why," Emerson said through gritted teeth. "All-Star, you're about to catch a fist in your face."

Quinn scoffed and brushed him off. "Please, you've never been in a fight in your life. *I,* on the other hand, have been in several." Quinn put his hands up in fists as if he were ready to box. "Lucky for you, these babies are rated *E* for Everyone- let's go."

"Rae, control your husband," Emerson said, not taking his eyes off Quinn. He was clearly pissed, but everyone in the room, including Gabby, seemed to be enjoying the entertainment.

Raelyn put her hands up in surrender. "You know what? A little over a year ago we were here and you were trying to bring shit up to make us fight. He couldn't hit you then because his arm wasn't healed…I say you have it coming."

Gabby snapped her head toward Emerson, incredulous. "You tried to make them fight?"

"I believe I succeeded, actually," he replied. "But I thought we were ready to put that behind us."

"Aw, come on, isn't this what you've been doing to me for a year?" Quinn asked. "Trying to make Rae regret her choice to be with me instead of going back to you? Payback, Asshole." He flipped Emerson off with both hands.

Gabby looked at Emerson again, one eyebrow arched, silently asking for confirmation that what Quinn had said was true. He tucked his tongue into his cheek before saying, "It's possible...that I was sort of...*combative* when they first got together. But, as I stated before, that's in the past. We can put all that behind us now." Gabby continued to eye him skeptically, so he continued defensively, "I mean it. I'm not remotely interested in breaking them up anymore. Look-" he gestured to Raelyn on the small couch, "I see her and it's just like...she's one of the guys. Just another bro. That's it."

Raelyn scowled. "Ouch. You didn't have to take it that far. I still got that V where you guys all have a P."

Chris and Jett chuckled on the couch opposite Raelyn and immediately stopped when her glare cut them off. Emerson rolled his eyes. "Rae, I've literally watched you inhale a Meat Lovers pizza while screaming at the refs during a Lions game from your couch. You're a bro."

Jett raised his hand. "I've also seen that."

"Can confirm," Chris added with a nod.

"I love it, baby," said Quinn. "As a matter of fact, talking about your bro-ish tendencies is making me a little hot." And then he began unbuttoning his jersey. It was like every gorgeous magazine cover ever made, but one-hundred times better because it was in the flesh. Gabby chewed the inside of her cheek to keep in any involuntary noises from escaping as he pulled his jersey open, showing off the ripple of hard muscles beneath.

Marco had no such intentions of keeping his thoughts caged in. "You and you," he said, pointing to Max and Quinn. "And I call middle."

Everyone looked at Quinn for his reaction. He looked contemplative before shooting his gaze to his wife. "Hang on, let me ask my wife how taking it from two guys at a time works."

Raelyn glared. "Oh. My. God. It was *one* time in college- you really need to get over that."

Gabby's jaw dropped and she shifted her gaze to Emerson. He gave a small nod then whispered in her ear, "Let me guess, she's not the perfect, fairy tale princess you were imagining her to be?" She shook her head with a silent laugh. This was going to be an interesting night.

A bottle of Chardonnay, two bottles of Pinot Noir, and some sparkling grape juice later, after darkness had descended on the summer heat outside and the guys had left for their night out, Gabby and the girls were still in the living room, laughing and swapping stories. It all felt so comfortable and familiar, and Emerson had been right- Gabby's initial impression of Raelyn or the one she'd created in her head was completely inaccurate. She wasn't remotely catty and there was nothing about her that implied she thought she was better than anyone. The topic of her ridiculous fortune only came up once, and it was just in reference to Quinn finding out just how much money she actually had when they'd joined their accounts after their wedding.

"He wanted to buy a private jet for a wedding present," Raelyn said after a sip of red wine. "I told him that the league already pays for us to fly first class everywhere, so why bother?"

"I think that's a guy thing," Gabby replied. "They like to throw their money around like it's going to show how impressive and huge their penis is."

The girls laughed.

"I don't know," Zoey said. She swirled sparkling red grape juice around in a fancy champagne flute. "Jett doesn't really do that. He's modest with gifts."

"Well, that's because Jett's penis is so ginormous, he doesn't need to brag about it," Raelyn said.

Lizzie groaned and made a puking noise. "Oh my God! That's my brother you're talking about! I do not need to hear about his…endowments."

Zoey's face turned a little pink and Raelyn apologized through a laugh. Gabby paused, her gaze shifting from one woman to the other. "Wait, so…did *you* and Jett…?" Gabby asked.

"No!" Raelyn practically shouted. "No, no. It was an accident. Me and Jett…" She shook her head vigorously. "I *did* make him go as my date to Amira and Brody's engagement party because…well, it was right after me and Emerson broke up and I heard he was taking someone so I didn't want to be the loser who showed up alone."

"So you took Jett?" Zoey questioned, looking both amused and skeptical. "Did you think Emerson would actually believe that was a thing?"

"I had a whole story made up," Raelyn explained. "The plan was to tell everyone how we'd been friends for so long and it just hit us at the same time- we couldn't believe we'd never realized it before. The man of my dreams was right there all along!"

"I remember Jett bitching about it," said Victoria. "He thought you were absolutely nuts for thinking it was going to work."

"Well, it would have worked if Jett were a better actor!"

Lizzie laughed. "Yeah, and if Emerson's bullshit meter weren't completely on point."

"I kept telling him to put his arm around me or hold my hand or do *something* to make it look like we were a couple," Raelyn said, laughing. "Honestly, I think he was terrified Quinn was going to jump out of the bushes and beat his ass even though he hadn't been home in six years."

"So, I'm guessing he *didn't* buy it?" Gabby asked.

"Not for a second, no," Raelyn replied. She shifted on the loveseat, turning to face Gabby. "How's everything with you guys? Still got the prank war going at work?"

How Gabby had managed to go this long without mentioning all the drama with Johnathan was a mystery. She was determined to put him out of her mind at least for the night, but apparently it wasn't meant to be.

"Actually…about work…" She explained everything, from the fundraiser over a month ago, to the phone call the previous Sunday, until that morning with her rapid rejections.

"Wait- *You* called Johnathan Yates out on his bullshit? You actually faced him and told him what a piece of shit he is?" Raelyn asked, jaw dropped.

Gabby nodded. "Well…yeah."

"Girl…Now, I'm not a pushover by any means, but that man scares the shit out of me."

"I'm not scared of him, I'm just annoyed. And I'm worried that he's got every law firm in town turned against me and I'm going to have to find a job somewhere else. I have money saved that'll get me by for now, not that I need it at the moment since Emerson's making me stay with him, but-"

"You and Emerson are living together?" Raelyn asked. The room went quiet and Gabby felt five sets of eyes on her all at once.

"Not technically, no. He's just being obnoxious and all protective, insisting that I need to let him take care of me."

"Holy shit…" Amira gaped. "You're staying in his apartment? And he's like…being nurturing?"

"He says he wants to spoil me. He practically begged me to let him," Gabby replied.

The room was silent for a few beats as the girls all exchanged glances.

"And you've been together for three months?" Amira asked, still in awe.

"Officially, I guess, yeah." Gabby nodded. She looked at Raelyn and debated whether or not she really wanted to ask what was on her mind. She liked feeling like she was special, like the things Emerson was doing weren't typical for him. That's what she'd thought over the past week, but she could find out for sure if she got the nerve to ask. "I mean, you dated him before. You know what he's like in a relationship…"

Raelyn took a deep swill from her wine glass. "Actually...it sounds different. I mean, he was a great boyfriend when we were together, but he liked to buy me stuff. Surprise me with nice gifts, expensive roses and things like that. While all that is nice, I think what you're getting from him sounds a lot more personal. Anyone with money can throw it around, but he's really giving you pieces of himself. His time and effort. That's huge...that's a big step for him and it's really intimate. You're not just some girl to him, that's for sure."

The conversation eventually transitioned to how Zoey and Victoria were doing with their pregnancies, how they were preparing and how Jett and Chris were responding. They'd both opted to wait to find out what they were having, but Zoey expressed that she was about to cave every time she found really cute baby boy stuff or really cute baby girl stuff at the store. Zoey's baby shower was about a month away, and she had a feeling she'd give in and ask the doctor to tell them the sex so she could put specific clothes on her wish list.

Amira said that she and Brody were starting to toss around the idea of trying for a baby. Raelyn groaned and threw herself back onto the couch cushions. Apparently Quinn was still insistent on impregnating her with nine boys so he could have his own family baseball team, but she had different plans.

"Let me guess," said Victoria, eyeing Gabby. "Being a lawyer, you're probably too work oriented to even think about having kids?"

Gabby shrugged. "I came from a really big family and I loved it. I know it's hard to work as much as I do- or as much as I'd like to, anyway- and have kids, but I definitely want kids of my own one day. A few of them."

"Does Emerson know you want kids?" Zoey asked curiously. "He completely freaked out when he found out *I* was pregnant."

"He did?" Gabby raised an eyebrow. After two months, it wasn't something they'd discussed yet.

"Oh yeah, and since then he's had some serious rants on why babies ruin everything," Zoey said. She lowered her voice in what was undoubtedly meant to be an impression of Emerson, *"How can I work all these hours and have a kid? If my wife works, we'll need a nanny and we won't even raise our own kids!'*

Raelyn joined in, *"I can't have an ugly nanny because she'll scare the baby, but if I have a hot one she'll probably try to seduce me. I'm not having my kids raised by an army of nanny sluts like I was!"* Her blue eyes flashed to Gabby. "If you do bring this up, just be prepared: There's a one-hundred percent chance he'll tell you about how he caught his dad in bed with his favorite nanny when he was seven."

Gabby rolled her eyes. "His dad's got him so convinced that he's destined to be just like him."

"Sounds like you're doing a good job of showing him that he's not," Raelyn said. "I think Kolbe helps a lot, too."

Gabby smiled. "Oh my gosh, that kid is too funny. I can't believe he and my little brother were friends before we even started working together."

"No way- you have a little brother, too? And they already knew each other?"

Gabby nodded and explained the short version of her life story and how her parents had three kids in Miami and another three in Michigan. She told her about Robby and how he and Kolbe are on the same travel baseball team and threw in a few brags about how good he was at the game. "He thinks he's the next Quinn Casey."

"I'll remember that," said Raelyn. "Quinn loves visiting local teams and coaching them. Maybe I'll have him stop by and meet the team. Actually- Zoey, maybe you should set that up."

"You got it!" Zoey lifted her glass of sparkling juice.

"He also has quite the crush on you apparently," Gabby added. She took a drink of her Chardonnay, feeling immensely more comfortable around Emerson's ex now that she'd gotten to know her. "So take that how you want. It would make his day to meet you, but if you don't want a fourteen-year-old ogling you, I totally get it."

"It can't be any worse than the grown men I put up with on the road," Raelyn replied. "Dean Bennett and Quinn are really close, so

Dean likes to fuck with him. I'll be in the therapy room talking to Quinn, and Dean will come in saying that he pulled a muscle in his groin again, asking if I could just *rub it out* like last time." The girls all laughed. "Seriously, I don't care what age these men are, if you have a big enough group of them, they all act somewhere between twelve and seventeen."

From the topic of immature men, the group quickly turned to Lizzie to dissect her dating life. It was impossible to keep up with. Apparently the girl had a new boyfriend every month, but she was currently flying solo and had been since her last breakup with some guy named Kyle. Her attempt to get in with the MLB players at the wedding back in June apparently had gone well until Jett decided to cock-block her from hooking up with Parker Preston. She'd been furious with her older brother and still seemed more than a little annoyed about it.

It wasn't until nearly one in the morning that the front door opened and a chorus of male voices filled the space. Chris and Jett collected their women, waving goodbye to everyone. Lizzie had been hitting the Chardonnay pretty hard and Quinn offered to give her a ride home since he hadn't been drinking all evening. Raelyn tossed back what was left of her glass of Pinot Noir and stumbled her way over to her husband.

Gabby watched as Raelyn put a hand on Emerson's arm and pointed at him. With as stern of a voice as she could muster in her wine-tipsy state, she told him, "Your girlfriend is kind of awesome. Don't fuck it up."

"I won't," Emerson assured her. His gaze slid over to Gabby still sitting on the couch and she smiled.

Quinn, Raelyn, and Lizzie said their goodbyes and left.

Gabby looked around for her brother and Max, and Emerson seemed to notice. "They took a cab home from the last bar. They'll be over in the morning to get their car," he informed her. "Ready to get going?" She slid off the couch and made her way over to him, wrapping her arms around his neck and pulling him in for a kiss.

From the kitchen, she heard Amira. "Aww...Emerson! You guys are like...a real couple. Isn't this so much better than those random hoe-bags?"

Emerson coughed a laugh. "Jesus, Amira. I'm sure Gabe really wants to be reminded of all that."

"Mentioning the random hoe-bags can't be as bad as them showing up during breakfast, can it?" Gabby teased.

"I'm sorry- what? Who showed up where?" Amira exclaimed.

"One of his former slam-pieces showed up this morning while we were eating breakfast," Gabby replied. She wasn't worried, and it was honestly funny to think about now.

Brody and Amira both eyed Emerson wearily. Looking tense suddenly, Emerson explained, "Olivia was just wondering why she hadn't seen me in a while...I told her I was no longer on the market and she left."

"And you saw this whole exchange?" Amira asked Gabby.

"It really wasn't a big deal. I'm honestly kind of surprised it hadn't happened sooner. Or more times. As long as they don't keep trying to come back, it's fine," Gabby said with a shrug. The four of them stood around the kitchen island now and she couldn't help noticing the tension and weird silence that had fallen over them.

Finally Amira cleared her throat and gave a curt nod. "Well good." She smiled at Gabby. "I don't think he'd get away with pulling the same shit on you that he did with Rae anyway. Not that Rae's weak, but somehow I feel like if he did that to you, there'd be castration involved."

Gabby felt Emerson go still next to her and saw Brody's eyes widen. *What the hell am I missing here?*

"What do you mean?" Gabby asked, forcing a smile into her tone. She glanced at Emerson who was staring at Brody- they looked like they were having a telepathic conversation. "What kind of shit did you pull?"

"I've-" Emerson cleared his throat, "I've been meaning to...circle back to this..." He looked the most uncomfortable she'd ever seen him.

There was sweat beading up on his neck. "It's about how me and Rae broke up-"

"Your breakup? You told me it was mutual..." Gabby questioned, her heart racing a mile a minute. Her anxiety level had spiked and she knew something bad was coming.

"Mutual?" Amira repeated. "*Mutual?* I'm sorry, what was *mutual* about her walking in on you screwing your legal assistant?"

Gabby blinked, certain she'd misheard. But Emerson wouldn't meet her gaze, and that told her everything she needed to know. "Is that true?"

She could handle his previous lifestyle. The hookups, the conquests, the steady flow of willing women in and out of his life. It was in the past. But...he was a cheater? He'd cheated on his fiance. The woman he'd been with for three years. They'd only been together for three months- what chance did she stand to make it last?

"Gabe, the first time it ever came up was when we were out to dinner with Kolbe and Robby. We weren't together, I didn't want to get into it in front of my brother, I really didn't think it would matter," Emerson explained, his tone calm and even. Completely in control. Just like he trained it to be when he found himself caught in a lie.

And just like that she realized she couldn't trust him right now.

"Okay, but it's come up at least a couple times since then and you continued to lie about it." Gabby kept her voice quiet, though she felt the shakiness of it as a feeling of complete betrayal ripped through her.

"I wanted to tell you," Emerson said. "I was going to a few times...I tried telling you, but..." He closed his eyes and let out a slow breath. "Listen baby, I could give you excuses or I could just admit that I messed up. I did. I should have told you. I shouldn't have let the distractions that came up save my ass for another day. I screwed up and I'm sorry."

Despite the fact that it was one of the best apologies she'd received from a man- no woman ever wants excuses, they just want an admission of guilt and recognition of the screw up- she didn't feel settled. There were still a hundred questions zooming around her head, but the middle of Brody and Amira's kitchen was not the place to get into all that. She swallowed hard and gave a small nod. Emerson reached for her, trying to put his arm around her waist, but she stepped away and around him toward the door.

"Thanks again for inviting me, Amira," she said, willing tears and frustration to hold off. "I had a lot of fun."

Amira glanced uncertainly from Emerson and back to Gabby. "Yeah, I'm glad you could make it. I'll let you know when the next one is."

Emerson followed Gabby out the front door to the car and they rode back to his apartment in uncomfortable silence.

Chapter 25

Fucking fuck.

Dammit.

Fucking Amira.

No, asshole, this is on you.

The entire ride home was torture. Gabriella didn't speak or look at him the entire way and he knew she was building her case, forming her argument and interrogation for when they got home. And he let her. He wasn't going to lie. He would tell her every little detail about his past that she wanted to know. Apologizing was only the first step. A simple apology and the admission that he was an ass for lying. It was a solid start. For the first time in his life he was pleading guilty and hoping for mercy.

The door to his apartment clicked shut behind him and he watched Gabriella move slowly ahead, looking around as though it was her first time there. He waited for her to say something. He wanted to make sure she was ready to ask him any and everything she needed to know. She made her way to the living room and he followed, leaning against the partition wall and waiting for his trial to start.

After what seemed like ages of listening to the clock ticking on the shelf, Gabriella turned to face him. "You were with her for three years…and you cheated on her," she stated, searching his face for a reaction or explanation, or maybe both.

Emerson nodded. "I did."

"She walked in on you and someone from work?" she asked. "Who?"

"Her name was Bianca…she was an intern."

"That's a little cliché, don't you think?" She was upset and had every right to be. He knew some of the things she would say would hurt, but he didn't care. He wanted to get through this. She could say whatever she wanted, accuse him of anything, call him whatever names in anger, as long as they resolved this. "How old was she?"

Emerson thought for a moment. "Twenty...two? I think. I don't really know much about her."

"How many times?"

His brow furrowed. "How many times did we hook up?" he asked, and she nodded. "Just once."

Gabriella stood in the middle of his living room with her arms at her sides, looking completely lost and vulnerable. He hated it. He hated that he was the reason for it. "Was it worth it?" she asked.

"No, of course not," he replied. Wanting so badly to reach out for her but knowing she needed her space, he shoved his hands in his pockets. "When you first asked me why we broke up I told you it was because she wasn't the one. I realized it maybe a week after I asked her to marry me. I thought she was, and I wanted her to be, but she wasn't. I should've been able to just tell her that, but I couldn't. I was a fucking coward. I didn't think I could explain it...I figured she'd keep trying to make it work and it was like I was suffocating. I had to do something to get out. Something that would ensure that she wouldn't keep trying to make it work."

Gabriella studied him for a brief moment, then asked, "Was Bianca the only one?"

His jaw clenched and he swallowed. "She was...the only one I had sex with."

Fuck, he hated himself for this. He hated talking about it, he hated that it was the truth, and he hated watching the woman he loved fall apart because two years ago he'd decided to be the biggest jackass on the planet.

"There were two other women...I don't even know their names. The first one was on a night like tonight- the guys split up for bar hopping, the girls did the same. There was this one bar where we were talking to this group of women, being stupid, buying them drinks and flirting with them. Nothing was going to happen, we were just having fun. This one girl was really tipsy and was getting ready to leave. They asked me to wait with them for their Uber. When the car showed up, she tried talking me into coming with them. I told her I couldn't, but then she kissed me before getting in the car. That's all it was, but Rae saw it. She and Amira were walking into the bar...she confronted me right away and I lied. It wasn't even anything- *she* kissed *me*. I had no intention of going anywhere with her, but...I still lied. I made Rae think she'd imagined it. I think it was a guilty conscience...like I knew it would happen sooner or later and was protecting myself."

Gabby was barely showing any emotion. She'd put on a mask of calm and all he wanted to do was scoop her up in his arms because he knew on the inside she was crumbling.

Against all natural instincts of self-preservation, Emerson willed himself to continue. "Then there was another similar to that. I was out with some guys after work and we went to a bar we didn't typically go to- one of the bigger places with dancing and a younger crowd. Again, I was drinking pretty heavily, flirting and buying drinks for these girls who were there for a bachelorette party. One of the girls asked me to dance and we ended up making out on the dance floor. She kissed me first, but...I didn't stop her."

Gabby's brow furrowed and she wrapped her arms around herself. "So how did you jump from a teenage make-out session on the dance floor to screwing an intern?"

"Bianca flirted with me relentlessly. It was a running joke. Even Rae knew about it. I'd get suggestive texts from her all the time, she'd flirt with me at work, make passes at me, and I ignored it," he explained. "Then...I don't know, I guess after those two girls, it's like I made up my mind that instead of telling Rae there was a problem, I was going to do something I couldn't take back or excuse. I was working late on a case and she'd been there the whole week with me. Then it just...happened. And then Rae walked in and...well, that was it."

"Why did she just happen to show up that night?" Gabriella asked. "Did she suspect something was going on?"

"No, she was…just coming to see me. It was my second week in a row working late, getting home after she'd already gone to bed."

The memory of Rae's face when she'd caught him was forever burned in his mind. He'd been so caught up in needing out, drowning in that desperate claustrophobic feeling he always got in relationships, that he hadn't considered how shitty he would feel telling her that it happened. He hadn't considered how hurt she would be. And when she'd caught him, the moment she'd stepped through that door was like some kind of curse breaking. Whatever selfish thoughts he'd had over the past several weeks dissolved and all he was left with was the cold, hard reality of what he'd done. Immediately he knew telling her the truth would have been a thousand times easier, even if he'd had to spend hours explaining it.

Gabriella was quiet again, chewing on her lip. "Was that the first time?" She met his gaze and he knew exactly what she was asking. He knew he'd have to tell her the truth about that, too. "Or had you cheated before?"

He shook his head sullenly. "It wasn't my first time."

"How many girlfriends have you cheated on?"

"All of them." The words were out of his mouth before he could talk himself out of it.

Her mouth parted, unsure of what to say. "*All* of them?"

"There haven't been that many I've called girlfriends, but yes…all of them."

Gabriella looked away and pushed a hand through her hair before lowering herself into one of the chairs. She kicked her heels off and the knot in Emerson's chest loosened just the slightest bit. Good, she wasn't planning on running out. At least not yet.

He stepped further into the room, needing to be near her but unsure if she would let him. He squatted in front of her, placing his hands on the cushion on either side of her. She was quiet and looking over him, beyond him, working through everything he'd confessed. When he felt the silence had stretched too long, he moved his hands from the cushion to the outsides of her thighs. It wasn't a possessive hold, just a light touch, grazing his fingers up and down her skin exposed by her floral romper. He lowered his head to the tops of her legs, closing his eyes and feeling like he needed to start praying she'd forgive him.

The silence was torture. He needed to know what was going through her head. What was she thinking? Did she hate him? What did he need to do to make it up to her?

He kissed her thigh, not in a sexual way, but because he needed to feel her skin on his lips. Raising his head to look at her, he pleaded, "Baby, tell me what you're thinking."

Still, Gabriella didn't look at him. Her lip quivered before she sucked it in, brushing her teeth over it. Emerson listened to her breathing and waited. "Honestly…" Her voice was barely a whisper, and the crack in her voice made his heart clench. "I'm kind of scared to ask anything else."

Resting his head back in her lap, he sighed. He didn't know if he was more upset with himself for lying to her or for being such a selfish prick in the past to begin with. He still wanted to tell her everything she wanted to know. Everything she needed to know to understand his past and know exactly what she'd gotten into with him. But even more, he wanted to assure her that she wasn't going to be another victim of his selfishness. Sure, it had only been a few months, but everything about her was different. He'd never felt this way about anyone and had no idea the level of emotions he felt for her even existed. It was like he fell harder every day. Everything she did, every second they were together, he found more to love about her. He wasn't letting her go. He couldn't. They would figure out a way to get past this. Whatever she needed to know that she could trust him and that he wasn't going to hurt her. That version of him was in the past, and she was his future.

"I'm sorry I didn't tell you sooner," Emerson said again. "I wanted to forget I was ever like that. I wanted to just put the past behind me and focus on now…on us. You see the best in me. You see things I'm not even sure are there, but I want them to be. More than anything, I want to be the man you deserve."

"You probably felt that way about Raelyn at some point, too," she replied.

Her voice was so distant and he could feel himself losing her. Panic took hold and he grabbed her hands. "When we were in Detroit you said that nothing you heard about my past would change how you feel now. You said you know the man I am now. Please baby, trust who I am now."

"I'm sure you think you mean that, but what about in a couple months? A couple years? Who's to say you won't think you need out then and fall back into old habits?"

"I won't-"

"But you don't know that!" Gabriella raised her voice and it flooded Emerson with relief. Maybe she was past being quiet and ready to work through it. Even if it escalated into a shouting match, it was better than sitting in silence and having no idea where her head was at on the subject.

"I do! I do know," Emerson insisted. "It's not the same. The way I feel about you already is nowhere near anything I've ever felt with any-one. It doesn't matter that it's only been a few months- I *love* you and I'm not leaving you."

"Maybe for now, but what if..." she hesitated, then her eyes set in a steely, unyielding glare. "What if I have an expiration date, just like all the others?"

Emerson bit down, clenching his jaw as she threw his father's words in his face. "I am *not* my father," he growled through gritted teeth. He'd always thought he was just like his dad, but for the first time she had him believing he really could be better. He wasn't about to let her faith in him die just yet. "I've made some shitty choices, I know. I've followed in that man's footsteps more than I'd care to admit, but I've never liked it. I've never felt good about myself while acting like him, doing exactly what he'd do. You've shown me how much better I can be, Gabe, and I'm not going back."

Gabriella looked conflicted, but still wouldn't meet his gaze. He brushed his fingers over her cheek and angled her head down to look at him. Her eyes were wet with restrained tears, but the dam wouldn't hold much longer. "Baby, listen to me…I love you so fucking much. You're right, I never thought I would do what I did to Rae. I thought I was past that. I don't just hate talking about it because it makes me look bad- I hate remembering how fucking awful I felt. How disappointed I was in myself. But even so, when we broke up, when the dust settled and the fighting was over and we went our separate ways, there was relief. Yeah, I still felt like shit for doing that to her, but I was glad it was over with just like I knew I would be. I never felt like I couldn't go on without her. I never felt like I needed her to feel whole. I never felt like she was *really,* truly mine." He brought her hand to his lips and brushed his lips over her knuckles. "But you're mine. I don't know how to explain it, I never thought I could feel like this about someone, but if I know anything to be true it's this. You were made for me, and I was made for you. The thought of ever having to be without you again knocks the fucking air out of my lungs."

Gazing back into those almond-shaped eyes, he watched her blink and the first tear rolled down her cheek. He brushed it away with his thumb, forcing himself to be calm even though his lungs were struggling for air, his heart was pounding too hard, and his stomach was doing somersaults. He needed to be strong and show her that he meant every word.

"I think…" Gabriella began. She swallowed and again Emerson wanted to kick himself for the hurt she was feeling. "It's late. Maybe we should just…go to bed. We can talk about all this in the morning."

Emerson searched her expression for a beat before nodding and getting to his feet. She slowly rose from the chair and led the way to the bedroom. Their movements were stiff and uncomfortable, everything was quiet and unsettled. He hated the thought of letting her go to bed upset or sad or whatever she was feeling. He hated even more that she was guarding her emotions so strongly and he had no idea what was going on inside her head. But he was the one who'd messed up. He was the one in the dog house and he fully deserved it.

They went through their before-bed routine in silence and it nearly broke him, but she needed her space and time to think. He'd rather have her stay and think than let her go back to her condo where she wouldn't have his presence to remind her of what they were fighting for. If she chose to fight for them to work. At the moment, he wasn't sure how good his odds were that she'd decide he was worth it.

But she was here. So that had to mean something.

Lying in bed, Gabriella curled on her side and faced away from him. After several long minutes of staring at the ceiling and feeling like she was an ocean away, he rolled onto his side and trailed his hand down her bare arm. She didn't acknowledge the touch, but she didn't push him away so he moved closer, wanting to hold her. He placed a gentle kiss on her shoulder and listened to the slow steady rhythm of her breathing, letting the sound soothe every worry from his mind as it lulled him to sleep.

In the morning, she wasn't there.

The space in the bed where he'd last seen her sleeping form was empty. Emerson's eyes flew open and he looked around the room. No one in the bathroom or the living room or the kitchen. She was gone.

Panic set in and he tried to come up with reasonable explanations. Gabriella loved him, she wouldn't just take off in the middle of the night without a word. Maybe she'd woken up early and went to pick up breakfast or Starbucks. He looked around for notes but found none.

Rushing back to his bedroom, he pulled open the drawer he'd cleaned out for some of her things. Most of what she'd stored in there was still there and he let out a breath.

The gym? Maybe she'd gone to the gym this morning without him. It was always the best way for him to work through frustration and clear out his head when it felt weighed down and cluttered. But her purple UnderArmor bag was still in his closet.

He tore his phone off the charger and sent her a quick text: *Good morning, gorgeous. Where'd you go?*

He waited impatiently but was met with silence, so he picked up and dialed. It went to voice mail. *God dammit!*

Fisting his hair, he willed himself to relax. She'd left her things behind. She was coming back. Maybe she just went for a walk or a drive to clear her head. *She'll be back.*

An hour and three unanswered phone calls later, Emerson was in his car driving to her condo, but she wasn't there either. He called Marco, wondering if she would have gone straight to his place if she were upset. Marco said that he was just about to head over to Brody and Amira's to get their car, but that he hadn't seen her.

Now, being her brother, that could've been complete bullshit. Marco could've been covering for her because she said she didn't want to see him. But hoping like hell that that wasn't the case, he accepted it and tried to think of where else she could be at seven o'clock on a Sunday morning. Where would she go if she was upset?

It hit him like a brick to the chest and he cursed. While his stomach squeezed and rolled uncomfortably at the thought of finishing their discussion anywhere her parents and younger siblings could hear, he stepped on the gas and made a beeline for her family's house.

Relief washed over him when he saw her Lincoln in the driveway, immediately followed by dread. What if she started yelling at him in front of her parents? In front of Lola, Robby, and Eliza? Did they really need to know all the shitty things he'd done in his past? Would it upset them even if he hadn't directly hurt Gabriella? He couldn't bear the thought of them hating him.

He'd always thought family- especially big ones were just a hassle. More trouble than they were worth, but he'd grown to enjoy the time he spent at the Cabrera house, even if most of their events centered around baseball. They'd had backyard barbecues, family dinners, and game nights over the summer and welcomed Emerson like one of their own. It wasn't something he was willing to give up. *She* wasn't something he was willing to give up. So, he got his ass out of the car and marched up the driveway.

When he knocked it was Gabriella's father, Carlos, who answered. Carlos gave him a small smile, and held the door open for him to come inside.

"I don't know what you two are fighting about," said Carlos, "but I'm glad you're here. She's stubborn…she needs someone who will chase her down when it gets tough."

Emerson offered the man a small smile in return and nodded, grateful that he wasn't shoving him out the door. He couldn't believe Carlos was rooting for them, but he held onto that knowledge like a prize. "Thanks Carlos. Where-?"

Carlos pointed toward the back sliding door that led to the small patio. Emerson thanked him and made his way outside.

The backyard was small, with a high privacy fence around it. There was one maple tree in the corner next to an old playset with a swing and slide that hadn't been used in a few years since eleven-year-old Eliza outgrew it. The patio was dated with uneven and cracked stone pavers, but everything about the setting was welcoming. It was worn. Well-used. There was no doubt that a lot of hours had been spent with family in that small backyard, and a knot grew in Emerson's throat at the comparison between his own childhood and the one that the Cabrera-Perez kids had experienced.

Sitting in one of the new wicker patio chairs with a blue floral patterned cushion was Gabriella wearing a light gray, oversized off-the-shoulder t-shirt with *Yale* across the front, and a pair of black leggings. Across from her was her mother, Evelyn. There was a small table between them with two mugs of coffee. The sound of the patio door sliding shut behind him caused Gabriella to look up.

"What are you doing here?" she asked, sitting up straight.

"What do you think?" he replied. "I woke up and you were gone. I tried calling you, but…"

Evelyn smiled at Emerson before standing up and reaching over to place a hand on top of Gabriella's. Evelyn said something to her daughter in Spanish, then walked past Emerson and back inside, giving them privacy.

Emerson took a few steps toward Gabriella and was about to take a seat, but she stood up instead. "I just needed some space," she said, keeping herself at a distance. "And time. I...I barely slept and I just don't know what I'm supposed to do."

"Well, I know what I'd like you to do, but I don't think that's how this works," Emerson said. He placed a hand on the back of the patio chair and looked across the table at the woman he was willing to do anything for. "I told you how sorry I am. I'm sorry I ever did those things, I'm sorry I lied, I'm sorry I let myself find ways to avoid telling you. But it's all in the past, Gabe. I'm just as disgusted with that guy as you are."

"I know," Gabriella said, her voice coming out rushed and a little breathless. "We talked- *you* talked- a lot about how you feel about everything, but I didn't get a chance to say much. I was still processing."

Emerson tilted his head. "And now?"

"And now I feel like I'm being forced to make this impossible decision," she explained. "Yes, you lied, but then you came clean about everything, and I appreciate that. I understand how hard it would've been to just bring it up when things were so great with us. It would've been like you were looking for a fight and I get that. I'm not really mad about that anymore."

A grin threatened to break out across his face, but a feeling in his gut stopped him. She wasn't finished speaking, and if her posture was any indication, he wasn't going to like what came next.

"I feel like I'm putting you on trial for a crime you haven't even committed...*yet.*" Gabriella swallowed and let her gaze travel over his face briefly. "And while things are amazing between us now, I can't help wondering...I won't be able to help wondering when it's going to happen."

A rush like the wind getting knocked out of him after a hard blow to the back nearly made his legs come out from under him. There it was. His fucking destiny laid out before him. The woman who'd made him believe in himself, who'd made him adamant to be so much more than what he'd been no longer trusted him. The truth about his past was determined to set the course for his future, and he had no say in the matter.

"You don't know that it will," he countered weakly.

"And you don't know that it won't." Her voice shook, but she steeled herself and stood up taller. "I love you so much already, and that love for you only gets stronger every day. I would be an idiot to take that risk. You've basically handed me the outcome of our relationship. You've admitted that you've never been faithful, even to the first woman you fell in love with. To the woman you asked to be your *wife*. How can I take that risk knowing those odds?"

"I wouldn't do that to you." Emerson clung desperately to every thought, every word that came to his mind, but he knew he wouldn't be able to win his case this time. His record was against him, the jury deliberated…the verdict was in: Guilty. He was a cheater, and that's all he'd ever be. Even if he wasn't anymore.

"I want to believe you," she whispered. "You have no idea how much I want to believe you, but I can't do that to myself."

"Yes you can," he urged. "You can. Just let me show you…*please*." Gabriella shook her head as he stepped toward her, closing the gap between them. He held both of her hands in his. "Love is always a risk, right? That's what everyone says. Love is a chance you have to be willing to take. Please baby…*please*, take a chance on me. Let me show you how much I love you. Let me show you how much I've changed because of *you*."

"I can't." Her voice cracked and a tear rolled down her cheek. "Emerson, if I did this and you…if you hurt me like that, it would break me. You don't understand."

Still holding her hands, he dropped to his knees in front of her. He didn't care how pathetic he looked or felt. He would go against all his rules, all the boundaries he'd drawn for himself, and he would beg this woman to stay. "Gabby, please. You know what we have is good. What we have is so, *so* good. Baby, please don't let this go. Don't give up on us. Don't give up on me."

Gabriella shook her head again and slipped her hands out of his grasp, wiping her tears away. Emerson grabbed her hips, desperate to hold on. He was losing her, but he couldn't. He leaned his head against her, eyes closed as his chest hollowed out. A lump formed in his throat and his breathing became labored as he grasped for anything that would save them. He began kissing her, across her lower abdomen, her stomach, her hip bones.

"Emerson, please…you need to stop." Gabriella's voice was thick with the strain of holding back sobs. He continued his assault of light kisses all over her skin until the first heavy sob broke out from her lips. He felt her stomach contract when she let it out. "Please stop…I can't do this. You need to go."

"*No*," he growled. "You love me and I love you and this is going to work. *We* are going to work. I don't care what happened in my past. You're not my past, Gabe, you are my future." He rested his forehead against her stomach again and willed his words to take hold. To work. To make her change her mind.

When Gabriella spoke again, her sobs and tears had cleared. Her voice was cold and distant. Trained. Forced. "I can't be with you, Emerson. I can't just wait around for you to get sick of me and find someone new. Because you will."

"I won't." Emerson gritted his teeth, determined to chisel his way through the wall of ice she was putting up.

"You will," she said. "You'll cheat on me just like you cheated on Raelyn and everyone who came before her. I'm not going to draw it out any longer." She stepped out of his grasp then and turned away without another glance back at him.

After several long moments of listening to his heavy breaths and the hammering of his heart come down like it was beating in slow motion, he brought himself to his feet. She was gone. He'd lost her. There was nothing else he could do but leave.

The swirling cloud of despair that was already overtaking him was without a doubt the worst sensation he'd ever felt. His heart was in physical pain, a tightness in his chest refusing to release its hold. He was sure he'd never felt this level of anguish, and his insides were assaulted by the rawness of it. To make matters worse was the knowledge that deep down, he knew he deserved it. After all the hurt and pain he'd inflicted on others, it was his turn to feel it all at once.

Accepting his fate, he turned around to make his way back to the front of the house. He stopped short and the desolation and guilt was magnified tenfold.

Standing just inside the sliding glass door was Kolbe.

His younger brother's eyes were as dark and hollow as he now felt.

Emerson's breath caught in his throat, but he forced himself to speak. "Kolbe, how much-"

Kolbe shook his head and his face crumpled. Disappointment, resentment, utter disbelief morphed his features. "You're just like him, aren't you?"

Rock...meet bottom.

Chapter 26

More than a week had gone by and Kolbe still wasn't talking to him. Another week and the kid would be starting high school, and Emerson wouldn't be there to hear about his first day, about his teachers, his classes, the girls. None of it. Because Kolbe wanted nothing to do with him since finding out just how much like their piece of shit father he really was- or at least had been.

Losing Gabriella sucked. It really fucking sucked. But losing his little brother was damn near unbearable. Kolbe was the only family he really had. The only family he wanted anything to do with. And now the truth was out about Emerson being a liar and a cheater, and yeah okay, maybe he deserved the hell he was living in.

"You should've seen his face, man." Emerson took a swig from the half-empty green bottle in his hand. He was sitting in Kalahan's Pub- Brody's very own backyard bar- with Brody and Tyler. He'd been MIA since Gabriella walked away and Kolbe dismissed him from his life, and was just now filling them in on what had happened just over a week ago.

"Fuck dude, that's rough," Brody said, then sighed heavily. "He'll come around though, don't you think? I mean, you're his big brother. He loves you."

"He looked up to me," Emerson retorted. "He thought I was the coolest and now I'm just another guy who let him down. Just like our dad…just like every other guy Maya's dated who won't stick around because they think Kolbe's too difficult. Fucking idiots…can't see what an awesome kid he is."

"What are you gonna do?" Tyler asked. "I know you. You're not just gonna let it go. You're the most obnoxiously persistent son of a bitch I've ever met…what's your plan?"

Emerson shook his head. "What is there to do? They don't make fucking Hallmark cards for this. *Sorry I'm a lying bag of dicks, but I'm still your brother- Please forgive me?*" He scrubbed a hand down his face. "I've stopped by his house a few times, but he's apparently been spending a lot of time at Robby's and I can't exactly go over there."

"So you and Gabby are done then, huh?" Tyler asked hesitantly. "You're not going to try to fix that?"

Emerson blew out a long breath. "I want to, but Kolbe's gotta come first and she needs her time anyway. She said she needed space and I kept pushing her for an answer, so she gave me one. I'm hoping that with a little more time and space, she'll change her mind. Maybe she'll realize what we had was too good to give up on. But Kolbe…that kid's not gonna make it easy on me."

Brody hummed and scratched his stubbly chin. "What would make Kolbe happy…?"

"Same thing that would make any fourteen-year-old boy happy," said Tyler. "A fourteen-year-old girl."

Emerson at least laughed a little at that. "Yeah, let me just go drive around looking for a minor my little brother will find attractive. That won't get me arrested."

Tyler chewed the inside of his cheek, then perked up. "He likes baseball, right? Take him to a major league game. Spring for the box tickets- you've got the money for that. He'll get to do something he enjoys and you'll have a chance to talk to him."

Grimacing, Emerson shook his head. "Nah, I don't want to force him to spend time with me. I was already fucking stupid and tried offering to take him school shopping…I even said I'd buy him a new iPhone since his screen is cracked, but he didn't go for it. He said if he wanted someone to buy his affection, he'd work harder to have a relationship with our dad. I didn't really have a good comeback for that."

"Ouch," Brody said with a wince. "He's got a point there though. He didn't grow up the same as you, always getting *stuff* in exchange for quality time and actually giving a damn."

Emerson groaned and slumped forward, resting his head on the glossy live-edge bar top. "He's never talking to me again."

His phone buzzed in his pocket and he groaned again, expecting it to be a work call. He was almost done with his current case and he'd been spending longer hours in the office, burying himself in his work to try taking his mind off the mess that was his life. When he pulled his phone out of his pocket, he was surprised to see that it was Kolbe's mom calling. He swiped to answer immediately. "Hey Maya."

"Hey! Are you working right now?" The familiar sound of relief in her voice made Emerson wonder if everything was okay.

"No, I finished up about an hour ago. What's up?"

"I have to work an overnight shift tonight and, well…the plan was originally for Kolbe to stay with Robby, but he got his ass grounded today, so…no friends for him for a while. Is there any way I can drop him off with you? If not, I'll just start his sentence tomorrow, but-"

"No- I mean, yeah, I can take him," Emerson replied, sitting up straight with new energy coursing through him. "I'm not home right now, but it won't take me long to get there. What time do you go in?"

Maya told him she'd be leaving in about twenty minutes to drop Kolbe off, so Emerson hopped off the bar stool, explained the miracle to Tyler and Brody and booked it back to his apartment. Finally some luck was coming his way. He was prepared for Kolbe to be moody and not want to talk to him, but what was he going to do? Jump out his sixth floor bedroom window?

Emerson made it to his apartment with enough time to change out of his work clothes and into a pair of gray chinos and a plain white t-shirt. His laundry was piling up and he was down to a couple pairs of chinos, basketball shorts, or the spandex workout leggings Gabriella had left behind. He was making a mental note to get some laundry started when there was a knock on the door.

Everything inside his chest felt liquid and squirmy. His pulse thrummed beneath his skin and he couldn't believe he was this nervous to see his brother. He didn't know what to expect on the other side of that door. Would Kolbe even look at him? Would he act like nothing had changed in front of Maya? Would he cause a scene and make Maya also think Emerson was a piece of shit? And if so, would she not want her kid around him anymore?

The knock came again and Emerson swiped a hand through his hair, took a deep breath in and out, and pulled the door open. Maya was in her scrubs and Kolbe was in a pair of tapered gray joggers and a black Nike t-shirt with his battered backpack slung over one shoulder. Kolbe was staring at his phone, acting completely indifferent.

"Thank you so much for taking him on such short notice," Maya said. She almost sounded out of breath, like she'd been rushing around to get there on time.

"I told you I would've been fine by myself," Kolbe grumbled. "I'm not a baby. I can lock the doors and put myself to bed."

"And have your friends over and trash the house when you're already grounded?" Maya retorted, her voice firm and leaving no room for argument. Hell, Emerson wouldn't even argue with her. "I don't think so."

"Exactly, I'm already grounded," Kolbe huffed. "Not like it could get worse."

Maya put her hands on her hips and stared at her moody son, one eyebrow arched dangerously high in challenge. "Mhmm, you go ahead and think that. And straighten out your attitude before I come get you in the morning."

Kolbe rolled his eyes. "Whatever."

Oh, to be a teenager again.

Maya may have been upset, but she still pulled her son into a hug and gave him a kiss on the cheek, which he winced and pulled away from. "I love you, baby. Be good for your brother." Kolbe grunted, eyes still glued to his near-shattered phone screen, and moved past his mom and Emerson into the apartment. Maya sighed. "I'm sorry to drop him off when he's like this. Teenagers, right?"

"It's okay," Emerson assured her. "I'll see if I can get him to talk about what's upsetting him."

"Thanks again. What time do you want me to come get him?" she asked. "I'm done at six, but he likes to sleep in."

"I don't have to be at work until eight, but I could probably push it and go in at nine if that helps you. I've been staying late anyway."

"Are you sure? That would be great if I could just run some errands when I get out of work, get them out of the way."

Emerson nodded. "Of course, yeah. If you really want to punish him I could take him to work with me. He'll be dying of boredom in fifteen minutes."

Maya laughed. "Now there's an idea. Okay, well I'll text you before I leave the hospital. Thanks again. You have been such a life saver, you have no idea how grateful I am that we have you here."

If only she knew how much having them around meant to him…

"Not a problem. I'll see you tomorrow."

After Maya left, Emerson turned to find the kitchen and living room empty. Kolbe had gone straight to his room and shut the door. That was definitely a first. He knocked on Kolbe's closed bedroom door and was met with silence. A moment later, some loud bass accompanied by mumble-rap was blaring from the bluetooth speakers Emerson had gifted his little brother on his previous birthday. Buying kids things that could get loud was a terrible idea at any age, it seemed.

Emerson sighed heavily and looked up to the ceiling. "There's a reason I'm not a father…I am *not* equipped for this shit." Then he turned the door knob and pushed his way into Kolbe's room.

Kolbe was on his full-sized bed leaning against the pillows, feet stretched out in front of him and crossed at the ankles. He scrolled through his phone with a glower, all moody teen angst, and didn't spare Emerson even a passing glance.

Okay, yeah, this doesn't work for me.

Emerson walked over to the speaker and flipped the switch, turning it off.

"What the fuck? I was listening to that!" Kolbe snapped.

Emerson's eyebrows shot up in surprise at the kid's attitude. It was hard not to reach out and swat him, but he didn't want to give Kolbe the reaction he was looking for. He was clearly pissed. Emerson knew his little brother would be mad at him and probably give him some grief, but he had no idea why he was pulling an attitude with his mom. He didn't know why he was grounded or what had even been going on in his life for the past week and a half.

"Yeah, well maybe we should keep it to *you* listening to it and not the whole damn building," Emerson said smoothly. Shoving his hands in his pockets, he took the few steps separating the dresser from the bed and lowered himself to the edge of the mattress. "What did you get grounded for?"

"Fuck off." It came out in a grumble, but Emerson heard it clear as day.

Okay, so he may not be a criminal defense lawyer, but he still knew how to put on a mask and act like that didn't twist the fucking knife in his gut.

"Kolbe, I know you're mad at me and you have every right to be-"

Kolbe snorted. "Thank you for validating my feelings, not that I fucking asked."

Emerson ground his teeth. This was harder than some random punk-ass kid with an attitude problem like the ones he'd dealt with right after law school. He'd done some work for a public defender near Detroit and no fucking thank you. Overworked, underpaid, and they had to deal with every little shit with a bad attitude that came across their desk and they couldn't say dick because most often it was court-ordered.

But Kolbe wasn't some kid. Getting cussed out by a twelve-year-old who's scared shitless that he might be getting sent to juvie was a lot different than hearing the disdain in his brother's voice. He'd grown used to the admiration and adoration- however ill-deserved it was.

"Listen, I know why you're pissed at me, but why are you taking it out on your mom? She works really hard to take care of you- you really shouldn't talk to her like that."

Finally Kolbe set his phone down and looked at Emerson. His eyes were narrowed into slits and the anger was palpable. "You're not my fucking dad, *Emerson.*"

That got his attention. Kolbe never called him Emerson. He was Will. To Kolbe, he'd always been Will. Sure, everyone else called him by his real name- except Robby now- but from Kolbe it felt a hell of a lot like an insult.

The corner of Kolbe's mouth pulled up into a humorless smirk. "Oh wait, or are you? I know it's kind of hard to tell you two apart these days."

Trying to remember how much of a pissed off smartass he'd once been, too, he again willed himself not to smack him or tackle him to the ground and force him to take it back. While they were brothers and wrestling was apparently a normal part of brotherly relationships, with the age gap and the way Kolbe had come into his life, he'd always felt more like a guardian. A mentor. They could mess around and have fun, but throwing fists and shoving each other around in anger wasn't part of the deal.

"Yeah kid, I know. My- *our*- dad was a real piece of shit. Still is. He's an asshole and he always has been," Emerson said, maintaining his calm, collected tone. Kolbe huffed and looked away, crossing his arms over his chest. "I know it can't be easy growing up without a dad, and I know I've told you this before, but you're really not missing out. Johnathan...growing up in the same house as him...it did a real number on me."

With a derisive snort, Kolbe remarked, "Yeah, growing up with both parents in a fucking mansion must've been tough."

"I would've taken a mom like yours any day," Emerson replied. "She goes to your games, knows what the fuck is going on in your life, wants to spend time with you. The mansion might paint a pretty picture-"

"But money isn't everything- says the guy who grew up with unlimited funds at his disposal."

"I didn't realize that's what you were upset about," Emerson said, knowing his brother was just throwing every resentment at him that he could think of. He wasn't pissed about how Emerson grew up compared to him, he was just pissed. Anything that could drive a wedge between them was fair game. "If it's money you want, I'll head to the bank tomorrow and transfer half my trust fund into that savings account your mom's got set up for you and we can go our separate ways."

"I don't want your fucking money," Kolbe grumbled.

"Never thought you did."

Kolbe wasn't looking at him, but he wasn't scrolling through his phone and he wasn't telling him to fuck off anymore, so Emerson guessed he was listening.

"I watched my dad cheat on my mom over and over, before I was even old enough to realize that's what was happening," he explained. "And my mom just...let it happen. She knew about it and she dealt with it. She wasn't happy about it, and I know it hurt her, at least in the beginning. I think now she's just accepted that this is the life she chose, but she didn't do a damn thing about it. And as much as I hated my dad for being the magnanimous dick-bag that he was, I resented my mother for never leaving. I resented her for being weak and letting him get away with it because she didn't want to give up the lifestyle she'd grown so accustomed to."

Kolbe shook his head. "I don't get it. If you hated him so much and you wanted her to leave...why would you act like him? Why would you put anyone through that? Didn't you hate yourself?"

"Not at first. In high school, I was a fucking nightmare. I was entitled and a complete egomaniac. I thought I could get away with anything and everything, and I toyed with people because I could. I played games with girls' feelings, I fucked around, saying the right things to make them feel special and then a week later I'd do the same with their friends. I'm not gonna get into the psychology of it, though I'm sure Isabel would tell you it has to do with a desperate need for approval since my parents acted like I was just some obligation, but that's what I did."

It was the first time he'd ever dissected his actions and feelings about his past behavior out loud, but it felt good to know he understood it. It felt like he at least had a reason for being a shithead, and it wasn't just part of his genetic makeup that he'd inherited from his father.

Clearing his throat, he continued. "Growing up with my parents as the primary example for what a relationship looked like was…not good. Johnathan Yates is a terrible fucking role model for young men. But it wasn't just my parents. A lot of kids I went to school with seemed to have similar experiences. So, rather than seeing how cheating and lying can hurt people, I took a whole different lesson from it. I learned that in every relationship there's a winner and loser. Someone who holds all the power, and someone who gets walked all over."

The look on Kolbe's face could *almost* be qualified as a smirk as he said, "I guess no one could expect you to want to be walked all over."

"Yeah…" Emerson sighed. "It's not true though- not in healthy relationships anyway. It should be a…partnership. You should both be on equal ground if you want it to work."

Kolbe was silent for a moment as he stared at the blank, cracked phone screen in his lap. "You don't think you and Raelyn were on equal ground? You wanted power over her?"

Letting out yet another heavy sigh, Emerson scratched his jaw and got ready to confess even more about the end of that relationship. "We were equal…mostly. It's one of the reasons I was attracted to her at first. I knew she wasn't like my mom…she wouldn't just let me get away with cheating. I respected her- still do. But it wasn't until I realized that she had power over me that I was desperate to get out."

Kolbe narrowed his eyes, the curiosity evident in his expression. "You think she would've hurt you?"

"No," Emerson answered honestly. "I don't think she realized she still had feelings for someone else."

The crease in Kolbe's brow deepened. "But All-Star didn't come back until a year after you guys were over."

"Oh, *now* you remember," Emerson said with a small laugh. Kolbe grinned. "No, he didn't. But after we got engaged, her parents threw us an engagement party at their house. I'd been there before, but I hadn't seen all of it. Rae gave me a tour and when we got to her bedroom, there were pictures of her and Quinn everywhere. From the time they were little kids all the way to the time they apparently made out at a high school championship game. She said they were just friends and that they hadn't seen each other in years and brushed it off, saying whatever she possibly could to get out of that conversation. I realized she didn't want to talk about him because she wasn't over him."

"So…what? So you cheated so she couldn't hurt you first?"

"Not exactly." He shook his head. "It scared the shit out of me to think that was a possibility…that she would leave me if this other guy ever came back around, but mostly it just got me thinking about what kind of love that must be. She hadn't even seen the guy in ten years and he was still so painful to talk about. I wondered if I'd feel that way about her if we went ten years without seeing each other. I loved her, but…not like that. I knew that even five years apart…hell, it's been two and I'm over her. It just hit me that she wasn't the one. And whether she knew it at the time or not, I knew I wasn't her one."

"Still doesn't excuse what you did," said Kolbe quietly.

"No, it doesn't," Emerson agreed. "I guess it seemed easier to fall back into what I knew than to face it. Hearing her say it out loud…that she was in love with someone else…Well, let's just say that didn't appeal to me. But I did hate myself after that. It was fucked up and I'm better than that. I thought I was past acting that way toward people, but it turns out fear and jealousy can be a real bitch."

"But you didn't think you loved her that much anyway."

"It's complicated. It's like I was pissed that I found out. Like…if I never would've seen those pictures, the rose-tinted glasses would've stayed on, and I would've felt like Rae was the one and everything would've been fine. I never would've asked myself how I'd feel if we had to spend time apart…I never would've realized that I was kind of a hopeless romantic in the sense that if I was going to get married, it had to be to someone I could never in a hundred years picture myself without."

Kolbe hummed. "Guess reality can be a real bitch, too." Then he grinned. "It does explain why you hate All-Star so much though. Shit, I was right. He *did* swoop in and steal her away."

Emerson let out a puff of laughter. "Well that stays between us, got it?"

Kolbe nodded, and Emerson felt the lead weight of an anvil lift off his shoulders. "I'm sorry I lied to you," he said. "I felt like I was protecting you. I wanted you to be able to look up to me...I wanted you to have a good role model and...well, I'm really not that. I am, however, unspeakably selfish at times, and having a good relationship with you made me feel like my family wasn't *entirely* fucked up. And I'd never had anyone look up to me before...I felt like I couldn't ruin the whole illusion of how perfect I was in your eyes."

His little brother scoffed, but there was humor in his expression. "Perfect? Okay, take it down a notch, fam."

Emerson shrugged. "It was nice to pretend that's what you thought anyway."

"I don't need you to be perfect," Kolbe said. "Just keep it one-hunnit, we'll be Gucci."

Narrowing his eyes, Emerson looked at his brother like he was speaking a different language. Because he was pretty sure that's exactly what it was. "I have no fucking idea what you just said."

"Keep it one-hunnit...One-hundred, like the number?" Kolbe explained- *sort of.*

"Okay?"

"Keep it real...be authentic."

Emerson arched an eyebrow, still confused and wondering where the hell these terms came from. "And the part about...Gucci? I don't have any Gucci- most of my suits are Armani..." He stopped at the look on Kolbe's face. "You're not talking about the brand."

"It just means cool. Like it's all good...it's Gucci."

"Why don't you just say that?"

Kolbe shook his head. "Damn, it's like teaching a whole new language."

"So just speak the one we both know!" Emerson exclaimed.

They both laughed and it tapered into silence, but a comfortable one.

At least until Kolbe said, "Gabby's pretty upset, you know."

Emerson's dark blue eyes flashed up to Kolbe's matching ones. "Because I lied to her?"

"She misses you," Kolbe answered. "She hasn't said it quite like that, but I can tell. So can Robby."

"Is she over at her parents' place a lot?" Emerson asked.

"Yeah, I think she doesn't want to be alone so much. She's been looking for a job. Did she quit after you guys broke up?"

Emerson scratched his jaw and sighed. "No...that's sort of a long story. Turns out Johnathan doesn't stop at ruining the lives of women *he's* involved with." That earned him a curious look, so he explained, starting with the weekend of Johnathan's fundraiser to finding out that he'd had her blackballed from several firms in the area.

"He actually said that to her?" Kolbe exclaimed, eyes wide and clearly offended. "And all that shit about her not being good enough or...from the same flock or whatever?"

"Stock, but yeah," Emerson replied, now sitting next to Kolbe on the bed with his own legs stretched out in front of him. "He's a real douche."

"Damn...sorry I said you were like him. That guy's a dick." Kolbe glanced down at his phone that lit up with a text message, but Emerson couldn't tell who it was from because of the cracks in the screen. Kolbe ignored it, but continued flipping his phone around in his hand. "You should get her job back or something. Maybe get her a new one. Does he know y'all broke up? Maybe he'd step back."

"Actually, I was sort of thinking about that...I know of exactly one person who wouldn't take the bait and probably wouldn't have anything Dad could blackmail him for anyway. He represents one of the most powerful firms in the area," Emerson said. It was an idea he'd been floating around, but there was sort of a catch. A complication. And then everything with Kolbe happened and fixing things with Gabriella had to go on the back burner.

"No cap?" Kolbe perked up. "Aight, bet!"

The general tone was excited and encouraging, but again, Emerson had no fucking clue what his little brother was saying. "How you go from perfect English to...whatever the fuck that is, I will never understand."

Kolbe didn't translate this time, but went back to normal English. "What are you waiting for? Go get her that job! Where is it?"

"I...can't."

"Why not?"

"Because the guy I'd have to ask...kind of hates me," Emerson said. The nerves that crept in every time he considered confronting this particular person were back in full force. "But he's got more money than our dad and would never consider giving him the upper hand on anything."

Kolbe shrugged. "Even better. Gabby finds out you went to this guy and helped get her a job...that would look good, right? Or...do you think this guy won't give her a job because of her relationship with you?"

"There's no relationship anymore," Emerson muttered bitterly.

"There's no relationship *right now*," Kolbe corrected. "You'll get her back."

"You think so?"

Kolbe suddenly looked thoughtful and wise beyond his years as his sapphire blue gaze met Emerson's. "Well...if you guys stayed broken up...would you still be thinking about her in ten years?"

He knew his answer immediately and was both overwhelmed and comforted by the truth of it. Overwhelmed because *holy shit*, he actually felt this way about a woman. But comforted because he just knew...he'd never been more sure of anything in his life.

The brothers shared a knowing look with nearly identical smirks tugging up the corners of their lips and Kolbe nodded. "Let's get you your girl back, Will."

Chapter 27

This is a fucking terrible idea if there ever was one.

A bad, dumb, terrible idea. Why the hell am I even here?

Emerson stood on a stone porch beneath a wide archway, staring at the enormous French doors with their frosted glass and black wrought iron design. His fingers twitched at his sides as he tried talking himself into ringing the doorbell. Knocking. Getting the fuck off the porch and driving away before anyone noticed he was even there.

Who was he kidding? The place had cameras at the gate at the end of the driveway, probably along the stone-paved walkway, and *yep,* okay, there was another one staring down at him from the corner of the covered porch. *Fan-fucking-tastic.*

With a heavy sigh, he reached for the button that would announce his presence, a sound like a four-foot windchime resonating through-out the massive French manor.

When the door pulled open Emerson had expected to see one of the many- hopefully new- maids in their traditional black knee-length dresses, but instead was met with familiar yet curious bright blue eyes.

"Emerson?" Raelyn looked confused, understandably so, as her cobalt gaze swept him from head to toe. A smile tugged up the corner of her pink lips as she said, "Wow, you look like hell."

"Thanks," Emerson muttered through gritted teeth. He knew he looked like shit. Though things between him and Kolbe had gone back to normal since their talk almost a week ago, he'd heard absolutely nothing from Gabriella which meant he was able to focus on the pain of losing her, allowing himself to feel the full force of it as it swallowed him whole.

He'd reached out, texting her after a few days apart, hoping that was all the space and time she needed to come around. He'd sent her flowers twice- a dozen of the purest white roses his money could buy each time- with a simple apology written on the card. He'd pestered Kolbe for information about her through his time spent with Robby. He'd even offered to host his and Robby's next sleepover, offering up his Xbox, PS5, his porn collection, or his soul if it meant getting an idea of what was going on with Gabriella. He was going absolutely insane. He never thought he'd be this guy, but here he was…the most pathetic, desperate fucking asshole he'd ever seen.

"What are you doing here?" Raelyn asked, her eyebrows pinching together.

"I could ask you the same thing," Emerson replied. "Don't you have a job on the other side of the country? No- wait, don't you *live* on the other side of the country? Why are you always here?"

"We're playing in St. Louis the next few nights and they finally hired a second PT so I can get some nights off," she explained. "And my parents got press box tickets, so we're meeting the team down there tomorrow."

Emerson nodded slowly. "Huh…I see. Well…I'm actually here to see your dad. Charlie…I wanted to talk to him about something."

Raelyn's eyebrows shot up in surprise. "You know he's still part of the I Hate Emerson club, right? He may actually be the president."

"President, founder, CEO," Emerson said, nodding again. "Yeah, I figured. But this isn't about me. I'm here for Gabby."

A look of understanding crossed Rae's face as she stepped aside finally to let him in. She closed the door behind him as his eyes took in the grand marble foyer, the curved staircase, the high ceilings, intricate moldings, and everything else about the space that made him feel like he'd just entered some kind of French castle museum. An interactive exhibit of French royalty combined with a modern-day chateau in the South of France.

"So, good ol' Johnathan's still being an asshat, huh?" Rae asked, leading him through the foyer and further into the depths of the house.

"Did we ever expect him to stop?" Emerson retorted bitterly.

Raelyn replied with a sardonic laugh of her own. "Fair point." She stopped in the living room where a couple of maids were washing impossibly high floor-to-ceiling windows. *"Ou est mon pere?"*

"Monsieur DeRose est dans son bureau, Madame," a young woman replied from her position on a ladder.

"Oooh, look at you," Emerson teased. "Upgraded to *Madame.*"

Raelyn thanked the maid with a quick *Merci*, and headed in the direction of Charlie's home office. "It just fits, doesn't it?" she replied, offering him a smile over her shoulder. "The first time they called me that it threw me off but I've gotten used to it."

"Madame All-Star," he teased again. "Yeah, that works."

She laughed. "You're just like the guys on the team. I'm officially Mrs. Quinn Casey. Sometimes I'm Dr. Mrs. Quinn Casey, but any identity I had before marrying him ceases to exist."

"Congrats, by the way," Emerson said, now walking beside rather than behind her. "I don't think I offered my congratulations before."

"Oh…thanks." She seemed caught off guard for a brief moment, but her smile returned. "I see being with Gabby finally made you get it."

"Get what?"

"What we had was *good* to some extent, but it doesn't even come close to being with the right one. I was still so angry at you a year later…then Quinn came back into my life and it was like I couldn't believe I'd ever thought anything else had felt right." Rae swept a hand through her long blonde hair, pushing it back just to let it tumble over her shoulders again. "That anger I'd been holding onto dissipated and eventually when I thought about you I just…I don't know, I guess I just hoped you'd feel the same about someone one day too."

Emerson offered a soft smile. He knew exactly what she meant, but at the same time it stung. The muscle in his chest squeezed and ached at the memory of Gabriella walking away from him two weeks ago.

"Yeah, I get it now. If what you feel for All-Star is half of how I feel for Gabby…" He shook his head. "It must've been fucking torture being away from him for so long."

Raelyn stopped walking and grabbed his arm to halt him, too. She pulled him around to face her and furrowed her brows. "What happened? You seem…sad. And you look like ass. Don't get me wrong, I love that part, but…did something happen?"

"You love that I look like ass?" he questioned, not sure if he should be amused or offended.

"Absolutely!" she said as if it were obvious. "Emerson, I've never seen you look anything less than impeccable, powerful, masculine perfection. And look at you! You've got purple bags under your eyes and your hair isn't styled, your skin is sickly pale, and *Jesus!* You forgot to trim your beard! It's like a whole two millimeters too long! What the hell happened to you?"

"I'm surprised Amira hasn't filled you in," he grumbled.

Although he knew it was his fault, *he* was the one who lied to Gabriella, he was still a little pissed at Amira for spouting it off the way she did. She'd tried to explain that she had little to no filter on a good day, but after a bottle and a half of wine, and after hearing the explanation that his and Rae's breakup was mutual, she got defensive for her best friend and angry that he'd written it off like what he'd done hadn't completely crushed her.

Raelyn continued to stare at him with that concerned look, so he scrubbed a hand down his face and over his almost unruly beard and explained, "Gabriella and I broke up. Well…she dumped me. And she won't take my calls or respond to my texts. I can't go over there because…well, she said she needed space and time to think. And then I pushed for an answer and she gave me the one I didn't want. But I need her back, Rae. I don't know how to make that happen but I do know I don't want to be without her."

"Why did she dump you? And when?" Rae's expression was genuine. Her concern, her disappointment for him, her empathy was all real, and he was reminded again of why he'd liked her so much in the beginning. Sure, she was gorgeous. Hell, there she was in front of him now, obviously having been spending time out back by the pool, wearing a white two-piece bathing suit with a navy blue sarong wrapped around her hips. Her sleek and toned muscles stretching the length of her perfectly fit body, her flawlessly sun-kissed skin and the smattering of freckles across the bridge of her nose, and that triangle bikini top showcasing small but perky tits that, once upon a time, would have made his mouth water.

Yeah, she was beautiful. But where her ass was rounded and sculpted, he wanted softer, fuller curves. Flesh he could dig his fingers into. Where her hair was long and bright, the color of sunshine, he wanted sultry waves, a thick, dark mane that was long enough to tangle his fist in, but too short to pull up into a bun. Breasts that overflowed in his large hands. He wanted full, plump lips to press his own against. To nibble, lick, and tease. Those dark, almond-shaped brown eyes, full of challenge, always pushing him to be more. To be better.

Fuck. He wanted Gabriella. So fucking bad. There was no doubt, no hesitation in his mind that she was meant for him. *Made* for him. No other woman had a chance. No one else would do or come close. She was it. She was the bar. And if he had to make an ass out of himself and take Charlie DeRose's verbal berating to get her a job, he'd do it. Nothing would stand in his way of showing her how much he cared. How badly he wanted her to succeed.

"Two weeks ago when we had our guys' night out and you girls all stayed in," he began, "Amira sort of let it slip in a very blunt way that the reason you and I broke up was…well, what it was. I hadn't told her about that yet. And that led to a long conversation about all the women I cheated on before you and…she decided she couldn't trust me. That it was only a matter of time before I did it to her, and that she'd be stupid to take that chance."

Rae's posture deflated and her expression was devastated. "Emerson…I'm so sorry." She put a comforting hand on his arm. "I mean, I see her point, but still…you didn't do anything wrong."

"I lied to her," he pointed out. "And that wasn't even the worst part of that day." He explained the conversation they'd had that night, finding her gone in the morning, and going to her parents' place to talk to her. "Kolbe's been spending a lot of his time there with Robby…"

"No!" Raelyn gasped, knowing what was coming. "Oh my gosh, he heard you? How is he? Is he completely shattered? Oh God, you should really fix things with him first-"

"I did," he interjected. "We talked and we're good now, so I can focus my energy back on Gabby."

"Do you really think she'll take you back just because you get her a job at my dad's firm?"

"No, but it's the least I can do since *my* dad is the asshole who got her fired and blackballed in the first place."

"So this has nothing to do with trying to get her back?" Rae questioned skeptically.

Emerson sucked the inside of his cheek in and nodded his head from side to side. "I'm hoping that maybe she'll at least talk to me. Give me another chance to see her or something. Anything, really."

Rae's small smile was filled with sympathy and hope for him. "I hope so, too."

And then their tender moment was interrupted by an angry voice that echoed in the empty hallway.

"What the hell is *he* doing here?"

Emerson's entire body cringed at first, but he forced himself to relax and exhaled, releasing the tension in his muscles.

"Dad! You remember Emerson, right?" Raelyn's voice was bright now, filled with amusement and sarcasm.

"Is this a joke?" Charlie DeRose asked flatly. "Tell me this is a joke."

"Charlie…good to see you again," Emerson said, giving a short and awkward nod of acknowledgement.

"It's Mr. DeRose to you. Or Sir," Charlie snapped. "What the hell are you doing here? Rae, did you let him into my home or do I need to fire someone?"

"It was me," Rae admitted. "But don't worry, Dad. He's not here for me, he's here to see you!"

Charlie's scowl deepened as he glared at Emerson. Charlie was not a particularly intimidating guy. He had a friendly face. He was tall and lean with a short beard and full head of hair that were both going gray, but he still looked youthful. His wrinkles around his eyes and laugh lines around his mouth gave the impression that he smiled and laughed often.

That being said, he may not be physically intimidating, but Charlie DeRose was powerful as hell. He didn't exercise that power or flaunt it- not like Johnathan. Charlie prided himself on raising his girls to be as normal and down to Earth as possible given their insane wealth and fortune. Most people with their money send their kids to boarding school, have nannies, and spend their weekends watching polo matches. Not water polo, but the regular kind. Like on horses. Because everyone in their social class also has horses that they board so that they can pay someone else to take care of them.

"You're here to see me?" Charlie questioned.

Emerson nodded. "Yes, sir."

"What the hell about?" He looked both confused and annoyed, but not lethal, so he'd take that as a win.

"I was wondering if you had any positions open at your firm." Charlie's eyes went wide with disbelief, so Emerson quickly added, "Not for me. For a friend...uh...she's a really good lawyer. Way better than me. She was top in her class at Yale-"

"If she's so amazing, why are you here asking for her?" Charlie asked.

"It's sort of...complicated."

"She was Emerson's girlfriend and when she met Johnathan he didn't like her for some reason- you know how he is, all high and mighty and that crap. He wanted them to break up so he got her fired and bribed and blackmailed a bunch of people at the firms in town so now she can't get hired anywhere," Raelyn explained quickly, almost all in one breath. "They broke up recently, but she's still having a hard time finding a job so...maybe you can give her one?"

Charlie listened to his daughter carefully before turning a narrow-eyed gaze on Emerson. "Why did you break up?"

Emerson sucked in a breath. "I guess she decided she can't trust me-"

"Smart girl," Charlie snorted.

Unclenching his jaw, Emerson continued, "But that's beside the point, Char- Mr. DeRose. It's not her fault that my dad decided to use his power for evil as he so often does. She's damn good at her job and her family lives here...My dad is trying to run her out of town to get her away from me and it's not right. If I have to move to get him to leave her alone I will, but I can't imagine Johnathan has anything over you that he could blackmail you for. You're a good guy, your firm is solid and honest, you'd be able to keep her from getting hurt by any more of my father's bullying tactics. Like I said, this isn't about me...I just want her to be happy."

Charlie's gaze was scrutinizing and he glanced from Emerson to Raelyn and back. "And you're telling me there's absolutely nothing in it for you? You're just trying to help her out of the goodness of your heart? Or whatever that thing in your chest is that keeps you going..."

Emerson shrugged. "I don't know if there's anything in it for me. Maybe she'll talk to me again...maybe she'll tell me to fuck off, I really don't know. But it's the right thing to do. It's the least I can do."

Turning to Raelyn, Charlie asked, "And you know her? What do you think?"

"I don't know anything about her work, but I *do* know that she told Johnathan Yates off to his face and that makes her a fucking hero in my book," Rae replied.

"Really?" Charlie raised his eyebrows, clearly intrigued. "No wonder he got so pissed off." The slightest trace of a smile pulled up the corner of his mouth, then he trained his gaze back to Emerson and the stern scowl was back. With the nod of his head he gestured down the hall toward his office. "Let's talk. I'll give you ten minutes."

The knot in Emerson's chest loosened and he let out a breath. "Thank you, Charlie- Sir. Mr. DeRose...Sir."

Rae's giggle met his ears and he turned to see her cautious grin. "Well...good luck in there. I'm heading back to the pool."

He was hit with a sudden realization and the urge to make things right as Rae turned around to head back down the hall. He grabbed her arm and pulled her to face him. "Rae...If I don't see you before I leave- *if* I come out of that office alive, that is...I'm sorry. About everything. And I'm glad you're happy."

A slow smile curved up her lips. "Thanks. I hope you get your girl back, Emerson."

He returned her grin before following Charlie to his office, and as the door closed behind him he felt lighter. His head was clearer and his chest looser. He wondered if this was how the Grinch felt when he decided to return the presents to Whoville. Gabriella or no Gabriella, he was determined to be a better man. The man she deserved. Because maybe convincing himself he was good enough was just as important as showing her.

Chapter 28

Gabby walked through the small office building downtown, only a short walk from her condo and overlooking the beach. Marco and Max showed her the three smaller rooms with large windows, offering plenty of natural light along with the open lobby that only needed a bit of a facelift. She didn't want her practice to be dark and stuffy like so many others, but sleek and bright. This was the second building in Gabby's price range that had popped up in the past month since she'd decided to go ahead with starting her own firm.

She was sick of the corporate savagery, the back-stabbing, the ability to bribe and blackmail. After getting turned down by nearly every firm in the area, she'd started contemplating her options. Moving wasn't one of them. She loved being this close to her family and that wasn't something she was willing to give up. Her Yale internship had been a highly coveted position with the prosecutor's office, but again, she wasn't interested in ruining lives and fighting to slam people behind bars for a living.

Of course there were pros and cons to working for the prosecution and working for the defense, but as a private criminal defense attorney, she could pick and choose her clients. She wouldn't have to represent anyone she felt sleazy protecting, and she could feel perfectly at ease balancing the scales of the justice system. Sure, she'd be defending people who were almost certainly guilty, but that didn't mean they deserved the maximum penalty of the law. She could defend kids who'd been dealt a bad hand or people who'd simply fallen on hard times. And, okay, yes she'd probably have to defend a few entitled assholes to keep her bank account comfortable, but she'd come to terms with that.

Marco had tabs on all commercial real estate in the area, and Max was a realtor so they'd been more than happy to help her find a space to call her own. Between them and her dad's construction business, she figured any repairs that needed done would be taken care of easily and she could be in her own building in another month. Her six-month plan was to have her practice up and running with a good name and a solid client foundation.

"This place is perfect," said Gabby, taking in the bright space and envisioning what it could be with some TLC. "It's really in my price range? Even being on the lake?"

"Well, I know a guy who'd be willing to give you a damn good deal on it," Marco replied with a wink. "He's got connections."

"You're sure this is what you want?" Max asked. "That offer from Charlie DeRose was a pretty sweet deal. It would be a hell of a lot easier."

Gabby sighed. The last thing she'd expected was to get a call from Charlie DeRose asking for an interview, and though she'd set up the meeting and had received a job offer, it didn't feel right taking it. Raelyn was sweet to do that for her, but she wanted to stand on her own two feet. Accepting help from her brother was completely different than accepting a job offer from someone who'd pulled strings. Not just someone. Her ex's ex. How weird was that? Too weird. Gabby appreciated the gesture, and though Raelyn was friendly and not at all the intimidating being Gabby had initially created in her head, she couldn't take the offer.

Distancing herself from Emerson's friends...his circle...just seemed like the easiest thing to do. It had been six weeks since she'd walked away from Emerson in her parents' backyard and she had to remind herself daily that it was the right choice. Marco and Max were hesitant to agree with her on that point, but they'd at least shut up about it finally.

"You know I couldn't accept that offer," Gabby said. "Besides, I'm over the corporate side of law. I know it would be different than working for banks, but I think this will be a good change. More personal. I'll actually get to know my clients and feel like I'm making a difference."

"Not to mention how you're going to rip the prosecution a new one every time you're in court," said Marco, absolutely delighted at the thought. "I can't wait to watch you in court for the first time." He dramatically slammed his fist down on the old, bulky desk that had been left behind in one of the rooms that would become an office. *"Objection!"*

Gabby laughed and shook her head. "Just remember that's my line and if you can't keep your mouth shut, you'll get thrown out."

Marco grinned and gave the office a look around again. "So you think this is the one?"

"I think so." She nodded.

"Let's celebrate! Trojan?" Marco nudged her and wiggled his eyebrows.

She glared at him intently. "Not a good idea. Besides..." she sighed and glanced down at her watch, "I have to be at the high school to pick Robby up from football practice in ten minutes."

"Ah, saved by the jock little brother. That kid's determined to play all the sports." Marco led the way back toward the lobby where Max promised to get paperwork around and come over later in the week with finance and leasing information to take the next step.

Gabby pulled into the parking lot where parents waited to pick up their kids from the freshman practice field. Her stomach churned with anxiety at the thought that she might see Emerson there. Kolbe was on the football team too, and it wasn't unreasonable to think his brother would be there to pick him up. She was actually surprised he hadn't used picking Kolbe up as an excuse to try and catch her in person, as much as he'd tried to get in touch with her since their breakup, but she hadn't seen him. Being the one avoiding him, she should have been glad, but she couldn't help the disappointment that settled in her gut.

Nausea still rolling through her as she stepped out of the car, she walked over to where the parents and older siblings waited for their little athletes to disperse from their huddle. She scanned the small crowd, something feeling off. Different. Was she sensing him? Was that even possible? However, to her relief- or her dismay, she wasn't exactly sure- Emerson was nowhere to be found. No sandy blonde hair, no deep, stormy blue eyes, no hulking Godlike form, no seductive smirks that should be an actual sin.

Okay, yes. Disappointment was the right word.

Gabby shoved it down and watched for her brother who walked off the field alongside his best friend. Kolbe had already pulled his phone out of his duffle bag and was texting as he laughed and talked to Robby on their way to where Gabby stood waiting for them.

"Hey Gabs," Robby greeted.

Kolbe smirked as he looked up. "Gabe! Lookin' good!"

Maybe she would see that signature smirk, though it didn't have near the same effect when given by the much younger brother.

"Will you stop hitting on my sister?" Robby grumbled. "She dated your brother, man. That's just wrong."

"Dat-*ed*," Kolbe emphasized. "Past tense." He glanced up at her, all charm and that obnoxiously knowing grin. "It's been, what? Six weeks? I'm sure she's over him by now, right?"

"Kolbe, you're eighteen years younger than me," Gabby stated.

As expected, Kolbe waved his hand and scoffed. "Age is but a number when it comes to love."

Gabby rolled her eyes. "Is your mom picking you up?"

"Nah," Kolbe said with a shake of his head. "She's working."

Worry filled Gabby's chest as she glanced around again, looking for the Demigod of a man who still had her heart in a vice grip, whether she liked it or not.

"Mom already said he could come with us," Robby said. "But they're having a date night so we were hoping you could take us to dinner. Lola's at Macie's house and Eliza is having a sleepover...so it's just us tonight."

"Oh…sure, we can go get some dinner," Gabby said, tension easing as her heart simultaneously sunk at the realization that she would not be seeing Emerson. "Did you have somewhere in mind?"

"How about that new sushi place?" Kolbe suggested, sparing a glance up from his phone.

Gabby's lip curled slightly at the thought. She liked sushi, but with the uneasy rolling of her stomach, she wanted to reject it immediately. "Are you sure? Is it just sushi or do they have other options?"

"Hibachi, I think," Robby said. "It's supposed to be really good. We should definitely go."

Clearly outnumbered, she sighed and waved them toward her car. "Fine. Maybe the soy sauce will cover up your football funk." Or maybe it would just mix with it and then she'd be sure to throw up.

Walking into the Hibachi/Sushi restaurant, Gabby was hit with the full force of soy sauce, raw fish, and all things pungent. She had to swallow a gag and immediately asked if there was any room on the patio for seating. It was October and the air was crisp, just tinged with the first hint of fall. It was a little chilly to sit outside, but there were heaters and the chance of gagging decreased tenfold.

The hostess led them through the restaurant, past several hibachi tables with large parties, smaller tables and cozy booths. Walking through the bar, Gabby did a double take at the sight of sandy blonde hair and a neatly trimmed, close-cropped beard. A black suit designed precisely for his broad, muscular form.

Emerson?

Yep. That was definitely Emerson. Sitting in a secluded booth…across from some petite blonde who was gushing over him with googly doe eyes. She looked young. Like…really young. At least ten years younger than him.

That. Fucker.

Gabby's surroundings faded. The nausea ebbed slightly, the noise and clanking of dishes, the cheer of excited guests watching their food get flipped and tossed and set on fire was muted. All she saw was him. And that girl. That fucking bitch. Whoever she was.

Nope.

Hell no.

Gabby straightened and huffed like a bull taking its charge and before she'd made a conscious decision, she was standing in front of their booth. Yelling.

"Are you fucking kidding me?!" she screeched. Her voice was so high pitched she barely recognized it as her own. "Who the hell- Is this for real? You're dating? You just...jumped right back in where you left off? What the *fuck*, Emerson?! How many- How could- You've sent me flowers *every* week since we broke up! You- I thought- Oh my God!" She pushed her hands back into her hair as she seethed, breaths coming in heavy, unsure if she was going to keep screaming or start crying.

Next thing she knew, Emerson was standing in front of her, his massive hands holding her flailing wrists still. "Gabriella...Gabby...*Gabe!*"

She glared at him and pulled back. *"Don't* touch me! I can't believe you...Have you been seeing new women all this time? Making me feel like you miss me, but finding comfort in these random-"

"I'm not seeing anyone," Emerson said, his voice calm but stern. "This is a client meeting, not a date."

Her brow furrowed and she glanced back at the young woman still seated in the booth. "What?" she breathed.

"A client meeting. For work. She's a potential client."

"Oh..." Gabby's surroundings started to come back. She was suddenly aware of the stares from onlookers, the shocked expressions of her brother and Kolbe standing only a slight distance away, Emerson's warm hands where they'd found her arms again, holding her. *God that felt right.* She cleared her throat and stepped back. "I'm...sorry." Then she let out a small embarrassed laugh. "Wow, I can't believe I just did that."

Emerson's sexy mouth curved into a smirk. *Damn that smirk.* "It's okay," he said. "Honestly, I can't believe it either. You've been avoiding me. Ignoring my attempts to get in touch...Glad to know you got my flowers though."

As the adrenaline came down, the nausea returned and she was rewarded with an additional headache. She needed a drink. Or a giant glass of ice water. Imagining how dazed she must look as she glanced around, she shook her head and took another step back. "Emerson, I-"

He closed the gap she'd put between them and rested his hands on her arms, just above the elbow, making sure she couldn't turn away. "We should talk later. Please..."

"I don't know-"

"Please, Gabe. Let me come over and we'll talk. If you want to set a timer and give me ten minutes, that's fine, but let's just talk. Please?"

Gabby shook her head, but no words came out. Instead, Robby stepped up beside her and took the reins. "She'd love to!"

"Robby!" Gabby hissed.

"What? It's been six weeks, Gabs, and you're no closer to getting over him. You owe it to yourselves to talk about this."

"Perfect!" Kolbe exclaimed, clapping Emerson on his shoulder. "Well, big bro, you finish up your client meeting and once your girl here drops us off, I'll text you and you can just...head on over. Maybe take some pajamas. Or don't."

Emerson snorted a laugh and looked down at his feet. Glancing up he said tentatively, "See you in a couple hours?"

Stuck. She was absolutely stuck because she knew what would happen if she let Emerson come to her condo and "talk things over." Sure, they'd talk. She could set that timer and as soon as it went off, they'd throw themselves at each other. Clothes would hit the floor, bodies would come crashing together, and they'd end up in a big tangled mess of sheets and complications and feelings that she was trying desperately to avoid.

But those blue eyes were so sincere. Pleading. And Robby was right. She was nowhere near getting over him, despite cutting him out for six weeks. Plus, she'd been feeling sick for weeks. She was attributing it to the stress of opening her own practice, not having a job, and hunting for prime real estate, but it had started when she made the decision to walk away from Emerson. Maybe they could talk and come to some kind of understanding or get closure.

"Okay." She nodded. "I'll let you know when I get home."

"If I haven't heard from you by eight o'clock, I'm just showing up," Emerson replied, that damn cocky smirk plastered over his handsome face.

And she couldn't help herself. She laughed, a small, breathy puff of laughter. "I would expect nothing less."

She offered a small smile as they turned back to the hostess to let her lead them back through to the patio when Kolbe piped up, "Hey, you know something? I just remembered I *hate* sushi. And the smell of soy sauce makes me dizzy. And I'm allergic to shellfish."

Gabby whipped around to face him before taking her seat. "Kolbe, you suggested we come here!"

"I took a pretty solid tackle at practice," he replied, though Gabby suspected he was lying. "I must've forgotten. What a nice coincidence though, huh?"

"Serendipity," Robby said, nodding along. The two teenagers grinned mischievously. And then they fist-bumped.

Gabby's jaw dropped. "You little schemers!"

The boys shrugged. "You know what sounds fire right now? A burger," said Kolbe.

"Ooh, yes!" Robby nodded. "Let's go."

Still stunned, she watched as the boys exited the patio, unable to believe how she'd just been set up, but also grateful she didn't have to sit through dinner smelling soy sauce and raw fish. And maybe a little grateful for those scheming teenagers for making her get out of her own way. Not that she'd ever admit that to them.

After dinner, Gabby dropped the boys off at her parents' house and headed back to her condo. Despite her affirmations and mantras to treat the meeting with Emerson as just that- a meeting. Business. Something that needed to be taken care of- she still jumped in the shower, shaved her legs until they were silky smooth, trimmed, plucked or waxed any other unsightly body hair, and did a full blow-out of her hair, making it fall in waves that now touched her shoulders.

"We are just talking," she said to herself, as she applied the first coat of Better than Sex mascara.

"Our clothes are staying *on!*" she insisted, pulling on a pair of black silky panties.

"I will not be hypnotized by that damn twinkle!" she assured herself, hiking her breasts up and doing a quick cleavage check in the mirror.

"This is a conversation," she told her reflection. "I'm getting closure and then he. Is. Leaving!"

With a spritz of her favorite perfume, she checked herself out in her full-size mirror. She was looking particularly casual in her pajamas. Never mind they were silky pajamas. Peach colored silk shorts with a turquoise swirling design, and a matching spaghetti strap top. The shallow V of her neckline offered just enough of a tease of what was beneath without being explicit. Yeah. Casual. Comfy. That's what this look said.

There was a knock on her door and she gave herself a few steadying breaths before answering. When she pulled the door open, she found Emerson still in his suit with a bouquet of flowers in his hand.

"Fffuck..." Emerson released his bottom lip from his teeth as he bit out the unexpected greeting. His gaze traveled the path up and down her body and he swallowed a groan. His eyebrows pinched and he looked like he might be in physical pain as he half-whispered, half-growled, "Dammit, Gabe. *That's* what you're wearing to...just talk to me?"

"What? They're pajamas. They're comfy." Her reply was supposed to sound aloof. Indifferent. But his damn twinkling eyes wouldn't stop roaming her body, making every inch of her skin feel hot. Making every piece of her want to reach out and pull him against her. Feel his body against hers. His mouth on her neck, his chest sliding over hers, his hard length moving inside her.

Oh no. This was a bad idea.

Emerson held out the fresh bouquet of roses and lilies. It was beautiful and bright, all yellows and oranges and reds, unlike the pure white roses she'd been getting from him for the past six weeks.

Six weeks. Suddenly the realization that her body had been deprived of this man for so long felt like a sin. Wrong in every way.

Gabby licked her lips and swallowed around the urge to throw herself at him and took the flowers into the kitchen, grateful for a reason to break her stare away and focus on a task.

"So," she began, pulling out a glass vase from beneath the kitchen sink, "what did you want to talk about?" Gabby busied herself with filling the vase with water, finding scissors to cut the stems short, and wishing there were more steps to putting flowers away than just those two.

"Are you really just going to wear those tiny shorts and expect me to keep my hands to myself?" Emerson's voice was low and rough. God, she'd missed that sound. That deep timbre she could feel to her core.

Gabby turned around and eyed him sternly. "I'm sorry, are you a caveman who's lost his ability to control himself?"

He shrugged. "Maybe around you."

She fixed him with a hard stare and he exhaled, gesturing toward the living room. "I'll just go to the couch so I can…sit on my hands."

Unable to help the quiet laughter that fell from her lips, she shook her head and followed him into the living room. Though Emerson didn't actually sit on his hands, he did shove them in his pockets before taking a seat on her couch. Gabby sat on the love seat adjacent to him and curled her legs beneath her. This also felt wrong. Being in the same room as him, being so close to him, but not able to touch him. Trying to keep her distance. The heat that danced between them was sweltering, yet they ignored it.

"You wanna tell me about your reaction at the restaurant?" Emerson asked, doing his best to conceal that arrogant smirk she knew he wanted so badly to flash. "I thought you were done with me."

"I was. I *am.* I…I don't know." Gabby sighed. It was the truth that she had no idea what had come over her. She hadn't made any conscious decision to approach him, she just knew that seeing him there with another woman was wrong. Absolutely wrong in every way. Like so many other things right now. "It just threw me, I guess. Seeing you for the first time in weeks, and then realizing you were with someone else. How would you have reacted if the situation had been reversed?"

Emerson scoffed and he shook his head, incredulous. "I would've fucking flipped. But *you* walked away from *me*, Gabe. You're the one who's been avoiding me, ignoring my calls, my texts, pretending I don't exist. You've shut me out for a month and a half and left me desperately asking my little brother for crumbs. Pieces of your life that he picks up on when he hangs out with Robby because I need to know what's going on with you. Your life, your career." He paused then and cocked his head to the side. "Why did you turn down Charlie's job offer?"

Gabby reared back. "How did you know about that?"

He leaned his head back and sighed heavily. "Don't be mad, I know you like to do things on your own, but it felt like it was the least I could do given my dad was the one making it impossible for you to get hired anywhere. I went to Charlie and asked if he'd consider hiring you."

Oh…well, that was new information.

But did it change anything?

"I didn't realize you guys were still close," said Gabby, contemplating what this all meant. Was it better or worse to think that Emerson had asked for the favor instead of Raelyn?

"We're not," Emerson said. "Honestly, I think the fact that you dumped me after discovering what I'd done to his daughter worked heavily in your favor."

For some reason hearing him say it so bluntly, that she'd *dumped* him, twisted something inside her. Broke her just a little bit. Is that what she'd done? Dumped him? Discarded him? She could've sworn she'd only done it to protect herself, but sitting across from him, watching his face, observing his posture and expressions, she wasn't sure who needed protecting from whom.

"I just decided to go a different route, that's all," she explained simply. "Thank you, though. I'm sure it wasn't easy to ask him for a favor."

He shrugged. "It's fine. As long as you're happy. That's all I want."

Silence hung between them, along with the stifling heat that wanted to pull their bodies together. Gabby chewed on her lip, watching as Emerson uncomfortably fidgeted with his tie.

"I'm not," she blurted out. When he peeked up at her with one eyebrow cocked she clarified, "Happy, I mean." *Shit, what am I saying? Am I trying to make this worse?*

"That makes two of us."

And the words kept pouring, the truth tumbling out as if she had no say in the matter. "I've been physically sick to my stomach. I can barely eat anything, I'm always nauseous. I'm so stressed out over everything and…I tried burying myself in this new work endeavor, but I miss you and it sucks. It sucks so much."

In one swift move, Emerson got up off the couch and knelt at her feet, taking her hands in his. "Then let's make this work. Let's be together. God dammit, Gabby, I miss you so fucking much. More than I knew was possible. What's the point in us both being miserable when we want the same damn thing?"

Inwardly cursing herself for being so honest and not having the strength to keep her mouth shut, Gabby groaned in frustration. "Because I remember why I had to walk away."

"You didn't have to," Emerson said, pressing his lips to her knuckles. "You don't have to now. Please, Gabby…give me a chance."

"I can't risk getting hurt that badly."

"You're *already* hurting. Take a chance on me, Gabe. It'll be fucking worth it. I swear to you, I wouldn't beg you to give me another chance if I didn't know. If I didn't understand that how I feel for you is *it.* That *you're* it. You are the greatest fucking thing I'm ever going to have and I know I probably don't deserve you, but I will try my hardest to be what you deserve. I will win you over every fucking day and never stop trying to show you how much I love you. Never stop trying to win your heart all over again."

Those damn blue eyes stared into hers, desperate and pleading. Those words were perfect and she could've sworn she felt them in her bones. There was no doubt he meant them. At least he meant them now. But how could she trust him? How could she just give him that chance knowing what she knew now? And how foolish would she feel down the road if their relationship ended just like all the others? Even worse, how would she feel if they were together for the next three years? Five years? Fifteen years? And he was still keeping those promises…Would she still be wondering? Just waiting for the inevitable?

Or could she put it aside? Would she be able to be with him and feel secure, just knowing that the love she felt from him, the love they shared was true and impenetrable? Was the future they could have together worth the risk?

"I know you love me, Gabe. I know you want this too," he pleaded. "And I know I'm asking a lot and I can't give you proof…but I want this so bad. I want you. I fucking need you."

"Loving you wasn't the problem." Gabby reached out and combed her fingers through his hair and he leaned into her touch with a sigh, closing his eyes. It felt so good to touch him, to see the look of relief on his face as she reached for him. She wanted so badly for this to work somehow. To know that his words weren't temporary.

"Tell me what I need to do, baby. Tell me what will make you say yes to giving us another chance. I need this and I know you do too. Please, baby, tell me what will make this better." Hearing Emerson beg was almost enough to make her crumple.

She let out a breath of humorless laughter, "Tell me it wasn't true. That you haven't actually cheated on all of your exes."

His mesmerizing, deep blue eyes met hers again in the low lighting of her living room and the corner of his mouth tilted a fraction into the smallest hint of a smirk. "I haven't cheated on all my exes."

Gabby blinked. "What? Then why would you-"

"Not anymore," he said, his grin growing, and she wasn't sure if he was grinning for her or himself. "I never cheated on you."

She huffed a small laugh. "Well I know that, but-"

"No," he cut her off. "I officially have an ex-girlfriend who I never cheated on. I know it sounds ridiculous, but this is kind of huge."

Gabby stared at him curiously, a little concerned because he looked like he was about to start laughing or jumping for joy.

"When I realized I wanted out of my engagement, I fell back on old habits. I decided to just default to what I knew. What I always did. But…I can't say that anymore. I no longer have this reputation weighing me down. I'm not the guy who's cheated on all of my exes anymore because you kind of killed my track record." His smile widened and his eyes twinkled. "The way I see it, I have a clean slate."

It was hard not to smile with him when he looked so joyous. He truly looked like some sort of weight had been lifted off his shoulders. A burden he'd been carrying, vanished. And though she was glad he looked so relieved, she wasn't entirely convinced. It had to be about more than just a reputation, right? An expectation that he kept for himself, and maybe that his friends got used to seeing.

"Do you really think that changes things?" she asked. "We were only together for a few months."

"Second longest relationship I've ever had," he replied proudly. "Gabe, I know I sound fucking nuts for being so excited about this but everyone expects me to be just like him…Just like my dad. I know I've made choices to be like him on occasion but I'm not him. He never would've felt ashamed or disappointed in himself like I did when I cheated on Rae. He never would've apologized and actually meant it. He wouldn't bother caring if she was happy now or not. He sure as hell wouldn't have thrown himself at a woman's feet- *twice*, might I add- and begged her to stay or to come back. I'm not him, and I don't have to fucking pretend I am ever again."

As much as she knew she hated the man, Gabby was sure she'd never felt more disdain toward Johnathan Yates as she did right now. Seeing the sheer weight of everything he'd put on his son- expectations, ridiculous beliefs and standards- was enough to make her want to absolutely destroy the man. But seeing Emerson's outright elation at this epiphany was worth putting all that aside. Johnathan didn't deserve a second of their time or an ounce of thought.

Gabby chewed her bottom lip as a smile threatened to break free and she considered her next move. "What if..." she began, voice shaky with both excitement and anxiety. "What if we take things slow?"

Emerson made a face and looked at her as if she'd offered her suggestion in Spanish. "No," he stated with absolutely zero space for argument.

"No?"

"Yeah. *No.*"

"I'm sorry, and why not?" she questioned.

"Because I'm already in love with you. Plus I've seen you naked…lots of times."

Ugh, that smirk. Cocky bastard…

"But what if that's the only way I'm comfortable trying this again?"

The smirk didn't leave his face. "Fine, then we'll *"take it slow"*," he said, with air-quotes. "But don't be surprised when the only thing slow that happens between us is the way I make love to you."

Gabby's eyebrows rose and her breath caught in her throat. Was her heart still beating? She should probably check her pulse.

Emerson stood and held out his hand for her but she only glanced at it skeptically. Her eyebrows pinched together as she looked from his hand up to his face. "Right now?"

He nodded.

"But-"

"Gabe…it has been six weeks. *Six. Weeks,*" he added again for emphasis. "My right hand has gotten exhausted and the left is just awkward and uncoordinated."

"You poor thing," she teased.

"I know. I almost spent eighty dollars on this blow-job simulating sex toy. But it was only nine and a quarter inches long so I was like, well that just won't do."

A laugh burst out of her lips. "Where in the world did you discover that?"

"Instagram."

Gabby shook her head, laughing as she took Emerson's hand. "My life has been so dull without you."

He pulled her to his chest and wrapped his arms around her. "I would imagine so. And mine has been hell without you." With his forehead resting against hers, he said in a low voice, "Gabby, I love you so fucking much. I meant everything I said about showing you every day what you mean to me and always winning you over. Please don't run out on me again."

"Well, we're at my place so there's a good chance I'll still be here in the morning," she teased, running her hands up the ripple of his abdomen and the hard, broad plane of his chest.

"I don't know about that. You're sort of a flight risk at this point. If you're not careful you're going to give me abandonment issues."

She smiled and lightly touched her lips to his. "I won't leave. I won't run away from you again. Just…please don't hurt me, Emerson. Don't make me regret trusting you."

"If you couldn't trust me, I would've left you alone. I never want you to hurt or feel pain because of me. I won't lie to you, I won't keep secrets from you, and I swear you'll never have to wonder if I've changed my mind. You're all I want. All I never fucking knew I needed." Emerson dipped his head and caught her mouth on his, breathing her in, kissing her so deeply, consuming, devouring. His tongue crashed into hers and she moaned as her body went pliant against his solid form.

Finally, all was right again.

Chapter 29

Soft, warm lips pressed against her neck. A firm, sure hand made a path up her legs, over the curve of her hips, trailing over her ribs before cupping her breast and teasing the taut peak of her nipple. Gabby let out a groggy moan as she moved against the hard plane of muscles pressing into her back. Her hips rocked back and she gasped when she felt the length of solid, silky flesh against her ass.

The previous night was a blur of heat and sweat, whispers and groans and praises, skin against slik skin, tongues and hands and mouths. Sweet kisses mixed with ravenous, unbridled fucking. After the first six ground breaking orgasms, Gabby was tapping out, swearing her body couldn't take any more. But Emerson had just kept them coming…and coming…*and coming.*

At one point she was actually worried her heart was going to explode or stop beating, and the last thing she'd see before she died was Emerson's gorgeous body and his stunning face in the glorious ecstacy of climax. And she was pretty okay with that.

It was morning and his hands were on her again, rousing her from sleep, and even though she was sore and still thought her body couldn't possibly take another orgasm, she was willing to risk it…if he insisted.

They'd finished off what was left of her one box of condoms in her nightstand, but Emerson hadn't seemed too concerned. She was still on the pill and he was completely lost to her. Lost to giving her pleasure and taking his own.

His hand slid from her breast down the front of her belly, over the small mound of flesh where she was grateful she'd had the foresight to keep waxing, and between her legs. Fingers teasing, dipping low and tracing her lips before coming back up to her clit, she moaned again and pushed her ass into his lap. She hissed when those practiced fingers found her still swollen and she could've cried at how sweetly her pleasure mixed with pain. Sensitive, but still yearning for him in every way.

"Wet for me again, are we?" Emerson's deep voice was gravelly with sleep and it made her shiver. How that voice could get any sexier was beyond her. It shouldn't be possible. But then again, a lot of things he'd shown her last night shouldn't have been possible. He really was a Demigod, wasn't he? He hummed against her neck. "What are we going to do with you, Miss Cabrera?"

She sighed, eyes still closed as she gave herself over to him. "Whatever you want."

"Can I put it in your butt?" he asked, pausing his movements while he awaited an answer.

"What? No!"

His chest deflated. "You said whatever I want, I had to know what all was on the table."

"Not that."

He grunted, then she felt his leg slip between hers. "How about you open up for me then, and I'll just slide in from behind?"

She did as he asked and his hand slipped away from between her legs to cradle the underside of her thigh, holding her in place so he could push into her. His cock was hard and ready, and he slid in slowly, teasing, taking his time and she gasped. Full. So full of him and it was so perfect.

"Fuck, honey, you feel so damn good," he groaned into her neck. He licked the shell of her ear and playfully bit her lobe as he moved himself inside her. "Keep playing with your clit. I wanna see you drive yourself wild with me."

Again she followed his instructions. She didn't know why she never questioned his direction, never fought him when he told her what to do in bed. There was no way it would fly any other time, but she was glad, relieved almost, to relinquish some of that control she always had gripped so tightly and hand it over to him. Despite everything, she trusted him. She trusted him to make her feel good, she trusted him to treat her the way she deserved, ways she'd never experienced at the hands of anyone else.

As his movements behind her became rougher and her fingers still worked between her own legs, her desperate pleas became gasps and pants. God, she was going to lose it. Her chest tightened and she just knew this was the time it was going to implode.

"Te quiero...aye, te quiero papi...Oh God," she keened, her voice straining as pleasure tightened and crested deep in her belly, between her thighs. "Emerson, *por favor...por favor, papi.*" He thrusted hard and long, the slow slide of his cock rubbing her everywhere she needed. Reaching and plunging, becoming one with her. Too much, it was too much. Holy hell, did he have any idea what he was doing to her?

"Shhh…breathe, baby. Just breathe," he whispered, sending tingling sensations all over her skin. "I missed this. Missed you. I love waking up with you. I love making you crazy for me. I love fucking you right…love knowing I'm the only one who knows what that means."

His words put her over the edge. Her muscles began to tighten and she sent her hips back harder, meeting his thrusts with need. No words, only sounds of absolute euphoria escaped her lips as the blissful shock of her orgasm trembled through her. Her body clamped around him and it was his turn to gasp and groan, sputtering incoherent, guttural curses as he shook against her, emptying himself inside her.

"Oh my God, I love you," he breathed. He enveloped her in both his strong arms as they allowed their bodies to relax, coming down from that untouchable high. "I love you, I love you…*fuck* I love you. This is so good. So perfect."

It was good. Completely perfect. So right.

Until- nausea. Roiling and bubbling up inside her so instantly. Gabby gasped and pulled away from him, a hand over her mouth as she booked it for the bathroom. She hunched over the toilet and let it all out. Her stomach clenched hard as it brought up everything she'd eaten and then some it seemed. Relentless. Completely relentless.

Once finished, she grabbed a cup and washed out her mouth then brushed her teeth. There was a light knock on the door. "You all right, baby?"

"I'm fine!" Gabby called back, hastily pulling out her drawers and looking for that small blue pouch that was the size of a credit card.

"Call me crazy but usually people who are fine don't puke their guts out first thing in the morning," Emerson reasoned from the other side of the door.

Found it! She pulled out the small tray of pills and looked at the days. Not that it would matter. All the pills on this pack wouldn't tell her anything about the last time she and Emerson had sex. If she'd accidentally skipped a pill or something. But she was diligent about that. And they used condoms most of the time anyway. Before last night she could only think of...one other time. In the shower at his apartment while she was living there...just over six weeks ago.

Her eyes went wide as she stared at the birth control pills in her hand, her chest heaving and threatening to hyperventilate.

No. No, no, no.

Not good.

We just worked things out.

Emerson doesn't even want kids.

There had to be another explanation. There *had* to be.

She was certain all the stress she'd been feeling was to blame for her nausea. Not being able to find a job, losing Emerson, a whole new career path and deciding to spend over half her savings to get it all started.

Gabby squeezed her eyes shut and forced herself to control her breathing. She swallowed around the realization that she had skipped a period in all the craziness of the last month and a half and was determined to look like she wasn't absolutely fucking terrified when she walked out of the bathroom. When she faced Emerson. She reminded herself there were several reasons she could be feeling sick and there were other explanations for missing a period.

She had to think about those things.

She had to hope for those things.

But placing a hand over her belly, she just knew.

"Baby?" Emerson called again.

Baby...oh my God. A baby. A knot lodged itself somewhere in her throat.

"I'll be right out," she replied, hoping she didn't sound as frantic and screechy as she felt. "Could you actually get me a can of Sprite out of the fridge? Marco was over experimenting with different spritzer recipes and I think he left some behind."

"Sure. Do I need to take you to the doctor? You said you'd been feeling sick for a while now. Maybe you should get it checked out."

Ha. She would indeed have to go to the doctor. But first she would rule out any of her other crazy theories. As soon as Emerson left, she would go to the closest drug store and get a pregnancy test. If it was negative, she would go to the doctor and make sure she hadn't in fact caught something. If it was positive...

Well, if it was positive, she'd find out if all those beautiful words and promises Emerson had made the previous night still applied.

Gabby blinked down at the stick in her hands with its bright pink plus sign.

Plus means positive. That would only make sense. So why wasn't it computing in her brain? She let out a shaky breath before tearing into the second test.

Three minutes later she was staring at two pink plus signs.

Dammit.

How was she going to do this? How was she going to tell Emerson that he was going to be a father?

A laugh bubbled out of her lips as she pictured Emerson on the first day she'd seen him. His cocky smirk as he'd eyed her up and down while holding the door open for her. Emerson Yates was going to be a father. Holy shit.

Gabby placed a hand over her stomach and tried to imagine the little blob growing inside her. How big was it now? The size of a pea? A chickpea?

Then she couldn't help the smile that broke through all the other stress. All the anxiety over how Emerson would take the news. This was something Gabby wanted. She'd always wanted to be a mother. She wanted a family like her own- maybe not six kids, but a support system. Kids whose siblings would be their best friends. She wanted to be the type of parent hers were. Hardworking and tough, but fair.

Would it be a boy or a girl? Would it have her dark hair and Emerson's stormy blue eyes? Would it have that cocky smirk and her Don't Mess With Me attitude?

She laughed. *Wow...look out world.*

She reveled in the possibilities, the new future that was laid out before her...until she threw up again.

Yeah, that part she could do without.

Back in her kitchen, she leaned over the sink and drummed her fingers on the side of her water glass, trying to plan out her next step. Her first reaction was to grab her phone and call Marco. Not telling him first felt wrong, but there was more to it than that. Sure, Marco would be ecstatic to find out he'd be an uncle. He'd also be thrilled to find out she and Emerson had worked things out, but he didn't know about Emerson's insistence on not being a father. Hell, Gabby didn't know a whole lot about it.

Most of what she'd learned had come from Zoey, Amira, and Raelyn. They'd mentioned that he absolutely did not want kids. They'd even suggested she let him know that *she* wanted kids just to make sure they were on the same page. He'd really only brought it up once, insisting that a child was the last thing he needed. Of course, that was all based on the fear that he was just like his father. After last night, were those fears still there? Would they come back?

Feeling a little traitorous for not immediately calling Marco with the news, Gabby grabbed her cell phone and found Zoey's number. Although Amira had been her second choice after Marco, Gabby knew that things between her and Emerson were complicated. She liked Amira, and was grateful for her honesty, but she didn't need Brody overhearing the conversation, and she thought Amira was a little...well...biased. She might exaggerate how much Emerson didn't want to be a father based on her own opinions about what kind of father he might turn out to be.

Zoey seemed like a neutral choice. She was always friendly and seemed to know Emerson well enough since he was Jett's friend. Zoey didn't have the anger or negative predisposition toward Emerson that Amira clearly had after how he'd treated her best friend. Not to mention, Zoey was currently pregnant, too. Maybe she could give her some advice and prepare her for what to expect.

After two rings, Zoey answered her phone.

"Hi Gabby!" Zoey's cheerful voice greeted her on the other end. "I feel like I haven't heard from you in ages! How are you?"

"That's actually a more complicated question than you'd think," Gabby replied, letting out a humorless puff of laughter. "Listen, I'm sure you're busy, but is there any chance we could meet up? I need to talk to someone...about Emerson."

"I heard you guys broke up," Zoey said sadly. "Is everything okay? He hasn't been around much since that happened. I just got a cliff-notes version from Amira."

"I ran into him yesterday actually. It's all sort of a long story but I need to talk to someone...someone neutral."

"Definitely not Amira then," Zoey replied, and Gabby could hear the amused smile in her voice. "I'm actually just working from home today. Quinn wanted me to fly to LA this weekend for a charity benefit I set up, but seeing as I'm a million weeks pregnant, I had to explain that I cannot fly right now." She laughed like she couldn't believe the man she worked for sometimes. "Why don't you just come by the house? Jett's working until seven, so it'll just be us."

"Perfect, I'll be there soon."

After ending the call, Gabby quickly slipped on a pair of tall boots and her black fall jacket and headed over to Zoey and Jett's house. She'd only been there a couple of times before, but it was welcoming all the same. Some people, like Jett and Zoey, like her parents, just knew how to make a house feel like a home. There was love and warmth in every corner, everyone was welcome at any time, and there were always plenty of goodies stocked in the kitchen.

Zoey and Gabby settled in the living room on the sofa facing the massive stone fireplace, each with a warm beverage in hand.

"So, what's up?" Zoey asked, curling her legs beneath her as she held her mug of decaf close.

"I almost don't know where to start," Gabby said with a sigh. "You obviously know that Emerson and I broke up several weeks ago because of his…past transgressions coming to light." When Zoey nodded, Gabby continued, "Well, my little brother and Emerson's little brother are sneaky little shits when they want to be. They set us up for an accidental, completely-by-chance run-in."

Zoey laughed. "I don't know your brother but if he's Kolbe's best friend, I can only imagine those two could get into some trouble. So, how did that go?"

Gabby explained her freak-out at the restaurant and agreeing to talk to him. She went over their discussion in as much detail as she could remember. "And we agreed to try again…and then he gave me so many orgasms I actually thought my legs were going to fall off." She'd been staring off into the corner remembering flashes of the previous night before glancing back at Zoey. She smiled sheepishly. "Sorry, you probably didn't need to be clued in on that last part."

Zoey put up a hand. "No, no, I'm glad you got some after six weeks. And also a little curious now. Emerson always hyped himself up about how good he was in the bedroom…I'm intrigued to know it wasn't all talk."

"He definitely walks the walk better than he talks the talk," Gabby said, a bit of playful suggestion in her tone. "And he's quite the talker, so that's saying something."

Grinning, Zoey said, "Well, I'm really happy for you. He was in rough shape after you broke things off...not that I blame you. I probably would have done the same thing, but I really do think you've changed him. I think of the Emerson I met almost a year ago and then look at him now and it's like he's a whole different person. You make him better and I think he just didn't know how badly he craved someone who'd push him. It's like how kids with strict parents are grateful for the discipline once they realize how everyone else who didn't have any discipline are all jerks."

Gabby laughed at the analogy then sighed. "On the subject of change..." She cleared her throat, unsure of how to approach the topic. "I don't know how to ask this without...well...You, Raelyn, and Amira were all pretty adamant that Emerson really doesn't want kids. He doesn't want to be a father. He's mentioned it to me before, but we haven't really gone into it."

Concern creased Zoey's brow as she took a sip of her coffee. "And you said you wanted a family. Are you worried that you're going into this relationship again wanting different things?"

Yes and no.

"Well, kind of. I just...It would be good to know. You said he has a whole speech about it or something..."

Zoey snorted. "Yeah. A whole list of reasons he shouldn't be a father. Reasons he doesn't want a kid, why they would just ruin-" Her eyes glanced down to where Gabby's hand self-consciously covered her stomach over her sweater, then they widened with a gasp. "Oh! Oh...my gosh...are you-?"

Gabby swallowed and nodded. Offering a weak smile, she tried to reel in the panic again. "How bad is it? How bad is he going to freak out when I tell him?"

"Did you know?" Zoey asked. "Before you ran into him again, I mean? Did you know last night before all the orgasms?"

"No." Gabby shook her head. "I knew I hadn't been feeling well and I'd barely realized I missed a period. I've been so stressed with so much going on and not having any sort of routine because I don't have a job right now. I got sick this morning and it just all came crashing into focus. The reality of it. I wonder if I'd been purposely ignoring it…like I couldn't handle another thing on top of all the other crap I was going through."

Gabby watched as a wide grin slowly crept onto Zoey's face. "What? Why are you smiling?"

"I'm sorry," Zoey said, shaking her head as if she could shake the smile off her face. "I just thought about how beautiful your baby is going to be. Your perfect complexion and his eyes. Oh my gosh, what if it's a girl and she has his sandy blonde hair and your lips? That might be a weird observation, but you have the right lips to be a lipstick model. It's not even fair."

Gabby couldn't help laughing. "Thanks. I just don't know what I'm going to do! What if he freaks out? What if he reverts back into thinking he'll be just like his dad?"

Zoey leaned forward to set her mug on the coffee table and looked as if she were searching for the right words. "He won't," she stated. "That man has a bigger heart than he lets on. His capacity to love is so much more than he probably even knows or gives himself credit for. When he found out about Kolbe he was furious with his dad that he could just treat his own son that way, that he could write him off like a check was enough to make up for not being there. I think that's sort of how he'd been treated as a kid. They bought him things and provided him with expensive *stuff*, but never time.

"Meeting Kolbe wasn't enough. He wanted to be a brother to him and have a relationship with him. He didn't have to but he wouldn't have it any other way. I think Emerson is lonely. I don't think he'd ever admit to it but that's my theory anyway. It's why he forces people to be his friend, it's why when he was single he could never spend a night alone. I think he grew up lonely, never had anyone who was really there for him, and he absolutely thrives on being there for other people. For the people who really mean something to him."

Gabby listened and let everything sink in. All these kind words toward a man so many people were so quick to write off as cocky and arrogant, selfish and cold. It warmed her heart to hear Zoey speak of him this way and know that she wasn't the only person who could see good in him. Maybe if he realized others could see it, he'd start believing in that part of himself more.

"So to answer your real question," Zoey said, meeting Gabby's eyes, "no, I don't think Emerson will abandon you and your baby. Not for a second. Though I won't lie to you, he will probably be dramatic. He might faint or go into shock for an hour, but he won't leave. He loves you more than he's loved anyone or anything, and if he had any doubts before, I think the last six weeks without you showed him just how much better his life is with you in it."

She gave a relieved smile. "Thanks. I think deep down I knew that, but I just really needed to hear it from someone else. Make sure I wasn't just deluding myself to believe that I really am different for him."

"Oh, you're definitely not delusional. He was a mess without you." Zoey reached out and put her hand over Gabby's. "The sooner you tell him, the better. I think in the spirit of your newly established relationship it would be best to not keep secrets for too long."

Gabby took a deep breath in and let it out slowly, nodding. "I'll tell him tonight."

Chapter 30

Gabby hadn't bothered to get too dressed up or do a whole lot of extra primping before heading over to Emerson's that evening. He'd called and asked her if she wanted to come over to his apartment and said that he'd make dinner. It had been cold and windy all day, and the sun that had been shining earlier was tucked behind gray clouds. The perfect night for staying in and watching movies under a blanket. So she tossed on a comfy sweater dress and stepped into some tall boots and rushed over, afraid that if she took her time she'd talk herself out of going.

She'd barely finished knocking when the door opened and Emerson pulled her inside, turning her around and kicking the door shut behind them. He held her close and kissed her hungrily. Need stirred below her belly and she almost forgot she had anything to be nervous about.

Emerson backed her against the kitchen island and lifted her, setting her down and pulling her legs around his waist. His lips were hot against hers, his tongue plunging into her mouth like he was starving for her. She definitely knew the feeling. Her hands slid beneath his slate blue Henley, feeling the hard dips, peaks, and valleys of his muscles.

"Hi," she breathed, smiling as he moved his mouth away from hers and began a trail of kisses down her neck.

"Hi gorgeous," he replied, mouth still moving over her, never missing a beat.

"Did you miss me?" Gabby teased.

"I went six weeks without you, baby. It's going to be a while before I can stop missing you."

"Well I'm here," she said. She scratched her nails down his chest and he moaned against her collarbone. "And I'm not going anywhere."

"Promise?"

Oh, he had no idea…

"Promise." Gabby let her head fall back and arched her back, pressing her chest toward him and letting him take the lead. It hadn't been her plan to have sex as soon as she walked through the door, but maybe it would ease the tension she was feeling. And maybe it would put him in a better mood to hear the news that would inevitably flip his world upside down.

"I want to take my time with you, but I need to be inside you so bad." Emerson pushed the hem of her dress up, shoving it over her hips and exposing her red silk panties. He groaned. "God, I love you in red."

"Oh yeah?"

"I'd love you in lime green or a potato sack," he said. "Or a lime green potato sack. But something about you in red…so fucking sexy."

"I'll test that theory," Gabby said, giggling. "For Halloween I'll dress in a lime green potato sack and see if you keep your word."

Emerson left one hand on her, gently rubbing and petting down the middle of her panties, and began unbuttoning and shoving his own pants and boxer briefs down. His cock sprung free, thick and hard, and Gabby reached for it instantly. She pumped her hand down the length of him, loving how warm and solid he was in her grasp.

When her eyes flickered up to his hooded gaze, she was struck by the depths of his stare. That deep blue swirling with lust and need, possession, and something sweeter. He braced a hand on the countertop beside her and leaned over her, inching himself closer. "Want me to fuck you right here in the middle of my kitchen?" he rasped. "You can have me right here, right now, or we can wait and you can have me in bed."

Gabby lifted his shirt up and over his head, dropping it to the floor. "Why not both?"

A deep, lustful sound rumbled through him as he peeled her dress off. "Good answer."

"Emerson," she whispered, touching his cheek, "I love you."

"I love you too, baby. Now just sit back and let me show you how much." He pushed aside the small scrap of fabric and pulled her to the edge of the counter. Aligning his dick with her opening, he trailed the tip down her center, just enough to get it wet, then back up. Slowly. Gabby thrusted her hips, asking for more but he didn't concede just yet.

"Emerson, please…" she begged, already grasping his shoulders. Letting her fingernails dig in and leave their mark. "I want you inside me…please."

He cursed. "Should I get a-?"

Gabby shook her head. "Not now. Please, I want to feel you. All of you. Nothing between us. *Please.*" Her chest was already heaving, panting.

His expression was almost pained just before he gave in and pushed into her, all the way to the hilt. Then his face was pure bliss. Relief. The feel of him inside her, of her wrapped so tightly around him again was like finding a missing puzzle piece. The fit was perfect, and when they came together they were finally whole.

He moved inside her, plunging deep, thrusting, giving and taking all he had. His hands gripped her hips, digging into her soft, round curves, and he covered her mouth with his. Tasting, teasing, sucking.

Gabby moaned and begged shamelessly. Needing him. All of him. Her fingers plunged into his hair and she pulled him over her, urging their mouths together even harder. Their tongues both licking and crashing together, making love of their own.

She was met with thrust after hard thrust as he fucked her harder, relentlessly. Pleasure swelled inside her, rising higher and higher until she was clinging to him. Her body went rigid as she cried out around her orgasm. The sheer intensity of it causing her to gasp and writhe wildly beneath him, unable to stop her hips from rocking up to meet his deep strokes over and over. The waves coursed through her, curling and twisting, cresting, but never wanting to fall. Her toes curled, her thighs held tight around his waist and she wasn't sure she would ever stop falling.

"Oh God," Emerson panted. "Fuck, you've got ahold of me so tight. Fuuuuck…" he drew out his groan as his eyes closed tight and he buried his face in her neck. His body was stiff and he was buried deep inside, holding himself there, all the way in as he came hard, shuddering and growling. Biting the nape of her neck, unable to move until his body was spent.

Gabby lightly scratched her fingers over the back of his neck, listening to him as he caught his breath.

A loud hissing sound caught their attention, followed by more hissing and rumbling.

"Shit!" Emerson straightened abruptly and pulled himself out of her, running around the island to attend to the food on the stove that was now boiling over. "I forgot I was cooking," he said, rushing to turn down the heat on the burners.

"What are we having for dinner?" Gabby asked, trying not to laugh at the sight of Emerson, naked and panicked in front of the stove. "And don't burn the goods, babe. I'll be sad if you spill boiling water on your penis and can't use it the rest of the night."

Quickly, Emerson grabbed a dish towel and held it over his crotch. "God, you really are the brains in this relationship, aren't you? I think I'll keep you."

Gabby's smile was somewhat forced as the anxiety began creeping back, though his back was to her anyway. Everything he said, she wanted to respond with something about him being a father.

Yes, I promise I'm not going anywhere because I can't very well take your child away from you.

I'm glad you want to keep me around because you might have to for at least the next eighteen years.

But she had to do this right. Calmly. Preferably sitting down and maybe after both his sexual appetite and hunger were satiated. Definitely not while he was standing naked in front of a pot of boiling water and a pan of bubbling, spattering pasta sauce.

She hopped off the counter and sidled up next to him. "Need help with anything? I know we're both master chefs, but I'm not below just taking bread out of the oven."

"Fuck! The bread...I forgot to set a timer!" Emerson scrambled to open the oven door, revealing a loaf of rather dark brown garlic bread. "Shit."

"It's okay," Gabby said with a laugh. "Here, I'll take it out and you just keep your penis away from the hot oven, please." Emerson backed up and she found a pair of oven mitts and pulled the well-done bread out. After setting it on the stove top, she tapped the crispy crust of the bread and grimaced. "Unless you want a trip to the dentist, I would advise we don't eat that."

"That's it, I'm hiring a fucking butler," Emerson said, throwing up his free hand that wasn't covering his junk. "Jett said spaghetti is the easiest meal to make and I can't even do that."

Gabby eyed the large bowl of greens with shredded cabbage, carrots, olives, and red onion. "That salad looks straight out of Olive Garden. I'd say you did pretty well."

He cocked a skeptical eyebrow in her direction but couldn't help the crooked smirk that slid over his face. "It does look pretty damn professional."

After the pasta finished cooking and the sauce had simmered and they'd assured that it hadn't burned, they moved everything to the table where Emerson had candles set in the middle. They both dressed again before sitting to enjoy their meal, Emerson lit the candles and turned off the bright kitchen lights in favor of the dimmer overhead light in the small dining area.

"Thank you for making me dinner," Gabby said, digging into her salad.

"Sorry for ruining it," Emerson replied.

"I'll take partial blame for that. I did come in and distract you."

"Well, I'll never be sorry for letting you distract me like that." He reached for the bowl of parmesan cheese that he'd grated himself, rather than using the sprinkle kind. "Oh! I almost forgot..." He stood and went to a cupboard where he pulled out two wine glasses and a bottle of chardonnay from the fridge.

Her heart sank. *I hadn't even thought about how I can't have wine for nine months!* She felt herself tense as he poured the delicious looking white wine into a glass in front of her then did the same for himself.

"I didn't know you drank wine," she remarked as he took his seat again.

"I don't, but I didn't want to drink whiskey with spaghetti and I'm out of Heineken."

Well, I hope you like it because you'll have to drink mine, too!

Emerson held up his glass and looked her in the eyes. His deep blues were swimming with hope and love and she sank right into it. "To a fresh start. To a love that stems from honesty, trust, and lots and lots of orgasms."

She laughed quietly as she clinked her glass to his. She could just...pretend to take a sip, right?

A love that stems from honesty...

It was a small thing, but she still felt deceitful. Then she remembered Zoey's words telling her not to keep secrets for too long. She was going to tell him, she reasoned. Tonight. Right after dinner. Or after they'd had a minute to let their stomachs settle.

Before the glass touched her lips she cleared her throat and set it back down. She straightened and held her hands in her lap, knowing that they'd be trembling if she left them where he could see them.

"Is everything okay?" Emerson asked, concern taking over his features. "Are you still not feeling well?"

"Everything's fine. I'm not sick...though I guess that doesn't mean I won't be again depending on what I eat."

His brow furrowed. "Think my cooking's that bad, huh?"

"No!" she said, then laughed a little. "No, that's not...I just. I have to tell you something. And I was going to wait, but the longer I hold off, the more I feel like I'm intentionally hiding it from you."

Curiosity now mixed with the concern on his face as he set his wine glass down, too. "Okay…"

"Emerson, you said a lot of wonderful things last night about being there for me and always showing me how much you love me. And you had this great epiphany about how you're nothing like your father, right? So…just try to remember all of that." Gabby took a deep breath. *Out with it, girl.* She met his gaze again. "I'm pregnant."

There was the slightest deepening of the crease in his brow and his lips parted a fraction, but otherwise he stayed silent. So she thought he might need further explanation.

"I didn't know last night," she went on. "I thought my not feeling well was because of stress. The stress of losing you, losing my job, not being able to find a job, and then deciding to spend a lot of my money on a building so that I can start my own firm, which I'm now realizing we didn't talk about last night. But that's my plan anyway. Or at least it was. I guess a baby might change things. But anyway…when I got sick this morning I realized I was late. Like a few weeks late. So I took a test. Actually I took a few tests because I sort of couldn't believe it. I actually have them all with me, they're in my purse. But they were all positive so…I'm pregnant."

Emerson continued to stare with that confused sort of expression. Slowly he leaned back and rubbed a hand over his jaw, scratched his beard. Then he cleared his throat and said, "Excuse me," before pushing himself out of his seat and walking down the hall toward his bedroom.

Gabby stared after him, wondering if she should follow, if he'd gone to get something, or if this was just him needing space and a second alone to process. Deciding it was likely the latter, she sat awkwardly in her seat, hands still folded in her lap as she waited for him to come back out.

And she waited.

And waited.

And then…she turned her attention curiously down the hall again as the sound of the shower turning on filled the quiet space.

He's…taking a shower?

Maybe he's trying to drown himself. Zoey did say he'd be dramatic.

Gabby stood up and found her purse, pulling out her phone and the ziplock bag with the four pregnancy tests she'd taken in it. After her visit with Zoey, she'd been overcome with denial and made a quick run to another drug store for more tests. Those tests seemed to think she was pregnant, too.

She smiled when she saw that she had two messages from Zoey already.

Zoey: Good luck tonight. Remember he LOVES you. No matter how he reacts. You're what's best for him and he knows it.

Zoey: Oh, and I forgot to tell you…Congratulations, mama.

With a quick glance toward the sound of the shower, she sent a response.

Gabby: He's in the shower. I told him…and then he excused himself to go take a shower. Any guesses as to what that's about?

It didn't take long before her phone chimed with a new message.

Zoey: I told you he'd be dramatic. Didn't expect that though. Can't wait to hear how this plays out.

Gabby: I'll let you know if there are any new and interesting developments.

Nearly twenty minutes later, while Gabby began clearing the table and packing up their dinner since she'd lost her appetite and imagined Emerson also had, she heard the shower turn off. She listened for him to come back out into the kitchen, but only heard the usual rustling of him doing his post-shower routine. The opening and closing of drawers, the buzz of his beard trimmer, and some other movements she couldn't quite decipher.

With the pasta and salad packed away in containers in the fridge, she re-corked the bottle of wine and was blowing out the two center candles when she finally heard his footsteps approaching. All anxiety was washed away and replaced by outright confusion. Befuddlement. And other words like that.

Her eyes narrowed and she tried to figure out what the hell to make of the sight in front of her. Emerson was cleaned up, dressed in one of his best suits and working the clasp on his rather expensive watch. He adjusted his tie with one hand and her gaze dropped to the manilla envelope and yellow legal pad in the other. His face, handsome as ever, was set in a mask of impenetrable focus. He looked like he was ready for a high profile court case.

With his free hand, he gestured to the table. "Have a seat," he said, making his way to the chair directly across from hers.

"Emerson…what are you-?"

"Please," he added, voice stern. All business.

She sighed. *And cue the freak out. I think…* Really, she had no idea what to make of his reaction, so she figured the best course of action was to go along with it. Best to get it over with and hear what he had to say. She sat down and folded her now steady hands on the table in front of her, staring across at him and waiting.

Emerson cleared his throat. "So, you are making the claim that you are pregnant. Is that correct?"

"Are you cross-examining me?" she asked, incredulous.

"Just answer the question, Miss Cabrera."

Her eyes narrowed to slits as she looked at him in utter disbelief. Finally she sighed and leaned back. "Yes, *counselor*, I'm pregnant."

"Do you have proof of that claim?"

Wow. They were really doing this. Gabby rolled her eyes and reached behind her for her purse that she'd slung over the back of her chair. She pulled out the Ziplock bag with the four pregnancy tests and slid it across the table toward him. Emerson hesitated before picking up the bag, and there was the faintest reaction as his eyes widened in surprise before the focused mask was put back in place. He put the bag down and set it aside, next to the manila envelope he had yet to bring into play, though she couldn't wait to see what his plan was.

Emerson nodded, pulled a pen out of the inside of his suit jacket and jotted down a few quick notes. Gabby rolled her eyes, too exhausted already to even try to see what he was writing. She folded her arms over her chest and continued to stare him down.

"The evidence supports the claim," he said. He clicked the pen and set it on the legal pad, then laced his fingers and set them on the table, fixing her with an unwavering stare of his own. "However the defense has some questions…some wrinkles that need ironed out." He reached for the envelope and opened it, pulling out his own evidence. First he pulled out a small blue pouch that contained the sleeve of birth control pills she must have left behind when she left. It was almost empty and she'd simply started a new pack when she realized she didn't want to risk coming back to collect the rest of her things. "Do you recognize this?"

"Yes."

"What is it?"

"My birth control pills."

"Birth control? Interesting." He nodded and pulled the sleeve out to examine what was left of the pills. "And you take these regularly, as directed?"

"I do."

"And birth control is said to be, what? Ninety-nine percent effective if taken correctly?"

"That sounds about right."

"Pretty solid protection then, wouldn't you say?"

"Apparently not solid enough," she retorted. This was getting ridiculous. But if this is what he needed to cope, she'd let him go through with it.

Emerson reached into the envelope again and this time pulled out a sleeve of condoms. "I assume you're familiar with these?"

It was getting difficult not to laugh, but she kept a straight face. "I am."

"How often would you say the defendant used these?" he asked. "Despite the plaintiff's insistence that Item A-" he lifted the birth control pills- "negated the need for Item B!" He raised the condoms.

"Almost every time."

"Almost. Every. Time," Emerson said slowly, tapping the condoms on the table with the emphasis of each word. "Not last night and not tonight, but you couldn't possibly know you're pregnant from that."

"That's correct."

"So, what do you think are the chances that, with the use of these two contraceptives, that *this-*"he picked up the bag of pregnancy tests- "could still happen?"

"I guess you must have super-sperm."

"Objection- Dodging the question!"

"Objection!" Gabby shouted back, bracing her hands on the table. "You can't object to a witness, only their attorney."

Emerson stood, also bracing himself on the table and leaning forward now. "The point, Miss Cabrera, is that you said that because you had *these* we didn't need *these!* But we still used *both* in order to avoid *this!*" He gestured toward the birth control pills, the condoms, and the pregnancy tests in sequence to emphasize his argument.

"I'm aware," Gabby said, voice hard as she stood up, leaning over the table and leveling her gaze with his. "But somehow it happened. Trust me, it wasn't my plan."

"How far along are you?" he asked, his voice softer as his focus dropped lower. Down to her stomach.

"I'm not sure," she replied. "I would guess six or seven weeks."

"I didn't see you for six weeks...you left your pills here. Did you...were you *with* anyone else while we were separated?"

Gabby reared back, offended. She watched as Emerson studied her, looking uncomfortable for asking the question but remaining quiet, needing to know. She scoffed. "No, Emerson. The baby is yours."

He gave one short nod. "Good."

"Have you been with anyone else?" she questioned, now that it was out there. She hadn't even considered that as an option, but if he'd been able to wonder, she thought maybe she should, too.

"No, Gabe. I haven't looked at another woman. Not with any sort of interest anyway."

Gabby's stare softened as she took in the worry on his face. Emerson was still looking toward her belly and it was clear his brain was swarming with thoughts, questions, and fears. She reached for him, cupping his jaw in her hand and he leaned into her touch like he always did. His head dropped and his eyes closed.

"Are we done with the courtroom drama?" she asked, gently scratching his neck.

He nodded. "Onto deliberation…What are we going to do?"

She let out a puff of laughter, though it was a nervous reaction and not remotely fueled by humor. "What do you mean? We're going to have a baby, Emerson. We're going to be parents."

He raised his head and met her gaze. He kissed her palm then straightened, smoothing a hand down his tie. "We'll get married."

"*What?*"

"It's the right thing to do. Our kid's parents should be married."

"Emerson…" Gabby shook her head.

"I want our kid to be happy. To know that his…or her- Oh *God*, what if it's a girl?" Emerson's eyes widened with fear before he shook it off. "I want our baby to know that we love each other. That we're happy and we're not going anywhere. We should get married."

"Because marriage is obviously the only way that works, I mean, just look at your parents," Gabby tossed back. Emerson chewed the inside of his cheek and looked away, but she reached for him again. "I know you grew up with all these ideas of what a perfect family is and how to keep up appearances, but our baby will know we love each other because we love each other. We'll show it in every way. And he *or she* will also know how loved they are. We don't have to get married to prove that."

Emerson was silent for a few beats before he walked around the table to stand in front of her. He slid his hand up her jaw, cupping her cheek as he smoothed his thumb over the arch of her cheekbone. "I love you, Gabriella. With everything I have and then some. And I promise I will love this baby just as much." Slowly, his other hand found its way to her stomach and he let out a contented sigh as he held it there. He dropped down, wrapping his hands around the backs of her thighs and placed a kiss on her belly before resting his head against her.

Gabby's heart could have exploded at the sight, and all at once her anxiety and fears were eliminated and replaced by bright images of their future. Watching him worry and dote on her when her belly got too big to do some things for herself, probably fighting when she tried to do them anyway. Seeing Emerson hold their baby for the first time and fall in love instantly. The warmth and love she knew that baby would feel as the three of them snuggled in bed, the little bundle between the two of them. Everything. It was everything she wanted and had no idea she ever needed.

Emerson pressed another kiss to her stomach, then leaned back on his heels before moving onto one knee. He reached into his inside jacket pocket and pulled out a ring. A beautiful emerald cut diamond with an intricate halo, and tiny diamonds sprinkled around the gold band.

She couldn't help the small gasp that escaped her lips and her jaw dropped. "Emerson…how…When did-?"

"I've had it for a few years," he explained.

Instantly, her eyes narrowed. "I swear, if this is the ring you asked your ex-fiancé to marry you with-"

"No! No," he laughed nervously. "No, this was my grandmother's. My dad's mom. She died when I was twenty-two, but we were close. The only person in my family I ever felt actually loved me…"

Gabby's heart clenched and she could have cried for his younger, lonely self.

"I love you, Gabriella. And we're going to have a family together. I'm not going anywhere and I want to be with you and our baby for the rest of our lives. I know it won't be perfect but I'll give you everything you need. Everything you ask for is yours. I just want to make you happy. I'll quit Warren & Blakely, we'll start our own firm as partners. Criminal law would be cool because I think we'd both be good at that. We'll buy a house with a yard and we'll have it all. Marry me, Gabby."

She looked down at him and knew he meant every word. God, she loved this man. And she wanted to marry him. One day…

So, taking a deep breath and releasing it she gave him her answer, "No."

His eyebrows shot up then furrowed, confused. "No?"

"Yeah. *No.*"

"Why not?"

"Because you're not asking for the right reasons." When he opened his mouth to defend himself, she cut him off, "I know you love me. And I know we're going to be together and raise this baby together, but…you're asking me to marry you because I'm pregnant."

"I'm asking because I want to marry you."

"Because you think it's the right thing. You think it's the right time and you just got me back and maybe you're terrified I'll run away again. But I promise I'm not going to run off with your kid."

"Gabe-"

"Were you going to propose tonight?" she challenged. "Before I told you about the baby, would you have proposed after dinner? Is that why you had the candles and the wine and all the romantic ambiance?"

"Well…no, but-"

"Do you have any idea when you would have?"

He hesitated and swallowed. "I hadn't really thought about it, but-"

"So don't rush it now. Let's be in love and let it just…be. I would like to marry you one day, but I want to know you're asking for the right reasons. Not because it's what's logical." She gripped his elbows and pulled him up to face her again. "I love you and I really think I'd like to be your wife one day, but let's just take it one major life change at a time, okay?"

Emerson peered down at her, gray swirling in the depths of those blue eyes, but they were still twinkling with mischief and desire. "I won't ask again," he said as if it were a warning. A last call.

"Yeah you will."

He smirked. "Yeah, I will." He dipped his head low and slanted his mouth over hers, sliding his tongue between her lips and inhaling deeply. One hand cradled the back of her head while the other pulled her flush against his body, heat licking over her skin, between her thighs, threatening to burst in her chest.

When he pulled away, her eyes struggled to flutter open. She was dizzy with the love of this man. "I put dinner away, but I can get it back out if you want..."

A low growl met her ears and sent a pleasant shiver down her spine, making her legs go weak. "I'm hungry for something else now, mami." He nipped at her bottom lip and began walking backward, tugging her along with him toward the bedroom.

"And what would that be, papi?" she teased playfully.

"You'll have to come with me and find out."

That coaxing twinkle in his eyes glinted with mischief and promise as she let him lead her to his bed. When he crawled over her, pushed inside her, he showed her with every move just how much he loved her. How much he would take care of her, be there for her. It was in each touch, each kiss, each sweet, breathless praise of her name. He took his time erasing her fears, proving that she was it. That she was the one. That she didn't have to worry or wonder.

Beyond a shadow of a doubt she knew this sweet, cocky, beautiful man was all hers.

Epilogue

It was June fourteenth, four whole days after Gabriella's due date and yet there she was. At the firm. Filing through cases as if she'd actually be able to take them on while she's on maternity leave. The woman was nuts. She hadn't quit working since the firm opened and started getting clients just over three months ago. Emerson tried to get her to hold off opening Cabrera, Yates, & Associates- well, Associate, really. Tyler was their only other employee at this point. Regardless, she refused, saying that she wasn't going to let a little thing like *being pregnant* keep her from working.

He'd tried to argue. Arguing with Gabriella was always fun. Arguing with *pregnant* Gabriella, however, was a suicide mission. So he'd dropped the issue for a while. Using a new approach, he'd tried to get Tyler, Chris, and Jett to make her see reason, and when she inevitably tore them all a new one, he resigned to the reality of his pregnant girlfriend taking on clients as long as she felt able.

"Honey, you doing okay?" Emerson asked, leaning against the doorframe to her office. Gabriella was frantically flipping through folders like she'd misplaced something urgent.

"Am I *okay?*" she repeated, her voice dripping with threat. "Emerson. I am like a million days pregnant. It's hot out. My feet are swollen, my stomach is the size of a beach ball, and I have to pee every five minutes. Does it sound like I'm *okay?*"

Emerson sucked his lips between his front teeth as he carefully calculated a response. "It sounds...like you're uncomfortable." Immediately, the expression on her face told him that was the wrong thing to say. So much for trying for empathy. He quickly added, "Which is totally understandable. Of course you're uncomfortable. Don't you think you'd be better off at home though? You could relax or take a nap. You know, once that baby gets here we won't sleep for like three months. That's what Jett said, anyway. Of course, that could be because they have a little girl. We'll have a boy and that'll make it so much easier."

Actually, they didn't know what they were having. Jett and Zoey had been so excited to wait and find out that they'd talked Gabby into thinking it was a good idea. Emerson wanted to know, but if she wanted to wait he supposed he could too. Jett constantly said he hoped Emerson was having a girl because he needed to experience the full weight of the type of person he'd been before meeting Gabriella. Emerson thought Jett was a dick for pointing it out and insisted that he had to have a boy so that little Maisie Miller could fall hopelessly in love with him.

Gabriella leaned over her planner and read some notes, "Okay, so…spicy food, exercise…sex! We have to have sex!"

"Right now?" Emerson questioned.

"It's the best way to induce labor. I need to get this baby out of me. *Please*, just do this for me."

He stepped into the room and closed the door behind him, locking it in case Tyler got back from his lunch early. "Are you sure?"

Her eyes narrowed. "What? Am I too round? We've been having sex all this time- I know finding comfortable positions has been an adjustment, but-"

"No," he laughed under his breath. "No, honey, you know I think you're fucking gorgeous, baby belly, swollen feet and all. I just…I think this is how the male praying mantis feels. Getting enticed into something fun and then he gets his head ripped off. I just want to make sure all my parts will stay intact if it doesn't work."

Finally she smiled as she walked around to the front of her desk. "I promise I won't rip off any appendages."

Emerson stepped toward her slowly before sliding his arm behind her, holding his hand at the small of her back. He pressed their bodies together and smoothed a hand over her protruding belly as he spoke to it, "Come on, baby Yates. We're ready to meet you. You gotta come out before your mom kills me for looking too comfortable or breathing too loudly."

The soft giggle that met his ears warmed his chest. He never thought he could be this happy in a relationship. Gabriella was everything to him. He would do anything for her, give her anything she wanted, find any and every way to make her happy. She was carrying this life for them, creating this beautiful baby that would be made up of all of their best qualities and hopefully none of their worst. His future was steady and solid, yet so full of possibility. There was no getting bored, no claustrophobic need for escape. Everything he held in his arms in this moment was all he'd never known he always wanted.

His lips pressed to hers, tongues sliding against each other as she sighed, leaning into him. Hands skating up her sides, over her breasts, palming and kneading, he felt himself growing hard as he coaxed out little moans from between her lips. Stunning. She was absolutely stunning. He loved her new curves, her soft skin that seemed to glow, and yeah, the pregnancy boobs were pretty fantastic.

He tugged her dress up and slipped his hands beneath the light cotton fabric for better access to those magnificent tits. Unclasping her bra and grabbing two handfuls of those swollen breasts, he lightly traced the pads of his thumbs over each nipple. Circling, sliding over the taut peaks. Gabriella's breathing increased and he felt the rise and fall of the swells under his palms.

Then she gasped, gripping his biceps. "Oh my God!"

"That good, huh?" He smirked against her lips before noticing something wet on the floor.

They both glanced down at their feet and back at each other with wide eyes.

"My water broke."

He nodded. "Your water broke."

"It's happening."

"Yep."

They stood unmoving for a few beats, just staring at each other as their brains processed everything in slow motion.

"We need to get to the hospital," Gabriella said, breaking the silence.

"Right." Emerson straightened, but didn't take his hands off her. "The hospital bag is in my office." He brushed his hand gently over her cheek. "You okay?"

She let out a breathy, "Yeah. And you?"

He smiled. "I'm good." Leaning forward, he pressed a kiss to her forehead. "Now let's go have a baby."

Nine hours later, Emerson was sitting next to Gabriella as she did her best to squeeze his fingers off. He wasn't stupid enough to complain- he wasn't the one whose genitals were being ripped open.

"Come on, honey, you got this," he said. He felt like a fucking liar. Like he was completely full of shit, sitting there as if he were totally calm when he was anything but. The strongest, most fierce woman he knew was in pain, making noises he was sure no human could voluntarily conjure unless...well, unless a fat baby head was squeezing its way through a hole that was way too small. He wiped sweat off her forehead with a cold washcloth and kissed her cheek. "You are so strong, baby. You're doing so good. Our baby's almost here."

"Another good push, Gabby," Dr. Bryant encouraged. "I can see the head. Just keep pushing."

"Oh, is that what I'm supposed to do?" she snapped. "All this time I thought I was supposed to suck it back in!" She let out a huff. "God, men are idiots."

"You're absolutely right," Emerson said. "We are all idiots." Agreeing with everything she said seemed to be the best option. "But our baby boy will be less of an idiot because you're his mother."

"You're never. Touching me. Again," she declared right before a final big push. She pushed and strained, yelling and cursing him the whole way.

When the doctor held something in his arms, he smiled up at them over the cries of a brand new life entering the world. "Well, say hello to your baby girl."

"Our what?" Emerson blinked and felt dizzy.

Gabriella's body leaned back into the pillows, finally relaxing with a heavy sigh. "It's a girl?" she asked, a smile on her face that was a complete one-eighty from the cursing, demonic expression only moments before.

"Yep. With ten fingers and ten toes," Dr. Bryant confirmed. "A healthy baby girl with a good set of lungs on her. Congratulations, you two."

Emerson stared at the bundle that was getting cleaned off, completely in shock. "I...I have a daughter?"

Gabriella reached for him, touching his arm. "Don't you dare pass out on me, Emerson. I stayed conscious through all that, I think you can handle this."

As the doctor worked between Gabby's legs to clean her up and do...whatever it is they do with the umbilical cord, a nurse handed Emerson the warm bundle, swaddled in a white and pink blanket.

He stared down at the small thing in his arms in complete disbelief. The breath knocked right out of his lungs as he held onto her and she nestled into him. Her crying soothed, already so trusting. Already knowing that he would never hurt her or allow anything bad to happen to her. After a long moment of letting his eyes take in her full head of dark hair, the little button nose, and pinkish skin, he slid his gaze up to Gabby. "We made this."

"Yeah, we did." Her smile was bright and teary-eyed.

"She's beautiful," he said, still breathless. He couldn't believe it. Something so new and so tiny had already stolen his heart. It didn't matter that for the past several months he'd been planning on raising a boy, or that he had no idea how to be a dad. This little girl in his arms was perfect, and he knew better than he'd ever known anything that he would protect her, give her everything, love her and make sure she never questioned it. His little girl would never feel alone, would never feel like she wasn't good enough. She was perfect. His heart swelled as he looked from his daughter to her mother, feeling more complete and more whole than he ever knew was possible.

"Holy shit, I fucking love her so much already," he said, nearly laughing even though he swore he was on the verge of tears.

Gabriella smiled. "Well, I don't think we can name her Emmett."

He laughed at their choice of name for the boy they were so sure they were going to have. "How about…Emilia?"

"You're really stuck on it beginning with *E-M,* aren't you?"

"You started it."

Still, her smile wouldn't fall off her face. "Emilia Maria Yates."

"Emilia Maria…that's fun to say," Emerson said with a grin. "I like it."

"Can I hold her now?" Gabriella stretched her arms out for her daughter. Reluctant to give her up, he passed the bundle over to the woman primarily responsible for this new joy in his life. Sure, she couldn't have done it without him, but she did all the hard stuff.

Watching Gabriella hold their daughter for the first time was almost too much. His heart was going to explode. There's no way he could have predicted this level of love existed. Impatient and feeling like he needed to be closer to them, he asked Gabby to scoot up a bit and climbed into the hospital bed behind her, letting his legs stretch out on either side of her so she could lean back against his chest. He pressed another kiss to her temple and looked over her shoulder at Emilia.

"Hey," he whispered into Gabriella's hair. "You realize what this means, right?"

"Hm?"

"Everyone we know can officially call me Daddy."

She let out an exasperated laugh and leaned her head back against his chest. "I'm trying to have a tender moment with *our daughter!*"

"I know, but it was too much. My chest is in physical pain from all the love right now."

"It's ridiculous, isn't it? My heart is so full right now. Like over-flowing to the point where I can barely take it."

Holding both of his girls, his whole fucking world, he wondered what the hell he'd done to deserve this. Even more, he wondered how he'd ever thought he could live without this. Without them. He rested his chin on her shoulder and reached out, touching Emilia's tiny little hand.

"Would now be a good time to ask if you're ready to marry me yet?" he asked.

Gabriella let out a contented sigh. "Not yet."

"Hmph."

"I still love you."

He grinned. "I know you do. And I'm not worried."

"No?"

"Nope." He shook his head, rubbing his lips along the curve of her neck. "It might take time but I think we both know...Emerson Yates always gets what he wants."

She turned her head so she could look at him and see his mischievous grin. "And *this* is what he wants? A wife and a kid?"

"More than he's ever wanted anything."

"Then I guess I'm in trouble, huh?"

That slow smirk curved his lips up just a little further, hooking into an expression that he knew made him look like the cocky bastard he was. He met her lips with a tender kiss before sliding his gaze down to their daughter who already had them both completely captivated. Those tiny fingers wrapped around his pinky and he was sure his heart stuttered, squeezing and overflowing with emotions he didn't quite know if he was equipped to handle.

Gabriella smiled and a small, joyful noise escaped as she watched Emilia hold on to her daddy.

He let out a breath, really working to keep those damn tears away now. "Honey...I think we're both in trouble."

THANK YOU FOR READING!

455

Thank you all for reading Emerson and Gabriella's story. I hope you enjoyed watching Emerson's transformation from book one until now, and maybe some of you even grew to love him as much as I did (even though I think we can all agree that Gabriella was really the one to crush on in this book). The characters in these stories have become so real to me in my head and I can't imagine how hard it will be when this series has come to an end. Luckily for all of us, these stories are far from over. Keep an eye out for the fourth installment, *The Closer* coming soon. Tyler and Lizzie's story is sweet, funny, new levels of sexy, and has elements completely unlike the previous books in this series. Thanks again for your support- You all keep reading and I'll keep writing!

www.ingramcontent.com/pod-product-compliance
Lightning Source LLC
Chambersburg PA
CBHW062105290726

48975CB00001B/115